∞⊃ EIGHT LAMENTATIONS ⊂∞
SPEAR OF SHADOWS

WITHDRAWN

WARHAMMER
AGE OF SIGMAR

EIGHT LAMENTATIONS
SPEAR OF SHADOWS

JOSH REYNOLDS

BLACK LIBRARY

For Deke, Andy and Greg. You guys know why.

A BLACK LIBRARY PUBLICATION

First published in 2017.
This edition published in Great Britain in 2018 by
Black Library,
Games Workshop Ltd.,
Willow Road,
Nottingham,
NG7 2WS, UK.

10 9 8 7 6 5 4 3 2 1

Produced by Games Workshop in Nottingham.
Cover illustrations by Johan Grenier.

A CIP record for this book is available from the British Library.

ISBN 13: 978 1 78496 667 6

See Black Library on the internet at

blacklibrary.com

Find out more about Games Workshop
and the worlds of Warhammer at

games-workshop.com

Printed and bound by CPI Group (UK) Ltd, Croydon, CR0 4YY

From the maelstrom of a sundered world, the
Eight Realms were born. The formless and the divine
exploded into life.

Strange, new worlds appeared in the firmament, each one
gilded with spirits, gods and men. Noblest of the gods was
Sigmar. For years beyond reckoning he illuminated the realms,
wreathed in light and majesty as he carved out his reign. His
strength was the power of thunder. His wisdom was infinite.
Mortal and immortal alike kneeled before his lofty throne.
Great empires rose and, for a while, treachery was banished.
Sigmar claimed the land and sky as his own and ruled over a
glorious age of myth.

But cruelty is tenacious. As had been foreseen, the great
alliance of gods and men tore itself apart. Myth and legend
crumbled into Chaos. Darkness flooded the realms. Torture,
slavery and fear replaced the glory that came before. Sigmar
turned his back on the mortal kingdoms, disgusted by their
fate. He fixed his gaze instead on the remains of the world he
had lost long ago, brooding over its charred core, searching
endlessly for a sign of hope. And then, in the dark heat of
his rage, he caught a glimpse of something magnificent. He
pictured a weapon born of the heavens. A beacon powerful
enough to pierce the endless night. An army hewn from
everything he had lost.

Sigmar set his artisans to work and for long ages they toiled,
striving to harness the power of the stars. As Sigmar's great
work neared completion, he turned back to the realms and saw
that the dominion of Chaos was almost complete. The hour
for vengeance had come. Finally, with lightning blazing across
his brow, he stepped forth to unleash his creations.

The Age of Sigmar had begun.

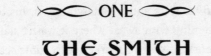

ONE

THE SMITH

Somewhere in the mortal realms, the smith raised his hammer. He brought it down, striking the white-hot length of metal he held pinned against the anvil with one fire-blackened hand. He rotated it and delivered a second strike. A third, a fourth, until the smoky air of the cavernous forge resonated with the sound of raw creation.

It was the first smithy, long forgotten save in the dreams of those who worked with iron and flame. It was a place of stone and wood and steel, at once a grand temple and a brute cave, its dimensions and shape changing with every twitch of the smoke that inundated it. It was nowhere and everywhere, existing only in the hollows of ancestral memory, or in the stories of the oldest mortal smiths. Racks of weapons such as had never been wielded by mortals gleamed in the light of the forge, their killing edges honed and impatient to perform their function. Beneath them were less murderous tools, though no less necessary.

The smith made little distinction between them – weapons were tools, and tools were weapons. War was no less a labour than ploughing the soil, and hewing down a forest was no less a slaughter, though the victims could not, save in rare instances, scream.

The smith was impossibly broad and powerful, for all that his shape was crooked, and bent strangely, as if succumbing to unseen pressures. His thick limbs moved with a surety of purpose that no mechanism could replicate. He wore a pair of oft-patched trousers and a battered apron, his bare arms and back glistening with sweat where it wasn't stained with tattoo-like whorls of soot or marked with runic scars. Boots of crimson dragon-hide protected his feet, the iridescent scales glinting in the firelight, and tools of all shapes and sizes hung from the wide leather belt strapped about his waist.

A spade-shaped beard, composed of swirling ash, and moustaches of flowing smoke covered the lower half of his lumpen features. A thick mane of fiery hair cascaded down his scalp, spilling over his shoulders and crackling against his flesh. Eyes like molten metal were fixed on his task with a calm that came only with age.

The smith was older than the realms. A breaker of stars, and a maker of suns. He had forged weapons without number, and no two were the same – a fact he took no small amount of pride in. He was a craftsman, and he put a bit of himself into the metal, even as he hammered it into shape. This one needed a little more hammering than most. He raised it from the anvil and studied it. 'Bit more heat,' he murmured. His voice at its quietest was like the rumble of an avalanche.

He shoved the length of smouldering iron into the maw of the forge. Flames crawled up his sinewy arm, and the metal twisted in his grip as it grew hot once more, but he did not flinch. The fire held no terrors for one such as him. Tongs and gloves were for lesser smiths. Besides, there was much to be seen in the fire, if you weren't afraid of getting close. He peered into the dancing hues of red and orange, wondering what they would show him this time. Shapes began to take form, indistinct and uncertain. He stirred the embers.

As the flames roared up anew, clawing greedily at the metal, he felt his students shy back. He chuckled. 'What sort of smiths are afraid of a bit of fire?'

He glanced at them, head tilted. Vague dream-shapes huddled in the smoke. Small and large, broad and gossamer-thin. Hundreds of them – duardin, human, aelf, even a few ogors – crowded the ever-shifting confines of the smithy, watching as he plied his trade. All who sought to shape metal were welcome in this forge, barring an obvious few.

There were always some who made themselves unwelcome. Those who'd failed to learn the most important lessons, and used what he'd taught them for bitter ends. Not many, thankfully, but some. They hid from his gaze, even as they sought to emulate his skill. But he would find them eventually, and cast their works into the fire.

The voices of his students rose in sudden warning. The smith turned, eyes narrowing in consternation. Talons of fire emerged from the forge, gripping either side of the hearth. Bestial features, composed of crackling flame and swirling ash, congealed. Teeth made from cinders gnashed in a paroxysm of fury. A molten claw caught at his arm, and his thick hide blackened at its touch. The smith grunted and jerked his arm back. The daemon lunged after him with a hot roar, its shape expanding as if to fill the smithy. Great wings of ash stretched, and a horned head emerged from within the hearth.

'No,' the smith said, simply, as his students scattered. He dropped the metal he'd been heating and caught the twisting flame shape before it could grow any larger. He had to be quick.

It shrieked as he dragged it around and slammed it down onto the anvil. Burning claws gouged his bare arms and tore his apron to ribbons, as flapping wings battered against his shoulders, but the smith's grip was unbreakable. He raised his hammer. The intruder's eyes widened in realisation. It warbled a protest.

The hammer rang down. Then again and again, flattening and shaping the flame into a more agreeable form. The daemon screamed in protest as its essence was reduced with every blow. All of its arrogance and malice fled, leaving behind only fear, and soon, not even that.

The smith lifted what was left of the weakly struggling daemon. He recognised the signature on its soul-bindings as easily as if he'd carved them himself. Daemons were like any other raw material, in that they required careful shaping by their summoner to make them fit for purpose. This one had been made for strength and speed and not much else.

'Crude, always so crude,' he said. 'No pride in his work, that one. No artistry. I tried to teach him, but – ah well. We'll make something of you, though, never fear. I've made better from worse materials, in my time.'

So saying, he plunged the daemon into the slack tub beside the anvil. Water hissed into vapour as parts of the creature sloughed away into motes of cinder, swirling upwards to float above the anvil. What was left in the tub was only a bit of blackened iron, pitted and veined an angry crimson, the barest hint of a snarling face scraped into its surface. The smith bounced it on his palm until it cooled, and then dropped it into the pocket of his apron.

'Now, I wonder what that was all about.'

It had been some time since he had been attacked in this place, in such a way. That it had happened at all spoke of desperation on someone's part. As if they'd hoped to prevent him from seeing something. He looked up at the cloud of floating cinders and reached to grasp a handful. He set aside his hammer and ran a thick finger through them, reading them as a mortal might read a book.

With a grunt, he cast them back into the forge and gave the coals a stir with his hand. An indistinct image took shape in the flames. Moments later, it split into eight, these clearer – a sword, a mace, a spear... eight weapons.

The smith frowned and stirred the coals fiercely, calling up more images. He needed to be certain of what he saw. In the flames, a woman clad in crystalline armour drew one of the eight – a howling daemon-sword – from its cage of meat, and traded thunderous blows with a Stormcast Eternal clad in bruise-coloured armour. She shattered her opponent's rune-blade, and the smith winced to see one of his most potent works so easily destroyed. He waved a hand, conjuring more pictures out of the wavering flames.

A bloated pox-warrior, one side of his body eaten away and replaced by the thrashing shape of a monstrous kraken, wrapped slimy tendrils about the haft of a great mace, banded in runic iron, and tore it from the hands of a dying ogor. An aelf swordsman, eyes hidden beneath a cerulean blindfold, ducked beneath the sweeping bite of an obsidian axe that pulsed with volcanic hunger, and backed away from the hulking orruk who clutched it.

Angrily, the smith swept out a hand, summoning more images. They came faster and faster, dancing about his hand like the fragments of a half-remembered dream – he saw wars yet unwaged and the deaths yet to come, and felt his temper fray. The images moved so fast that even he couldn't keep track of them all. Frustrated, he caught those he could, holding them tight, only for them to slip between his fingers and rejoin the flames. The time had come around at last. He would need to make ready.

He ran his wide hands through his fiery hair and growled softly. 'Best get to work.' He turned and fixed several of his students with a glare. 'You there – stop skulking and find something to write with. Be quick, now!'

His students hurried to obey. When they returned, bearing chisels and heavy tomes of stone and iron, he began to speak. 'In the beginning, there was fire. And from fire came heat. From heat, shape. And that shape split into eight. The eight were the raw stuff of Chaos, hammered and sculpted to a killing edge by the sworn forgemasters of the dread Soulmaw, the chosen weaponsmiths of Khorne.'

He paused a moment, before continuing. 'But as the realms shuddered and the Age of Chaos gave way to the Age of Blood, the weapons known as the Eight Lamentations were thought lost.' In the fire, scenes of death and madness played themselves out, over and over again, a cycle without end.

Grungni, Lord of all Forges and Master-Smith, sighed.

'Until now.'

Elsewhere. Another forge, cruder than Grungni's. A cavern, ripped open and hewn from volcanic stone by the bleeding hands of many slaves. Fire pits and cooling basins occupied the wide, flat floor. Racks decorated the uneven walls, and hackblades, wrath-hammers, weapons of all shapes and sizes, hung from them in disorganised fashion.

At the heart of the forge, within a circle of fire pits, sat a huge anvil. And upon the anvil, a hulking figure leaned, head bowed. Sweat rolled down his muscular arms to splatter with a hiss upon the anvil. His crimson and brass armour was blackened in places, as if it had been exposed to an impossible heat.

He inhaled deeply, trying to ignore the weakness that crept through him. He had infused the daemon with some of his own strength, in the hopes that it would prove a match for the Lord of all Forges. Or at least last longer than a handful of moments. He consoled himself with the thought that it was not every man who could match wills with a god and survive.

'Then, I am no mere man,' Volundr of Hesphut murmured to himself. 'I am Forgemaster of Aqshy.' A warrior-smith of Khorne. Skullgrinder of the Soulmaw. He had forged weapons without number, as well as the wars in which they were wielded. He had raised up thousands of heroes, and cracked the skulls of thousands more.

But for the moment, he was simply tired.

'Well?'

The voice, cold and soft, echoed from the shadows of the forge. Volundr straightened, skull-faced helm turning towards the speaker who sat in the darkness, wrapped in concealing robes the colour of cooling ashes. Qyat of the Folded Soul, Forgemaster of Ulgu, was more smoke than fire, and his shape was seemingly without substance beneath his voluminous attire. 'He saw,' Volundr rumbled. 'As I predicted, Qyat.'

A second voice, harsh and sharp like shattering iron, intruded. 'You seek to excuse your own failure, Skull-Cracker.'

Volundr snorted. 'Excuse? No. I merely explain, Wolant.' He turned, pointing a blunt finger at the second speaker, who stood beyond the glare of the fire pits, his profusion of muscular arms crossed over his massive barrel chest.

Wolant Sevenhand, Forgemaster of Chamon, was a brass-skinned, eight-armed abomination, clad in armour of gold. Seven of his arms ended in sinewy, fire-toughened hands. The eighth ended in the blunt shape of a hammer, strapped to a mangled wrist in an effort to correct a long-ago injury. 'If you think you can succeed where I failed, then try your luck by all means,' Volundr continued.

'You dare–?' Wolant growled, reaching for one of the many hammers that hung from his belt. Before he could grab it, Volundr snatched up his own from the floor and slammed it down on the anvil, filling the smithy with a hollow, booming echo. Wolant staggered, clasping his hands to the side of his head.

Volundr pointed his hammer at the other skullgrinder. 'Remember whose smithy you stand in, Sevenhand. I'll not suffer your bluster here.'

'I'm sure our bellicose brother meant no harm, Volundr. He is a choleric, self-important creature, as you well know, and prone to rash action.' Qyat unfolded himself and stood. He loomed over the other two skullgrinders, a tower of lean, pale muscle, clad in black iron. 'Even so, if he is so rude as to threaten you again, I shall lop off another of his hands.'

'My thanks, brother,' Volundr said.

'Even as I will pluck out your eye, if you continue to stare at me so balefully,' Qyat added, mildly. He spread his thin hands. 'Respect costs men like us so little, my brothers. Why be miserly?'

Volundr bowed his head. 'Forgive me, brother,' he said. Weak as he was, he was in no shape for a confrontation with a creature as deadly as the Folded Soul. Wolant was bad enough, for all that he was a brute. He set the head of his hammer down on the anvil and leaned forwards, bracing himself on the haft. 'Wolant is right. I failed. The master-smith knows. And now he is aware that we know, as well.'

Wolant growled. 'If you had not failed–'

'But he did, and so new stratagems must be forged in the fires of adversity.' Qyat pressed his hands together, as if in prayer. 'The Crippled God cannot be allowed to take from us that which is ours.'

Wolant laughed. 'Ours, Folded Soul?' He spread his arms. 'Mine, you mean. Perhaps yours, if I am unlucky. Or someone else entirely, for we three are not alone in our quest. Our brother forgemasters begin their own hunts. The Eight Lamentations call to we who forged them, ready to spill blood once more.' Seven fists shook in a gesture of challenge and defiance. 'Only one of us may earn Khorne's favour by recovering them. Or had you forgotten?'

'None of us have forgotten,' Volundr said. 'We have each chosen our champions, and cast them into the realms to seek the Eight. But that does not mean we cannot work together against those outside our fraternity.' He shook his head. 'Grungni is not our only foe in this endeavour. Others seek the Eight as well. If we do not work together, we will–'

Wolant clapped four of his hands together, interrupting. 'Nonsense. The greater the obstacle, the greater the glory. I came only out of respect for the Folded Soul's cunning. Not to join my fate to yours. My champion will acquire the Eight Lamentations for me, and the skulls of your servants as well, if they get in his way.' He laughed again, and turned away. Volundr watched him stride towards one of the great archways that lined the cavern wall, and wondered whether he could split the other smith's skull while his back was turned.

Qyat chuckled softly, as if reading his thoughts. 'Would that you could crack his thick skull on your anvil. Though I would be forced to slay you in turn, brother, should you choose to break the iron-oath in such a way.'

Volundr grunted. The iron-oath was the only thing keeping the remaining forgemasters from each other's throats. The truce was a tenuous thing, but it had held for three centuries. And he would not be the one to break it. He gestured dismissively. 'It will be more satisfying to snatch victory from him. My champion is most determined.'

'As is mine.'

Volundr nodded. 'Then may the best champion win.' He turned his attentions to the fire pits and gestured, drawing up the cinders and sparks into the air. He stirred the smoke, casting his gaze across the mortal realms, seeking a singular ember of Aqshy's fire. When he found it, he cast his words into the fire, knowing that they would be heard.

'Ahazian Kel. Last of the Ekran. Deathbringer. Heed your master's voice.'

In a land where the moon burned cold, and the dead walked freely, Ahazian Kel heard Volundr's voice. Though it was like heated nails digging into his mind, he decided to ignore it. Given the situation, he thought Volundr would forgive him. Then again, perhaps not. In any event, it was done and Ahazian gave it no more thought.

Instead, he concentrated on the dead men trying to kill him. Deathrattle warriors, animated skeletons still wearing the tattered remnants of the armour that had failed them in life, emerged from the shadows of the great stone pillars extending to either side of him. They pressed close in the moonlight, crowding the wide stone avenue. Rusted blades dug for his flesh, as corroded shields slammed into the ranks of his followers, bowling several of them over.

Ahazian gave little thought to the bloodreavers' plight. The living were a means to an end, and the dead merely one more obstacle between him and that which he sought. Ahead of them, past the ranks of the dead, at the end of the pillar-lined avenue, were the open gates of the mausoleum-citadel. Two skeletal giants, carved from stone, knelt to either side of that immense aperture, their skulls bowed over the pommels of their swords. Somewhere, a funerary bell tolled, rousing the dead from their slumber of ages.

Deathrattle warriors flooded the avenue. They marched out between the shadowed pillars, or from within the mausoleum-citadel, singly and in groups. Not just the dead native to this place, but even those who'd been slain here more recently heeded the tolling of the unseen bell. Though their bones had been picked clean by the jackals and birds that haunted the ruins, he still recognised the sigils that adorned their ruptured armour – the runes of Khorne and Slaanesh, the baleful glyphs of a thousand lesser gods, all were in evidence among the silent ranks of the enemy.

In Shyish, there was only one certainty. One the gods themselves could not defy. It was a land of endings, where even the strongest would eventually falter. There could be no true victory over that which conquered all. That didn't stop some from trying.

But conquest was not Ahazian's goal. Not today.

He stood head and shoulders taller than even the tallest of the tribesmen who fought alongside him. His broad frame was hidden beneath razor-edged plates of crimson and brass armour, and the skull-visage of his helmet curved upwards, coalescing into the rune of Khorne, clearly marking his allegiances. Heavy chains draped his form, their links decorated with barbs, hooks and the occasional scalp.

He was surrounded by a phalanx of savage tribesmen, culled from the lowlands of this region. The heads of their former chieftains slapped against his thigh, their scalps knotted to his belt. If there were a simpler way of making others do what you wished, he hadn't yet found it. The bloodreavers wore rattletrap armour scavenged from a thousand killing fields. It was decorated with totems meant to ward off the dead, even as their flesh was painted with ashes and bone dust, to make them invisible to ghosts. None of these protections seemed to be working particularly well at the moment. They didn't appear to mind.

The bulk of the bloodreavers fought fiercely to either side of him, hacking and stabbing at the silent dead. Ahazian held the vanguard, as was his right, and pleasure. The Deathbringer surged forwards like the tip of the spear, his goreaxe in one hand, skullaxe in the other. Both weapons thirsted for something this enemy could not provide, and their frustration pulsed through him. The thorns of metal set into their hafts dug painfully into his palms, opening old wounds, so that his fingers were soon slick with blood. He didn't care – let them drink, if they would. So long as they served him faithfully and well, it was the least he could do. Blood must be spilled, even if that blood was his own.

He chopped down through a shield marked with the face of a leering corpse, and splintered the bones huddling beneath. Brute strength was enough to win him some breathing room, but it wouldn't last for long. What the dead claimed, they held with a cold ferocity that awed even some servants of the Blood God. One of the many lessons his time in Shyish had taught him. 'Onward,' he snarled, trusting in his voice to carry. 'Khorne claim him who first dares to cry hold.'

The bloodreavers closest to him gave a shout and redoubled their efforts. He growled in satisfaction and drove his head into the rictus grin of a skeleton, shattering its skull. He swept the twitching remains aside and bulled on, dragging his followers along in his wake. A spear struck his shoulder-plate and shivered to fragments, even as he crushed the spine of its wielder. Fallen skeletons groped for his legs, and he trampled them into the dust. Nothing would be allowed to stand between him and his goal.

What lay beyond the gateway was his destiny. Khorne had

set his feet upon the path, and Ahazian Kel had walked it willingly. For what else could he do? For a kel, there was only battle. War was – had been – the truest art of the Ekran. Its reasons did not matter. Causes were but distractions to the purity of war waged well.

Ahazian Kel, last hero of the Ekran, had sought to become as one with war itself. And so he had given himself up to Khorne. He had offered the blood of his fellow kels in sacrifice, including that of Prince Cadacus. He cherished that memory above all others, for Cadacus, of all his cousins, had come the closest to killing him.

Now, here, was simply the next step in his journey along the Eightfold Path. He had followed that path from the Felstone Plains of Aqshy to the Ashen Lowlands of Shyish, and he would not stop now. Not until he had claimed his prize.

Ahazian let the rhythm of war carry him forwards, into the midst of the dead. Slowly but steadily, he carved himself a path towards the gateway. Broken, twitching skeletons littered the ground behind him. His followers shielded him from the worst blows, buying his life with their own. He hoped they found some satisfaction in that – it was an honour to die for one of Khorne's chosen. To grease the wheels of battle with their blood, so that a true warrior could meet his fate in a more suitable fashion.

He swept his skullhammer out, smashing a skeleton to flinders, and suddenly found himself clear of the enemy. A few dozen bloodreavers, stronger than the rest, or simply faster, stumbled free of the press alongside him. He did not pause, but forged on, running now. The bloodreavers followed him, with barely a backwards glance between them. Those who were still locked in combat with the dead would have to fend for themselves.

The forecourt of the mausoleum-citadel was lit by amethyst will o' the wisps, which swum languidly through the dusty air. By their glow, he could make out strange mosaics on the walls and floor, depicting scenes of war and progress. Statues, weathered by time and neglect, lurked in the corners, their unseeing eyes aimed eternally upwards.

Ahazian led his remaining warriors through the silent halls. The bloodreavers huddled together, muttering among themselves. In battle, they were courageous beyond all measure. But here, in the dark and quiet, old fears were quick to reassert themselves. Night-terrors, whispered of around tribal fires, loomed close in this place. Every shadow seemed to hold a legion of wolf-fanged ghosts, ready to spring and rip the tribesmen apart.

Ahazian said nothing to calm them. Fear would keep them alert. Besides, it was not his duty to keep their feet to the Eightfold Path – he was no slaughterpriest. If they wished to cower or flee, Khorne would punish them as he saw fit.

The sounds of the battle outside had faded into a dim murmur. Shafts of cold light fell from great holes torn in the roof above, and the amethyst wisps swirled thickly about them, lighting the path ahead. Ahazian swept aside curtains of cobwebs with his axe, and smashed apart toppled columns and piles of obstructing debris with his hammer, clearing the way.

The spirits of the dead clustered thick the deeper they went. Silent phantoms, ragged and barely visible, wandered to and fro. Lost souls, following the paths of fading memory. The ghosts displayed no hostility, lost as they were in their own miseries. But their barely intelligible whispers intruded on his thoughts with irritating frequency, and he swiped at them in frustration whenever one got too close. They paid him no mind, which only added to his annoyance.

When they at last reached the inner chambers, his temper had frayed considerably, and his followers kept their distance. He found himself hoping for an enemy to appear. An ambush, perhaps. Anything to soothe his frustrations.

The throne room of the mausoleum-citadel was a circular chamber, its rounded walls rising to a high dome, shattered in some long-forgotten cataclysm. Shafts of moonlight draped the ruined chamber, illuminating the fallen remains of broken statues, and glinting among the thick shrouds of cobwebs and dust that clung to every surface.

'Spread out,' Ahazian said. His voice boomed, shattering the stillness. His warriors shuffled to obey. He stalked towards the wide dais that occupied the centre of the chamber. It was topped by a massive throne of basalt. And upon the throne, a hulking shape sat slumped. Broken skeletons littered the floor around the dais and upon the steps, the scattered bones glowing faintly of witch fire.

Ahazian climbed the dais warily. It was almost a given in this realm that a silent corpse was a dangerous one. But the broken form slumped on its throne didn't so much as twitch. The heavy armour was covered so thickly in cobwebs that its crimson hue, as well as the bat-winged skulls that decorated it, were all but invisible. As he drew closer, he felt a touch of awe at the sheer size of the deceased potentate. The being had been massive, as was the great, black-bladed axe that hung loosely from one fleshless hand, its edge resting on the ground. The corpse wore a heavy, horned helm, topped by a frayed crest.

He scraped away some of the cobwebs with the edge of his axe, revealing a long, gaping rent in the filthy chest-plate, as if some wide, impossibly sharp blade had passed through the metal and into whatever passed for the dead man's heart. 'Ha,'

Ahazian murmured, pleased. At last, he'd found it. He buried his goreaxe in the armrest of the throne and thrust his hand into the wound. Spiders spilled out, crawling up his arm, or tumbling to the floor. He ignored the panicked arachnids and continued to root through the mouldering chest cavity, until his fingers at last closed on that which he'd fought so long to find.

He ripped the sliver of black steel free of the husk, and there was a sound halfway between a moan and a sigh. He held his prize up to the dim light. A splinter, torn free in the death-strike. It was a fragment from a weapon – and not just any weapon, but one forged in the shadow-fires of Ulgu. One of eight.

'Gung,' Ahazian said, softly. The Spear of Shadows. Called the Huntsman by some, and the Far-Killer by others. Once hurled, Gung would always find its prey, no matter how far they fled, or the distance between caster and target. Not even the veil that separated the mortal realms could prevent the Far-Killer from slaying its quarry.

The metal sliver seemed to tremble in his grip, as if eager to return to its nest within the corpse. 'No, little fang, the time has come for you to awaken and lead me to that which I desire.' He dropped the fragment into a pouch on his belt. If Volundr were right, the sliver would lead him to the Huntsman. The piece was sympathetic to the whole, and one called out to the other. All he had to do was get it away from the remains of its victim.

As he made to descend the dais, he heard a sudden thunder. It lengthened into a drumming pulse, and he realised that it was the sound of hooves on a stone floor. His men turned towards the doors as they were smashed open, and a wedge of mounted warriors crashed into the chamber. Coal-black steeds snorted and screeched as they galloped towards the startled bloodreavers. Their riders wore obsidian armour and carried long spears and swords. Pale, feminine faces glared out from within several of the baroque, high-crested helms, while the faces of the others were hidden behind bestial visors. The horsewomen had isolated and hacked apart most of his surviving men before Ahazian could do more than shout a warning.

As the butchery continued, one horsewoman broke away from the rest and urged her steed towards the dais. Ahazian waited. He was confident in his ability to hack his way free, if necessary, but his curiosity had got the better of him. The rider slipped from the saddle in a clatter of mail, and strode towards the dais. As she drew close, Ahazian caught a whiff of old blood. He chuckled. 'I did not expect to see one of your sort here.'

'My sort are everywhere. This land belongs to us, after all.' She spun, hacking through the upraised arm of a bloodreaver as he rushed towards her. She swatted the dying man aside, and gutted a second, as he sought to capitalise on her seeming distraction. She turned back to him. 'However many of you creatures infest it currently.'

Ahazian shrugged. 'I am merely a pilgrim.'

'A loud one. You Bloodbound make quite a racket, when you're of a mind.' The vampire smiled, exposing a fang. 'Then, I've never been against a bit of noise from time to time.' She swept her sword out in a casual gesture, removing a bloodreaver's head as the wounded man staggered towards her. 'Screams, for instance.'

Ahazian rolled his neck and loosened his shoulders. He was looking forwards to matching blades with her. The thirsty dead were known to be competent warriors, if nothing else. 'Are you the queen of this bone pile, then? Have I offended you with my presence?' He took a step down the dais. His weapons twitched in his hands, eager to bite unliving flesh.

'I am not a queen, but I do serve one. And she requests that which you've come to pilfer.' She extended her sword. 'Hand it over, and I may let you depart with all of your limbs intact.' She smiled. 'Then again, maybe not.'

'Tell your queen that she can have from me what she can seize, and nothing more.'

The vampire nodded, as if she had expected as much. 'If that is your wish, I shall simply have to take it from you.'

'You think to kill me, pretty one?' Ahazian gestured welcomingly with his axe. 'Come, step up. Let us see if you are as eager to lose blood as to drink it.'

The vampire sprang up the dais, quicker than he'd expected. She moved with deadly grace, despite her armour. Her sword scratched a line across his chest-plate, knocking him back a step. Annoyed, he swatted at her with his skullhammer. She eeled away, her blade licking out across his bare bicep, and sprang back as his axe chopped down, splintering the surface of the dais.

'Fast,' he murmured, approvingly.

'Faster than you.'

'We'll see.' He spun his axe lazily. As her eyes flicked instinctively to follow it, he struck at her with the hammer. She twisted, catching the blow on her palm. His axe bit at her thigh, and she was forced to retreat.

Her followers slid towards him, black steel shadows, quicksilver swift. His warriors were all dead, or dying. He was alone. He smiled, pleased. There wasn't enough battle for everyone. Their blades darted at him from a dozen directions, and he was hard-pressed to deflect them. Some slid past his guard, to score his armour or pink his flesh.

He roared in anger and swept his goreaxe out in a wide arc. One blood knight, slower than the rest, screamed as his blow caught her in the side. She whirled away, armour crumpled and the ribs beneath caved in.

He pursued the wounded vampire as she rolled down the steps. The others followed him, as he'd hoped. He turned, catching one in the face with his hammer. She collapsed, head reduced to ruin. A second shrieked as his axe tore across her arm. The force of the blow pitched her across the chamber.

'Is that all you've got?' he laughed. 'I am a Kel of the Ekran, leeches. I was weaned on blood, and my lullaby was the clash of swords. I am war itself, and no creature, dead or alive, can stand against me.'

'Too much talking,' the first vampire said, as she rose up behind him. Her sword slid easily between the plates of his armour and into his back. Ahazian bellowed and lurched forwards, ripping the weapon from her grip. His axe slipped from his hand. A blessed agony ripsawed through him, setting his nerves alight. Pain was a warrior's reward, and he welcomed it. He turned, hammer raised.

The weapon crashed down, narrowly missing her. She leapt onto his back, her weight causing him to stagger. She clawed for the hilt of her sword. He twisted, snatching her from her perch and slamming her flat against the floor. Holding her pinned with his hammer, he groped awkwardly for the blade. 'Treacherous leech,' he grunted.

'All's fair in war,' she hissed. Her fist cracked across his jaw, knocking him sideways. Her strength, while not equal to his, was still impressive. As he staggered, she lunged to her feet, set a boot against his back, caught the hilt of her sword and ripped it free in a spray of blood. He howled in agony. Breathing heavily, he cast about for his axe.

Spotting it, Ahazian snatched it up just in time to block a slash from her sword. The other vampires circled them, waiting for an opening. Every fibre of his being demanded that he stay and fight – that he prove his superiority, or die in the attempt. But what was the point of such a small death? Khorne would barely notice. No, better to quit the field and seek a more glorious destruction. One worth his time.

He rose to his feet, and they edged away. The wound in his back had already clotted and begun to scab over. It would take more than that to seriously injure a warrior of his pedigree. He laughed, low and long. 'This has been amusing, pretty one. But I have more important matters to attend to than this dance of yours.'

Ahazian jerked forwards, towards the closest of the blood knights. The vampire, unprepared, fell beneath a flurry of savage blows, and then he was past them. Before they could stop him, he caught one of the coal-black steeds by its rough mane and hauled himself into the saddle, thrusting his hammer through his belt as he did so. The animal twisted, trying to bite him, but a swift blow made it think twice. He jerked the reins, and slammed his heels into its flanks. The animal leapt forwards with a despairing shriek. He leaned low over its neck, urging it on to greater speed.

He burst from the mausoleum-citadel, riding hard. The dead waited for him, in the moonlit silence beyond. The bodies of his bloodreavers lay scattered about, in heaps and piles. Soon, they would rise and join their slayers, to fight eternally – a fitting reward for them. Ahazian Kel laughed as he readied his axe. He would chop a path to freedom, before the vampires could follow. Let them pursue him, if they would. Let all of the dead souls in this realm muster against him. It did not matter.

One way or another, the Spear of Shadows would be his.

~∞ TWO ∞~

VOLKER

It was not the first time that the skaven had attacked the City of Secrets. Nor, sadly, would it be the last. Excelsis attracted enemies the way dung attracted flies. And the only way to deal with flies was to swat them. Luckily, in his time in the Realm of Beasts, Owain Volker had become quite adept at swatting flies of all shapes and sizes.

The gunmaster stood in one of a handful of hastily dug trenches that sprawled between the skaven and the half-finished walls of Excelsis. The trenches, dug in the hard earth by duardin picks, were reinforced by sandbags and wooden duckboards. Firing steps marked the rearmost trenches, allowing the hand-gunners of the freeguilds – the city's mortal defenders – to ply their trade in relative safety. Volker's trench was farther back from the front line, where the artillery crews of the Iron-weld could deliver their munitions without fear of immediate reprisal.

He let out a slow breath, and pulled back on the trigger of

his long rifle. He had compensated for windage and elevation, and calculated the powder load accordingly; all second nature to him now. Preparing a shot was an instinctive act rather than a conscious one, and accomplished with impressive speed.

The ball traversed the rifle-bore and spiralled along a swift, stable trajectory. By the time he felt the kick of the shot through the ironwood stock, the ball had already found its target. The skaven, a black-furred brute clad in red war-plate, with a wooden back-banner heavy with skulls, snapped backwards, snout first.

Nearby ratkin scattered in all directions, seeking cover, before the body completed its journey to the ground. Volker frowned. Normally, there was precious little of that on the wild plains of the Coast of Tusks. But the skaven were inveterate builders, despite lacking any sense of craftsmanship. They had swarmed over the pitiful shanty towns that clustered like barnacles in the shadow of the Bastion – the great wall that nominally protected the city – tearing them apart and putting the wood and stone to use as crude defensive works.

Now, in the ruins of those wretched slums, the vile ratmen and their loathsome kin readied themselves for the next push. He lifted his rifle and stepped back. 'What do you think?' he asked his companion.

'A fair shot, lad.' The speaker was a duardin, heavy-set and round-faced beneath his carefully groomed beard. Makkelsson was a paragon of duardin virtues – gruff, observant and stubborn beyond reason. All of which made him a natural artillery engineer. The cannon he oversaw sat behind and just above them, on a carefully constructed wooden firing platform. To the side of the platform, at the foot of the steps and stacked carefully behind a protective pavise, was a small hill of powder barrels and shot.

The cannon was an old weapon, a survivor of the Great Exodus, and its age-blackened barrel was marked with scenes from long-forgotten wars. Makkelsson's gunners, human and duardin alike, sat on the platform and spoke loudly in Khazalid – the ancestral tongue of the Dispossessed. The first thing all members of the Ironweld had to learn was the duardin language. It just made things easier in the long run.

Makkelsson clapped Volker on the shoulder. 'The ratmen will be scurrying around like mad until one of them gets up the minerals to take command.' He leaned against the trench wall and offered Volker the flask he'd been sipping from. Volker took the flask gratefully and washed the taste of powder and smoke out of his mouth.

'I hope it takes longer than last time.' Volker took the range-finder from his eye. The monocular goggle, composed of half a dozen gold-framed glass lenses of varying sizes, helped him to focus on the target, no matter the range. He'd painstakingly cut and fitted the lenses himself, in his first year as an apprentice to the engineers of the Ironweld Arsenal.

'The miners say they can hear things scurrying, down in the dark,' Makkelsson murmured, tapping the duckboards with a foot. 'The rats are digging down even as they hold us here. Spend too long killing them up here and we'll never find them all below.'

'And so? There's not a rat living that can gnaw through the Bastion's roots.' Volker offered Makkelsson his flask back. 'If only the perimeter walls had been completed, they'd never have dared show their whiskers in the open like this.' He glanced back towards the city.

The thick, high walls of the Bastion loomed over the southern plains, square and imposing. Its towers were lined with siege-cannons, their focal lenses glinting in the ochre light of the setting suns. Above the walls, Volker could make out the vast cloud-wreathed shape of the Spear of Mallus – a broken chunk of the world-that-was, cast down into the Sea of Tusks generations past. The city had grown up around it, spreading outwards from the bay thrown up by the Spear's tumultuous arrival. From its sprawling docklands to its floating towers, Excelsis offered opportunity and sanctuary to all.

But while the offer was for all, not everyone enjoyed the largesse equally. Before the Bastion and stretching well past the line of defensive trenches were ramshackle slums, stacked atop one another like teetering cages; a stifling network of rookeries and tangled, uncobbled streets, at the mercy of the elements and worse, until such time as the Bastion could be extended to encompass them.

The city was growing swiftly. Too swiftly, according to some. And the city's walls had to be broken down and reconsecrated with every new district added. The last consecration had begun almost thirty years ago, and still wasn't complete, thanks in part to the too-frequent earthquakes that rocked the region. And while parts of the Bastion remained unconsecrated, the outer city was vulnerable to attack.

The skaven had chosen their moment well. Only the warnings of the Collegiate Arcane had given the city's guardians time to prepare a suitable defence for those unconsecrated areas. Even then, they'd lost an entire district of the slums to the skaven. If the ratmen managed to retain their foothold here, they'd be almost impossible to root out. Volker was determined to do his part in seeing the loathsome creatures eradicated. While he'd come of age in holy Azyrheim, amid the wonders of the Ancestral City, Excelsis was his home now.

The traditional leather coat of a gunmaster wasn't his only protection. An intricately wrought breastplate, decorated with a stylised representation of Sigmar's thunderbolt, protected his torso, and he wore thick leather gauntlets and reinforced boots. An artisan pistol was thrust through his belt and two repeater pistols were holstered at the small of his back. A satchel of shot-cylinders and powder-loads sat beside him on the ground, within easy reach. A weapon's use was in direct proportion to the availability of ammunition. Words of wisdom from his mentor, Oken.

The old duardin had taught him everything he knew about the art of gunsmithing and more besides. Oken had shown him what it meant to be a member of the Ironweld Arsenal, and the burden of responsibility that came with it.

To be a member of the Ironweld was to be heir to the triumphs and losses of two nigh-extinct cultures, to walk the line between two fallen worlds, and pay homage to both, in word and deed. The masterwork long rifle he held was a thing of precise beauty, crafted according to these tenets. It had never failed him, even as he had never failed to care for it. Care for your weapons and they care for you – another bit of insight from Oken.

Volker smiled, thinking of the irascible ancient. The duardin was old, even by the standards of the Dispossessed. But like many duardin, age had only made him that much tougher. He remembered the first time they'd met, over a blacksmith's anvil. He'd been a child then. He recalled the way Oken had deftly repaired a broken toy, thick fingers moving with surprising delicacy. 'Do you want to learn how?' he'd asked, after he'd finished, his voice like stones rattling in an iron bucket. And Volker had.

His smile faded. He wished Oken were here now. The old grouch was a comfort to have around, though Volker would never dare say so aloud. Comfort was something he sorely needed at the moment.

He was the youngest gunmaster in the Ironweld, barely thirty winters. Once, he'd thought that might buy him the respect of his fellows. Instead, it had only made things harder. Herzborg and the other gunmasters resented him, and their influence counted for more than his, here on the fringes of civilisation. Not that he had any influence, really.

Volker had no aptitude for politicking, only for weapons. He could pluck the wings from a rotfly with an artisan pistol, but couldn't navigate the sullen currents of influence within the Ironweld without three guides, a map and several torches.

Case in point – his current position. Acting as a glorified handgunner, rather than among his fellow officers crafting strategy back in the Bastion. Or even in command of his own artillery detachment in the field. It stung. Makkelsson noticed the look on his face and chuckled. 'Better off out here, lad. Fresh air. Powder in your lungs. Healthy.'

'Healthier for who? I – ah. Look who it is.'

Makkelsson turned and frowned. 'Now I know we're in trouble.'

Volker laughed. Old Friar Ziska stumped towards them, his profusion of bells and chains creating a mighty racket. The Sigmarite priest wore threadbare robes, which did little to conceal his muscular form. An abundance of prayer scrolls flapped about him, sewn into the robes. Select passages from the Book of Lightning had been tattooed on his bald head and chest, and his bare feet stamped on the duckboards. Ziska was one of the Devoted of Sigmar, and about two charges light of a load. If he'd been let loose to inspire the men, someone was expecting an attack soon.

'And thus did Sigmar smite the perfidious realms with his storm, and cast his bolts of blessed fury, to free these lands from wickedness,' the priest bellowed, ringing the largest of his bells for all he was worth. 'Thus are served all who challenge Azyr, and the might of the Heavens.' He strode down the gun line, his chains rattling and his bells jangling. He carried no obvious weapons, but Volker had seen the good friar crush an orruk's skull with the bell he held. It was crafted from meteoric iron, and as deadly as any blade.

Makkelsson shook his head. 'Manlings,' he muttered.

'We are a devout folk,' Volker said, smiling.

'You're devout,' Makkelsson said. 'He's *bakrat*.' He tapped his head. 'Got a bad seam running through him.'

'Inspiring, though.' Ziska had begun to sing a somewhat bawdy hymn, and the cannon crews were clapping and whistling in time. 'In his own fashion,' Volker added, lamely. He turned back towards the enemy lines, watching as black shapes mustered in the ruins. 'They'll be making another push soon.'

'Aye. They've been gathering their courage for the past hour.'

'Too much open ground out there,' Volker said. 'They'll have the advantage of numbers, and the space to use them.'

'Better a rat in the open than in the tunnels,' Makkelsson said. 'At least this way we can see how many we kill.' The duardin tugged on his beard, expression thoughtful. 'I wonder what the bounty is on skaven tails, these days?'

'If I thought the Small Conclave would actually pay it, I might find out.'

Makkelsson snorted. 'True. Never met a more tight-fisted bunch.'

Volker looked at him. Makkelsson shrugged. 'Tight-fisted for humans, I mean,' he clarified.

Volker chuckled, and sat back against the wall of the trench, his long rifle leaning against his shoulder, the stock braced between his knees. He pulled a rag from his sleeve and began to wipe the rifle down, removing excess powder from the firing mechanism. Makkelsson sank to his haunches, watching Volker work.

'You treat that rifle like a *rinn*,' he said, approvingly. He fished a pipe from his smock, filled it, and lit it with a spare fuse. A smell like the sour shadows of the deepest coastal caverns rose from the bowl. 'Oken taught you well.'

'That's the only way to do anything,' Volker said. 'Or so the old grump says.'

Makkelsson laughed, a deep sound, low and rumbling. 'Aye, he is that.' He looked around. 'He'll be sorry he missed this.'

Volker paused. 'Really?'

Makkelsson frowned, considering. 'Probably not.'

A single, winding note filled the air. Volker looked up. 'I guess someone took charge,' he said, gathering his feet under him and standing up, as Makkelsson hurried back to his cannon. Warning bells began to ring, up and down the line. The duckboards reverberated with the tread of armoured demigods, as the hulking, black-clad shapes of the Sons of Mallus moved through the travel trenches towards the front line.

A retinue of the black-armoured Stormcast Eternals took up positions in the gunners' trench, ready to defend the Ironweld's precious artillery from any skaven who managed to get this far. Volker eyed the gigantic warriors surreptitiously.

It had been almost a century since the Gates of Azyr had been flung open and Sigmar's storm had raged forth to reclaim the mortal realms. Volker could remember his grandmother's stories of those first, harrowing days and the demigods who had marched into the maw of Chaos, carrying with them the hopes of the free peoples. The Stormcasts had fought battle after battle against the enemies of Azyr, and forged alliances with old allies and new. Only when the Realmgate Wars had at last ended had those first courageous colonists been allowed to step forth and claim their ancestral birthrights.

Now, with time and tide behind them, Excelsis and the other Founding Cities were permanent footholds in the mortal realms. And so long as men like Volker manned the guns, they would remain so, whatever the cost. But it helped to have allies such as the Stormcast Eternals. Excelsis was home to no less than three Stormkeeps, manned by warriors from three Stormhosts, including the Sons of Mallus.

The roar of war-machines split the air. Volker heard Makkelsson snarl a command, and the cannon belched death, adding its bellow to that of the rest of the artillery detachment. From further back he heard the shrill shriek of a rocket battery. The rockets soared overhead, racing to meet the advancing skaven.

Volker laid his rifle against the edge of the trench and flipped down his range-finder. He flicked through the selection of glass lenses until he found the correct one and leaned forwards, the rifle's stock braced against his shoulder. He selected a target and fired – another pack-leader. Pick off the leaders, and the rest of the rats would scurry back into their holes. Without waiting to see whether his shot had hit, he began to reload.

Around him, the Stormcasts had moved into position, shields raised and warblades ready. He prayed they wouldn't be needed. If the skaven got this far, there'd be little chance of stopping them. The firing platforms shook to their struts as rocket batteries and cannons fired. Handgunners opened up as well, filling the air with powder smoke. A solid wall of shot met the skaven, and tore those at the front of the advance to shreds.

The skaven that reached the front line of trenches found themselves face to face with freeguild guard, bolstered by retinues of Stormcasts. Those who weren't slain out of hand scrambled back across the wasteland between the slums and the trenches. In the forwards trenches, duelling war-cries sounded, as the men of the Iron Bulls and the Bronze Claws regiments celebrated.

Volker lifted his rifle. 'They're retreating,' he said.

'They always retreat,' one of the Stormcast said. Her voice thrummed through him like the echo of fading thunder, familiar and welcome, though her accent was strange. Her name was Sora. He'd got to know her somewhat in the weeks since the skavens' arrival. 'It is their primary strategy.'

Volker laughed. 'And a masterful one it is. Let's hope they stick to it.'

She looked down at him. 'If they run too far, we will not be able to kill them.'

Makkelsson piped up. 'They won't be able to kill us, either. That's the important bit.' Murmurs of agreement rose from down the line. The Stormcast looked around, as if puzzled.

'I would not let them hurt you,' she said. She removed her helmet, and inhaled deeply. With her close-cropped silver hair and bright blue eyes, she put Volker in mind of some hill-country matriarch. Which, like as not, she had been, before Sigmar had chosen her to fight in his name. He couldn't help but wonder who she had been, before the blessed lightning had carried her to Sigmar's side so long ago.

Volker smiled. 'Good to hear, Sora.' Sometimes, he wondered how she felt about being referred to as a 'son'. Then, given what he knew of her, he doubted she thought about it much at all. Sora was a pragmatic soul.

She stared at him for a moment, and then chuckled. She rubbed his head, nearly knocking him from his feet. 'Sometimes you remind me of my grandson, Owain.'

'Oh?'

'Then I remember that he's dead, and I am sad again.' Sora

was the friendliest of the Iron-sides, though that wasn't saying much. She shook herself, as if to banish the old hurts, and said, 'They will return.'

'They always return, sister. That, too, is a constant of their foul race.'

The newcomer's voice was deeper than Sora's by a distinct magnitude. It did not echo so much as simply crowd out all other sound. The Stormcasts turned as one, and bowed their heads in respect. Volker turned as well.

The Lord-Celestant had come. He stalked down the trench line, one palm resting on the pommel of his sheathed rune-blade, his hammer held low by his side. His sigmarite war-cloak was immaculate, despite the mud, blood and soot that stained everything else. His black war-plate seemed to soak up the light of the lanterns. If Sora was a giant, then Lord-Celestant Gaius Greel was a giant among giants.

His broad frame barely fitted in the trench, and he had to step carefully to avoid cracking the duckboards. As he approached, men and women sank to their knees or bowed their heads reverentially. It wasn't often that one of Sigmar's chosen walked among them. 'Are you well, sister?' he rumbled, looking at Sora.

'I still stand, Lord-Celestant.'

'So I see. And you, gunmaster?' The black gaze slid towards Volker. Greel's eyes were like chips of obsidian flecked with silver. His gaze was a solid weight on Volker's soul. The gunmaster fought the urge to kneel.

'I am unhurt, thanks to Sora,' he said, fighting to keep his voice even. 'Thanks to all of you. The Ironweld owes you a debt.'

Greel reached up and unclasped his helmet, pulling it off with one hand. 'It is good of you to say, son of Azyr.'

'He is a considerate boy,' Sora murmured.

Greel snorted. 'As you say, sister.' His features were the colour of marble, beneath a shock of night-black hair. He looked like a statue that had come to life, rather than a man. Volker had heard the whispers – Greel had fallen in battle more than once, and had returned twice over. Each time, he had come back... changed. Less than human, more than mortal. Even his own warriors seemed uncomfortable in his presence at times.

Greel himself was the very image of gloom; a permanent scowl was etched into his pale features. Up close, Volker could see that his black armour was pockmarked with impact craters and the marks of enemy blades. Twists of hair bound in silver and other trinkets hung from his gorget and shoulder-plates. Volker had heard from others among the Ironweld that these items had been collected from the innocent dead, as if Greel sought to make himself into a walking memorial for those whom war had unjustly claimed.

A shout from the outer trenches drew Volker's attention. He turned, lifting his rifle. 'Another attack?'

'Refugees,' Makkelsson said, peering through a telescope. 'Looks like they're trying to run the gauntlet.' He frowned as he said it. 'Poor fools. The freeguild won't let them through.'

Volker cursed. There were more than a few people left out there, in the slums the skaven had claimed. Sometimes, after an attack, they made a run for it. They rarely made it. 'Are they turning them back? That's tantamount to murder!' He whirled, glaring up at Greel. 'Tell your warriors to help them.'

'I will not.'

'They'll die.'

Greel nodded. 'Perhaps.'

Volker stared at him. 'The skaven will kill them. Or worse.'

'Your concern does you credit, though it is foolish.' The Lord-Celestant of the Iron-sides loomed over him, his expression mild.

'Better a fool than heartless,' Volker retorted.

Greel stared at him for a moment, before turning away. 'Perhaps you are right,' he said, simply. 'But it is a discussion for another time.' Shouts from the forwards trenches filtered back. Volker heard the crash of guns. Greel pulled his helmet back on. 'Eyes front, Iron-sides. The enemy is upon us.'

Through his range-finder, Volker watched the skaven advance once more. This was the largest assault yet, and the refugees scattered, seeking their hiding places. With a start, he realised the previous assault had just been a probe, testing the strength of the forwards trenches. The skaven swept forwards in a great, chittering swarm, thousands of fur-covered figures packed so tight that Volker had trouble telling where one ended and another began. The front ranks carried crude wooden shields, marked with ruinous sigils, and cruel spears.

Behind the ranks of spear-rats marched a line of armoured overseers, who cracked barbed whips over the heads of the scuttling warriors and shrieked orders. Around them flowed a tide of less uniformly equipped skaven – malnourished beasts, wearing little more than rags. These frothed and squealed shrilly, and the resulting cacophony rolled ahead of the advance, washing over the trench line.

Volker didn't bother to pick his targets. He couldn't miss at this range. And every dead skaven was one less that could kill him. The artillery detachment spoke eloquently, sweeping the front ranks of the enemy from existence. But still the skaven came on, desperate now to get under the range of the guns. They scrambled over the dead and dying, flinging themselves into the forwards trenches, attacking the volley gun crews and the freeguild soldiers. Men died beneath wave after wave of hairy bodies.

The Stormcasts stationed in the trenches moved to cover

the mortals' retreat. But even fighters as doughty as the Sons of Mallus could be dragged down by sheer weight of numbers. The crackle of ascending lightning marked the death of more than one of Greel's warriors. Volker whispered a prayer as another bolt of azure lightning arced skywards.

The skaven weren't stopping this time; even a barrage of rockets wasn't enough to dissuade them. Worse yet, they were bringing up their own guns. Volker spotted jezzail teams moving into position, setting up their heavy pavises to best take advantage of the freeguild's own defences, as the rest of the horde scurried on.

Wounded men were carried through the travel trenches, back towards the city. Fresh units of handgunners and freeguild guard from the Stormblessed regiment moved to bolster the defences. A powder barrel went up nearby, filling the air with smoke and dirt.

Volker's hands ached, and his eyes stung from the heat and powder. He continued to load and fire, his actions automatic and unconscious. He could hear little save the roar of the big guns and the screams of men and skaven. Then, there was a roll of thunder. He paused and turned. The Sons of Mallus thumped their shields again.

'Remember Hreth,' Greel rumbled, as he clambered over the lip of the trench. His warriors echoed his words as they followed him into battle. Even Sora. They advanced towards the oncoming skaven, hunched behind their shields, swords extended through the gaps. Warplock jezzails cracked as skaven claimed the trenches for their own. Several Stormcasts were punched backwards as warpstone bullets tore through their shields.

Volker concentrated on picking off the skaven gunners. His fingers grew numb, so swiftly was he reloading. The Sons of

Mallus crashed into the enemy like a battering ram. The skaven broke and flowed around them, racing towards Volker's trench. 'Makkelsson,' he called out, 'they're still coming!'

'I see them, lad,' the duardin roared. Besides the pistol shoved through the engineer's belt, he and his crew were armed only with their tools. It would have to be enough.

Volker set his rifle aside and drew one of his repeater pistols. The skaven were too close now. The freeguild were falling back – regrouping, he hoped, rather than retreating. The skaven swept forwards in a red-eyed wave, their chittering filling the air. Volker backed away from the edge of the trench, the heavy pistol levelled.

He pulled the trigger as the first pointed snouts appeared. Skaven shrieked and fell, but more poured into the trench. He dropped the emptied pistol and clawed for the second. He was forced to use it to parry a spear thrust. His fist snapped out, catching his attacker in the snout. The skaven tumbled backwards. Another darted past it and he readied himself, but it wasn't him it was after.

The skaven raced towards the stack of powder barrels, its eyes bulging in terror or frenzy, or both. It was carrying a hissing, crackling device in its paws – an explosive of some kind. Volker turned, too slowly. He fired. The skaven pitched forwards, but the explosive kept going. Volker looked up, a warning on his lips. He saw Makkelsson's eyes widen. 'Oh, *kruk*,' the duardin said, in the moment before the barrels went up and the world went white. Time seemed to shatter, and Volker's perceptions with it. For an instant, everything stopped.

Then the force of the resulting explosion slammed Volker backwards, into the wall of the trench. He collapsed, wheezing, his skull echoing from the explosion. Dazed, he searched for Makkelsson. The barrel of the ancient cannon had split open. Fire raced along the trail of spilt powder and oil, filling the trench with smoke. Volker pounded on his head, trying to clear it. He spotted Makkelsson lying nearby, a look of surprise on what was left of his face. The rest of the cannon's crew had suffered the same fate as their engineer. They lay where the force of the explosion had hurled them, flames crawling across their broken forms.

His vision blurred. Pain stretched across his scalp, and he reached up. His fingers came away red. Unable to focus, he stared into the flames. Something took shape within the flickering haze of oranges and yellows. At first he thought it was a cannonball. But then he realised that it was a head – a duardin head, but stretched and swollen. It twisted in the flames. No – it was the flame, and the smoke as well. A face made from heat and cinders. A face he recognised, for it was emblazoned on every forge, and on the memory of every mortal who'd ever picked up a rifle.

Grungni. God of Metal. The Master-Smith.

A voice thrummed through him. It did not speak in words, but in sound: hammers striking hot metal, the hiss of molten gold, the roar of the forge. Volker sagged back, clutching his head. It was too loud, too much. He screamed.

His cries were answered by chittering laughter. Dark shapes sprinted along the trench line, their blades gleaming in the firelight. Skaven. He fumbled for the artisan pistol in his belt, but his hands were numb. His panicked breath thundered in his ears. He didn't want to die this way, in front of the god.

Grungni turned. Flames roared up, sweeping down the line. The skaven went up like torches, without even a squeal to mark their passing. The god turned back, his forge-spark eyes fixed on Volker. He nodded, his mane of smoky hair swirling. Then he was gone, as if he had never been. Volker lay back.

He heard a voice call his name. Dazed, he turned. Sora clambered towards him.

Volker blacked out before she reached him.

Kretch Warpfang, Grand High Clawmaster of Clan Rictus, studied his lieutenants through slitted eyes. They were nervous, which was good. The fear-musk rose from them in pungent waves. They had failed to take the enemy trenches, and knew well the consequences of failure. He was in no hurry to pass that judgement, however. It was more satisfying to let their fear build to a crescendo – sometimes, the weaker ones even went insane.

He slumped on his throne, shrouded in war-plate that was now too large for his shrunken shape. The throne, once the skull of some subterranean monstrosity, was now a conglomeration of bone and scrap metal, covered in jagged runes, carved by the hands of slaves. Those hands now decorated the top of the throne, their fingers sealed in animal fat, and made over into candles. The light they cast was sufficient to fill his command-burrow.

The dim glow played across the plunder of a thousand campaigns – the barest scintilla of a grand collection. The light was reflected, too, in the eyes of the dozens of mutated plague rats that squirmed noisily in the tall iron cages hanging from the ceiling of the burrow. The cages were strangely formed, with esoteric mechanisms built into the underside of each.

Warpfang was old by the standards of most mortal races. By the standards of the skaven, he was impossibly ancient. For more than a century he had crouched at the top of the bone-heap that was Clan Rictus, sustained by potent magics and an enduring savagery that had not dimmed with age. His fur was the colour of dirty snow beneath his war-plate, and old scars ran through its thinning follicles, twisting and turning on themselves. They were a map of a life violently lived.

There were more than scars marking his withered limbs, however – his body was shot through with flickering veins of eerie green light. An oily jade miasma seeped from his pores and stained the edges of his armour black. Part of his splotched muzzle had calcified into a scar of shimmering warpstone. The replacement fang that had earned him his name had set strange roots within him. The warpstone fed on him, even as it sustained him.

It had changed him, somehow. Made him stronger. Smarter. It had given him the strength to claw his way up through the clan hierarchy, until he found himself at the top – alone and unchallenged. A good place to be, for any skaven.

A sure sign of his status were the guards who surrounded his throne. Few skaven leaders were brave enough to allow large bodies of armed underlings in their presence. Especially guards like these – the deathvermin. Greybacks, larger even than the black-furred skaven who filled the ranks of the stormvermin. They wore slate-coloured armour over thick crimson robes, and razor-crested skull helms, which concealed all but their fangs and whiskers. Each was armed with a heavy, serrated blade, taller than a clanrat, and hooked at the tip. The hilts of these blades were wrought to resemble the face of their god, and at its core, each weapon had a hair plucked from the mane of the Horned Rat himself.

The deathvermin were no more loyal than any other skaven, but they were far more impressive-looking than most. And even in his decrepitude, Warpfang had few doubts as to his supremacy as a warrior. Had he not earned a place of honour in the councils of the Scarlet Lord? Had he not collected the beards of the Firewalk Kings, to make himself a cloak? Even now, he could throttle any who dared challenge him.

Warpfang lifted his paw and flexed it. He felt the strands of warpstone grind against his bones. Green light flared briefly beneath his skin, and his lieutenants drew back. Warpstone was valuable, but deadly. It could make a skaven's fortune or kill him stone-dead. Warpfang chittered in amusement. The braver lieutenants were quick to join in, eager to ingratiate themselves. He silenced them with a gesture.

'Well, what have you to say for yourselves?' he growled. His voice had assumed a particular resonance since the warpstone had spread to his larynx. It was deeper now than any skaven could hope to replicate. At the sound of it, the quicker-witted lieutenants flung themselves to the floor, grovelling for all they were worth. The rest followed suit a moment later. Warpfang took note of the last to do so, and twitched a talon at the clawleader of the deathvermin. The big skaven hefted his serrated blade and stalked forwards.

The offending skaven, realising his mistake, squealed and attempted to flee, but too slowly. The deathvermin pounced, heavy sword sweeping down with finality. The lieutenant dropped, skull cleaved, legs twitching. Warpfang grunted in satisfaction. 'Either be better fighters, or quicker, yes-yes?' he rasped, studying the surviving lieutenants.

The lieutenants nodded agreeably to this wisdom. The stink of fear filled the burrow. He gestured to one of the lieutenants. 'Skesh – stand. Report-explain, yes?'

Skesh stood, hesitantly. The melted remains of numerous candles clotted the bridge of his helmet and the grooves of his shoulder-plates. Dirt stained his armour and he stank of machinery. His dark paws clenched and relaxed, just above the hilt of the war-pick hanging from his belt. 'We have made greatly-much progress, Clawlord, yes-yes.' He began to rub his paws together. 'Much tunnelling and digging and gnawing, oh most savage of potentates.'

'Yes,' Warpfang said. It was an obvious lie. Skesh's scroungers were in charge of the sapping efforts. They'd gnawed hundreds of tunnels since the beginning of the siege, few of which had proven to be of any use. The cursed duardin had tunnels of their own beneath the city, and they were prepared for such efforts. Skesh was a veteran tunnel-sneak, but he had his limits – and he was out of his depth here. Warpfang considered killing him, then decided to allow the lie to stand. Skesh would repay his mercy by redoubling his efforts. 'Good-good. You please me, Skesh.'

Skesh twitched in surprise. The other lieutenants glared at him murderously, even as they murmured in unctuous agreement. Warpfang fastened his gaze on another – a scar-faced starveling called Kleeskit. 'The latest attack failed. Explain.'

Kleeskit voided his bowels.

Warpfang leaned forwards. 'Was that an apology?'

Kleeskit shuddered, causing his war-plate to rattle. Up until the bowel-voiding, it had been suspiciously clean. Warpfang had no patience for warriors who did not fight. He leaned further, crooking a claw beckoningly. Kleeskit stumbled forwards, whining. Warpfang's paw snapped out, catching him by the muzzle. With a sharp jerk, he snapped the other skaven's neck. The body collapsed at the foot of his throne. 'Krizk – you are clawleader now. If you fail-disappoint me, I will gorge on your innards, yes-yes.'

Krizk, a heavy-set skaven, clad in the scavenged remnants of what might once have been duardin war-plate, grovelled in thanks.

Warpfang sat back. He pounded a fist against his throne.

'I want the man-things driven back. I want the storm-things driven back. I want the duardin-things driven back and then slaughtered. I want-need this now-now.' He pointed at the huddle of lieutenants. 'You will do this thing, yes-yes. And soon.'

They scrambled out of the burrow, fighting and shoving to be the first. Warpfang sighed. They would not do the thing. It was beyond them. But they would keep the enemy occupied and penned in, until his allies got under way.

He glanced up as the rats in the hanging cages began to squeal as one. The animals stiffened, their throats bulging, jaws wide. Thin arcs of emerald energy billowed from the mechanisms beneath each cage and sparked between them, until all were limned in a shimmering glow. The squealing rose in volume and stretched into a new sound – a voice.

'*–hear me?*'

'I can hear you, Quell,' said Warpfang. 'Your farsquealer works better than I expected, renegade. Perhaps you are as much the engineer as you claim to be.'

'*Many thanks, oh most brutal of despots. This humble skaven is pleased that you are pleased, and grovels at your feet.*' Quell snickered. '*Or not.*'

Warpfang restrained a growl of anger. The renegade warlock engineer could be infuriating, when he put his mind to it. It was no wonder the arch-warlocks of Skryre had put a price on his mangy head. But so long as he produced results, Warpfang would refrain from collecting it. 'Is your war engine ready, renegade?'

'*Yes-yes, most esteemed Clawlord. A few more tests – hardly any – and then we will crush the man-things, yes-yes. And you will be adjudged as a most puissant warlord, most astute, most brave-fierce, yes.*'

Warpfang snorted. The renegade had promised him a weapon

47

capable of smashing down the immense Bastion that protected the City of Storms. But as yet, he'd seen no evidence of any such thing. 'I care only about the walls, Quell. Smash-shatter them for me, or I will make sure your masters know where to find you.'

Quell chittered in amusement. One of the rats burst into flames and slumped, consumed by the energy flowing through it. Another followed, and then another, until all of the strange cages were full of dying, burning rats. Quell's chittering broke apart and faded away, lost in the crackle of flames.

Warpfang grunted in annoyance. Much as it irked him, he would have to trust that Quell knew his business. Excelsis would fall, and its treasures would be his.

He signalled one of the deathvermin.

'Get more rats for the cages.'

THREE

THE GREAT MAKER

Volker turned Makkelsson's flask over in his hands. It was still intact, though blackened by the heat of the explosion that had claimed its owner's life. Carefully, he unscrewed it and held it up. 'May your soul ever descend, and find comfort in the deepest glimmering, my friend,' he said, saluting Makkelsson before taking a swig.

He sat on the edge of the unconsecrated section of the Bronze Claws Bastion, looking out over the battlefield. Wildfires swept the plains, putting a halt to all hostilities for the moment. Both sides were regrouping. The skaven seemed to have no intention of leaving. Fresh freeguild troops filed through the trenches below as their battered comrades trudged back into the city. The Sons of Mallus, inured to war, remained at their posts. Greel and his Iron-sides would hold that savaged patch of ground until there was nothing left to defend, and even then they would not retreat unless ordered to do so.

Volker took some small comfort in that. Not much, but some.

Flesh tore and bone broke, but sigmarite held firm. He raised the flask again. 'To Sigmar's storm. May the rain fall on the just and unjust alike.' Another swig. The liquid burned going down.

Nearby, a raven croaked, as if in agreement. Dozens of the black birds perched on the edge of the Bastion, watching the trenches below with the keen interest of carrion eaters. As one, the birds swept into the air and away, towards the sea.

He glanced over his shoulder, watching them vanish into the dark. This part of the Bastion lay in the shadow of the Spear of Mallus. The mountain of rock rose high into the air, a jagged reminder of the world-that-was. A tombstone for a dead world, consumed by Chaos and spat out. Or so the stories went. Volker didn't know how much of it he believed. There were so many stories, and seemingly so little truth to any of them.

What he did know was that without the Spear, Excelsis wouldn't exist. The Spear bled secrets and prophecies into the aether. If you stood on the docks at midnight, it was said you could hear the wind whispering answers to questions no one had asked. He wasn't sure how it worked – no one really was. Not even the mages and would-be prophesiers who'd flocked to the spear, looking to profit from its incessant auguries.

He glanced up, at the floating towers and observatories of the Collegiate Arcane, which circled the Spear in a slow, unending gavotte. They had been there almost since the beginning, cast into the air not long after the Stormcast Eternals of the Knights Excelsior had raised the wedge of black iron and dark stone they called the Consecralium. The Stormkeep crouched amid the western districts like a hungry ghyrlion, its ramparts studded with trebuchets and ballista.

Not all of those celestial engines were aimed outside the city walls. Volker had heard the stories – whispers of brutal pogroms and mass executions. Of thousands put to the sword or drowned in the rising tides of the harbour, on suspicion of heretical worship. Of the great crypts beneath the Consecralium, where the bones of suspected dissidents were held and, on occasion, questioned by a gathering of Lord-Relictors and the amethyst mages of the Collegiate Arcane. Even death was no escape from the justice of Azyr.

Volker shivered and took another slug from the flask. Sometimes he wondered what he'd hoped to find by coming here, to the edge of civilisation. Not that there had been anything for him in Azyrheim. A life spent in the smoky halls of the Ironweld, fiddling with broken mechanisms. Perhaps a high rank would have come his way eventually. More likely he would have remained a minor engineer, with nothing to show for his efforts but a bad back, weak eyes and a beard in need of a good combing.

He rubbed the stubble on his chin, suddenly aware that he needed a shave. More than that, he needed food. His stomach gurgled encouragingly. He could smell cooking fires and roasting meat, wafting up from the Veins. The outer city was waking up, as the sun set.

'I thought I'd find you up here.'

Volker turned. 'Master Jorik,' he said, politely.

Jorik Grunndrak was the most senior member of the Ironweld Arsenal in Excelsis – the Master of the Arsenal. It had been Grunndrak who'd assigned him to the trenches. Not out of any malice, Volker knew, but to keep him out of the way of Herzborg and his cronies.

The cogsmith was old. Older even than the Warden Kings who held council in the deep citadels below Excelsis. Rumour had it that he'd seen Sigmar close the last Gates of Azyr, and helped craft the runes that kept the Three Brethren inviolate for five centuries.

51

Jorik stumped along the edge of the Bastion, unlit pipe clenched between his teeth. He wore heavy, rune-marked armour over thick robes, and had his thumbs tucked into his belt. He carried no visible weapons, but that didn't mean he was unarmed. 'Feeling sorry for yourself?' he growled.

'I'm toasting the memory of a friend.' Volker sloshed the flask.

Jorik nodded sombrely. 'Makkelsson. I heard. A good engineer. His name will be inscribed beside those of his predecessors, once the cannon is repaired.'

Every artillery piece in the Ironweld was marked with the names of those who had died overseeing its function. Volker knew of at least one volley gun that had so many names inscribed on each of its barrels, there was no room for any other decoration.

'Herzborg wants your head,' Jorik continued. 'He's decided you're to blame for it all.' Claudio Herzborg was currently the highest-ranking gunmaster in Excelsis, and a scion of the ancient Houses of Thunder. His blood was of the purest Azyrite stock, as he took pains to remind others at every available opportunity. He surrounded himself with a circle of similar minds and they spent most of their time attending the galas and balls that seemed to occur daily in the stormstone halls of the city's Noble Quarter.

Volker nodded. He'd expected that. 'Going to give it to him?'

Jorik laughed. 'No.' The old cogsmith sat down beside Volker with a grunt. 'It wasn't your fault, you know. I'm told you performed your function with all due efficacy.' He smiled grimly. 'Lord-Celestant Greel was very complimentary.'

'It wasn't enough.'

'You're young yet, to carry those tools,' the cogsmith said. He gestured, and Volker handed him the flask. The duardin drank. 'They weigh heavy on you.'

'I oversaw the rifling of those handguns myself,' Volker said, absently. He gestured to the trenches below. 'A good job, that. Imparts just enough spin to keep the ball on track.' He tapped his head. 'I did the calculations up here.'

'And that reason, among others, is why you hold the rank of gunmaster.'

'Herzborg wouldn't agree.'

'Herzborg is a fool,' Jorik said. 'He's here because of his blood, not his brains. He's aggravated every real officer in the city, according to General Synor.'

Volker frowned. 'The same might be said of me.' He'd heard the whispers throughout his career – mostly from men like Herzborg – that his mother had used her position on the Grand Conclave of Azyrheim to place him in the Ironweld, so that she might influence it through her son. But then, such rumours flew thick and fast in Azyrheim.

'Possibly. But the Arsenal knows its own. That you're here is proof enough.' Jorik handed the flask back.

'Herzborg doesn't think so. Nor do many of the others.'

'And so? I do not see Herzborg here. I did not see him in the trenches. That is what counts here, lad, not words.' Jorik scraped at the bowl of his pipe with a flat knife. He tapped the blade against the bottom of the bowl, emptying it. 'Besides, it's good to have influential kin. No duardin worth his beard would look down on a man for that. It's only sensible, after all. Kin are the only ones you can trust.' He put his pipe between his teeth. 'A saying my cousin Oken is fond of.'

Volker looked at him, startled. 'Oken…?'

Jorik nodded. 'An old clan, ours. Venerable even when the world was young. We dug our way out of one world and into another, ahead of an all-consuming fire, or so the story goes. We left a lake enclosed by mountains, and came to new waters

53

and new mountains. Formed a new clan from the ruins of the old.'

'Oken never talked about it much.'

'That sounds like him.' Jorik concentrated on packing his pipe. 'Haven't seen him in some time. Not like him, to go so long without sharing a drink.'

Volker shook his head. 'No, it isn't.' He sighed. 'I wish he was here.'

'I suspect he does as well.' He lit his pipe carefully, scraping the edge of the blade across the rim of the stone bowl. He puffed contentedly. 'You know where he is?'

'No.' Volker peered at the cogsmith. An odd line of questioning. What was Jorik getting at? 'Do you?'

'No,' Jorik said. He puffed more fiercely, and sparks danced above the bowl of the pipe. 'But I know someone who might.' He turned, smoke curling about his face. 'And they want to speak to you, lad.'

Volker felt a chill at the cogsmith's words. The chill only grew as he noticed the shape the smoke was taking.

A face. The same face he'd seen in the fires of the destroyed cannon. A face he'd half convinced himself was nothing more than a hallucination, brought on by the stress of near death. A face that was as familiar to any member of the Ironweld as their own.

Volker shot to his feet, heart hammering. 'The Great Maker,' he whispered. The Smith-God had not been seen in the mortal realms for nearly a century. Some said he had followed Grimnir into whatever darkness awaited fallen gods. Others, that he had simply grown tired of serving as Sigmar's armourer, and had struck out on his own. A few claimed that the runelords of the Dispossessed knew, but if they did, they weren't telling.

Eyes like sparks met his own and the mouth moved. There

was no sound, but he heard what the apparition said nonetheless. A time. A place. The location stretched across his mind like smoke. It was somewhere in the outer city – what folk called the Veins. He knew, without knowing how, that once he started walking he would find where he was supposed to go. He hesitated. 'Is it – is it really him?'

Jorik puffed contentedly on his pipe. 'I wouldn't know about that. I merely pass along the message.' He cocked an eye at Volker. 'I'd suggest doing as he says, though.'

Elsewhere.

In his dark cave, Volundr, Forgemaster of Aqshy, crushed embers between his fingers and read futures in the trickling soot. Not the future, or even a future, but many different ones. Paths and destinies untaken and unfulfilled. In the fires of his forge could be read the life of all the realms, for good or ill.

He turned, gesturing. 'Bring him.'

His assistants lurched forwards, dragging the slave between them. They were large brutes, descendants of the Raxulian herds that had once haunted the crater rim of Klaxus. Shaggy and crimson, the beastmen wore muzzles of brass and leather wired to their skulls, and their horns had been shaved and capped with gold. Their smocks were stiff with years of bloodstains, and scars left by fire and lash cut deep trails through their flesh.

The slave was new – a recent capture, from some minor battlefield. A hundred warlords owed Volundr a tithe of flesh and bone for every victory earned with the weapons he crafted. Most of the slaves were put to work in the quarry pits and bone fields, but some were fit for a more important purpose.

The man struggled, even now. Limbs broken, flesh scarred, he struggled. His breath came in tortured gasps, through ragged lips. The stink of the battlefield was still on him, the blood of friends and enemies alike still fresh on the tatters of his clothing and armour. He gargled curses in a liquid tongue – some hill dialect from Chamon, Volundr thought. 'The anvil,' he said, stepping back.

His assistants did as he bade, forcing the captive's head and shoulders down on the scalding surface of the anvil. The man screamed and thrashed. Volundr lifted the chains he held, and the second, smaller anvil that dangled from them. 'You were brave,' he intoned. 'And thus does Khorne reward brave men.'

His assistants leapt back with bestial speed as he swung the anvil up, and brought it crashing down on the slave's head. Bone splintered and flesh tore as the wounded man's skull ruptured at the point of impact and was reduced to shivering fragments. The blood seeped into the surface of the anvil, causing the pitted metal to grow white-hot. Volundr carefully gathered the bone fragments up, and dropped them into the fire pit.

One of his assistants whined eagerly. Volundr grunted and gestured. 'As you will.'

The beastmen fell upon the body ravenously, tearing at it. They stuffed gobbets of cooling meat through the grilles of their muzzles, and painted their fur and manes in blood. Volundr watched the creatures for a moment. He almost envied them such simple pleasures. But such was not for him. Not any more.

He touched the scarred surface of his chest-plate. He could still recall the feeling of the lightning coursing through him. The hammer blow of Sigmar's wrath, called down on his head by a dead man, shrouded in iron. One of Sigmar's chosen.

The sky-god had returned with a vengeance. And war had come with him. Not the little wars of the Age of Blood, but a conflagration unlike any other. A fire so great that it had spread to every corner of every realm, and drawn every eye to its glow. For the first time in a long time, Khorne knew the peace of total war.

His champions had grown fat and lazy, barring a few. Now, those who remained were lean and eager to prove themselves. They cast themselves into the fire, heedless of the risks. That was all Khorne asked of most of his followers: that they show courage, and leave a river of blood in their wake.

'But he asks more of those of us with the wit to hear,' he murmured. All of the blood had seeped into the anvil now. In the resulting steam, he saw Ahazian Kel riding hard across the dusty plains of Shyish. Dark shapes pursued him – the servants of a dead queen. Volundr growled, low in his throat.

Unacceptable. But there was nothing to be done, save hope that he had chosen well. Ahazian knew where to go, and would have to reach it on his own. The iron-oath prevented him from doing anything more to aid his champion.

Not that Ahazian Kel needed aid. The Ekran had only been defeated, in the end, by their own ferocity. They had resisted every army sent against them, until Khorne, at last, set his hooks in the kel – the warrior princes who'd ruled the Ekran. Slowly, surely, working with a subtlety only rarely displayed, Khorne had twisted their martial honour into something savage. Their empire had collapsed in an orgy of violence, leaving behind only ruin.

Ahazian was not the only kel to survive, whatever he claimed. But all were like him – unfit for command, desirous only of battle. They would never rise to lead great armies in Khorne's name, but their services were highly sought after by those who did. As warriors they had few equals. But would skill alone prove enough for the task ahead?

That the Eight Lamentations were stirring now was a portent

worth heeding. The weapons scented war the way a hound scented prey. Though the battle for the All-Gate was at a standstill, the realms still thundered with the cries of the slain. The Three-Eyed King stirred in his keep, making ready, and the Chaos gods watched him, and plotted.

As his fellow forgemasters plotted. They had all gone their own ways, seeking the advantage. The iron-oath was coming to its end and soon they would be at each other's throats once more. Whichever one of them succeeded in this quest would face an alliance of the others. They could not allow one of them to stand above the rest. Better death than subservience. Thus did the Blood God control the hearts and minds of his servants. Even those whom he clearly favoured.

Volundr frowned. Khorne had spoken to him in a dream. His thunderous whispers had drawn him from the haze of pain that had been his constant companion since Klaxus and the shattering of the Black Rift. Khorne had spoken to him then, as well.

In his dream, the god had shown him things – impossible things. Nurgle huddled, blinded and injured, in his manse, his servants in disarray. Tzeentch spreading his wings, ready to ascend when the Blighted One descended – as Khorne had ascended when his rival Slaanesh had vanished. The ancient pacts were undone, the old balance askew. Where there had been Four, there might now be Two, if Nurgle succumbed.

And perhaps soon, only One.

Khorne would be that one. For was Khorne not the strongest of the Four, and the eldest? All that was had been his in the beginning, and would be again. And to that end, as mightiest of the Four, was it not fitting that his strongest champions carried those weapons forged at his command?

Thus had Khorne commanded his forgemasters to find those things that had been lost, and lay them at the foot of his throne of skulls. Even now, somewhere in the black seas of infinity, those who were worthy enough to wield the Eight Lamentations in Khorne's name were being gathered. And so Volundr would find the eight weapons and become Master of all Forges, rather than simply one.

Something croaked.

Volundr looked up, alert. A raven sat perched high above him, watching him with its glittering black eyes. The bird cocked its head and croaked again. It almost sounded like laughter.

'A spy, then?' Volundr hefted the chain, and the war-anvil that dangled from it. The bird leapt away, in a skirl of loose feathers. Volundr watched it sail away, into the depths of the cavernous forge. Unease gnawed at him.

'Ride swiftly, Ahazian Kel. For both our sakes.'

Volker strode through the folds of the salt-mist that permeated the Veins, one hand on the pistol in his belt, his rifle leaning across his shoulder. The mist slunk in from the sea every evening, to curl through the knot of rickety buildings that rose about him, inundating every nook and cranny.

The quality of the structures that lined the cobbled streets declined steadily the further away from the city centre one got. Here, it was a warren of cramped wooden cages, one set atop the next. Shadows pooled thickly in arterial alleyways, and gas lamps cast a hazy glow across the misty streets. Pools of stagnant water occupied dips in streets slick with night soil and tallow. This effluent clumped against the edges of the gutters, alongside the beggars and the drunks, and worse things besides.

As he passed an alleyway, someone coughed discreetly. He caught a glint of steel out of the corner of his eye and paused.

They'd been following him for a few streets now, he thought. Not surprising. Good-quality weapons fetched a high price on the docks. No one was safe in the Veins – roof runners and alley-men took their prey with impunity. He swung his rifle down, into the crook of his arm, his thumb on the hammer. 'Think carefully, friends,' he said. 'How much are you willing to pay, to take what I have?'

Moments passed. He considered a warning shot, and then discarded the idea. It would be a waste of a bullet he might otherwise need. He was just about to speak again when he heard the splash of retreating footsteps. The alley-men had chosen to seek less well-armed prey. He sighed, shouldered his rifle and continued on.

Besides the ever-present smell, the tangled streets were full of sound and colour, beneath the muffling folds of the salt-mist. Even with the skaven scratching at the gates, life went on. It was the nature of the realm, and the city raised on its soil displayed that savage zest for life in every aspect of its function.

Here in these streets, the descendants of the lowborn fisher folk who'd made the Coast of Tusks their home rubbed shoulders with off-duty freeguild guardsmen and glowering duardin. The majority of the city's population lived and worked in the Veins, whether they wanted to or not.

Market stalls occupied every corner and crossway, with merchants from as far away as Vindicarum hawking their wares. Meteors and motes readily changed hands, the coins of meteoric iron being among the most commonly traded currency. But there were more esoteric forms of legal tender on display – quicksilver ingots, crudely shaped coins of ur-gold, iridescent scales harvested from dragon hatchlings. But above them all were the glimmerings – crystal vials of vaporous secrets and prophetic whispers, gleaned from the shard of Mallus occupying the bay. Some hoarded these to trade later, while others consumed them for their own illumination.

Volker paused to watch as a swarthy man in cerulean robes pried loose the stopper on one such vial and inhaled the contents. The coloured vapour seeped into his lungs and the man doubled over, coughing. When he straightened, he had a horrified expression on his face. He screamed and staggered, clawing at his head. His friends rushed to help him as he sank to the street, weeping. Not every secret was worth knowing. Volker quickly moved on.

Grungni's message pounded in his head like a drumbeat. The shock of it was beginning to wear off, and Volker felt a twinge of trepidation. It wasn't every day that one met a god. Especially a god not one's own.

A doorway lantern crackled and Volker tensed. It had sounded like laughter. Overhead, a raven croaked. He looked up, but the bird was nowhere in sight. He realised that he'd turned down a blind alley and stopped. The lanterns here were crude things, barely flickering. But they blazed to impossible brightness ahead of him, as if to light his way.

A chill ran through him as he caught sight of a shadow on the wall. It hunched forwards in the light of the lanterns, shaggy and huge. Eyes like sparks fixed on him as the shadow turned, one massive paw beckoning him on.

The ground trembled beneath his feet, echoing with strange reverberations. Unthinking, he clasped the hammer-shaped amulet that hung around his neck. Normally he gave it no thought, but here, now, he desired nothing more than the comfort the sigil of Sigmar offered. The rumble receded. The glow of the lanterns had faded to a soft radiance. In the luminous haze, he thought he saw a face – Grungni's face. The god spoke, as he had on the battlefield, without sound.

Volker nodded slowly. When the gods called, a man had little choice but to go. He continued on. The lanterns flickered out behind him as he passed them. There was a strange glimmer ahead, and a new, more tangible unease rose in him. The way forwards was blanketed in thick webs. As the lights played across them, strange colours rose from within their patterns. It was almost hypnotic.

Dream-spiders. Volker grimaced in disgust. He eased through the webs of unfulfilled prophecy, ignoring the whispered promises and half-glimpsed visions that rose up whenever he tore a strand. To give in to the colourful lure of the webs was to risk winding up just one more smiling, blood-drained corpse in the back alleys of Excelsis. Spiders the size of rats scuttled from his path, their iridescent bodies glinting eerily in the dark.

A strand of web brushed against his cheek, and visions danced before his eyes. He saw himself falling from a great height, something black and terrible swooping towards him. His heart jumped with the echoes of a phantom pain, and he staggered. His mouth tasted of ashes. He thrashed his way free of the webs using his long rifle to tear them, and stumbled towards the end of the alley. There was a door there, set into an incongruous stone frame.

A massive hand reached out of the dark and caught him.

'No go,' a deep voice rumbled. Volker looked up. The ogor looked down. The brute was twice his height, and clad in crudely beaten plates of iron, over threadbare trousers. He was bald, save for a tightly wound scalp lock, and flowing moustaches that hung to either side of a toothy grin. Indecipherable brands marked his grey flesh – most were primitive in design, but one was immediately recognisable as the duardin rune for 'forge'.

'I'm expected,' Volker said, hesitantly. He kept his hand away from the pistol in his belt. The ogor held a hammer in his other hand, and one swing of it would be enough to pulp Volker's skull, if he wasn't careful.

The ogor said nothing. Instead, he lifted the hammer and gave the door a resounding tap, shaking it in its frame. Then he set the weapon lightly against Volker's shoulder. 'We see,' the brute said, almost cheerfully. 'If no, I smash your skull, yes?'

Volker swallowed thickly, and nodded. 'That seems entirely reasonable.'

They didn't have to wait long. The door opened and a wizened, bearded face peered out. 'What?' a thin voice wheezed, from within the bramble of white hair.

'He is expected,' the ogor growled, peering down at the newcomer.

'Is he?' The face turned to Volker. 'Are you?'

It was a duardin, Volker realised. But a very old one. Older even than Jorik or Oken. So old that all that wasn't absolutely necessary had worn away, leaving a narrow blade of a duardin. Axe-sharp eyes studied him warily.

'I am.'

'He is,' the newcomer said, glaring at the ogor. 'Why'd you stop him?'

'I guard door,' the ogor said, patiently.

'Yes, but he's expected.'

The ogor shrugged. 'So I knock, yes?' He grinned and shoved Volker towards the door, nearly knocking him off his feet. 'You are expected.'

Volker looked back and forth, trying to make sense of the exchange. The newcomer grumbled impatiently. 'Are you coming in or not?' The door swung inwards. Volker had to duck to enter. It was smaller than it looked.

Heat enveloped him as the duardin shut the door. The red

glow of firelight stained rough-hewn stone walls. From outside, the building had merely been another wooden tenement, but inside it was something else again – larger than it ought to have been, impossibly vast. He turned, and saw strange runes carved into the stone frame of the door. They shone with an orange light, and he quickly looked away.

'A realmgate?' he asked softly. His voice echoed, even so.

'No,' the old duardin said. He was scrawnily built, beneath the thick furs that draped his form. His hair was wild and unkempt, as was his beard, and old scars marked his hollow cheeks. 'Don't be daft. Realmgates are big things. Loud.' He turned and beckoned Volker. 'Now, be silent and follow me.' He limped away, moving as if the very act of walking pained him.

Volker looked around, trying to pierce the haze of smoke that clung to everything. He had the impression of immense pillars rising along curved walls. The runes etched into their circumference glowed with heat, and red cracks ran through the dark stones of the floor. He could hear the sound of hammers ringing down on steel and stone, and the quiet murmur of voices, somewhere beyond the pillars. But he could see nothing save vague shapes and the scarlet glow of forges. Sweat ran down his face and neck. What was this place?

The old duardin led him along an uneven path. Volker stumbled more than once, and nearly fell after colliding with a hunched shape. He backed away, apologising to the grumbling figure. The old duardin grabbed him by the coat. 'Stop bothering them, you daft fool. Can't you see that they're working?'

'I can't see anything,' Volker protested.

'*Umgi*,' the old duardin said, derisively.

Volker jerked free of his grip. 'I know what that means.'

'Then you are not wholly ignorant.'

'Why am I here? What is this place?'

The old duardin flushed, and jabbed a thick finger in Volker's chest. 'This place is sacred, umgi. A place only for those who seek it. That is not you.' The vehemence in the duardin's voice startled Volker.

'I meant no offence,' he began, in halting Khazalid.

'Do not sully our tongue with such inferior pronunciation,' the duardin growled, eyes narrowed. Spittle flecked his beard. 'If you must speak, use your own language. You would not borrow the tools of another – why do you feel free to borrow words?' He poked Volker again. 'Are you a thief, then?'

Volker shook his head. Before he could reply, a deep voice did so for him. 'He is no thief, Vali, my son. No more than Sigmar is a thief, or the Six Smiths. No more than any of those who seek this place out, to learn what I have to teach them.'

The old duardin – Vali – stepped back. He bowed his head, a disgruntled look on his face. Volker turned slowly. He could feel the power of the being standing behind him, like warmth blasting from a furnace. Driven by instinct, he sank to one knee, head bent, before he could get more than a glimpse of the squat, massive shape.

'Rise, son of Azyr,' the god rumbled. His voice echoed through Volker like the reverberation of a hammer striking metal, dragging him to his feet. He felt at once scalded and frozen, like a chunk of metal thrust first into flame and then into water. Malleable, and yet brittle, as if the god broke and reshaped him with every word.

There was warmth there, and kindness. A craftsman's consideration. But also a lurking ferocity that sent a thrill of primal fear shooting through the roots of Volker's soul. He tried to push it aside, to concentrate on what he could see. He had never met a god before, and woven in amid the fear was a faint thread of curiosity.

Grungni was clearly a duardin, but a duardin the size of an ogor. He reminded Volker of one of the great statues that lined the deep paths the Dispossessed had carved beneath the city. He was dressed in a stained, much-patched smock over his bare torso. His thick arms were crossed over a chest like a powder keg, and bandy legs supported his bulk.

It was the last thing that most struck Volker about the god's appearance, even more so than his beard of smoke and mane of fire. It was impossible to believe that those small, bent legs could support such a massive frame.

Grungni chuckled. 'They were broken, long ago.' He reached down and patted his thigh. 'By my own hammer, no less. An insult I spent an eternity attempting to repay.'

'Did you?' Volker asked, before he could stop himself.

Grungni smiled. 'It depends on your perspective. One could say that I am even now in the process of paying it back.' His smile widened, displaying teeth like hot cinders. 'Some grudges are best nurtured.'

Volker shuddered. The god's smile put him in mind of a cannon's muzzle in the moments before it belched fire and smoke. 'You summoned me here.' It wasn't a question. The duardin did not question their gods. They spoke, and the gods replied, or not, as they wished. He wasn't a duardin but he knew that much.

Vali growled something beneath his breath. Grungni's smile faded. 'Go, Vali. I would speak with our guest.' The old duardin bowed low and retreated, still grumbling. Grungni sighed. 'You must forgive him. Vali is old. I have kept him by my side for more years than I can count. Selfish of me, perhaps. But then I am old as well, and set in my ways.'

Volker said nothing. It seemed rude to interrupt the god while he was talking. Grungni's eyes twinkled and he held out his hand. 'May I?' Volker handed him the long rifle. Grungni took the weapon and examined it carefully, murmuring to himself as he ran his fingers along the rifle's length. 'A good weapon, this. Old technique – duardin?'

Volker nodded.

Grungni chuckled. 'I can feel the memory of its shaping still clinging to the barrel. A light touch, but skilful. You should be proud.'

'I had help,' Volker said, mouth dry.

'The best craftsmen do, whether they admit it or not.' The god's voice grew sad, and Volker felt it, in his heart. 'Once I had the help of many like myself.' He held out the rifle, and Volker took it gingerly. The wood and metal were warm, and felt somehow lighter, as if the god's touch had changed the weapon in some indefinable way.

'We had a sister, Grimnir and I. Aye, and more than one. Brothers too. Sons and… and wives.' He paused and shook his head. 'Our voices shaped the realms of metal and fire, and the roots of more realms besides. Our song drew up the stones from the seas and our hands crafted the mountains.' Grungni frowned. 'Or maybe I misremember. I am old, as I said, and I have lived many lives. Older even than he who sits upon the throne of Azyr.'

His voice grew soft, like the crackle of dying fire. 'Sometimes, I think I am older than all that ever was. I see my brother marching into the snowy north, axe in hand, crafting a road of enemy skulls. Then I see him again, wreathed in fire and falling away into legend. Both are him, and yet not.'

Volker said nothing. The words were not meant for him, he knew. That he was here was incidental. Grungni spoke to the shadows on the smithy wall, and the flames that roared in the unseen forges, not to him. Not to a human.

The god laughed softly. 'And what is a human, Owain Volker, but untempered iron, awaiting the heat and the hammer's touch?'

Volker stiffened. Had the god read his mind, or were his feelings so plain?

'Both and neither.' Grungni reached out and caught him behind the head with one massive hand. Volker froze. The strength in that hand could crush his skull like an egg. The heat of Grungni's palm blackened the ends of his hair. The god studied him with eyes like melted gold. Finally, he released Volker and stepped back, as if satisfied. 'Yes. Oken was right. There is steel in you, son of Azyr. Good.'

'Oken? Is he here? What–?'

Grungni smiled. 'All in good time. But first, come. There are others you must meet. Time is short and we have much to discuss.'

∞ FOUR ∞

EIGHT WEAPONS

Grungni led Volker deeper into the smoke and heat of the smithy. The god ignored his questions, and eventually Volker fell silent. He contented himself with listening to the sounds of industry echoing from the hazy depths. There were many such places in Excelsis, buried deep within the halls of the Dispossessed.

But this place was something else again. A hidden smithy – or was it? Were they even in Excelsis any more? There were no windows, and he couldn't hear the city; only the sounds of hammers striking metal, and voices murmuring in conversation. He caught snatches of those discussions drifting on the smoky air, and the strange accents of their participants. Deep, rough growls conversed with softer, silken tones, between the crash of metal on metal. Duardin voices, some of these, and human as well, but others were less identifiable.

Was this a temple of some sort? Or was it a school? Out of the corner of his eye, Volker caught sight of a clockwork shape scuttling into the dark, its gemstone eyes winking in the firelight. More shapes, arachnid and gleaming, scampered along the walls, their gears clicking softly. He gripped his rifle more tightly.

Unable to restrain himself any longer, Volker cleared his throat, trying to catch the god's attention. 'Why am I here? Does it have something to do with my – with Oken?'

'Oken is my servant. One of many.' Grungni glanced at him. 'Did you know that?'

'I – no. No, he never said.'

'And why would he?' Grungni hooked his thumbs into his belt. 'He served me loyally and well, for years without number. Not so long as some, but longer than others.'

'But what does that have to do with me?'

Grungni stopped and fixed him with a level stare. 'Oken is missing.'

He ran his hand through his smoky beard, tearing some of it loose. He held it out to Volker, who watched in awe as the smoke shaped itself into a face – battered and old. Oken. The duardin was like a lump of granite someone had chiselled a face onto as a joke. 'He was searching for something, at my behest. I believe he found it.'

Volker looked up, and then away. He couldn't bear to meet Grungni's gaze for long. There was an awful weight to it, and a sadness that threatened to overwhelm him. Like the last fires of a dying city, or a beacon that would never be answered. 'What – what was it?'

'Something dangerous.'

Volker closed his eyes. 'Is he alive?'

'That is what I wish to know. That is what I called you here to find out.'

Volker frowned. 'Why me?'

Grungni shrugged. 'Why not you?' He gestured. 'I saw your face in the fire, lad, and heard your name in its crackling. It's a fool who doesn't listen when such things speak. Especially a god.'

Volker shook his head. 'But–'

'Enough. It is time to meet the others.' Grungni gestured. A doorway rose out of the haze, sloping and squarish. It was not a duardin door, with precise angles and tidy corners. Instead, the frame was composed of three massive stone slabs, one balanced atop the other two. The slabs were all different sizes and the frame was sloped haphazardly. A rough-cured curtain of leather hung within the frame, runes marked on its folds with soot and ash.

Grungni swept the curtain aside and stepped within. Volker made to follow, but found that he had to duck to do so. Had their seeming magnitude been a trick of the light or had Grungni simply changed size? Nothing here was what it seemed.

Confused, he stepped into the chamber beyond. The air was different here, clean and thin. Cold as well. His breath plumed before him, despite the fire that crackled in the forge built into one wall. The fire cast its orange light over a small stone chamber, rough-hewn but clean, with thick furs covering the floor. A round table occupied the centre of the room, with eight chairs set up around it. Three of the chairs were in use.

The woman drew Volker's eye immediately. She was tall and dark, with a mane of tightly bound serpentine black locks spilling across her shoulders and down her back. She wore battered war-plate the colour of tarnished gold over well-worn, if good quality, clothing. Leather gloves covered her hands, and vambraces made from hundreds of coins of all denominations protected her forearms. A golden helmet, wrought in the shape of a gryph-hound's head, with a coif of bronze feathers, sat on the table in front of her.

She grinned widely as Grungni showed Volker to the table. 'He's very fancy,' she said. She bent sideways and studied Volker's feet. 'Good boots, though. I respect a man who knows the value of good boots.'

'Thank you?' Volker said, uncertain as to the proper response.

'Zana,' she said, as she straightened up.

'What?'

'Zah-nah,' she elaborated, sounding out the syllables. Her accent was fluid. The Chamonian dialect of the celestial tongue was a liquid thing, harsh in some places, soft in others. 'Mathos. Zana Mathos.'

Volker blinked.

She peered at him for a moment, then looked at Grungni. 'Is he addled?'

'I'm not addled.'

'Oh good, I was worried. We're already well stocked with addle-pated lunatics. Isn't that right, Roggen?' She looked at the burly man sitting beside her.

He smiled genially. 'You would know, Zana.' He rose and extended his hand to Volker. His accent was coarse, as if he had only learned to speak Celestial a few days earlier. 'I am Roggen, of the Ghyrwood March.'

Roggen was heavy with muscle beneath his armour, and his thick, tattooed arms were bare from shoulder to elbow, showing off numerous serpentine scars. A similar scar bisected his right eye, and vanished within his thick beard. His bronze-coloured war-plate was decorated with curling vine motifs and what might have been sylvan faces, which seemed to study Volker with cool disinterest. The ragged tabard he wore over his armour was the colour of tree moss, and a helm crafted in the shape of a stag's head, complete with curved, thorn-like antlers, sat on the table.

As Volker took his hand, he realised that Roggen's gauntlet wasn't made of iron or bronze, but some sort of incredibly tough fibre. The big man noticed his look and chuckled. 'Ironwood,' he said. He knocked on his chest-plate. 'Hard as metal, but it lives and breathes.'

'And in the spring, it sheds leaves everywhere,' Zana said. She leaned back in her chair, legs crossed on the tabletop. 'Burns easy, too.'

Roggen shrugged. 'At least I do not have to take it off when I fall in the water.'

'Do you fall in the water a lot, then?'

'Do you get set on fire often?' Roggen retorted. Zana laughed.

'Maybe we should ask him,' she said, jerking her chin towards the third chair. 'Though he hasn't so much as told us his name since he arrived.'

The third chair was occupied by a scowling duardin. He was squat, thickly muscled and distractingly unclothed. His only concession to civilised sensibilities was a loincloth made from the black scales of some great beast, and a wide belt of the same, strapped tight about his midsection. He wore a helmet crafted in the shape of a rearing dragon, open at the top to allow a thick crest of crimson hair to spring forth. The plaits of his massive beard were bound in gold and capped by iron hooks that clattered dangerously with every turn of his head.

A fyreslayer, Volker realised. He'd never met one of the strange duardin before. He bowed low, as a gesture of respect. 'Owain Volker,' he said, simply.

'Lugash, son of no runefather, scion of no lodge,' the duardin growled, scratching at one of the many golden runes hammered into his flesh. An abundance of short-hafted fyresteel throwing axes were thrust through the rawhide loops of his belt, and a cruelly barbed war-iron sat on the table before him, alongside a hook-bladed axe. His thick fingers traced the sigils carved into the axe's haft as he stared a hole in Volker. 'Another manling,' he said, finally, looking at Grungni somewhat accusingly.

'Aye and what of it, nephew?' Grungni chuckled. 'Grand-nephew, rather. Many generations removed.'

'You are not the god of manlings, Maker.'

'Am I not? Do you own me then, child of my brother?' Grungni's deep voice was even, but Volker could hear the undercurrent of warning in his words. 'Who am I the god of, Lugash of the– '

'Do not say it,' Lugash roared, heaving himself to his feet. His runes flared, and Volker backed away as heat bled off the duardin.

Grungni frowned and brought his hands together, almost gently. The glowing runes went cold and dark. Lugash staggered, as if all the strength had been wrenched from him.

'Who are you to tell me what I can, or cannot, say? You are the blood of my brother, and so I am oathbound to show patience – and yes, kindness, even. But my patience extends only so far. Do not let my brother's fire drive you to rashness, as it did him.'

Lugash fell back into his seat, his expression surly. Grungni shook his head. 'Grimnir was much the same,' he said, absently. 'Always seeking offence where none was meant. He craved it, the way a drunkard craves ale. Insult was his milk and impatience was his meat. And now he is dead, and his children look to me.' He sounded weary.

'Dead, but not gone,' Lugash said.

'No. Not gone. And death is not the end.' Grungni sighed. 'But I did not bring you here to speak of my brother, fascinating as he was.' He turned to the open forge and thrust his hand into the flames. He grasped a handful of hot coals and spilled them into the concave dip at the centre of the table. Fire roared up. Volker stared at it, seeing indistinct images in the crackling flames.

'Sit, son of Azyr. My story is long, and you are tired.'

Volker suddenly realised that the god was right. He was tired, and had been for some time. Adrenaline and curiosity had kept him on his feet thus far, but it was fast wearing off. He took the empty seat and laid his long rifle on the table. Grungni nodded, pleased.

'Four children, from four realms. Enough to make a start, I suppose.' He stumped around the table, waving a hand over the head of each of them in turn. 'Chamon, Ghyran, Aqshy and Azyr. Metal, Life, Fire and the Heavens. I've made better from worse, and no mistake.'

'That almost sounds like an insult,' Zana murmured.

Grungni smiled. 'No insult intended, Zana. As you well know. How long have you served me, daughter of Chamon?' He set his hand on the back of her chair. Zana straightened.

'Years, my lord,' she said, with no trace of her previous sarcasm.

'You were a vagabond when you came to me. An exile, worth more dead than alive. And now...' Grungni gestured. 'Now you are something better.'

The god turned, trailing smoke from his beard and hair. It curled behind him, making strange shapes in the air. He traced his hand along the back of Roggen's chair. 'And you, son of Ghyran. How long have you fought under my banner?'

Roggen knocked on the table. 'Six seasons, Maker, and proudly. I am a Knight of the Furrow, and such was my oath upon taking up the sword.'

Grungni nodded, and looked down at Lugash. 'Lugash, blood of my brother. We know our bargain, don't we? No more need be said of that.'

Lugash closed his eyes and muttered something. He looked as if he were praying.

At last, Grungni turned to Volker. 'These others have served me for some time. Will you join their number?'

Volker hesitated. What was being asked of him here? His hands found the hammer-shaped amulet again. Grungni shook his head. 'Fear not. I am not a greedy god, lad. I ask only your sweat, not your soul. Roggen's first fealty is to the Lady of Leaves. Lugash serves the memory of my brother. And Zana…' He paused. 'Who do you worship, lass?'

Zana shrugged. Grungni laughed, and the room shook from his mirth. 'Maybe it's me, eh? No shame in it.' He looked at Volker. 'You see? Sigmar still has first claim on your spirit, but I need your steady hand and keen eye, gunmaster. And Oken does as well. What say you?'

Volker stuffed the amulet beneath his chest-plate and nodded. If Oken was in danger, there was no choice. The old duardin was a friend, and a Volker never turned their back on a friend. Whatever the consequences.

Grungni smiled. 'Good.' The god reached into his smock and retrieved a lump of black iron. It was streaked with raw, red veins and Volker thought he glimpsed what might have been a face on one facet. Grungni bounced it on his palm, and then tossed it into the fire at the centre of the table. There was a sound like tearing sailcloth, and something rose from the flames. It had no shape, but was of all shapes – as if it were a thing of potential, rather than certainty. Monstrous mouths screamed silently, as chains of embers held it trapped in the bowl. Its elemental shape convulsed, glaring in all directions at once.

'What in the nine glorious ores is that?' Zana hissed, making the sign of the hammer over her heart. Volker did the same, feeling the weight of his amulet around his neck.

'A daemon,' Lugash said, fingering his axe. 'Or it was.'

'It was a message,' Grungni said. 'Or a warning, though the sender did not intend it so. Look – see.' He gestured, and the fiery entity writhed as polished facets of red glass blossomed from its semi-liquid shape. In the glass, Volker could see faces, movement, people and places. Grungni caught his questioning look and nodded. 'A daemon is more than its form. It is sorcery itself, hammered and shaped by the summoner's mind. Those drawn into these realms by mortal hands take on something of their master – a bond of memory binds them together. And in that bond are the seeds of intent and cause.'

He raised one wide hand, and the shape in the bowl stretched with agonising slowness. Volker could not hear the daemon's screams, but he could feel them in his teeth and in his joints. As the entity stretched, more facets surfaced in its roiling substance. Images swam within them. Scenes of antediluvian destruction, as monstrous warriors battled among themselves across broken, bloody ground.

Volker heard the clash of weapons – not normal ones, these, but something else. A great, iron-banded mace, gripped by a slab-muscled giant, connected with a massive gate of bone and iron, and shattered it into a thousand flinders. Volker jerked back instinctively. He'd felt the resonance of the blow, some-how. 'Sharduk, the Gate-Smasher. Forged from the remains of the last great gargant-kings of the Golden Peaks. No port-cullis or doorway can stand against it, whatever its thickness or the magic warding it.' Grungni's voice came from some-where behind him.

A second facet. An emaciated creature, covered in runic

brands and scarification, swung and snapped a chain-whip. Men and women in amethyst armour died, their souls torn from the withering flesh by the barbed links. 'Charu, the Soul-Lash. Each link crafted with a single, ruinous purpose. To hook the soul, and bind its strength to that of the one who wields the Lash.'

Lash and wielder faded, replaced by a brawling barbarian chieftain clad in furs and crude armour. A stiff crest of hair rose from his shaved pate, giving him a bestial appearance. The strange, ridged cestus gauntlet he wore only added to this impression. The gauntlet flexed, the hooked talons tipping each finger glowing with a savage heat. 'Sunraker, the War-Claw. A crude thing, built by crude hands, but no less deadly than the others. The heat of its touch is enough to melt stone, or even the scales of a dragon.'

Another facet rose, replacing the barbarian and his fiery claw, revealing instead a shadowy warrior clad in armour made from some tarry substance. The warrior hefted a spear with a wide, leaf-shaped blade. Grungni's voice became hard. 'Gung. The Huntsman. The Spear of Shadows. But whisper a name or hurl it at a target and it shall seek them out, wherever they are, whatever the distance. Even the membrane between realms is no barrier to its murder-lust.'

Grungni reached over Volker's shoulder and clasped the facet. He twisted the substance of it, the way a blacksmith might twist a length of hot iron, trapping the flickering image and making it larger. 'These weapons, and four more like them, each equal in power and malevolence, were – are – called the Eight Lamentations. They were forged in the fires of Khorne's wrath by his chosen forgemasters.' The god growled as he spoke, and Volker sensed an abiding rage there. One he was glad was not aimed at him.

'Eight forgemasters, one for each of the mortal realms, crafted eight weapons from the raw stuff of Chaos, which infused existence. Eight weapons fit for a god, or the champion of a god. But these weapons were lost amid the madness of the Age of Blood, when the Dark Gods made war upon one another, and the Gates of Azyr were shut.'

Grungni continued to twist and mould the facet of daemon-substance, smoke rising from his hands as he worked. 'Some were hidden by the Dark Gods themselves, for such weapons, in the right hands, could harm even them. Others were passed from vanquished to victor, until they were dropped on some nameless battlefield and forgotten. And a few were found by those who sought only to contain them – my children and my children's children.'

The daemon essence squirmed in Grungni's grip, bubbling like molten metal. But the god continued his work. 'In those bleak final days, as the Khazalid empires crumbled, several of the Eight were found and hidden away where their creators might never find them.' Grungni sighed. 'But nothing lasts forever. The drums of the ur-war, the all-war, beat anew and those terrible tools stir in their slumber of ages. They call out to be wielded, and their calls will be answered.'

He held up the facet. It resembled nothing so much as a tiny city. Excelsis, Volker realised with a start. The god had shaped it in miniature, from the daemon's boiling essence. 'The foundations of Excelsis were old when this realm was young,' Grungni said. He laid his smoking creation on the table, his eyes closed. 'It was a ruin, even then. Some ancient cataclysm, perhaps. That was always Grimnir's contention. I had my own theories.'

He looked at Volker. 'The realms were born from the life blood of a dying universe. And in that blood were impurities. Things that should not, could not be, but somehow were.' As he spoke, his voice grew distant and deep. The flickering light of the forge became star-motes, swirling in the black between worlds. Grungni's form, so solid a moment ago, seemed to stretch and thin like smoke, until Volker found himself somehow standing in the palm of the god's hand. He looked up, his heart thundering in his chest.

Grungni returned his gaze with eyes like twin suns. His beard and hair were a celestial inferno, growing brighter with every passing moment. Volker raised a hand to shield his eyes. He could barely breathe.

'That is what the Eight Lamentations are. Not just weapons, but impurities – motes of cosmic filth, honed and sharpened to a killing edge.' The god's voice came from everywhere and nowhere, echoing up from within him, and roaring down from on high. A hammer striking iron. Volker sank to one knee, lungs straining against the heat.

'But I will reforge them. I will break them and reshape them to a more pleasing purpose. I will make ploughshares from them, if I must. All these things I will do. And you will help me. You will be my hammer, and the realms my anvil.'

Abruptly, the heat vanished, replaced by a cool breeze. Volker opened his eyes. He was still sitting at the table. The others looked as dazed as he felt. The daemon essence rising from the centre of the table had hardened into a tree of black iron. Smoke seeped from it. As he watched, cracks appeared. All at once, and very quietly, it crumbled to pieces. He glanced at the miniature Excelsis and saw that it too was gone, reduced to a pile of black dust by his elbow. He looked at Zana, who was staring at the dust.

'Vindicarum,' she said, softly.

'No, it was Phoenicium, I am certain,' Roggen said, intently. He looked at Volker. 'Was it not?'

Volker shook his head. Before he could reply, Lugash said, 'You wish us to find these weapons, then.' His voice was harsh, and Volker wondered what he'd seen. Why had Grungni showed them the Founding Cities? Questions heaped themselves at the back of his mind, but he could not give voice to them.

'No, nephew. Just the one, for the moment.' Grungni, back to his normal size, circled the table, hands clasped behind his back. 'My servants search for any sign of the others, even now. But one is here – in Ghur.' He traced the shape of a spear in the air, using smoke from his beard. 'The Spear of Shadows. One of my servants was on its trail–'

'Oken,' Volker interjected, before he could think better of it.

Grungni looked at him, and nodded.

'Yes. He sent me a message some days ago, saying that he'd found the location of the spear, and intended to recover it. But since then... nothing.' He gestured, and the fire in the forge blazed brightly. 'I can see all of my children in the flames. But not him. He is not dead, for I would know it. So, you will find him.' He swept the table with his fiery gaze. 'And with him, the Spear of Shadows.'

A moment of silence followed Grungni's words. It was broken by a laugh from Lugash. The duardin slapped the table. 'Find him? Where do we even begin? The trail must be long cold.' He shook his head. 'Best find a death-mage, Maker.'

'He sent a message,' Volker said.

Lugash peered at him. 'So?'

'So where did he send it from?'

Grungni smiled, obviously pleased with Volker's logic. 'A library. The greatest library in all the lower realms – the Libraria Vurmis, in the city of Shu'gohl.'

Zana whistled. 'The Crawling City.'

'What is this "crawling city"?' Roggen asked. 'Is it dangerous?'

'Depends on how you define dangerous.' Zana scratched her chin. 'It's on the back of a bloody great worm, I know that.'

Volker had never visited the city of Shu'gohl, but he'd heard plenty of stories. Mostly from Oken, who had visited it often, though he'd never said why. It had been freed from the grip of the skaven early in the wars and had slowly regained prominence as one of the great trading hubs of the steppes. Thousands of merchants, pilgrims and travellers of all sorts arrived every day, seeking passage on the ancient basket lifts, which connected the worm's back to the ground far below.

Zana frowned. 'It'll be hard to reach. Especially from Excelsis. The Amber Steppes are several days' hard riding from the coast, and most of that's orruk territory.'

'There are duardin roads, but they're no safer than the overland routes,' Volker said. 'More dangerous, some of them.'

'You speak as if you are afraid, manling,' Lugash sneered. 'Does your courage shrink at the thought of facing enemies closer than a cannon's range?'

'Only a fool lets an enemy get so close,' Volker said.

Lugash flushed, but Grungni silenced him with a curt gesture. 'Hush, nephew. You'll have plenty of opportunities to wet those blades of yours.' The god frowned. 'I am not the only one searching for the spear. There are others, even now, who are on its trail.'

'Could one of them have something to do with Oken's disappearance?' Volker asked.

'It is possible.' Grungni idly sketched smoky shapes on the air. Weapons, Volker thought, though the shapes dissipated almost immediately. 'The portents are no more clear on this subject than any other.'

'Maybe we should visit the Prophesiers' Guild,' Zana said.

Volker laughed. The Guild house stood at the heart of the

trade quarter, and was the most heavily defended building in the city. Every augury wrenched from the Spear of Mallus, no matter how large or small, passed through the Prophesiers' Guild. There they were refined and codified, before being auctioned off to the highest bidder.

Grungni made a dismissive gesture. 'The secrets and lies they peddle are no true prophecies. More like hints and glimpses. Useless to one who can hear the voice of the fire. Worse than useless, for they muddle otherwise clear perceptions.' He shook his smoky head. 'No, the gunmaster has the right of it. You must follow the trail wherever it leads.'

None of them argued. For all of his informality, Grungni was still a god, and when a god commanded, mortals could not help but obey. Zana sighed. 'I do know of a way we can get there, and quickly. It'll take some haggling, though.'

'And that is why I chose you, daughter of Chamon,' Grungni said. 'You are the only mortal I know of to bargain with death itself, and come out the better.'

Zana laughed. 'That was easy, compared to what I have in mind.' She sat back. 'The Kharadron have a berth in Excelsis, near the docks. One of their captains owes me a favour.' She frowned. 'Just the one, though.'

Volker blinked, surprised. The aether-vessels of the Kharadron were a common sight these days, but the sky-borne duardin were still something of a mystery. Despite their shared origins, they had little in common with the Dispossessed clans, and indeed, seemed to regard them as little more than penniless vagabonds. The Dispossessed, for their part, seemed to hold their cousins in similar distaste.

From his expression, Lugash shared their opinion. 'Aether-swilling cowards,' Lugash muttered. 'What sort of duardin forsakes stone for sky, I ask you?'

'Wise ones, given the ground was crawling with Arcanites and Bloodbound,' Zana said. 'At least in the sky they only have to worry about harkraken and the like.' Volker shivered, thinking of the immense, tentacled nightmares that haunted the upper aether of most realms. Even the skies of Azyr were not free of the predacious aerial monstrosities. 'Old Captain Brondt will take us, and complain the entire way.'

Grungni nodded. 'I will make it worth your while, lass. And his as well, if I must.' That last was said with some reluctance. A duardin was a duardin, all divinity aside, Volker mused.

Zana bowed her head. 'You always do, Maker.' When she looked up, she was grinning. 'But I'll hold you to it, nonetheless.'

Grungni gave a rumbling laugh and clapped his big hands. In his mirth, the god seemed to fill the room, and his fiery mane blazed as brightly as the flames in the forge. 'I wouldn't have it any other way. When you find Oken, you will find the Spear of Shadows. Or so the flames say. Return both to me, if you can.'

He gestured, and a door Volker hadn't noticed before swung open. It was an old door, battered and swollen by damp. A sea breeze whistled through the opening. Volker could hear the creak of rigging and the squalling of seabirds. Grungni rubbed his hands together. 'You said this Captain Brondt's berth was near the docks, yes?'

Zana nodded. Though they were obviously no strangers to Grungni's power, she and the others appeared somewhat taken aback by such a casual display. Like his people, Grungni seemed to have little time for mystery or enigma. Even so, Volker couldn't help but recall that he'd been nowhere near the docks when he'd arrived.

'How far does this place extend?' he asked, in awe.

Grungni shrugged. 'As far as it needs to.' His smile faded. 'Be watchful and wary. There are spies abroad in every realm,

seeking word of the Eight. Trust no one, save that you must.'
At this sobering dismissal, the others rose from their seats and
headed for the door. Roggen said something, but Volker wasn't
paying attention. Instead, he was thinking about all that had
happened. Things were moving quickly. Too quickly to process.
A day ago, the skaven had been his biggest concern. And now–

'Life comes quickest when you least expect it,' Grungni said,
studying him. 'It has always been thus. An agile mind will
adapt, while others are overwhelmed.' He sighed. 'The world
is not in the habit of waiting for permission before it changes.'

'I never thanked you for saving me,' Volker said. 'From the
skaven, I mean.'

'You'll repay that debt, I have no doubt.' Grungni's eyes narrowed. 'You have a question. Speak. I will do my best to answer
it, before I send you on your way.'

'Why did you abandon Sigmar?' It wasn't the question Volker
had intended to ask. Somehow, he thought the god knew that.

Grungni smiled. The expression came easily to him, but like
a gemstone it was a multi-faceted thing. Every smile was different, with a different meaning. From his studies, Volker knew
that there were whole volumes of metal-bound books in the
deep libraries of the warden kings, devoted to translating the
expressions of the gods. The duardin took such things seriously, as they did most things. 'Did I? Is that what he claims?'

'I – no. I don't know. People say…'

'Oh, well, people. Very informed, people.' Grungni tapped
the side of his head. 'Mortals, lad, are creative things. And stories are tools, like any other. Sigmar and I are allies. I am no
more his servant than he is mine. I swore an oath to aid him,
but it is up to me to fulfil that oath how I see fit.'

'The Eight Lamentations,' Volker said, grasping the god's
point.

Grungni nodded. 'Sigmar seeks to reforge men, to purify souls and minds. I've never been one for that sort of thing. But weapons, now... weapons are meant to be reforged. To be repurposed.' Sparks danced in his eyes. 'You know this as well as I.'

Volker nodded. 'I will find Oken, Maker, and the spear,' he said, in Khazalid.

Grungni clapped him on the shoulder. Volker tensed, but the god's touch was surprisingly light. 'I know. That is why I chose you, Owain Volker.' Something in the way he said it sent a chill down Volker's spine, and suddenly the image he'd seen in the dream-spider's web – of something dark, seeking his life – rose up in his mind.

Before he could ask Grungni about it, the god produced a familiar satchel from nowhere – Volker's ammunition bag. It bore the seal of the Ironweld, and contained his extra shot-cylinders and powder. But like his long rifle, it somehow felt lighter than before. He hefted it wonderingly, noting the golden threads that now ran through the thick burlap. 'A weapon's use is in direct proportion to the availability of ammunition,' Grungni said. 'And I have seen to it that your powder will always be dry, and never run low. Use it wisely.' The god stepped back, arms crossed. 'Go. The others are waiting.' Volker slung his satchel across his chest, bowed and turned towards the doors.

He felt the weight of Grungni's gaze on him the entire way.

Elsewhere, in the Realm of Beasts, a long-sealed gate was opening.

The Jaws were simply named and crudely formed. They had stood inviolate for untold centuries, sealed by the hands of Gorkamorka himself, or so the shamans of the great orruk clans claimed. The ancient realmgate was nothing more or less than the jawbone of some long-dead monstrosity, thrust into the earth and split open by the axe of Gorkamorka so that his favoured children might have a road to fresh conquests. But those conquests had proven elusive, and the dead made for poor sport, especially when they had the advantage of numbers. So the two-headed god had sealed that which he had cracked open. And sealed it had remained, for years without counting.

Until today.

The bone gateway, its binding sigils worn smooth by time and weather, began to glow with a pale, amethyst radiance. Crackling strands of light stretched like a new-spun web between the edges of the gateway as it began to swing wide. There was a sound like an animal's roar, and then the light blazed upwards. The air took on the consistency of water, and strange, spectral shapes raced from the depths of the light, screaming hideously.

In the sprawling, ramshackle camp that had grown up around the Jaws, orruks brawled cheerfully among themselves, unaware of the light or what it brought. Greenskin tribes from all across the Amber Steppes made an annual pilgrimage to the Jaws, awaiting the day Gorkamorka would see fit to reopen the realmgate. Only the most devout – and violent – were allowed to make camp there, and as new tribes arrived, fights inevitably broke out. Entire wars had been fought for the honour of camping close to the Jaws for a single night. But as the first of the screaming wraiths sped through the camp, all internal hostility was set aside, replaced by sudden and intense interest.

Bosses bellowed and mobs of boys scrambled out of the camp and up the slope leading to the Jaws, waving their choppas joyfully. Something was coming out of the gate, and every orruk wanted to be the first to meet it.

The black horse and its red-armoured rider burst from the

pulsing light. Ahazian Kel gave a wild, whooping laugh as his vision cleared and he spotted the orruks barrelling towards him. The orruks roared in response. Ahazian released the animal's reins and snatched his hammer from his belt.

He had ridden hell for leather across the lowlands of Shyish, through storms of bone dust and howling maelstroms of feral wraiths. Several times he'd been attacked by flying shapes or dark-clad riders. He'd allowed none of it to stop him.

The splinter of Gung hung from a rawhide thong about his neck. It was almost painfully cold, the chill radiating through his armour and into the flesh beneath. The discomfort was good. It kept him focused. He leaned forwards in his saddle, arms extended. The first orruk died quickly, skull cracked open. The second lived, but lost its hands and the choppa it had held. The black horse shrieked angrily and lashed out with its hooves. Ahazian laughed and followed its example, striking again and again. The orruks swirled like a green tide, but soon enough the horse broke away from them and pelted down through the camp. More orruks sought to bar his way, and he urged the horse to run them down.

The blood sang through his veins, hot and swift. He wanted to turn, to drop from the saddle and meet the greenskins in battle. His weapons howled in his mind, desirous of death. They yearned for murder, the way a man might yearn for the love of a woman. But there was another sound in his mind, warring against the whispers of his weapons. A soft crooning, like the voice of some distant singer.

He knew, without understanding how, that the voice belonged to Gung. The Huntsman was singing a killing song, one that echoed across the realms. A song that he could hear, thanks to the piece of it in his possession; a song that would lead him right to it.

So distracted was he by the song that he failed to notice the orruk charging to intercept him. The brute roared and leapt, landing on the back of the horse. The animal staggered, nearly falling. But the black horses of Shyish were made of sterner stuff and instead of falling it began to buck and kick. Ahazian fought to remain in his saddle, even as the orruk attempted to twist his head off. The creature snarled. It had lost its axe, and now gripped the horns of his helmet. Ahazian drove the haft of his goreaxe into the orruk's belly. The spiked pommel punched through the creature's crude armour and into its stomach.

If it felt any pain, it didn't show it. Instead, its grip tightened. Ahazian's neck began to ache. Spots danced before his eyes. He twisted and flung himself from the saddle, carrying his opponent with him. They struck the ground hard and rolled over and over in a bone-crushing tangle. When they slid to a dusty stop, Ahazian shoved himself to his feet, weapons in hand. The orruk lurched after him, bloody froth coating its tusks. Ahazian swung his skullhammer. The creature ducked and tackled him. He drove the pommels of both weapons into the orruk's hard skull, again and again. The orruk drove him back, his heels digging a trench in the dirt. He struck it again and again, until the thick bone of the brute's skull at last crumpled. The orruk slumped with a gurgle.

Ahazian stumbled back, breathing heavily. He stared down at the creature. A worthy foe. Slowly, he lifted his hammer in salute. 'May Khorne grant your soul the battle you crave,' he murmured. He turned, and saw his horse standing nearby. It glared balefully at him, but made no attempt to flee when he moved to recapture it.

He began to mount, stopped, and looked back at the orruk. His stomach rumbled. It had been some days since he'd eaten.

'Waste not, want not,' he murmured, as he led the horse towards the body. It had been some time since he'd tasted orruk.

He wondered if it was as good as he remembered.

>⊂◯ FIVE ◯⊂<

CAPTAIN BRONDT

The harbour district of Excelsis was very much the nerve centre of trade in the city. Bustling and vibrant, it seemed worlds removed from the shabby squalor of the Veins, or the elaborate styling of the noble districts.

Instead, as befitted the oldest district of the city, it had been constructed in the style of the tribes who'd fished the waters of the bay for generations. Structures made from the calcified bones of leviathans, fused together with a mixture of sun-baked mud and animal dung, predominated among the stalls and shacks of the harbour.

Grungni's door had opened off the back of a fishmonger's, in Go-By Street. No one had paid them any mind as they trooped out. But then, the wharfs were the sort of place where one kept one's eyes on one's own business. The sight of freshly slain corpses, either in the gutters or dangling from a signpost as a grisly warning from one of the many street gangs that plagued the harbour, weren't uncommon.

The air was thick with the smells of salted fish and exotic spices, not to mention the more lingering aroma of overflowing gutters. Beneath it all, Volker could detect the tang of the oldest Ironweld armouries in the city, still crafting arms and armour after a century. Everything that was Excelsis had grown outwards from the bay and the Spear. Here in the docklands, the first adventurers from Azyr had arrived, seeking a new life. A variety of languages and dialects hummed through the air like music, including the rough growl of Ghurdish tribesmen and the harsh rasp of natives of the Hot Seas, in Aqshy.

They passed a trio of light-weavers, crafting shapes in the air with the aid of small, concave mirrors in order to entertain a growing crowd. The shapes were part of a story – one of the heroic deeds of the god Tyrion. The light-weavers all wore the symbolic blindfold, marked with the device of the daystar, and sang softly as they manipulated their mirrors. The crowd cheered and whistled as the image of Tyrion lopped the head from some monster.

Elsewhere, merchants hawked their wares to sailors and fisherfolk, as tattooed members of the Fate's Favoured patrolled the streets, on alert for any sign of rival gang members. Volker eyed the latter, noting the lines of tiny script that covered their faces and shorn scalps. It was said that they tattooed themselves with their own fates, as whispered by the Spear, and that the hand that wielded the needle was always that of the Burning Man, the gang's mysterious leader. Few had ever seen him, and fewer still admitted that he actually existed. Certainly not the officers of the freeguild or the worthies who made up the Small Conclave.

The gang members gave Volker and the others a cursory inspection, but showed no sign of further interest. Indeed, they gave the group a wide berth. Volker suspected that it was mostly due to the way Lugash glared at them. The fyre-slayer looked in the mood for a fight, and wasn't picky about his opponents.

Lugash grunted softly. 'Look. Up there.'

Volker looked. Several ravens were perched on the overhanging edge of a roof. 'The birds?' he asked, confused.

'Yes,' Lugash muttered. 'I've seen those carrion birds before.'

'There is a siege going on.'

'Not here. In Aqshy. The Felstone Plains.' Lugash narrowed his eyes. 'Same birds, I'm certain of it.'

'Are you sure?' Lugash looked at him. Volker raised a hand in surrender. 'Very well. But there's nothing to be done about it now. Unless you want to throw a cobblestone at them.' The duardin glanced down, as if considering, but shook his head.

'No sense alerting them,' he growled. He looked at Volker. 'Next time, though, you put that fancy handgun of yours to use, manling.'

'Point and I'll shoot,' Volker said. Lugash grinned, and Volker immediately regretted the promise. He glanced up, but the ravens were gone. Idly he wondered if they were the same birds he'd seen before, on the Bastion. He pushed the thought aside and inhaled, trying to clear his lungs of the lingering weight of forge smoke.

That proved to be a mistake. He coughed as the wind shifted, and the stink of the tanneries enveloped him. Eyes watering, he turned to the others. 'The aether-berth is closer to the bay, I think.' He'd rarely had call to visit the docklands after his arrival. Even the freeguild stayed away if they could help it. It was left to the captains and local merchants' associations to police themselves, for the most part.

'We must retrieve my steed first,' Roggen said. He looked around, clearly bewildered. 'There was a stable, near the harbour. After I came ashore I left her there.' He carried a set of bulky saddlebags over one broad shoulder.

'There's a stable on Hookjaw Street,' Volker said. 'Has a shark on the sign?'

Roggen nodded eagerly. 'Yes, that is the one. We must get her.'

'No, we mustn't,' Zana said. 'It'll still be here when we get back, provided no one sells it while we're gone.' Like Roggen, she travelled light. She had a wool blanket bundled up and tied across her chest with leather straps, in the manner of the freeguild. Inside the folds of the blanket would be food and kit, as well as any valuables she carried.

'Sell her?' Roggen looked aghast. 'But she is mine!'

'So?' Zana shrugged. 'Property is for the rich and the careful.'

Before she could continue, the air was split by a crack of thunder. It echoed through the streets, silencing the merchants in their stalls, and the bawdy songs of drunken sailors. The thunder was followed by the piercing crash of artillery. Zana and Roggen both spun towards the sound, their hands on their weapons.

Volker chuckled. 'Those are the primus line batteries – volley guns, mostly. The wildfires must be dying down.' The skaven attacks were like clockwork, on a clear day. They'd probe the trench line, fall back and come again, when someone new took charge.

'You can tell what kind of gun it is by the sound?' Roggen asked, baffled.

'Can't you?'

'His people don't use them,' Zana said. 'The Lady of Leaves doesn't care for flint and steel. She prefers creeper vines and poisonous thorns.' She shuddered. 'And those bark-kindred of hers are worse.'

'The sylvaneth?' Volker asked. 'I've never seen one,' he added, somewhat wistfully.

'Oh, you have,' Lugash grunted. 'You just didn't know it. Sneaky sorts of things, trees. Always where you least expect or want them.' He frowned. 'Like the sea. Water – pfah.' He spat on the ground. 'What sort of thing is that, to make an ocean out of?' He sniffed. 'Lava. Now there's a proper liquid – so hot it'll scald your eyeballs.'

Zana rolled her eyes. 'So why did you leave home, if you miss it so much?'

Lugash glared at her. 'None of your concern, woman. I am oathsworn to the Maker, same as you manlings. Though why he needs you, I don't know.' He looked away. 'Maybe he's getting senile.'

'Do gods get senile, then?' Zana prodded.

Lugash ignored her. Volker shook his head.

'The stables are this way from here,' he said to Roggen, catching the thread of conversation before it could escape entirely. He gestured, 'We'll cut through Jaeger Lane.' Jaeger Lane was a cramped artery connecting the Veins and the docklands. It was a rowdy patch of alehouses and cheap eateries, where young blades from the Noble Quarter went to indulge in licentious behaviour, and would-be revolutionaries plotted against the Grand Conclave. A statue weathered to featurelessness marked the largest crossing – the Jaeger for whom the area had been named, possibly.

'Just leave the beast here,' Zana said, as they followed the winding lane. 'It'll be no use where we're going. More of a hindrance, in fact.'

'I go nowhere without my steed,' Roggen said, stubbornly. 'She grows anxious without me. She is very sensitive.'

'I'm not sure we should be taking an anxious horse with us,' Volker said. 'Or a sensitive one.' He'd never been a fan of horses, even the clockwork ones the Ironweld used to haul its

95

artillery trains on occasion. They were temperamental beasts, with a tendency to snap at unprotected flesh.

Roggen looked confused. 'Horse?'

The doors of the stable slammed open, stirring the hay scattered across the ground. An ear-splitting screech echoed through the courtyard as half a dozen stable hands spilled out, shouting and cursing. They were clad in padded armour and masks, and they stumbled out into the courtyard, dragging a massive shape in their wake with heavy chains and straps.

The beast was hooded, in the same way a falconer might do for his birds. Even so, its thrashing sent the stable hands floundering. It clawed at them, tearing gouges in their quilted vests. They scrambled from its path as Roggen whistled sharply. The heavy shape lunged towards him, and he sidestepped it, tearing the hood from its head as he did so. 'Oh hell,' Volker murmured, as he realised what the thing was.

'Yes,' Zana said.

The demigryph shrieked in what Volker hoped was recognition as it swung around to face Roggen. The big beast was covered in brownish, shaggy fur and vibrant green feathers. Dark ironwood armour covered the creature in places, and it wore a heavy saddle. With a sinking sensation, he suddenly realised just what sort of knightly order Roggen belonged to. He looked at Zana, his eyes wide. 'You could have warned me.'

'Why? No one warned me, the first time.' She sighed and shook her head. 'And he's such a mild sort, too. Never saw it coming.'

Volker turned back to the reunion of beast and rider. He had seen the carnage a squadron of such creatures – and their riders – left in their wake. The mountains and forests of Azyr were home to a sizeable population of demigryphs, and many of the ancient chivalric orders of Azyrheim, such as the Myr-midites and the Sons of Breton, sent their aspirants to stalk and break the beasts to their will.

Most failed. Only the most determined of warriors could tame a demigryph. And even then, they'd bear the scars for the rest of their life. The massive creatures were larger than any stallion, and far more bloodthirsty. They could dismember a fully armoured warrior with ease, and made little distinction between friend and foe.

The beast rose up on its heavily muscled hind legs and landed its fore claws on Roggen's shoulders, nearly knocking the big man to his knees. It stood twice again as tall as its master, though Roggen seemed used to such displays. He caught the tip of the hooked beak and bent it away from his face. 'Easy, Harrow. There's a girl.' Harrow shrieked again, and followed it with a dull clacking as her mad, amber eyes noticed Volker and the others. The brown tail began to lash as the demi-gryph shoved away from her rider and fell onto all fours with a rattle of armour.

'Keep that beast away from me,' Lugash growled. He raised his war-iron menacingly. 'Else I'll crack its skull. See if I don't.'

The demigryph hunkered down, head tilted, beak half-open. She hissed, her claws scraping the street. Roggen caught the scruff of her feathered neck. 'Well, stop waving weapons at her. I told you – she's very sensitive.'

'It's a bloody great murder-cat is what it is,' Zana said, eyes narrowed. 'Why'd you even bring it? Or have you forgotten what happened last time?'

'That was an accident,' Roggen said, defensively. 'She didn't mean any harm.'

'It ate Capollino!'

'Only his leg.' Roggen stroked the demigryph's neck, and

murmured soothingly. 'And the Maker crafted him a new one, didn't he?'

'Who was Capollino?' Volker asked.

'A very unlucky fellow,' Roggen said, somewhat apologetically. 'She was just playing, really, but he started screaming and... well.' He knocked on Harrow's beak. 'She gets excited easily. Instinct, you see.' The demigryph snapped at his hand. Roggen frowned and pried the hook of her beak out of his gauntlet. 'You are not making a good first impression, Harrow. Be polite.'

'That ship has sailed, I'm afraid,' Zana said, one hand on the hilt of her sword. 'It's not coming with us, Roggen. I refuse to be in a confined space with that thing.'

Roggen frowned. 'You would not separate a knight from his steed?'

'Cheerfully.'

Roggen opened his mouth. 'She could come in handy,' Volker interjected. 'Provided you can keep her under control?' He glanced at the knight, who nodded.

'I can try,' Roggen muttered, looking mulish. Seeing the look on Zana's face, he quickly added, 'She will be on her best behaviour.'

'That's what he said last time,' Zana growled. 'But fine. Your funeral. It goes in the hold, and gods help you if it eats something it's not supposed to, because they'll pitch it and us out of the ship. Without landing first.'

That settled, they followed the winding streets down to the docks, Harrow padding beside Roggen, the big knight tightly gripping her reins. Excelsis harbour played host to countless vessels. A forest of masts and sails rose over the waters from merchant fleets and the warships of a hundred fledgling empires, flourishing in the wake of Sigmar's return.

The aether-berth rose above them all. It was the single new structure amid the old. A tower of bone and wood, higher than any ship's mast, surmounted by a structure of the Kharadrons' own design – a wide platform, easily the size of one of the larger streets below, topped by a globular watch-station, crafted from bronze and steel. Anchor-jetties extended in seemingly haphazard fashion from the curves of the station.

Aether-frigates and ironclads, the mainstays of the Kharadron fleets, occupied these aerial wharfs, their bulky, blade-like proportions out of place next to the sleek towers and magical vessels of the Collegiate Arcane. The vessels were heavy lengths of riveted metal and bulbous aether-endrins, resembling nothing so much as the seagoing ironclads some clans of Dispossessed made use of, save that they sailed above the ground, rather than on the water.

Duardin clad in aeronautical gear and weatherproof uniforms busied themselves about the base of the tower, overseeing the loading and unloading of cargo or arguing loudly with harbour officials. Others clad in the heavy war-plate the Kharadron called arkanaut armour, their faces hidden behind stylised masks, stood guard, aethershot rifles held across their chests.

Volker stared up at the docked vessels in awe. He'd seen the aethercraft of the Kharadron at a distance, but seeing them this close was something else again. Whereas the duardin he was familiar with preferred to dig down, these had soared upwards. 'Magnificent,' he murmured.

'Unnatural is what it is,' Lugash said, glaring upwards. 'Floating in the air. Like birds. Or worse.' He spat. 'No way for a proper duardin to live.'

'You mean half-naked, in a volcano?' Zana asked.

Lugash looked at her. 'It's not my fault your thin manling

skin can't handle the weather,' he said, huffily. 'You should grow thicker skin.'

'And then hammer gold into it.' Zana looked up. 'Brondt's vessel is the larger one – not the usual frigate or ironclad. It's a long-distance hauler. He had some bright spark of an endrin-rigger make modifications, last I heard, to improve the old scow's speed.'

'It's called the *Zank*, as you well know, woman,' someone growled, in a voice like wind rushing through a metal tunnel. Volker looked down and saw a broad form stumping towards them. The duardin was dressed in battered, midnight-blue aeronautic gear, over a tan uniform. He wore a dark coat of some slick-looking material, with thick fur cuffs and collar. What little of his face could be seen within the bristly thicket of iron-grey hair and beard was burnt bronze by the wind and weather. He clenched a smouldering cheroot between thick, yellow teeth. 'She's the finest Makaisson-class hauler in the fleet, and don't you forget it.'

Zank meant cleaver, or thereabouts, Volker thought. An appropriate name for such an ominous-looking vessel. It had the curved hull common to Kharadron vessels, but it was twice again the length of the frigates moored above and around it. Strange weapons lined its decks, and studded its armoured hull. An ancestral figurehead of dark gold glared down from the prow. It reminded him of Grungni, with its billowing beard and wide face, and for a moment, it almost seemed to be looking down at him…

'Gunmaster.'

Volker started. 'What?'

'I'm introducing you,' Zana hissed. 'Apologies, Brondt. He's a bit deaf.' She tugged on her ear. 'Artillery is loud. As I was saying, meet Captain Njord Brondt.'

'I'm well aware of the noise the ground-pounders make.'

Brondt eyed them with ill-concealed displeasure. As Zana spoke, he extracted his cheroot and tapped ash onto the ground. 'Give me one good reason I shouldn't have you tied to a skyhook and fired out over the bay, woman,' he growled.

'Two reasons,' Zana said, fingers held up. 'One, I saved your stumpy rear from that harkraken – remember? And two, we're on a mission from a god.'

Brondt frowned. 'Which god?'

'Does it matter?'

'It does to me.'

'I thought you Kharadron didn't believe in gods,' Zana said.

'We don't. That doesn't mean we're foolish enough to annoy the wrong one without cause. Which one – Sigmar?' He hesitated. 'Nagash?' he asked, more softly.

'The Great Maker.'

Brondt examined the glowing tip of his cheroot. 'Fine. What do you want?'

'A ride.'

'Where?'

'Shu'gohl. I know for a fact it's on your route.'

Brondt looked past her, at Volker and the others. 'All of you?'

'Yes.'

Harrow screeched.

'And that thing?'

'Yes,' Roggen said, frowning.

Brondt grinned. 'That's worth two favours.'

Zana cocked her head. 'One.'

Brondt puffed on his cheroot. 'Two.'

'One and a half.'

'Deal,' he said. He spat on his hand and held it out. Zana did the same, and they shook hands. 'There's room in the hold for livestock. And passengers, come to that.'

Zana's face fell. 'No cabins?'

'Not for one and a half favours.' Brondt's grin never wavered. 'It's dry and warm. Better than sleeping above decks.'

Zana sighed. 'Fine, you old grumble-miser. But you still owe me half a favour, and don't you forget it.'

Brondt's grin slipped. 'I never forget a debt,' he growled. 'Artycle six, point three of the code states–'

Zana shook her head. 'I know, I know.'

Brondt frowned, then turned and bellowed to several of his crew. They ambled over, in no particular hurry. Brondt growled at them in rapid-fire Khazalid, then turned back to Zana. 'They'll show you to your quarters.' He puffed on his cheroot. 'It'll take a day or thereabout to get to the Crawling City. Barring any difficulties. Like last time.' He looked closely at Zana as he said it.

'That was an accident,' she protested.

'The cost of repairs alone–' he began, stabbing the air with his cheroot.

'I didn't hear you complaining at the time,' she snapped. 'Besides, you beat Brokrin to the find, didn't you? And the *Drak Ang* took twice as much damage as the *Zank*...'

Brondt turned away, dismissing her. 'Get on board before I change my mind.'

As they allowed Brondt's crew to guide them into the aether-berth, Volker looked at Zana. 'What happened last time?' he asked, quietly.

Zana ignored him, her face set. He exchanged glances with Roggen. The big knight grinned and patted Harrow's beak. 'I am very excited, whatever happened. It will be my first time flying.'

Volker nodded. 'Yes. Let's just hope it's not our last.'

* * *

Ahazian Kel sat before a crackling fire, cooking his evening meal. His seat was what was left of the body of the orruk that had leapt on his horse. The rest of it was impaled on sticks and slowly roasting over the fire. He'd acquired a taste for orruk-flesh in the Ashdwell, in his youth. The beasts were best cooked alive, but even dead they had a decided tartness.

His weapons sat within easy reach, and his helmet was at his feet. His scarred features were relaxed as he stared into the fire, imagining the glories to come. Idly, he toyed with the fragment of Gung, rolling it between his fingers. He reached for a chunk of orruk, snatching the smoking meat from the fire.

'You are close.'

Ahazian looked up from his meal. The hank of orruk flesh bubbled on the bone, roasted to perfection. He finished chewing and swallowed. 'I know.' He flicked the fragment, where it dangled. 'It… sings.'

Volundr nodded. 'Qyat of the Folded Soul sang an ancient song of murder as he shaped Gung. The echo of that song still reverberates through the spear, giving it life. The song will grow louder, the closer you get to the weapon.'

Volundr's shape wavered in the firelight. He was not truly there, Ahazian knew. Just a sending, cast into the realms by the Skullgrinder's will, and the daemonic fires of his forge. Volundr sat, hands dangling between his knees, head lowered. He looked tired. The fires of his gaze burned low. Ahazian peered at him, and took another bite of orruk. 'Are you well, Skullgrinder?'

Volundr gestured dismissively. 'It is of no matter.' He straightened and passed a hand over the fire. 'You are being followed.'

'I know.' Ahazian cracked the bone and scraped at the marrow with a finger. 'I keep hoping they will catch up with me, but no luck so far.'

'Arrogance is healthy in a warrior. But it must be tempered by wisdom.'

Ahazian licked marrow from his finger thoughtfully. 'As you say.'

Volundr grunted, visibly annoyed. 'Our enemies are not solely mortal. You must be cautious. The Crippled God is not to be trifled with.'

'You speak as if you know him.'

Volundr fell silent. Ahazian waited. The Skullgrinder would speak when it suited him, and not before. After long moments, the warrior-smith said, 'I was born a slave. In the chattel-pens of the Furnace Kings. You know of them?'

Ahazian nodded. 'They forged weapons and armour for the servants of the Dark Gods, before the Azyrites cast down the Bale-Furnace and scattered its rulers. Stunted brutes. Like duardin, but twisted and cruel.' He grinned around a mouthful of orruk. 'They made good blades, though. There are warlords who'll trade a thousand slaves for just one axe forged by the Furnace Kings.'

'They deserved their fate,' Volundr rumbled. 'They were weak. Decadent. I saw as much, the day the Crippled God came and cracked the Bale-Furnace.' He stared at his hands. 'They had stolen his secrets, and turned them to bitter ends. He arrived in an explosion of heat and fire, roaring curses and wielding a great hammer. Not a warhammer, but a blacksmith's hammer. And with it he shattered our chains and cracked the great furnace. The Furnace Kings fled into the depths of their mountain, rather than face him.'

Ahazian blinked in surprise. 'He... saved you?'

'More than that. He taught me his arts. Some of them, at least.' Volundr looked up. 'And those lessons served me well, in the trials that followed.' He laughed harshly. 'He was quite angry, when he learned of my betrayal.'

'Why did you betray him?' Ahazian asked the question before it occurred to him that it might be wiser not to.

Volundr's gaze grew hot and bright, like a fire newly stoked. 'Your purpose is not to ask questions, Ahazian Kel. Yours is but to seek out that which I desire, and bring it to me.'

Ahazian bristled at the Skullgrinder's tone. 'And so I have sworn, warrior-smith.' He cast the bone he held into the fire. 'And the oath of a kel is as iron itself.'

Volundr laughed again, but softly this time. 'And that is why I chose you, son of Ekran. Do not fail me.'

His form flickered and faded, like smoke on the wind. A moment later, he was gone. Ahazian grunted and reached for another piece of orruk. He was still hungry, and he had a feeling he would need all of his strength in the days to come.

∞ SIX ∞

TOOLS OF THE MAKER

Volker woke suddenly. Heart hammering, eyes bleary, he was uncertain for a moment of where he was. He looked around the relatively clean, dry confines of the aft hold of the *Zank*, lit as it was by aether-lanterns hanging from the support beams. These cast a soft, ruddy glow over the crates, casks and sacks that filled the hold.

Despite the cheery ambience, it was cramped, especially with the demigryph, Harrow, occupying a third of it. Volker sat up carefully, still unused to the ship's swaying. He could feel the hum of the vessel's aether-endrin through the crate he sat on. His nose was full of demigryph stench. It smelled a bit like he imagined a chicken coop full of wet cats would.

Zana sat across from him, sharpening her blade with slow, practised strokes of a whetstone. She smiled as he stirred, but said nothing. Lugash lay nearby, his helmet's brim tipped so that it covered his eyes, his weapons crossed beneath his head as a makeshift pillow. He snored noisily. Roggen had claimed the only clear part of the hold for himself, and now moved slowly, practising his blade work. None of them seemed particularly bothered by the stink of the restive animal sharing their space.

Volker watched Roggen, trying to recall what had woken him. His dreams had been tangled knots of unease that prevented total rest. There had been something dark pursuing him down a corridor of sound and light. A malign force, singular in its purpose and resolve. But his dreams hadn't been all bad – he'd dreamed of Oken as well.

More a memory, that, perhaps. Not of the duardin himself, but of his voice, deep and rough, as he conversed quietly with Volker's mother. Catrin Volker had not been amenable to her son's apprenticeship with the Ironweld at first. But Oken had convinced her. Volker remembered that they'd spoken often, that tall, brittle woman and the short, sturdy duardin. They had known each other since her childhood, at least.

In truth, he didn't know how long Oken had been acquainted with his family. Once, the old duardin had let slip that his clan owed the Volker family a debt, one older even than Oken himself, though he'd refused to elaborate further. But then that was the duardin way, at least among the clans of the Dispossessed. Debts were shameful things, to be honoured but never spoken of in polite society. He wondered if that debt had anything to do with why Grungni had chosen him.

That only brought more questions, however. What prevented Grungni from simply finding these Lamentations himself? Why use mortal servants at all? Divine prerogative, or something else? Then the same might be asked of Sigmar – why didn't the God-King lead his armies to war personally, as he had in ages gone by?

Uncomfortable with that line of thinking, Volker distracted

himself with exploring the satchel Grungni had given him. He hadn't thought to do so before he'd succumbed to the fatigue that had been dogging his trail since the battle.

His suspicions were proved correct; the satchel was his, but subtly changed somehow. He could feel rune magic radiating from it, though he could see no markings save the insignia of the Ironweld, picked out in gold and crimson. Grungni had done something to it, though what, Volker couldn't even begin to guess.

He checked the powder-loads and shot-cylinders for signs of tampering, but found none. Normally, he carried half a dozen reloads for the repeater pistols and a small quantity of shot and powder for the rifle and his artisan pistol on him at all times, but the satchel would keep him supplied for weeks, if he were sparing. He had the alchemical tools and training to make more powder and shot if necessary, too.

'How can you stand carrying all of that?'

He looked at Zana. 'You've carried a field kit before, surely?'

'Yes, but my field kit doesn't clatter like an ironmonger's wagon.' She tossed him something. 'Brondt sent down food while you were snoring.'

Volker caught the chunk of hard brown bread and took an eager bite. He chewed carefully, eyes closed, enjoying the acrid tang and coarse texture. When he opened his eyes, Zana was watching him closely. 'Not many men can get past the first bite of duardin bread,' she said. 'Not without a lot of wine.' She held up a wineskin.

'It's an acquired taste,' Volker mumbled around a second mouthful. He swallowed. 'Goes well with a bit of *chuf.*' He looked around hopefully. Zana snorted and took a swig of wine, before tossing him the skin. He washed his mouth out and turned at a sudden shrill screech. Harrow was turning about in her stall at the far end of the hold, tapping at its sides with her beak and paws. There were bloodstains on the slats, which Harrow had been investigating eagerly since the *Zank* had hauled anchor and departed Excelsis.

'They bring cattle, sometimes,' Zana said, as they watched the demigryph snuffle at the stains. 'Use them as bait for the megalofins. Brondt sells the meat in Shu'gohl. The worm-folk don't get much meat that doesn't come with feathers or too many legs.'

'You sound like you've travelled this way before,' Volker said. He tossed the bread back to her, followed by the wine. Zana caught them easily.

She laughed. 'More than once. It's cramped, but quick. And the Kharadron can always use another quick hand with a blade, whatever they claim. Speaking of which...' She gestured towards Roggen with the bread. 'That's enough practice, sir knight. Come eat before you fall over.'

Roggen let his sword dip and turned. However long he'd been at it, the Ghyranite seemed none the worse for wear. Nevertheless, he gratefully accepted the offer of food and drink. He tore off a hunk of bread, made a face, and swallowed cautiously. 'Did they make this with stones?' he mumbled.

'Probably. Your sword... it's wood as well?' Volker asked after a moment, studying the blade the other man held.

Roggen nodded, still chewing. 'Made from the seedpod of a devourer plant.' He turned the dark sword over so that Volker could see. Thick, vein-like undulations connected the sharpened blade to the leather-wrapped hilt. The pommel stone was a pearlescent gem, uncut and heavy. 'You have to whittle and scrape away the excess sap and fibres after you shatter the pod. Then you layer the pieces, one atop the other with a slather of the sap between them. You have to press on it for days, squeezing and leaning, until it's flat enough to begin carving away all that is not blade.' He held up the sword. 'It takes weeks. But when you are finished – ha!'

He pivoted, bringing the blade down. It hissed as it parted the air. He turned, holding up the blade. 'It will cut through metal as easily as it does wood.' He looked at the bread he held. 'Though maybe not this.' He handed it back to Zana ruefully.

'You wouldn't catch a duardin using a blade of wood, no matter how sharp,' Lugash grunted. The fyreslayer still lay on the deck, eyes closed.

Roggen smiled. 'Who do you think taught us how to make these?'

'There are duardin in Ghyran?' Volker asked, somewhat taken aback. He'd heard stories, but never paid them much mind.

'Some,' Zana interjected. 'The root-kings. A proud folk, but shy. They delved deep, and rarely surfaced, and then only to trade.'

Roggen nodded, a sad look on his face. 'Some say they abandoned the world when the Lady of Leaves vanished into the Athelwyrd.' He sighed. 'Perhaps they will return one day, just as she did. I should like to meet them, just once.' He sheathed his sword, picked up a nearby bucket and went to tend Harrow. Brondt had grudgingly provided fodder before their departure, after Zana had pointed out that a hungry demigryph was bound to be troublesome. Roggen pulled a hunk of scaly meat from the bucket and tossed it to the demigryph, which chirped in pleasure. The meat glistened strangely in the lantern light as the creature tore at it, and Volker felt his stomach twist.

'Megalofin,' Zana said. 'It's quite good, if you cook it properly.'

'You seem to have an opinion on everything,' Volker said, smiling. Zana laughed. She had a rough laugh, like something worn thin. Everything about her spoke to a life hard lived. He'd met her sort before – sellswords and coinspinners. They fought for anyone who could pay their fee. Most had served in one army or another, even the freeguilds of Azyr. Some freeguild captains hired entire companies of such war-dogs to fight the battles they didn't want to waste other troops on.

Volker had fought alongside such troops more than once. They were brave enough, but they had a distressing tendency to value their own lives over whatever cause they had pledged themselves to. And yet, this one had pledged herself to a god. And not just any god, but one whose oaths were as iron.

'It's one of the drawbacks of an interesting life, gunmaster. I expect I could say the same about you.' She eyed him. 'You're young for your rank. Are you a hero, or just lucky?'

'I hunted megalofins, once,' Volker said, avoiding the question. 'From a blind. They feed on mountain goats and the like, in the high places of Azyr. Dive down and snatch up anything they can get their teeth in.' He frowned, thinking of the immense shark-like beast as it had pierced the clouds and swum down through the snowy air, jaws impossibly wide. He hefted his rifle and peered down its length. 'Never doing that again.'

Zana smiled. 'Easier from the deck of an aether-ship, but probably not by much. Brondt has it down to an art – hook them quick, let them tire themselves out, and then pummel them senseless. Once they're dead, it's just a matter of cutting them up and salting the meat. It keeps practically forever, or so I'm told.'

'You *have* lived an interesting life,' Volker said. He hesitated. 'What were you before?' he asked.

'Before I became a sellsword, you mean?'

Volker flushed. 'Yes.'

'I served in the freeguild, in Vindicarum,' she said, running the stone along the length of her sword. 'Gold Gryphon regiment. Got promoted to captain, eventually.'

'What happened?'

'What makes you think something happened?' She laughed at his expression. 'You're not wrong, though – something did.' She laid her sword across her knees. 'And I'd wager that it's the same thing that caused you to be here, rather than standing in some draughty chamber, poring over maps and arguing strategy.'

'Politics,' Volker said.

She tapped the side of her nose. 'Got it in one. Maybe you're as smart as you look.' She took off her glove and ran her thumb along the edge of the blade. 'I made enemies. Highborn Azyrite brats, with comfy positions bought for them by their mothers and fathers.'

Volker frowned. That described him as well, though he didn't think it prudent to admit as much. He continued wiping down his long rifle. 'They forced you out?'

'Eventually.' She squeezed her thumb. Volker watched as a bead of blood welled up. She sucked on the injured digit for a moment before continuing. 'One too many duels, even for Vindicarum. Too many dead Azyrites. And a price on my head, besides.'

'A price...?'

Zana grinned. 'Like I said, I made enemies. What about you, gunmaster?'

Volker paused, rag in hand. 'No, no enemies. No friends either.' He suddenly felt the weight of Makkelsson's flask sitting in his coat, and touched the pocket it rested in. 'Not any more, at least.'

'Count yourself lucky,' Lugash growled. 'Friendship is a chain of obligation that weighs heavily on the weak.'

Volker glanced at the doomseeker, uncertain how to respond. The fyreslayer was worryingly volatile, and they were trapped in a confined space. Lugash glared at him, as if daring him to reply.

'Spoken like a doomseeker,' Zana said. 'No wonder your lodge kicked you out.'

'They didn't kick me out,' Lugash said. 'My lodge is no more. Their name is dust, and their deeds nothing more than ash.'

Zana nodded. 'Maybe you should've died with them.'

Lugash was on his feet, weapons gripped tightly. 'What was that?'

Zana stood. 'You heard me.' She pointed her sword at him. 'Did you run? Or maybe you simply weren't worth killing.'

Volker exchanged worried glances with Roggen, and let his hand drift towards the grip of his artisan pistol. If Lugash made to harm her, he might have no choice. Duardin were tough though – a single shot, carefully placed, wouldn't kill him. And Sigmar only knew what would happen if he shot the doomseeker and didn't kill him.

Veins of ur-gold glimmered on the duardin's heavily muscled form, like cracks in some ancient statue. His beard bristled, and his eyes were wide and staring. 'Say it again,' he snarled. 'Say it to my face.'

'I thought I had. But then it's hard to tell with you duardin, misshapen lumps that you are.' Zana twitched her sword, as if in invitation.

Lugash stared at her in silence for long moments. Then he gave a gap-toothed grin. He threw back his head and laughed. It was not a pleasant sound, and Volker didn't remove his hand from his pistol. But it appeared that Zana's baiting had had the intended effect. The fyreslayer shook his head, still chuck-ling. 'You are brave, umgi. If your folk had more like you, they wouldn't need us to fight their battles for them.' He paused. 'Then maybe that's a good thing.' He turned and made for the bulkhead hatch. 'I'm going to get some air. It reeks of demigryph down here.'

Roggen paused in his exercises to sniff the air. 'She doesn't smell that bad.'

Zana chuckled and shook her head. 'You took quite a risk, there,' Volker said. 'He might've killed you.'

'No, he wouldn't have. He wanted an argument, so I gave him one. Fyreslayers are like that – prickly. They need conflict the way we need food and drink. Without it, they go a bit crazy.' She frowned. 'Crazier, I should say.' She looked at Volker. 'Speaking of crazy duardin, known Oken long, then?'

Volker smiled at the segue. 'He taught me everything I know.' He gestured to his weapons. 'Everything I am, I owe to him. Without him, I wouldn't be anything to speak of.' He chuckled. 'Just another highborn Azyrite brat.'

Zana blinked. 'Ah. That'd have been a waste.'

'I like to think so.' Volker set his rifle aside and retrieved his artisan pistol. Oken had taken his education in hand, though he'd never said why. And if his mother knew the reason, she hadn't shared it with him. One more secret. Catrin Volker was good at keeping secrets. But then that was practically a way of life in Azyrheim.

He hadn't seen her in years. Not since he'd decided he was more suited to a life in Ghur. For better or worse, she'd abided by his decision. He frowned and tried to concentrate on disassembling the pistol. Normally he could do it blindfolded. But he'd been rattled since Grungni had first appeared to him.

Being a gunmaster was to ritualise routine. Weapons had to be oiled and cleaned, calculations made and adjusted. Not just his, but those of the men nominally under his command.

Artillery pieces required constant supervision to keep them in working order. Granted, you could fob it off on to your assistants – if you could afford assistants – but there was no substitute for doing it yourself.

'He might be dead, you know. Grungni didn't say it, but...'

Volker paused. 'He might,' he said finally, completing the reassembly. 'Then, he might not.'

'Is that why you came?'

He looked at her. 'Is that so strange? He's my friend.'

She leaned back. 'Strange? I suppose not. Everyone knows you Azyrites are touched in the head. Too much time spent with your god shouting at you, I suppose.'

'I've never seen Sigmar, let alone been shouted at by him.'

'Maybe Grungni will introduce you.'

He studied her. 'Why do you do that?'

'What?' She looked at him, her expression unreadable.

He shook his head. 'I think Lugash had the right idea. I'm for some air. Excuse me.' He stuffed his pistol into his belt and left the hold, angry at himself. She was right, whether he wanted to admit it or not. Oken might very well be dead. And this would all be for nothing. The thought resonated through him like a sour note.

As he followed the cramped stairwell to the upper deck, something else occurred to him. Zana had spoken of Oken as if she knew him as well. He paused, wondering if he should go back down and ask her. He dismissed the idea a moment later; it didn't matter. He was forced to flatten himself against the wall several times on his ascent as Kharadron bustled past him, going about their business. The duardin paid him little attention, and the few attempts he made at striking up conversation were ignored.

Volker climbed to the deck, and was immediately struck by

a cold wind. The glow of the aether-endrins kept the vessel free of frost, but that was about it. The wind whistled, coiling around the struts and across the rails. Night had fallen, and the savage stars of Ghur gleamed like the eyes of immense beasts, out in the dark.

The deck curved upwards at the prow, and everywhere he looked, hoses, ropes and stiff iron struts rose to meet the globular aether-endrins. It was a forest of esoteric machinery, and the engineer in him wanted nothing more than to begin taking it apart, then and there, to figure out the secrets of its function.

The deck rolled strangely beneath Volker's feet. It wasn't like walking on a sea-going vessel. It was smoother, somehow. He found an out-of-the-way spot near the starboard rail and turned to study his hosts. The duardin were hard at their various duties.

He knew next to nothing about the Kharadron. What little he'd heard made them out to be as different from the Dispossessed as the fyreslayers were. All three shared a common ancestor in the Khazalid empires, which spread across the mortal realms during the Age of Myth. But all three had diverged greatly from the course set by their ancestors.

The Dispossessed venerated tradition above all else. They clung tightly to half-remembered rituals and centuried grudges, as if they could hold onto the last glimmerings of their former greatness through sheer will. The lodges of the fyreslayers, on the other hand, had developed their own rituals and a greatness all their own in their isolation.

And the Kharadron, from what little he knew of them, seemed to have shed the oldest Khazalid traditions in favour of survival. They had abandoned all that made duardin duardin, and become something other, yet familiar. A strange folk, with strange ways.

He turned, and spotted a solid form crouched on the curved snout of the prow. Lugash hunched there, a fingerbreadth from falling, staring out into the dark. He wondered what the fyreslayer was thinking about. It was probably best not to ask.

Volker sighed and leaned over the rail. Startled, a raven took wing from a dip in the hull, and sailed away with a croak of recrimination. Far below him, the grassy expanse of the Amber Steppes stretched from horizon to horizon. Occasional tumbledown hills and craggy expanses of stone jutted from the grasslands like tombstones, marking the last resting places of fallen empires. The Ghurlands were full of forgotten kingdoms. The great Waaagh!s of Gorkamorka had broken them, and the servants of Chaos had finished off those that remained. Now, only a few nomadic tribesmen called the grasslands home. He could see the glow of their campfires from this height, dozens of them, many hundreds of leagues apart. Tiny motes of humanity, adrift in the dark.

In the end, that was what it was all about, Volker thought. That was perhaps why cities like Excelsis had been founded. For all their flaws, they would serve as beacons to the scattered children of men, calling them home. Excelsis and the other Founding Cities were the seeds of a new beginning. One for all mortals.

He blinked as something glimmered in the dark. Not starlight, or the glare of a fire down below, but something almost… metallic. He leaned forwards. The clouds had thickened, and faint seams of glittering radiance ran through them.

'Star-dust,' Volker murmured. He had seen such motes before, as a child. They swirled about the highest peaks in Azyr and collected in the thickest clouds.

'Is that what they call it where you're from, then?'

He turned. Captain Brondt stood behind him, chewing on

his ever-present cheroot. The duardin joined him at the rail. 'Surprised you're able to breathe, manling. Usually your kind can't tolerate these altitudes.'

Volker inhaled. He hadn't even thought about it. 'This? This is mild, compared to where I was born.' He looked up. 'I could almost touch the stars from my crib.'

Brondt grunted. 'Could you now?' He swept his hand out, and caught a fistful of the sparkling motes. They clung to him like dust. 'Aether-gold – the breath of Grungni, some call it. Rich seams run through these clouds. Through the whole realm, really.'

'It's beautiful,' Volker said.

'It's more than that. Without it, our ships wouldn't fly. Our cities would fall from the skies. Our people – our society – would crumble, as that of our ancestors did.' Brondt stared at his hand. 'It's everything.'

'Are you a miner, then?'

Brondt chuckled. 'A speculator, let's say. I come before the miners. To see what there is to see.' He sighed. 'A good life, if you're of a certain turn of mind.' He gestured to the clouds. 'We're not the only ones who hunt it. The harkraken and other, worse things, eat it. No idea why, since they prey on flesh as well as aether. They can smell it for leagues and they'll go after a ship carrying it quicker than you can spit. Case in point–'

He reached and caught a handful of Volker's coat as something monstrous surged up through the clouds below and rose towards them with a sound like an avalanche. Volker had an impression of thousands upon thousands of triangular teeth, each the size of a man, lining jaws as wide as the Bastion, before a wall of pebbled flesh rose past the rail for what seemed an eternity. The *Zank* rocked, its aether-endrins groaning with strain as it was displaced by the sudden arrival. Klaxons blared and shouts of alarm rose from the crew as the force of the entity's passing sent a reeking torrent of wind crashing across the deck.

Brondt shoved Volker back, and turned. 'All hands to the guns,' he roared. 'Man the belaying valves! It looks like we're not the only ones in the sky tonight!'

Volker stared upwards as the monstrosity continued to rise past the aethercraft. Hillocks of aether-barnacles dotted its belly, and he thought he saw the shattered remains of other craft dangling from its immense flanks, their hulls crushed and splintered. 'What is that thing?' he shouted, a burst of primitive fear coursing through him. Nothing could be that big and still fly – it defied all logic.

Brondt laughed. 'Not a what, manling – a who!' He grinned fiercely. 'It's the Great King himself, come to see who's invading his territory!'

Elsewhere on the Amber Steppes, the Jaws sagged open for the second time in as many days. Amethyst lightning frenzied forth, causing the corpses that lay about it to jerk and dance. Those orruks who had survived the deathbringer's arrival had soon after plunged into the open realmgate, seeking a fight.

They'd got one. And paid a high price for it.

The monstrous shape that burst forth from within the Jaws issued an ear-splitting shriek of challenge as it entered this new realm. It had been a bat, once. An enormous bat, larger than any such creature should have been, but a natural creature nonetheless. Now, it was anything but.

The terrorgheist screamed again as it hauled itself out of the realmgate. Folded wings gouged the bloody soil as the rotted remains of its spear-blade nose twitched in phantom hunger. It wore the tatters of a once-fine livery and war-plate, as befitting a beast that had, in life, been ridden to war by one of the long-dead dukes of Gheist.

Now its rider was like it, a thing cold and dead.

Adhema, last noblewoman of a fallen kingdom, did not think of herself as such. Blood still pumped in her veins after all, stolen though it was. Heat filled her, at the thought of battle, or the hunt. That was life enough for now.

Her armour and blade were spattered with the tarry blood of orruks, and her nose full of their rancid scent. They had come boiling out of the gate like hungry insects, and she'd been forced to carve herself a path through their ranks. An amusing diversion, but one she'd had little time to indulge in.

She jerked the reins, bringing her monstrous steed to a lumbering halt. The massive chiropteran hissed in protest and squirmed beneath her. It smelled blood. And where there was blood, there was prey. Leaning over the pommel of her saddle, she studied the crude encampment. It was empty now, abandoned by the living and occupied only by the bodies of the newly slain.

She clambered from the saddle and dropped to the ground. The terrorgheist grunted, but a single gesture was enough to calm it. She knew little of the necromantic arts, but enough to control such a simple spirit. Carefully, she moved through the camp, stopping to taste the air every so often.

Her quarry had come this way. His particular scent – like hot iron and roasted meat – hung heavy amid the greenskin miasma. But she had no idea which way he'd gone. She sank to her haunches, and traced the faint indentation of a horse's hoof. The hard soil did little to capture the tracks of those who trod it.

Adhema.

The voice echoed like soft thunder in her mind. Adhema

rose from her crouch. Dead orruks littered the ground in all directions; they had been killed recently, and with great violence. Her quarry had definitely come this way, and not long ago. 'I hear, my lady, and I await your command,' she murmured, still studying the battlefield.

He was sloppy, this deathbringer. All force and no artistry. A whirlwind of carnage, lacking even the barest subtlety. Yet even so, he fought with cunning. There was a mind there, beneath the muscle and brass. That made him dangerous. Behind her the terrorgheist gave a rumble of impatience. The hungers that had driven it in life had grown doubly fierce in death, though it no longer required meat in its belly.

Have you found him yet? Neferata's voice was like the rustle of dark silk. It sang through Adhema's blood, as it had done many times throughout the centuries. Her blood was Neferata's, and Neferata's hers, and wherever she went in the realms, her mistress was there with her. Like a shadow on her mind.

'No, mistress. He was here, but I have lost his trail.' She looked up, shading her eyes against the light of the pale, reddish moon. She felt the flicker of Neferata's anger and hurried to excuse her failure. 'It's one of your own stallions he's riding. No faster steeds exist than those bred in Nulahmia.'

And who let him take that steed, sister?

Adhema winced. 'He killed her before he took her horse,' she murmured.

A dark chuckle tumbled through her mind. Her mistress was amused, at least. That counted for something. 'I can track him, but it will take time.'

Something we do not have.

Adhema frowned. 'We are immortal. Surely that is the one thing we *do* have.'

Neferata sighed. *We are not the only wolves on this trail, sister. My agents in the courts of the great powers send warning – the Eight Lamentations are known now. Vast mechanisms have begun to turn, and spies slink forth from the Varanspire and the Inevitable Citadel, to seek the weapons out.*

Adhema felt an elemental chill slither down her spine. If the Three-Eyed King had dealt himself into this game, could the Great Necromancer be far behind?

But he is, dear sister. We are his hand in this endeavour, though I grant we move without his acknowledgement. In any event, it is not Archaon himself who strides forth, but one of his courtiers. This is, as yet, a game for pawns, not kings and queens.

Adhema frowned. She had no illusions as to her importance in the scheme of things, but it rankled nonetheless. 'As you say, mistress.'

Ah, my dear, sweet, Adhema. So fierce, so eager to spill blood. But I need you to think like a player of games, not a warrior. He is ahead, yes, yet the solution is not to pursue him, but to anticipate him.

'He has the fragment,' Adhema protested. That she'd failed to acquire the fragment herself still stung her pride. She'd been unprepared for the deathbringer to flee, as he had. Usually they fought to the death – theirs.

Which he follows blindly. He is a blunt object, stampeding in whichever direction the wind takes him. But you, my dear, are a swordswoman. Think like one!

Adhema paused, considering. 'If I follow him, I risk a confrontation. But there must be some other way of telling where the spear rests – some other source of information.'

The servants of the Crippled God obviously think so, for they hurtle southwards across the Amber Steppes even now. Neferata laughed. *Such clever creatures, the sky-duardin, to build such magnificent vessels. Look, sister – see!*

Adhema gasped as her vision was overridden by that of another. The world spun crazily, erratically, and her skull echoed with the high-pitched squeal of bats. Through their manifold eyes she saw a strange armour-plated craft cut smoothly through the clouds, travelling south. The world returned to normal a moment later and she staggered, clutching at her aching head.

My apologies, sister, I often forget how difficult some find it, looking at the world through different eyes. Still, you saw?

'More than I realised. I know where they're heading.' Adhema straightened. 'The Crawling City.'

And why might they do that? Neferata's purr said she knew the answer already.

'Something is there. Something that will lead them to the spear.' Adhema turned and hauled herself up onto the terrorgheist's neck. The monstrous bat-thing emitted a shriek of eagerness as she slammed her heels against its tattered flesh and hauled on the reins. It leapt into the air with a single beat of its ragged wings.

'And I will find it first.'

SEVEN
THE GREAT KING

The Great King.

The words sent a tremor of fear through Volker. There wasn't a soul in Excelsis that hadn't heard the stories of the mountainous megalofin – a shark-like beast that swam through the skies of the realms and even the void itself, as easily as its smaller, aquatic cousins did the water. The megalofins were immense – easily the size of Kharadron aethercraft, or larger. But the Great King was larger still.

It was the king of all megalofins, a vast monster that had hunted the skies of Ghur since the realm had first congealed. Some whispered that it had been trapped within the realm by some ancient force, seeking to be rid of it. Others that it was one of the fabled god-beasts. All Volker knew was that the mere mention of it could cause even orruks to flinch in primordial terror.

The passing of the megalofin caused the *Zank* to tumble awkwardly off course. Endrins moaning with effort, the vessel righted itself. Kharadron in heavy arkanaut armour hurried to the rails, manning the aethershot carbines and sky cannons. Belaying valves howled as the craft heaved to. The shadow of the megalofin draped over them like a second night. Brondt squinted up at it as it rose high above them.

'Always forget how big the bastard is,' he muttered. 'Like one of those flying islands in Ghyran, only angrier.' He turned and bellowed an order. Aethershot carbines swivelled on their firing stands, following the beast as it began to circle back. Given its size, Volker estimated that they had several minutes before it got close again.

'Surely we're not going to try to fight that thing.' Volker's palms itched. He wished that he hadn't left his long rifle in the hold.

'Don't be daft. We're making a run for it.'

'To where?'

'There.' Brondt pointed. Volker followed his gesture and saw a bobbing light in the distance. '*Zonbek*,' Brondt continued. 'A glowbeacon lighthouse. We establish them along the better trade routes. Keeps the harkraken and megalofin at bay. Mostly.' He flicked ash from his cheroot. 'More beasts in these skies than stars above.' He peered at Volker. 'You're not from here. Got the look of Azyr about you. Something about the eyes.' He gestured with two fingers for emphasis.

'I am.'

'I hate Azyr. The air is too clean. Too cold.' Brondt grinned. 'You seem all right, though. Bit dull, but that's what comes of clean air.'

Volker snorted. 'And where do you come from, then?'

'Barak-Mhornar.' He reached into his coat and extracted a curious mechanism. It resembled a compass or a pocket watch, or both. He flipped it open and studied the spinning dial, keeping one eye on the massive shape of the Great King circling above. 'Above the Straits of Helsilver, somewhere near the Brasslok Mountains, depending on the aether-currents.' He closed the mechanism with a click and stuffed it back in his coat. 'A profitable enough port.'

'As profitable as a place called the City of Shadows can be,' Zana said. Volker turned as she joined them at the rail. 'What's going on?' she asked, checking the buckles on her armour. 'Are we under attack?'

'Of sorts.' Brondt craned his neck.

'Where's Roggen?' Volker asked.

'Still below, trying to keep his beast calm. If she gets loose, excited as she is, things will turn very unpleasant very quickly.'

'One monster is more than enough,' Brondt said. He pointed. 'Crafty bugger. Those were skyhooks rattling from his carapace. He knows us well, the old devil. I heard Brokrin almost downed him, a year back, but that was likely just wishful thinking on his part.'

Zana stared at the distant form of the megalofin and cursed. She glared at Brondt. 'Can't this heap of yours go any faster? Outrun him?'

'Maybe. If we get to the *zonbek*, he'll peel off and go bother someone else. Sensitive eyes, the King. That's why he only hunts at night usually. I'd heard he was sighted in other skies of late, or else I'd have been better prepared.'

Zana frowned. She looked around. 'Where's Lugash? Wasn't he up here?'

Volker turned. 'He was on the… prow…' The prow was unadorned by the hunched form of a fyreslayer. He turned to Brondt. 'Did you…?'

Brondt didn't look at him. 'Don't ask me. I've been a bit preoccupied, what with the giant megalofin trying to eat us. If

127

you've lost one of yours, I'm not liable. Artycle eight, adden-dum three of the code clearly states–'

'Hang the code, and hang you, if he's dead,' Zana hissed.

'He's not dead,' Volker said, leaning over the rail. He caught a flash of red on the side of the aether-endrin. 'He's up there.'

Brondt paled. 'What in the name of the Maker is he doing up there?' He rushed to the rail and craned his head. 'Come down, you hot-blooded idiot,' he shouted. 'You'll crash us for sure!' A string of expletives followed as Brondt shook his fist at the fyreslayer.

Volker saw Lugash's sturdy form scuttle onto the top of the spherical endrin. He could hear the duardin laughing, and wondered if he meant to hurl himself off the ship and onto the beast. He glanced at Zana. 'One of us should go after him.'

She held out her fist. 'Gold, silver, copper?'

'What?'

A sound like a typhoon swept over them. The Great King was making its approach, tatters of cloud trailing from its teeth. Volker cursed. 'Never mind.' He gripped the rail, ready to haul himself over, wishing once again that he had his long rifle.

'What are you doing, Azyrite?' Brondt snapped, catching him by the arm. 'Are you mad? There's no way I'm letting you climb out there.'

'What about Lugash?'

'What about him? Let the maniac look after himself.' Brondt turned as one of his crew shouted something. He spun back and shoved Volker towards Zana. 'You two – stay out of the way. This is company business and I'll not have you mucking it up.' He stumped along the rail bellowing orders. 'All ahead full, batten the hatches and ready the belaying valves. Njord, Bron – I want those carbines aimed down his bloody throat. He wants a piece, let him earn it.'

He turned back to the approaching megalofin. Its jaws widened, as if it would swallow the vessel whole. 'Fire,' Brondt roared. There was a harsh grumble as the ship's weapons spat aetheric fire across the sky. The approaching monster shuddered, more in surprise than pain, Volker thought. He lifted his artisan pistol, though he knew it would do little good, and saw that Zana had half-drawn her own blade. She smiled ruefully at him, but before either of them could speak, a beam of impossibly bright light enveloped the *Zank*.

There was a thunderous rumble as the Great King twisted in mid-lunge, rolling away from the light and the hammering guns. The great beast cannoned past the aethercraft, shaking it to its rivets, and dived away into the clouds with a flick of its massive tail. A bow-wave of air buffeted the ship, but it remained on course. Brondt shouted triumphantly and pounded the rail with his fists. 'Ha! Don't like that, do you, your majesty?' He turned to Volker. '*Zonbek*, just like I said.'

The glowbeacon lighthouse rose opposite them, piercing the clouds like a ray of sunlight caught in amber. It was a tower of sorts, balanced on an array of aether-endrins, which served to keep the edifice afloat. Jetties extended out from its base in a wide circle and high, fortified walls enclosed the central structure. As they passed it, Volker could see that both the walls and lighthouse behind them were bristling with weapons, and duardin.

Brondt waved cheerfully to the Kharadron on the walls. 'They'll keep us in the light until we reach port.' He hooked his thumbs into his belt and let out a long, slow breath. 'That was a close one – thought he almost had us there.'

'So did I. Why did you chase the bugger off?' Lugash growled, as he clambered over the rail. The fyreslayer's runes were glowing red-hot, as were his eyes. He had his axe in his hand and a murderous expression on his face.

Brondt glared at the other duardin. 'Because I didn't fancy being eaten today, doomseeker. Unlike some.'

'Coward,' Lugash spat.

'Practical,' Brondt countered, eyes narrowed. 'There's no honour in a profitless death. Especially against a monster like that. It's not an enemy to fight, it's a storm to outrun.'

'So you say,' Lugash said. He took a threatening step forwards, but halted as Volker stepped between them. 'Out of the way, manling. This *wazzock* and I have business.'

'The only business we have can be conducted in the length of time it takes me to throw you off my ship,' Brondt snarled, reaching for the cutlass-like blade sheathed on his hip. Zana caught him and pulled him back. Volker raised his pistol. Lugash grinned.

'Found your courage, then?'

'I never lost it. I just don't like wasting resources.'

Lugash snorted. 'Is that a threat?'

Volker cocked the pistol. 'Yes.'

Lugash hesitated. Then he stepped back, and spat at Volker's feet. 'I could smell ur-gold in that thing's belly. It sang through my blood.' He turned away, and Volker lowered his weapon. That was all the explanation they were going to get, he suspected. He holstered his pistol and let out a shaky breath.

Zana whistled. 'I've seen fyreslayers march through balefire without flinching. Think that toy of yours would've done anything to him?'

'No. But it would've bought me enough time to get out of the way.' Volker bowed low to Brondt. 'My apologies, captain. Our comrade is… volatile.'

Brondt sighed and waved Volker's apology aside. 'You mean he's a doomseeker. He's worse than that overgrown gryph-hound in the hold.' He shook his head. 'No matter, though. You'll soon be off my ship, and good riddance.'

'Admit it, you'll miss me,' Zana said.

'You've got half a favour left,' Brondt growled. 'After that, we're even.'

A shout from one of the crew brought a smile to the grizzled duardin's face. 'Finally,' he grunted. 'Best get your other friend up here, Mathos. He might want to see this. It's not every day one sees the Crawling City in all its monstrous glory.'

Yuhdak of the Ninefold Path, last prince of the City of Tiers, slumped with a sigh, his head aching from the strain of his effort to control the great beast. Its mind was a reef of primeval desire and if the sorcerer were not careful he would batter himself to pieces against it. Greater souls than his had come up short in a duel of wills against the antediluvian monstrosity known as the Great King.

The megalofin was ancient, even by the standards of one who had lived for centuries. It was the oldest thing in these skies and bore the scars of a lifetime of constant battle. It had devoured harkraken and chimera packs, and defeated all who sought to invade its territory – even Gorkamorka himself had failed to put a permanent end to the Great King, it was whispered. The enormous megalofin still hunted the sea of stars, so there was some truth to the tale, Yuhdak supposed.

He looked up as its shadow passed over the outcrop he sat on and swam up through the clouds, back into the high darkness where it normally lurked. It was a beautiful thing, in its way. It defied complexity – a smooth mind, of simple hungers. 'Well, a failure, but an honest one,' he murmured. There would be other opportunities, and soon.

Yuhdak smoothed his multicoloured robes with a graceful

gesture. His armour was crafted from iridescent glass, each facet a different hue. His war-mask was carved from cracked crystal and mimicked the shape of a daemon's leering face. It was open at the back, allowing his mane of thick hair to spill across his shoulders. The blade resting at his hip was curved, and its sheath richly ornamented.

Though magic was his weapon of choice, he had been taught the arts of the blade early and well, as befitted a prince. He fancied there was no greater swordsman in all this brute realm than himself. And if there were, he scarce had wish to meet them.

Yuhdak sank to his haunches and commenced drawing ritual shapes for a new working in the dirt. The Eight had surfaced often, in the centuries since their disappearance. The weapons would seek out wielders and be used, before vanishing once more. Rumours about the reasons for this sprouted fast and thick amongst the servants of the Ruinous Powers. Among the rows of chained tomes and stalking shelves of the grand libraries of the Forbidden City, the servants of chance whispered stories of the being known as the Daemoniac Conundrum.

A trickster without equal, the Conundrum was preeminent even among such deceivers as the Queen of Foxes or the Changeling. Malevolent and treacherous, the entity had been banished from the Forbidden City – the only being to suffer such a fate – but that had not curtailed its love of japes and jests. Its favourite joke was to steal away some item of great value and hide it within a labyrinth of its own construction.

Such structures, or the remains thereof, dotted the realms – folded citadels and furling castles. In Ghur, it had supposedly raised the Howling Labyrinth – a maze of amber and bone – to house the Lamentation known as Marrowcutter, the sword of fire. Yuhdak had been party to the discovery of the blade almost a century before, and witness to its loss in the final moments of the labyrinth's destruction.

Some said that the blade wasn't the only one of the Eight that the Daemoniac Conundrum had hidden. Legend had it that he had snatched Starcracker, the black hammer of the heavens, from the hands of Sigmar himself, as the God-King sought to bend it to his will, in the wake of the theft of Ghal Maraz. The Conundrum was said to have secreted it somewhere deep within the shadowed reaches of Ulgu.

Thankfully Gung, the Spear of Shadows, had been hidden by mortals rather than a daemon. That made things somewhat easier. He heard a flutter of wings and stood, as something alighted nearby. 'You're back. Good.' He dusted off his hands. 'Tell me, my lady, what does your flock see?' he murmured respectfully, as he turned to the dark-clad woman now standing behind him on the rocky outcrop.

She wore a narrow helmet shaped like the skull of a raven, from beneath which her hair spilled down across her shoulders and the black feathers of her cloak. Obsidian mail peeked through her dark robes, black on black. She had no name that he was aware of. The Ninety-Nine Feathers no longer thought as men, and names were considered nothing more than an affectation. She was simply the Daughter of the King of All Ravens, and the mistress of the cabal. That was enough.

She turned, her dark eyes gleaming with ancient knowledge. 'Many things,' she said. Her voice was harsh, like the croak of a raven. 'We see the wars that are waged in the hollows of the moons, and the great rivers that shape the roots of the mountains. We see the ratkin swarming towards the high walls of a city on the Coast of Tusks. And we see the servants of the forgemasters, racing to and fro.'

Yuhdak nodded encouragingly. 'And where are they racing to, my lady?'

She cocked her head, birdlike. 'Here and there.'

Yuhdak laughed softly. He nodded again. 'So I gathered. Could you be more specific? What of him whose trail we followed from Shyish?'

She stared at him unblinking. Then, 'The closest seeks the Spear of Shadows.'

'Which is somewhere in this savage realm, according to the auguries,' he said, gesturing expansively. 'But we know not where. And merely to follow him is to risk losing it, for he will not give it up easily. He is a Kel of the Ekran, and they are not known to be especially reasonable. Instead, we must anticipate him.' He turned, considering. He had many auguries at his disposal – the cards that hung from his belt, encased in silver, the sands in their sigil-sewn pouch, or even the rune-marked bones, which rattled softly in their square case.

But sometimes, a soul needed no augury to choose the right path. Instead, he merely needed to listen to the voices within, and heed them. He pointed towards what appeared to be a distant mountain range, moving slowly across the steppes. 'There. Creeping across the Amber Steppes. Shu'gohl, the Crawling City. There is a great repository of knowledge there – the Libraria Vurmis. What we seek is there, if anywhere.'

She looked at him in silence. He read the question in her body language. 'The duardin,' he said simply. 'Grungni's servant. That is where he went, before you lost track of him. The answer will be there.' Several of the Ninety-Nine Feathers had followed the duardin for weeks, dogging his trail through ruins and over mountains, even as more members of the flock kept watch on others throughout the mortal realms.

She nodded. In an eye blink, she was gone. A raven swooped

away across the grasslands, in the direction he'd indicated. He sighed thoughtfully. She was a princess, and he a prince, yet their dalliance was but for a moment. An intertwining of two fates, soon to part. He would miss her, but such was the way of it.

The services of the Ninety-Nine Feathers could only be bartered for or won. He had done the former, selling a handful of ill-tempered memories from his youth, for the loyalty of the raven-cabal. As war-mages they were without peer, and the bidding wars for their oaths were fierce indeed.

For the moment they were his to command, and he would make full use of them. They were his eyes and ears in the realms of men, spying out those who would deny him his triumph. They had followed the airship, and its passengers, from the Azyrite city, and through their eyes he had seen the moment to strike.

He had hoped to stymie the Crippled God's servants by crashing the vessel they travelled on. And it was still possible that he might do so. They had bloodied the Great King, and the beast's rage would smoulder for days. It had a long memory for such a simple brute. If necessary, he would point the monstrosity at the aethercraft and let nature take its course. But only if his servants found the information they needed. Otherwise, it would be necessary to follow these mortals, and hope that they led him to what he sought in a timely fashion.

Despite these worries, the hunt was proving more entertaining than he'd expected. The Eight Lamentations were scattered throughout the mortal realms, hidden in some cases or else wielded by the ignorant. Eight weapons of great power, capable of turning the tide in the wars to come. Or so Archaon, the Grand Marshal of Chaos, thought. Why else would the Three-Eyed King send his chosen servants to seek them out?

That it might simply be a game – a way for a bored potentate to pass the time – had crossed Yuhdak's mind on more than one occasion. Even if such were the case, it did not diminish the pride he felt in being among those granted the honour of undertaking the quest. Whatever the true purpose of his search, he would complete it, and perhaps prove himself worthy of joining the Varanguard.

Either way, the Eight Lamentations would belong to Archaon, and with them the Three-Eyed King would reap a great and terrible toll from his enemies.

∞ EIGHT ∞

CRAWLING CITY

Adhema clung to the side of the immense worm, her armoured fingers digging into its thick hide. It was like climbing some vast, breathing mountain. She had allowed her terrorgheist to fly free, and hunt the steppes as it willed. Entering the worm-city required more subtlety than the shrieking bat-beast could muster.

So she climbed, hand over hand, moving more swiftly than a mortal – especially one in full armour – could have. It was no tricky thing to avoid the watch towers that clung like fungal growths to the worm's flanks. More difficult were the sweeping beams of reflected light, which swept the grasslands below, and the worm's flesh, searching for enemies. The worm-folk had been attacked too often to be entirely lax in their security measures.

Often, she was forced to pause in her ascent, to wait for a searching beam to pass away. In those moments, she entertained herself with the thought of what she was going to do to the deathbringer when she finally caught him. The servants of Khorne could endure much before they expired. And she had learned the torturer's arts during her time among the desert tribes of the Great Emptiness. Neferata insisted that her servants availed themselves of a well-rounded education.

He had killed several of her sisterhood, and deserved a painful death as his reward. To kill a mortal was but to pay homage to death. To slay an immortal, however, was to do that which death had forbidden. Her foe had broken that law and thus must pay the price.

Once such thoughts might have disgusted her. Then again, maybe not. In her youth, when her heart still beat, she had thought that the sum total of the world was her father's kingdom, and that world was good. She remembered climbing into bed using the backs of her servants as a stool, and the archery lessons with screaming targets – peasants, mostly, and a few criminals. Her father had believed that blood was the best teacher of all and had schooled her accordingly. Such was the way her family had always ruled Szandor.

Szandor the Proud. Szandor the Cruel. Where gibbet cages hung in every market square and the enemies of the aristocracy were impaled on short stakes so that their agonies might last for hours, if not days. Szandor, where hymns in praise of the Undying King were sung on high holy days and a tithe of flesh was offered up to his servants.

Szandor, the last gasp of resistance in western Shyish. Neferata had seen to that. The Mortarch of Blood had wielded the might of Szandor as a swordsman might wield a blade, bleeding the enemy of days, weeks, months. Until at last the blade broke, and she cast it into her opponent's face, to make her escape.

But not alone. She took the firstborn daughters of the great families with her. She took them, and made them fit for purpose, full of spite and anger. Adhema grinned, and licked her teeth. Her fangs, like those of an adder, or a wolf, the better to bite out the throat of the enemy. Neferata's catch were the orphans of a thousand murdered kingdoms, united in their hatred of the Ruinous Powers. But hatred alone wasn't enough. Like anything, it had to be honed to a killing edge.

Despite the intervening centuries, she could still hear the voice of their teacher as he schooled her and the others in the arts of war. The Blood Dragon himself, the finest warrior Shyish had ever seen. How Neferata had coaxed him down from his mountain, Adhema did not know. But she was grateful. By his hand had the lessons of her father been built on, and in some cases, discarded entirely.

It was the nature of time that the old ways gave way before the new. Wit replaced weapons, and cunning became the anticipator of carnage. For her queen, war was a game of applied strategies. An artistic endeavour, equivalent to painting – every brushstroke another stratagem, every subsequent dab of colour a new factor applied to the problem. The realms were vast, and the war that raged across them was not a single conflict, but a thousand smaller ones, each one with its own purpose and peculiarities.

Szandor had been one such. She paused, staring up at the yellow moons. In Shyish, they were silver and dead, scoured of all threat by the will and whim of the Undying King. Here, they swelled with obscene life. It was said by the liche-monks of the Dead Vaults that whole tribes of the Chaos-tainted prowled the lunar crags of the Beast-Moons, their forms warped into howling mockeries of wolves. She had fought such creatures before, and had enjoyed it immensely. They died as easily as any other living thing.

Above her something cawed. She looked up, frowning.

Carrion birds – ravens – circled overhead, their raucous cries trickling down towards her. To her eyes, far keener than those of a mortal, something about them seemed off. They left a stain on the air, as if by their very nature they offended the laws of this realm.

She watched the ravens circle and dart down, into the city. A slow grin spread across her face. Those were not natural birds. Her mistress had been right. 'Well, this has suddenly become more interesting.'

She scuttled up the side of the worm, moving more quickly now, heedless of the beams of light that occasionally swept over her. Men in the watch-posts stared in alarm as an inky black shape clattered past, moving more swiftly than they could perceive, in fits and starts, between one eye blink and the next.

And soon it was out of sight, and no more than a fading memory.

Shu'gohl, the Crawling City, squirmed ceaselessly across the grasslands of the Amber Steppes. The immense, segmented form of the worm stretched from sunrise to sunset, carrying a city of several million on its back. It devoured all in its path with unthinking hunger, and some days great herds of beasts stampeded ahead of it, seeking safety.

Shu'gohl was but one of ten – ten great worms, driven up onto the surface in aeons past by great rains. Someday they might descend once more into the cavernous depths of the realm, but for now, they were content to continue their mindless perambulations.

Like Shu'gohl, many of the ten bore some form of metropolis upon their back, and had done so since before the Age of Chaos. The oldest stories claimed that the ancestors of the worm-folk had fled to those fleshy heights in order to escape

Gorkamorka's hordes. Isolated and ever-moving, they had ignored the tides of Chaos sweeping across the realm. Until the eyes of the Dark Gods had at last turned towards them.

A few had fallen to Chaos, in those final fraught decades before the opening of the Gates of Azyr. Guh'hath, the so-called Brass Bastion, had carried tribes of Bloodbound in slow pursuit of Shu'gohl, as had Rhu'goss, the Squirming Citadel. Both ancient beasts had been cleansed by the efforts of the Stormcast Eternals, and the worms themselves continued their journeys, only dimly aware of the wars waged upon their backs.

But Shu'gohl was the greatest of the worm-cities, despite all that it had endured in its centuried life. The Crawling City had flourished in the wake of its liberation from the skaven of the Clans Pestilens, and was now once more a major port of call for travellers from across the realms. Volker could believe it.

His eyes were drawn to the ever-present storm that flickered across the great worm's head – the Sahg'gohl. The Storm-Crown. A temple complex had been constructed there, aeons past, and a realmgate raised, connecting the city to the Luminous Plains in Azyr. That realmgate was open now and travellers passed through it freely. 'May it always be so,' Volker murmured, lifting his amulet and touching it to his lips.

'Gods below, it's the size of a mountain,' Lugash growled from nearby. He stared down at the vast, crawling shape with wide eyes. The wind caught at his beard, causing the blades woven into it to rattle and clatter. 'What does it eat?'

'Everything,' Zana said, leaning over the rail. 'Anything. It once devoured an entire kingdom, bit by bit, over the course of a century.' She pulled on her helmet. 'Thankfully it's slower than the day is long.'

Volker shook his head. An odd saying. Maybe days were longer in Chamon. He peered over the rail. Shu'gohl was longer than he could take in at a glance. Even at this height, its distant segments vanished over the horizon. A slow, sonorous grinding marked its eternal journey, and an omnipresent dust cloud, thrown up by its undulations. The city on its back was a narrow strip of creation, rising up from within the bristles that coated the worm's hide. Smoke rose from its highest towers, and beams of light, cast upwards by immense mirrors, swung across the darkening sky.

The Kharadron vessel swooped silently towards a group of the tallest of the bristle-towers, where aerial docklands, built from hair, skin-plates and other assorted materials, stretched in the round. Like Excelsis, Shu'gohl had made the sky-borne duardin traders welcome. Docking was apparently a complex process involving venting the belaying valves and what seemed like a lot of shouting.

When the *Zank* had subsided in its berth, boarding ramps were extended to the rough, spongy jetties. Brondt saw them off with a glower. 'Goodbye, good luck, good riddance,' he said, one hand resting on the pommel of his cutlass. He pointed at Zana. 'Mathos – don't bother me for at least a year.'

Zana saluted him airily. 'Half a favour, Brondt.'

He sneered and turned away, to vent his frustration on his crew. 'He likes me, really,' she said, stepping aside so that Roggen could lead Harrow off the vessel. The demigryph snapped at an unwary Kharadron, prompting a flurry of curses. Roggen apologised profusely, and tried to hurry the demigryph towards the cunningly designed lift network. Volker sighed.

'Maybe you were right about the beast.'

'No. Roggen wouldn't have abandoned her willingly.' Zana clapped him on the shoulder. 'Besides, as you said, she might come in handy.'

'Worst comes to worst, we can eat it,' Lugash said, stumping past them.

The lift – a platform suspended by pulleys and thick ropes of braided worm-hair – carried them to the streets far below, at a speed just short of ridiculous. Volker felt the bread he'd eaten trying to climb back up out of his stomach, even as they reached the bottom.

The city was a forest of high, swaying setae towers rising above cramped, squirming streets. Bridges and walkways made from worm-scale and hair connected these towers to one another and the street. It was like looking up into some vast web, full of colour and sound. Mirror plates hung from the towers reflected criss-crossing beams of lantern light down into the streets, and up into the heights. Even at night, Shu'gohl was as bright as day.

'Do they fear the dark so much, then?' Roggen asked, looking around. People moved to and fro across the cracked, uneven streets. The ground underfoot twitched tremulously. Volker stumbled more than once. It would take time to get used to.

'Not the dark, but what's in it,' he said. He shifted his long rifle onto his shoulder. 'The skaven took this city once. They fear that happening again. And not without cause, I suspect.' He gestured to the base of a nearby tower, where strange, hairy hides were nailed up. 'There are still skaven, deep in the worm. Gnawing away at it, as they do everything.'

'We hunt them, in the bleeding season,' a voice said. Soft but strong, with a strange guttural accent. Volker and the others turned. A woman clad in thick robes and a curious type of scale armour strode towards them. Coiling, worm-like sigils marked the hem of her robes, and the hammer symbol of Sigmar had been etched onto every scale of her armour. She was pale, as all the folk of Shu'gohl were, and her long hair was almost white, though Volker judged her as being younger than himself. 'When the gut-shafts expand, and grow slick, we descend into Olgu'gohl and burn back the infestation for another year.'

'Olgu…?' Roggen began, trying and failing to pronounce the odd syllables. Harrow chirped and rubbed his shoulder with her beak. Absently, he patted the beast.

'The Squirming Sea,' the woman said. She bowed her head. 'I am Nyoka Su'al'gohl. I have been expecting you.' She pressed her fist into her palm and bowed. She wore heavy, ridged gauntlets, and silver bells were threaded through her hair. They made soft harmonies as she moved. 'Sahg'mahr bless and keep thee.' She straightened. 'The Builder sent word. I am to escort you to the Libraria Vurmis.'

'The – Grungni, you mean?' Volker said. Of course the god would have someone waiting on them. Grungni left little to chance, it seemed.

She nodded. 'The Builder, yes. Come. You must be eager to see it.' She turned away. Volker and the others shared a look. He cleared his throat.

'See what?'

She glanced at him. 'The book.' She spoke as if to a child. He wondered if all the worm-folk were so abrupt. Perhaps something was being lost in translation.

Volker hesitated. Zana pushed him aside. 'What book?'

'The duardin book.' Nyoka frowned. 'Why else would you come to a library?'

Zana shrugged and looked at Volker. 'She has a point.' She gestured. 'Lead on.'

Lugash stepped between them. 'Wait a moment – why should we trust her? She could be a spy.' He glared at Nyoka. 'Going to lead us into an ambush, then?'

'If I were, I would not admit it, just because you ask,' Nyoka said.

Lugash blinked. 'Good point.' He sniffed. 'I'll be watching you.'

'Good. That way you will not get lost.' Nyoka gestured. 'Stay close. The city is crowded this time of year, and outsiders can become easily disorientated.'

As they walked, Volker studied his surroundings with an engineer's eye. Shu'gohl had grown in the century since its liberation, upwards and outwards, or so he'd heard tell. The streets were almost as crowded as those of Excelsis, though it was far more peaceful. Freeguild warriors in grey uniforms patrolled the streets alongside the members of the infamous Setaen Guard in their dark robes and polished armour. The Guard wore full-face helms, wrought in the shape of writhing tendrils, and mail hoods, further lending them an air of subdued menace.

Volker noticed a definite tension in the air between the two groups. Hostile looks and knots of discontent on street corners, swiftly dissipated by the attentions of the freeguild. The city was by no means a powder keg, but it wasn't especially friendly either.

Like Excelsis, the narrow streets had their share of traders cluttering the path. Some worm-folk, but there were others as well, among them grim-faced duardin merchants, selling weapons and tools, and colourfully robed desert nomads, selling spices and salt. He saw a scar-faced ex-freeguilder hawking strange jewellery, which still stank of the sea bottom, and a thin, hollow-cheeked woman handing out religious tracts. She pressed one into his hand before he could get away, and said, 'Nagash is all, brother, and all are one in him. In death, all are equal, and all are safe...'

Lugash spat a curse, startling the woman. She vanished into the crowd as they pushed away from her. Lugash shook his head. 'You manlings have too many gods.'

'I only worship one,' Volker said, feeling for his amulet. The Nagashites weren't the only ones out in force. He saw white-robed and golden-masked Hyshites walking in single file, their heads bowed and their arms crossed, and a coven of wild-haired forest-brides singing eerie hymns in praise of the Lady of Leaves on a nearby street corner.

Nyoka spotted his gesture and smiled, pleased. 'You are one of the Devoted?'

'I – yes,' Volker said. 'You as well, I take it.' He motioned to her armour. She nodded.

'I carry the hammer in his name, and proudly.' Her hands flexed, and she cast a speculative glare at the forest-brides. They began to dance wildly, attracting a crowd. 'I have made grist of his enemies, for the mills of heaven.' Startled, Volker glanced at Zana, who smiled grimly. Nyoka was a war-priestess, then. Like old Friar Ziska, though hopefully she wasn't mad as well. But then, perhaps you had to be a little mad to make your home on the back of a monster.

Mad or not, Nyoka – or the trappings she wore – commanded respect. People made way for her, bowing and making the sign of the hammer. Even the Nagashites stepped aside, though with far fewer smiles. As in Excelsis, all faiths were welcome, but only one was truly honoured. That much was evident from the wayshrines that littered the streets.

Volker wasn't the only one interested in their surroundings. Roggen stared openly, clearly impressed. He held Harrow's reins tightly, and when the demigryph suddenly lurched to the side, he was almost dragged off his feet. The beast padded towards a noisome stall, where a bespectacled trader hawked a bevy of exotic animals – infant merwyrms glaring out of their glass bowls, scaly peryton eggs and a chained ghyrlion were among his merchandise.

The ghyrlion, its thorny mane clattering, snarled once at the demigryph before slinking away beneath the egg baskets. The colourful birds in their cages shrieked and squawked in growing panic as Harrow approached, but the demigryph had eyes only for a bevy of mangy wolf-rats, crouched in heavy wooden cages. The trader's patter stuttered into silence as Roggen finally halted his steed's advance.

The wolf-rats screeched in their cages, lashing hairless tails as they bit at the bars. The feral rat-creatures were as large as gryph-hounds, and almost as vicious. Roggen gestured to the merchant, and reached for his coin purse. Volker couldn't hear what they were saying, but given what he'd seen of Harrow's appetites so far, he could guess.

'What is he doing?' Nyoka asked. She watched the transaction in puzzlement.

'Buying his beast a treat,' Zana said, in disgust. The merchant kicked the cage open and leapt back as the wolf-rat burst free. The slavering vermin darted towards Roggen, jaws wide. Harrow gave a scream of joy and swatted the animal from the air. The demigryph's blow snapped the wolf-rat's spine, and it flopped limply to the street. Harrow ducked her beak and lifted her prey easily. Roggen smiled and patted the beast.

'She was hungry,' he said, when he noticed the stares of the others.

'She's always hungry,' Zana snapped. Harrow chirped at her as she swallowed a chunk of the wolf-rat's carcass in that peculiar, avian fashion. Zana made a rude gesture.

'Best to keep her fed, then,' Volker said, attempting to head off any argument. He'd been trying to keep a map of the route they were taking in his head, but it was proving impossible. The streets of the Crawling City seemed to change shape constantly, as the worm moved across the steppes. The towers and walls shifted position with frustrating regularity, and the only unchanging routes were the walkways and rope bridges high above. He turned to Nyoka. 'Where is the libraria, exactly?'

She pointed. 'There. The Dorsal Barbicans.'

The barbicans rose over the worm's middle, separating the more affluent districts of the city from the lesser. The high walls were built from hardened ichor, fossilised hair and ironoak timbers, procured at great expense from Kharadron traders. Or so Nyoka claimed, as she led them towards the plaza that housed the barbican gates.

The crowds were thicker here, and the noise and smell was almost overpowering. Nyoka dived into the sea of humanity without hesitation. Volker realised belatedly that this was the city's main thoroughfare, as he narrowly avoided being flattened by an ironmonger's cart. The woman pulling it only paused long enough to bark a curse before forging ahead. There was no order to things – you pushed in where you found room, and only kept your place with a judicious use of elbows and harsh language. Street performers threaded through the crowd, dressed in distracting colours, and adding to the confusion with their nonsense songs and acrobatics.

'Keep a hand on your gear, Azyrite,' Zana murmured, from close behind him. 'I've spotted at least two pickpockets.' She elbowed someone in the chest, knocking the man out of line. His protests were swallowed up by the crowd.

'Have you warned Roggen?'

'No need. Only an idiot would try to sneak close to that beast of his. But you're carrying enough hardware to earn a good thief a year's wage.'

Volker, no stranger to the perils of the urban jungle, nodded and dropped a hand to the grip of his artisan pistol. He thrust his rifle out like a cane, prodding people from his path. People glared at him, but no one spoke up.

The plaza was made from dyed and polished setaen tiles, which had been placed to form an intricate mosaic, the meaning of which escaped Volker. Statues of the great heroes of the city's history lined the edges of the plaza, gazing benignly down on the tide of people moving through the gates. A few guards, mostly freeguild, stood watch, but they made no effort to impede the flow of traffic.

As they passed through, Volker looked up and saw timber bridges passing between the outer walls and the inner. The inner walls spread outwards from a domed structure, like the spokes of a wheel. This central structure had been built around a great encrustation on the worm's hide, and had only grown larger as the city swelled. High, square walls rose in a hexagonal shape towards a vast dome, covered in mirror-plates. Scattered among the mirrors were stone archways, each connected to one of the timber bridges.

The whole edifice crouched on a dais of hardened and carved ichor, and slanted slab steps cascaded down each side. There were more guards sitting or standing on these steps, leaning on their weapons. They watched as tired and thirsty travellers collected water from the bronze taps of the great barrels scattered about the courtyard. The barrels were rain siphons, Volker knew. Rainwater built up in them, and they were communal property – they had passed dozens of them, coming from the aetherdocks. He knew there were similar barrels, though much larger, atop each of the setaen towers. The water from those was mostly filtered down to the fungal farms in the dorsal districts, and the breweries and steam-houses of the anterior. The people of Shu'gohl had adapted well to their curious environment.

At the centre of the courtyard sat a statue. The crowd broke and flowed about it, like water around a rock. The statue was immense, and symbolic rather than realistic, carved from the hardened ichor of the worm. Vague shapes, standing in formation, spears and blades thrust out towards some approaching enemy. Other shapes lay as if wounded, or dead. Wreaths of hair and gold were set against the statue's base, alongside bunches of strange, pale blossoms and piles of rolled parchments or folded papers. 'What is all that?' Volker asked, as they neared it.

'Prayers for the honoured dead,' Nyoka said.

Volker looked at her. 'Who were they?'

'They are who I am – the Vurmite Order. The Order of the Worm,' Nyoka said, looking up at the statue. There was something like awe in her voice as she spoke. 'When the foe burst upon us, we Vurmites defended the holy segments, for the grace and the light of Sahg'mahr, as was our oath and duty. Under a guard of forty, we sent off the most valuable tomes in their possession. The rest fought here, and gave their lives on the steps of the Libraria Vurmis in the name of our Lord Sahg'mahr.' She laid a hand against the base of the statue, where what appeared to be names had been chiselled. 'Their names – as well as the names of those who've fallen since – are inscribed here, so that all who pass by might see them.' She took a breath, and seemed to steady herself. She looked at Roggen. 'Your beast will not be allowed in the library. It must remain out here.'

Roggen frowned and stroked Harrow's beak. 'Will she be safe out here?'

Nyoka smiled gently and made the sign of the hammer. 'As if Sahg'mahr himself were watching over her.' As Roggen tied

Harrow's reins to the statue, Nyoka led Volker and the others up the stairs, and out of the press of people. Volker checked his satchel, making sure everything was in place. When he looked up, he found that the freeguild guards had snapped to attention and were blocking their way.

Lugash stepped towards them with a curse. 'I knew it. An ambush.'

Nyoka glanced at him, startled. 'Not of my doing, I assure you.'

'Then you'd best tell these fools to move, woman. Or I'll help them along.' He leered at the guards. 'And I promise you, they won't enjoy the experience.'

'Still yourself, fool,' Zana hissed. 'We're not here to murder freeguilders.'

'Then why are you here?' The voice was sharp, and harsh. A man, older and clad in similar fashion to Nyoka, stood at the top of the steps, his hands resting on the haft of a war-hammer. Old scars marred his grizzled features, and his scalp had been shorn smooth. A broad, bristling beard spilled down his barrel chest. He squinted at them through a gold-rimmed monocle. 'Well?' he continued. He hefted his hammer and pointed at them. 'Speak now, or answer to a higher power. It matters not to me.'

He waited for a beat, and then, with a shrug, said, 'So be it. Take them into custody.'

At his command, the guards levelled their spears and began to advance.

❋ NINE ❋

LIBRARIA VURMIS

Adhema slunk through the curved canyons of shelves that filled the Libraria Vurmis. Her nose wrinkled at the smells of dust and age. Even as a mortal, she had never liked libraries. If knowledge could not be held in the head, what good was it? Especially secret knowledge. But Neferata insisted that her handmaidens learn to read, and do so widely and often. The great libraries of Nulahmia had been things of beauty, before their destruction; ancient, lamp-lit vaults, filled floor to ceiling with the wisdom of untold ages.

While this library was not so big as those, it was no less impressive. The central chamber accounted for most of the building's space. The vast room was occupied by hundreds of curved, freestanding shelves, packed so close together that there was barely enough room to move between many of them. There were four levels, each one slightly smaller than the previous, rising towards the inner curve of the dome, connected by many spiral staircases. And every level was crammed with shelves.

She suspected that on some of those shelves were volumes that Neferata's agents were even now scouring the realms for. They sought particular volumes for their mistress' pleasure, including books of verse written by the great poets of the Golden Age, and the alchemical texts of Chamonite philosophers. Her agents were even in Shu'gohl, haunting the book markets of the dorsal districts.

The servants of Nagash – and by extension, Neferata – were everywhere. They had flooded from Shyish not long after the opening of the realmgates leading to Azyr. Thousands – millions – of souls, carrying the word of Nagash to the farthest reaches of the mortal realms. Those in Shu'gohl were mostly mortal. Simple death-worshippers seeking the peace of the grave. But they had their uses.

She licked her lips. She could still taste the blood of the one who'd met her, and guided her to the libraria. He had offered it up ecstatically, and she had granted him that which he desired – oblivion, and oneness with the Undying King. His fellows would dispose of the body after the traditions of Shu'gohl. It would be tossed off the side of the worm, to feed the beasts that travelled in its wake.

Of course, now that she was here, she'd found that she'd been anticipated. Or rather, Neferata had. She grinned, wondering if she should alert her mistress to that fact. She'd seen the first ravens as she'd slunk in through the open windows that lined the curve of the roof, while some sort of argument erupted in the courtyard. Too many, and too quiet, to be natural. They had the whiff of the unnatural about them – a staleness that was soul-deep. Like something drained of all vitality, but still alive. Their feathers were too clean, their eyes too shiny.

Chaos, then. Only the servants of Chaos could so perfectly mimic the form of the thing and miss all the subtleties of its existence. The gods of Chaos were ruinous idiots, and their followers were little better than mad dogs.

They'd been hunting something, those birds. So she'd hunted them in turn, slinking from shadow to shadow, quiet as an evening mist. Even in full armour, Adhema could be quiet. A trick of the blood. The Dragon had taught her to fight, but Neferata had gifted her with silence. She froze as an unwary scholar nearly bumped into her. The man was small, and his dark skin tattooed in the fashion of the Ghurean Sea-Kingdoms. He could not see her, for she did not wish to be seen, but he paused nonetheless. Some animal instinct compelled him to look around, eyes narrowed.

Her hand clamped tight about the hilt of her blade, and her thirst, so recently sated, rose up again as his heartbeat thundered in her ears. She loomed over him, teeth bared, for just a moment. Then she was past him and striding away. The thirst raged within her, demanding satisfaction, even as she forced it back into its cage. It was a beast that could never be tamed, not fully. The soulblight grew worse with every year, hollowing her out and making her over into a thirsty ghost, haunting her own corpse.

A fair trade, that. An eternity of thirst, for an eternity of revenge on those who'd humbled her people. An eternity to draw spite's full measure from those who thought themselves blessed of the gods. An eternity of service, in return for an eternity of glory.

And what glories they were. Skulking and hunting for ancient weapons, ones she wouldn't even be allowed to wield, most likely. Neferata didn't trust her that far. Ah well. 'Thy will be done,' she murmured, a slight smile curving her lips.

She stopped, watching as the birds grew agitated. They flew swift and silent, gliding through the shelves on black wings. She followed, moving quickly.

They'd found what they were looking for, and that meant she had as well.

'This place is a holy place, and one not meant for common rabble,' the old priest growled, as he swept his warhammer out in a gesture of righteous anger, indicating Volker and the others on the steps. The freeguild warriors formed up around him on the steps, the points of their spears glinting in the reflected light. They had a hard look to them, as befitting experienced soldiers. The campaign markers on their armour spoke to their status as veterans of some of the worst fighting this realm had seen – Lion Crag, Slothstone, a dozen others. All of them bore the sign of the hammer prominently on their gear, too, or in some cases tattooed on their flesh.

Such open devotion was not strictly frowned upon in the freeguilds, though it differed from company to company. Sigmar was their lord and master, but it was the opinion of many freeguild captains that the God-King likely preferred his warriors to keep their minds on the battlefield, rather than worrying about questions of the soul.

'If you will not speak freely, perhaps it is best that you be put to the question,' the priest continued, in a voice as hard and as cold as the wind. He raised his free hand, and Volker heard a clatter. Zana cursed.

'More of them,' she muttered. Volker glanced back, and saw a knot of uniforms moving through the crowd towards them. So far, no one was paying much attention to the confrontation, but that would change if there was swordplay. Volker frowned. What was going on here? It was as if these men had been waiting for them.

'Lay down your arms, or brace your souls for judgement,' the priest said. He lifted his hammer, preparing to order the soldiers to attack.

Nyoka stepped forwards quickly, arms spread. 'Wait – Lector Calva. They are here as guests of the Libraria Vurmis. I was asked to–'

'Yes, and by whom, I wonder.' Calva's metal-shod feet rang as they descended the steps. 'Certainly not by me. Which is odd, as this place is my responsibility.'

Nyoka stiffened. 'It is the Vurmite Order's responsibility, you mean.'

'Yes, but I am responsible for the Order. Ergo, the Order's responsibilities are mine. Or do you disagree, acolyte?' Calva's stern gaze swept over the group as Nyoka bowed her head. Not in shame, but anger. Volker could see the muscles in her jaw tense. Calva's lip curled slightly as he took in Lugash, who returned his sneer with interest. 'What an odd grouping, this.' Calva stopped as he came to Volker. His eyes widened slightly. 'You are Azyrite.'

'I am.'

'From Azyrheim?'

'Third district,' Volker said. He bowed. 'Gunmaster Owain Volker, of the Second Excelsis Expeditionary Force.'

Calva frowned. 'Ironweld, are you?'

'I have that honour.'

'I would debate the use of that word.' There was an undercurrent of disgust there. Volker winced. Not every Azyrite looked with favour upon the duardin. Just as many saw in the opening of the realmgates an opportunity to purify Azyr of what they considered to be impure elements. Calva studied him. 'Sigmar, in his wisdom, sees fit to give your sort much leniency. But we are not in Azyrheim, and I am not Sigmar. Merely a humble servant of the Order of Azyr.' He shook his head. 'It has fallen to me to see that the Devoted of this city follow where the storm-winds blow, and not fall to the many heresies that plague these lower realms.' He took another step towards Volker, resting his hammer in the crook of his arm. 'What do you seek here, gunmaster? Why did this worm-girl scurry off to collect you, upon your arrival? Come to that, why come in such a secretive fashion?'

Volker wasn't sure how to answer. How did this man know so much? He glanced at Nyoka, whose face was flushed with anger. He recognised that anger, for he'd known it before, and felt a twinge of sympathy. He cleared his throat. Before he could speak, Lugash did so for him. 'And what business is it of yours, manling?' the duardin growled.

'I thought I had explained that – you must be as dim as you look, fyreslayer.' Calva smiled thinly. 'I was sent by the Grand Theogonist herself to see to the reorganisation of the Order of the Worm. For too long have they flouted proper celestial doctrine, in favour of benign heresy. If the Church of Sigmar is to retake its place as the guiding faith of man, all must follow its tenets, as laid down in the Age of Myth. Though I do not expect you to understand that, given that your folk worship a broken deity.'

Volker tensed, expecting an explosion of anger from the duardin. Instead, Lugash laughed softly. 'Yes, we do,' he said. 'But that is neither here nor there. We have business in this hall of words, and you will not keep us from it.' He drew his war-iron and scraped it against his axe. The runes stamped in his flesh began to glow, and Lugash's grin widened. 'Though you may try, if you like.'

'You willingly consort with this… creature, acolyte?' Calva spat, glaring at Nyoka. 'Perhaps you should have been purged from the Order, along with the others. It is becoming clear to me that your kind lack the spine to–'

'To what?' Nyoka said, meeting his glare. 'You have no cause to prevent them from going in. The Libraria Vurmis is open to all who seek knowledge, lector. That is one of the central tenets of our oath. We died to keep this knowledge safe for all, not to lock it away for a privileged few.'

'They died in Sigmar's name,' Calva said, stiffly.

'And now you dishonour their sacrifice,' Nyoka countered, not softly. Her words rang out over the courtyard. People had stopped, noticing the confrontation for the first time. Now they began to huddle, and a murmur of discontent rose. Calva grimaced. Whatever his faults, the old priest was observant enough to recognise what was happening.

It was becoming clear to Volker that the tension he'd noticed earlier hadn't simply been his imagination. They'd walked into the middle of something that had been building for some time. It didn't surprise him. The Grand Theogonist was well known for attempting to expand her influence beyond the Hallowhammer cathedrals of the devotional districts. She regularly harangued the Grand Conclave, attempting to bully them into allowing her witch-hunters greater freedom to act.

'You dare...?' Calva said. But more quietly. 'Perhaps you have more spine than I gave you credit for.' He glanced back at the libraria, considering. Then, with a disgruntled sigh, he stepped aside. 'I do not know what is going on. But if I discover that it is heretical in nature, I will see you burn in the fires of righteousness.' He gestured sharply, and the soldiers stepped aside, allowing them to pass. Volker felt Calva's eyes on them the entire way as they climbed the stairs and entered the library.

'Someone warned them we were coming,' Zana murmured as they entered.

Volker nodded. 'So it seems. Has this happened before?'

'Once or twice. Factions within factions, gunmaster.' She smiled crookedly. 'An alliance is not a friendship, and you know as well as I do that even Azyrheim has its share of skulduggery.'

She laughed. 'For all that he is a god, Grungni has never been very good at keeping his intentions secret. And there are many in his employ who serve two masters.'

'You don't seem concerned.'

She shrugged. 'Should I be? I know who I serve.' She eyed him. 'What about you?'

'In this? I have no doubts.'

'Good.'

'Even so, if others are on the same trail...'

'More than likely what we seek is resting in some dusty tomb somewhere, lost and forgotten by everyone. That's usually the way of it, in my experience. Tomb-robbery is something of a sport in my homeland.'

'I'm not here to rob tombs,' Volker said. 'I just want to rescue my friend.'

Zana nodded amiably. 'So you are. And I wish you luck with that. Myself, I'm here to earn a fee.' She rubbed her fingers together. Volker couldn't help but chuckle, despite the worry gnawing at him.

They passed a number of robed acolytes in the entry hall, mostly worm-folk, with pallid skin and thin faces. But there were also several Azyrites, all bearing the star and hammer sigil of the Order of Azyr prominently somewhere on their person. All of them were engaged in quiet consultation or conversation, and barely noticed the odd group.

At the end of the entry hall, a set of wide double doors marked the entrance to the central chamber. A pair of heavily armoured acolytes, armed with double-handed warhammers, guarded the doors. They allowed the group to enter without comment, though one smiled genially at Nyoka and murmured, 'Well done, sister.'

Volker glanced at the rounded walls as they passed through

the doors and saw that they were decorated with carefully crafted bas-reliefs, depicting scenes he thought were from the history of the Vurmite Order. When he asked Nyoka, she nodded. 'What is history, but a worm crawling through the soil of time?' she said, with an air of recitation. 'That is why this place was chosen. From here, we could see the past–' she gestured in the direction of the worm's tail, '–and the future, all at once.' She motioned towards the worm's head.

Volker whistled softly, impressed. 'It reminds me of the celestial galleries, in Azyrheim. Books and scrolls gathered in the final days, before the Great Exodus. Millions of them, more than anyone could read in a lifetime.' He looked at her. 'Will you be punished for aiding us?'

'No,' she said. 'Calva is lector, true, but he is also an outsider. We allowed him here, as we allowed the freeguild, and they have only the authority the Setaen Council allow.' She sighed. 'We thought – my people thought – that it would be wise to show hospitality to those who risked so much in order to free us from our enemies. But gratitude has its limits.' She shrugged. 'We will abide, as we always do. The storm blows and we endure it. When he is gone, those he has expelled will return and take up their duties once more.'

'Here's hoping there's something for them to come back to,' Lugash said. 'A fool like that tears down more than he builds.' The duardin had been silent since the confrontation.

'I am sorry,' Nyoka said, looking down at him.

'Why? He's the one who insulted me,' Lugash said.

'I am sorry, nonetheless,' Nyoka said again. 'The Builder... has long been a friend to our Order. But there are some among the Devoted who see other gods as distractions at best and thieves at worst.' She smiled, slightly. 'They think Grungni wishes to steal us away.'

Volker snorted. 'That's ridiculous.'

'Not so,' Roggen said. 'The Lady of Leaves seeks worshippers from all races and peoples. So too does the King of Bones. Perhaps the Thunderer's servants are right to be afraid. There are many who remember the stories of the black days after the Gates of Azyr closed shut, and the God-King abandoned his people...'

Nyoka frowned. 'He did not abandon us. Not willingly.'

'And yet it happened,' the big knight said. He shrugged. 'It is no bark off me, for my folk have always held faith with the Lady of Leaves and her children. It is she to whom we pledged our swords in the days before Chaos came.' He looked around. 'I have never seen so many books. Are there words in all of them?'

Nyoka blinked. 'Yes.' She shook her head. 'There were more, once. Before the skaven took the city. They destroyed many priceless manuscripts – knowledge that can never be reproduced.' She reached up, and stroked the bindings of several books. 'We have done what we could. The acolytes of our order scour the realm for lost wisdom, to bring here to safety. Where all might have the chance to learn.'

Volker looked around. Though there was little room for them, there were a few heavy, oaken tables piled high with tomes. Scribes occupied them, hard at work, copying out the information within, for delivery to wealthy or influential patrons. Here and there, men and women with the look of mages or philosophers sat in quiet discussion of some grimoire or other. 'You mentioned a book,' he said.

'The one Oken found, yes.' Nyoka smiled slightly at his look. 'I heard you mention his name. I knew him, though not well. He was quite scholarly for a duardin. He came here many times over the years. Searching for this book or that scroll.'

Volker opened his mouth. Closed it. She was right, now that he thought about it. Oken was more scholarly than the majority of duardin. Had that been why he came here so often? Just to make use of the library? 'So he was,' he said, finally. 'You say this one he found?'

'Oken journeyed into the worm-sea with us, last bleeding season, seeking the ancient ruins there. He found nothing, save a bit of gold, marked with strange sigils. He claimed it was a book, and seemed very excited by it, though it was like no book I've ever seen.'

'Do you still have it?'

Nyoka gestured. 'Follow me. I had it brought out of the vaults, before I came to get you.' She frowned. 'Like as not, that is what alerted Calva.' She led them through the labyrinth of shelves, nodding occasionally to this person or that.

As they walked, Volker happened to glance up, and noticed a raven, hopping along the top of the shelves. He paused, wondering how it had got in. The bird eyed him as it hopped, as if trying to keep him in sight. He was about to dismiss it when he remembered the ravens in Excelsis. And then later, on Brondt's craft. He felt a sudden chill. What if Lugash had been right earlier, when he'd claimed the birds were spies?

Before he could say something, the first bird was joined by a few more. Ahead of him, Nyoka came to a halt. 'What-?' Volker looked over her shoulder and saw several heavy tables in a natural clearing among the shelves. On one was a peculiar standing rack, from which hung what appeared to be a series of golden beads, bound in leather. Examining it was a figure in black. Two acolytes of the Order lay on the floor, seemingly unconscious. Both had been armed, but their weapons lay nearby, out of reach.

'Who are you?' Nyoka demanded. 'What are you doing here?'

The intruder turned. She wore a black helmet, shaped like the skull of a bird, and black mail and silks beneath her cloak of black iron feathers. Her hand slapped the hilt of the curved blade she wore on her hip as she spun. She drew it with a flourish. 'Brothers – peck their bones,' she called out, in a high, clear voice.

The ravens perched on the shelves and archways leapt into the air as one. They swooped towards Volker and the others, croaking. As they drew close, the birds underwent a startling metamorphosis. Their forms expanded, stretching and twisting to become slim obsidian-clad warriors, bearing curved, talon-like blades. They attacked as one, in a flurry of loose feathers and harsh cries.

Lugash cackled. 'Guess I was right, eh, manling?'

✖ TEN ✖

NINETY-NINE FEATHERS

The black-clad warriors raced forwards, more swiftly than Volker had thought possible. He barely managed to draw one of his repeater pistols before the first of them was on him, blade flashing towards his head. He blocked the blow with the repeater pistol, but was forced back against a shelf. 'Look out,' he shouted.

'We've got eyes, manling,' Lugash snarled as he bounded towards the warriors. The doomseeker roared as he drove a shoulder into one's midsection, knocking him backwards. As the warrior staggered, Lugash whipped his war-iron out in a wide slash, opening his opponent's throat to the bone.

Volker drove the haft of his pistol into his foe's head, gaining enough room to fire. The warrior exploded into a whirlwind of feathers, and the shots passed harmlessly through it. Volker twisted aside as a sword erupted from the whirlwind to chop into the shelf.

To his left, Zana caught one of the black-robed warriors by

his cowl and drove him head-first into a bookshelf. The former freeguild captain turned and drew one of the long knives from her belt as another raven-man lunged at her. She whirled beneath his blow, her knife flashing up and across the gap between his helmet and his armour. The warrior staggered back with a strangled gurgle, clutching at his throat. Zana kicked his legs out from under him and stooped to finish the job.

Volker lost sight of her as his own opponent swept towards him, moving in a swirl of feathers. The raven-warrior spat an incantation, and the black feathers shot forwards like arrows. They tore through his coat and nicked his flesh. He threw himself aside as his attacker hurtled by. The raven-warrior's boots slammed into the side of a bookshelf and he propelled himself after Volker, who'd fallen to the floor. Volker rolled onto his back and levelled his artisan pistol. The warrior's eyes widened as the pistol's hammer snapped down with a flash. The ball punched through the black-clad killer's skull in a spray of gore.

Nearby, Roggen roared and upended a table, sheltering behind it as an arcane blast cascaded over its surface. The table began to warp and twist as the fossilised hairs from which it was constructed suddenly regained their plasticity. Tendrils of bristly hair writhed about the knight as he cursed and hacked at them. Volker scrambled to his feet and moved to help him, reloading as he went.

Lugash barrelled past them, his weapons wet with blood. The ur-gold hammered into his flesh glowed with a hot light, burning to ashes the feathers that jutted from his flesh. He leapt up onto another table, and vaulted towards the black-clad woman. She gestured, and the doomseeker went flying into a shelf. Such was the force of the impact that the ancient shelf toppled backwards, striking another. Luckily, this one was more sturdy, and it stayed upright. Lugash fell to the floor in a cascade of books and scrolls.

Volker heard Nyoka shout something and the writhing tendrils of the table abruptly went slack as a golden radiance suffused it. He glanced at the priestess, and she gave him a brief nod. He levelled his pistol. Her eyes widened and she dropped to the floor as he shot the raven-warrior rising up behind her. He helped her to her feet, as her attacker staggered back. 'Are you all right?'

'Yes. But I wish I had brought my – ah!' She stooped and snatched up a warhammer belonging to one of the fallen priests. She spun it easily, and struck the wounded raven-warrior as he tried to get to his feet. 'Sahg'mahr provides,' she shouted, cheerfully. Whirling the hammer, she confronted another. Volker turned and fired with his repeater pistol, clipping a shelf as his target vanished. Cursing, he began to reload.

He saw Roggen and Zana, back to back, trading sword blows with raven-warriors. Elsewhere, Lugash was scrambling to his feet, and Nyoka was fending off a darting attacker with brutal sweeps of her borrowed hammer. He avoided a crackling bolt of eldritch energy as it seared the air black. He twisted and fired, forcing his attacker to duck away. He couldn't tell how many of them there were. Four were dead, for sure. But there were easily twice that number left. He scanned the chamber, searching for their leader. If he could get to her–

'If you could get to her, what?' a quiet voice murmured in his ear.

Volker froze. The inner edge of a curved blade rested against his throat. 'Your thoughts are as loud as thunder, Azyrite. And your intentions are as bright as day. I could not help but hear them.' The blade twitched. 'Drop your weapons.'

Volker's repeater pistol clattered to the floor. The raven-woman laughed softly. 'All of them. No – wait.' Volker hesitated. 'Take that one in your belt, and shoot the duardin. He offends me.' Volker frowned. Something about her voice insinuated itself into him, echoing strangely. Despite his attempt to resist, his hand twitched towards his artisan-pistol. Sweat beaded on his skin as he tried to stop himself. But her voice pulsed through him, chaining his will. His head was full of the sound of flapping wings and the harsh crying of ravens.

Then, suddenly, it was gone. The pressure on his mind lifted and he tore his hand away from the pistol. The blade was removed from his throat and he quickly stepped away, turning as he did so and snatching up his repeater pistol.

A second figure stood behind the woman in black, sword-tip pressed to the back of her neck. 'Hello,' the newcomer said. 'My name is Adhema. What's yours?'

'Death,' the woman said, still staring at Volker.

'Mmm, no. No. That is a title which you may not claim, little sparrow. Though I encourage you to try, if only to see what will happen.'

'It is the only name that would mean anything to you,' the raven-woman said. 'It is the only name you will get.' She smiled thinly. 'Today, at least. Tomorrow, who is to say?' She threw back her head and screeched. Volker dropped his weapon and clapped his hands to his ears. As the shrill cry reverberated through the chamber, the remaining raven-warriors leapt upwards, shedding mass, their forms twisting back into those of birds. The flock rose upwards in a screeching storm of feathers. Their leader joined them a moment later and the whole flock spiralled up and away, through the open windows set around the curve of the dome.

'There is something you do not see every day,' Roggen said, staring upwards.

'If you're lucky,' Zana said. She pointed at the newcomer. 'Her sort, I've seen too often for my liking.' She laid the flat of her blade across her shoulder. 'You are a bloodsucker, aren't you?'

'And if I am?' The woman was tall and dressed in black armour of a curious design, its ridged plates covered in baroque adornment. Her helm was also tall, and topped by a black crest of hair. She planted her sword point-first in the floor and rested her hands on the crosspiece.

Volker spoke up before Zana could reply. 'Thank you,' he said.

The vampire eyed him and then nodded.

'You are quite welcome…?'

'Volker. Owain Volker.' He bowed slightly.

She did the same. 'Lady Adhema, late of Nulahmia and the court of the Queen of Mysteries.' She straightened with a smile. 'It was my pleasure, Master Volker. One must aid fellow travellers, mustn't one?'

'Fellow travellers?' Volker repeated.

'What else would you call us?' the vampire said, blithely. 'Given the path we walk, after all? And we are on the same path.'

'What do you think you know?' Zana demanded.

'I know many things. An infinite array of things, in fact. Eternity is a good teacher.' She pointed her sword at Volker. 'For instance, I know who you serve. The Crippled God. Grungni.'

'Are we supposed to be impressed by that?' Zana said.

'A little, yes,' Adhema said.

'I suppose you serve him as well,' Volker said, doubtfully.

Adhema laughed. It was not a pleasant sound. Almost like the scream of an excited cat.

'Not even remotely, mortal. I serve She Who Illuminates the Eternal Night.' Adhema shrugged. 'Others of my kind might play coy in that regard, but as my mistress has reminded me on so many occasions of late, I am but a blunt instrument of her will. So, I share my secret freely.'

'And at length,' Lugash said. 'Do all vampires talk about themselves so much?'

'Only when we're in need of stimulating conversation.' She looked at him. 'Feel free to go dig a tunnel, or whatever it is your folk do.'

'Enough,' Volker said. He looked down at the corpses. 'Who were they? What were they here for?' He nudged one of the bodies with his long rifle.

'Nothing good,' Nyoka said, holding up a feather. 'They are members of the Ninety-Nine Feathers. Skinchangers and sorcerers. One of the war-cabals of the Sideways City. They serve the King of All Ravens, or so the stories say.'

'The–' Volker began, confused.

'The Changer of Ways,' Zana said, softly. She looked around warily, still holding her sword. 'Are we sure they're gone?'

Nyoka nodded. 'If they weren't, we wouldn't be alive.' She dropped the feather she'd been holding and wiped her hand on her robes. 'They don't leave witnesses.'

'Then how do you know about them?' Lugash said, eyeing her.

'They came once before. Many years ago, when they were sworn to the service of another. He sent them here to steal something. We – my order – stopped them. We captured one, and he bargained for his life, trading knowledge for release.'

'You let him go?' Lugash growled incredulously.

'No,' Nyoka said softly. 'But we added his knowledge to our own, and gladly. Knowledge is power, master duardin. It is our bulwark against the darkness, even in these troubled times.' She traced the image of the hammer etched into her gauntlets. 'Even unto the end of the worm's journey.'

'However you learned of them, they serve a new master now.' Adhema rolled one of the bodies over with her foot. 'More gods than Grungni desire the Eight Lamentations, and those gods have many servants. Indeed, I followed one such to this realm. I had assumed he might come here. Instead, I find these.' She shrugged. 'Still, lucky for you, eh?'

'Luckier still to kill you now, leech.' Lugash raised his axe menacingly. 'The dead can't be trusted. Especially the kind that can talk.' He took a step towards the vampire, but before he'd got very far she jabbed the tip of her sword to his nose. Lugash froze. The vampire had moved faster than any of them had been able to follow.

'And here I was speaking so sweetly,' Adhema said, silky menace evident in every word. 'I can speak more harshly, if you like. Perhaps I'll cut you a third ear, to facilitate your listening.'

'Or you could forgive him, and join our company,' Volker said quickly, ignoring the astounded looks the others gave him. Adhema glanced at him. 'It's clear you're after the same thing we are. Why not pool our resources? We might get further working together than apart.'

Adhema grinned. 'And what about when the day is won?'

'Let us win it first, and then we can talk.'

Adhema cocked her head, as if listening to something. Then her grin matured into a smile. She lifted her blade from Lugash's nose and sheathed it with a flourish. 'Wise words, from one so young.' She pulled off her helmet and ran a hand through her tangled locks. She had a narrow face, aristocratic and hard. Red eyes met his own. 'I look forwards to fighting beside you… Owain.'

Nyoka cleared her throat. 'The Feathers may well serve a new master, but they appear to be searching for the same thing as last time.' She gestured to the book, as she checked over the unconscious men.

'They were after the same thing you are,' Adhema said, leaning against a shelf. 'The same thing I came for, as well.' She smiled at Nyoka's look of consternation. 'A secret is only as good as the people who keep it.' She gestured to the beads. 'Though what this one is, exactly, escapes me.'

'It is a bead book,' Lugash said softly. 'Ordinarily, they'd hang from an iron frame. This one must have been lost.' He ran his calloused fingers along the rune-marked beads, mouth moving silently.

'Shu'gohl gnaws the earth as it passes,' Nyoka said. 'Many ancient places now reside in his gullet. Perhaps the remains of one of your people's lodges are among them.'

'What does it say?' Volker asked.

'It's an old dialect – one of the Far Lodges, I think. Those who were cut off with the coming of Chaos.' He frowned. 'It's incomplete. There's something about a weapon, and a fortress...' He began to read. 'They were once part of the Lofnir lodge, but there was a disagreement of some sort, as there always is, in lodges of a certain size.' He smiled bitterly, as if reminded of a private joke. 'Falnekk, twelfth son of Hardrekk-Grimnir took one-sixteenth of the lodge's gold, as well as a *grumdael*, into the gaze of the sun, there to set his vault among the deep roots of the *thunwurtgaz*...'

Volker mouthed the words, wracking his brain for a translation into a more familiar dialect. The words were almost like those he was familiar with, but not quite. 'An artefact?'

Lugash nodded absently. He blinked. 'That can't be right. It says they went to the great forest of Gorch, bearing ur-gold and an artefact won in battle.'

Volker frowned. 'A forest? That seems unusual.' He'd heard of Gorch. It was the largest forest near the Coast of Tusks, stretching for untold leagues and thick, besides. It was said, by those who'd had the bad fortune to skirt its edges, that it was always night in Gorch, for no light passed through its ever-growing canopy.

'There must be a mistake.' Lugash made to examine the beads more closely. The duardin sounded almost insulted. 'Proper duardin don't live in trees.'

'Except for the ones who do,' Zana said. A sudden clatter interrupted any reply Lugash might have made. The sound brought them all around, weapons drawn. Zana laughed. 'Look who finally showed up.'

'What is this blasphemy?' Lector Calva roared. He stood amid the devastation, surrounded by freeguild soldiery and accompanied by several other warrior-priests. He raised his warhammer threateningly. 'What have you fools done?'

'Killed some Chaos filth. You're welcome.' Lugash dragged one of the corpses up by its hood of feathers and then dropped it. 'Where were you, by the way? Haranguing the faithful?'

Calva glared at the fyreslayer, his face purpling with anger. Nyoka stepped between them. 'Our brothers are injured. See to them.' Her voice had the ring of authority. Volker studied her as she faced the apoplectic lector. She might be an acolyte now, but had she always been one? Or had Calva's arrival brought more changes than just the obvious? Her acquaintance with Grungni was beginning to make more sense.

The other priests snapped into action, hurrying to the aid of the unconscious men. Calva's glare found new targets, but he made no attempt to stop them. His authority was apparently as tenuous as Volker had suspected. The lector looked around, frowning. 'The air smells of witchery.'

'They are – were – sorcerers,' Nyoka said, handing her hammer to one of the other priests. He took it gingerly, wincing at the blood and brain matter clinging to it. 'And they have paid the price for it.'

'Not them,' Calva said. His monocle gleamed as he fixed it on Adhema. 'Take that *thing* into custody.' The freeguild started forwards, weapons lowered. Volker unslung his long rifle and cocked it. The sound was loud, as he'd intended. The freeguilders stopped. They knew that sound. Calva did as well.

'Again,' he said, heavily. 'Again, you would put yourself between the righteous and the unrighteous. Why?'

Volker didn't reply. Nor did he aim the weapon at anyone in particular. He simply waited, with the patience of a gunmaster of the Ironweld. 'What are you doing, Azyrite?' Zana murmured, coming to stand behind him.

Volker had no answer for her. In truth, he didn't know why he was doing it. Gratitude, perhaps. Or pragmatism – the vampire knew things, that was obvious. He still wasn't sure why she'd bothered to intervene, but until he had reason to suspect otherwise, she might prove a strong ally. And even if not, he'd prefer to keep her where he could see her.

'Negotiating, I think,' Roggen said. He leaned on his sword, seemingly at ease. 'He does it very well.'

Calva ground his teeth, looking from one person to the next. His face went through several interesting contortions and hues, as he visibly fought to control his temper. Then, with a sigh, he said, 'This place has seen enough violence. Go – take your leech and go.'

He glanced at Nyoka, but said nothing. Merely glared. A hard glare, that, but wary now; not quite so arrogant. Nyoka, for her part, merely nodded serenely. She looked down at Lugash. 'You remember what you read?'

'Of course I do,' he growled. He tapped the side of his head. 'Duardin don't forget.'

'Good. Then we should get out of here, before your lector changes his mind.' Zana sheathed her sword with a clatter. She glanced at Adhema. 'You could say thank you.'

Adhema smiled. 'I could have handled them.'

Zana nodded. 'Maybe you could have, at that.' She grinned. 'Spared you the effort, though. So a little gratitude would be nice.' Adhema clicked her heels together and bowed mockingly. Zana looked at Volker. 'Sure you don't want to shoot her?'

He shook his head. 'Not today.' He started towards the doors. 'I fear we might need her, before we're done.'

Ahazian Kel rode through the shadows of great worms, hunched low over the neck of his steed. Arrows jutted from his back and shoulders, his arms, and one singularly annoying one from his throat. It made cursing difficult, and he dearly wished to curse.

The riders had come upon him suddenly. Vurm-tai nomads – worm-riders. Some steppe clans had taken to following the migration routes of the great worms and picking over what was left in their wake, or raiding the caravans that travelled to and from the worm-cities. He glanced up at the heaving bastion of segmented flesh that blocked the horizon from view and shook the earth beneath the hooves of his steed.

It was as dark as night here, in the lee of the great worm, Rhu'goss. Ancient wounds, carved by the efforts of thousands of slaves, marred its hide. Once those wounds had boasted of the glory of Khorne. Now, healed and scabbed over, they spoke of defeat, and challenge. What had once belonged to the gods had been taken and made weak once more, by the storm of Sigmar. Fresh rains had washed away sour ichor, and closed the unhealing wounds sliced into the great beast's flesh at the order of its conqueror.

Far above him he could just make out the watch towers and defensive emplacements clustered at irregular intervals along the beast's flank. Having been conquered once, the inhabitants of Rhu'goss were determined never to let it happen again. Mirror-lights shone down like stars, sweeping the grasslands for any sign of trouble. Great horns blew warning notes as one such beam passed over him and his pursuers. He paid them no mind.

Ahazian turned, tracking the outriders as they sought to intercept him. They were a dark folk, burnished by sun and rain, and clad in scavenged armour decorated with worm-scale, furs, and feathered back-banners rising above their heads. Their horses were spotted, long-limbed beasts, with tangled manes, protected by boiled leather armour. The nomads weren't archers by inclination. That they'd tagged him as many times as they had was due more to volume than skill. Like his own folk, the Vurm-tai preferred the cut and thrust of honest battle. Each rider carried a profusion of weapons for that purpose.

They would try to knock him from his steed or cripple the beast. Then they would surround him like wolves around a crag-elk, wearing him down until a killing blow could be delivered. Ahazian grinned, despite the pain. A fine people. An honourable folk. It was a shame he'd have to kill them. But needs must, and he was getting hungry besides. As was his steed. He reached down and slapped the black stallion's neck. 'Time to hunt, pretty one.'

The black horse squealed eagerly. They'd come to something of an understanding, in the time since they'd galloped through the Jaws and into this realm. Both of them were hunters, and eaters-of-men. Both were content to serve, so long as their needs were met.

The riders were closer now, veering towards him, arrows nocked and ready to fly. So close he could see feral grins stretching across weather-beaten faces, and old scars marking leathery skin. How long had they ruled the shadow-steppes, in the protective thunder of the worms? A century? More? They had never been conquered, these folk. Never bowed to any power, Ruinous or otherwise. They worshipped the worms and their own strength.

It would be a pleasure to teach them of their folly.

Ahazian tore the arrow from his throat and hauled his legs up onto the saddle. Perched there, one hand tangled in his steed's mane for balance, he hefted his goreaxe. His skullhammer whined in resentment, consigned to his belt for the moment. 'Patience, my friend, patience,' he murmured. 'Good things come to those who… *wait.*' As the word left his lips, he left the saddle, leaping towards the closest rider with a joyful yell.

He crashed into the startled nomad, knocking him from his saddle. They fell in a tangle and Ahazian buried his axe in the man's skull. His steed leapt upon the nomad's, sinking its teeth into the other horse's throat. Ahazian kicked his way free of his victim, retrieved his axe and drew his hammer.

It had been hours since his last bloodletting. It might as well have been a century. He slammed his weapons together and laughed. 'Come then, my friends – come and fight. But sing your death-songs now, to save time.'

A horse galloped past. He ducked the swing of an axe and smashed the animal's legs out from under it. The beast rolled, screaming. Its rider was on his feet quickly, hurt but moving. He flung himself at Ahazian, single-bladed axe raised over his head. He was a tall man, snake-thin, wearing rough leathers beneath a loose cuirass made from worm-scale and braided animal hide. The only bit of metal on him was his helmet – a battered conical war-hood with a curving visor over his eyes. He spat something in the worm-tongue as he chopped down at Ahazian. The deathbringer twitched aside and drove his skull-hammer into his opponent's spine, shattering it.

Horses circled him. More arrows came, but fewer now. Warriors slid from their saddles, whooping in eagerness. Some had brightly painted shields decorated with furs and feathers, while others carried long spears with thin, fang-like blades. Those with shields smacked them with the flat of their weapons, chanting eerily, as the rest converged. The worm continued on its way, unaware of the drama playing out in its shadow.

Ahazian turned, trying to keep all of his enemies in sight. Thirty, at least. Despite their numbers, he smiled. A good fight, this. Not his best, but… adequate. Nearby, his steed continued to feast on its screaming prey and he smiled in amusement. Such a beautiful beast. He hoped he would not have to kill it.

The noise of weapons hammering shields began to annoy him. What were they waiting for? An invitation? He raised his weapons and spread his arms, waiting. A warrior stepped forwards out of the crowd.

'Zig-mah-HAI!' the warrior bellowed as he slammed his axe against the surface of his shield. For the first time, Ahazian noticed the azure zigzags that marked their arms and armour. Crudely rendered lightning bolts. Sigmarites, then. No wonder they had pursued him so fiercely. The others took up the chant, stamping their feet and whistling.

His own people had worshipped Sigmar, before the coming of Khorne. The Skull-Splitter. The Hammer of Witches. They had cast captives and slaves into the fire by the hundreds, all in his name, but the storm-god had never so much as spoken to them. He preferred his people to be sheep, not wolves. And the Ekran, for all their faults, had most certainly been wolves.

Ahazian stretched, cracking his neck and rolling his shoulders, loosening them. 'Come on then. Let us give the Skull-Splitter a show.'

The warrior sprang towards him, axe raised. Ahazian met

him. His axe sheared through his opponent's, even as his hammer crushed the man's shield. The warrior staggered, a look of anger on his face. No fear there, only frustration. Ahazian kicked him in the chest, pulverising his ribs. He pursued the wounded man and casually pulped his knee. The warrior fell, and Ahazian took his head. He reached down and hooked the head with the tip of his axe, holding it up. He flung it at the feet of the closest nomad. 'Next.'

One by one they came to die in the shadow of the worm. He could not fault their determination, or their courage. Axes and blades scarred his war-plate and his flesh, but he never slowed or stopped. He had held his own against hundreds. Thirty was nothing; a drop of blood in the ocean he'd already spilled. And would yet spill, once the Spear of Shadows was his. The thought drove him on, faster and fiercer.

To hold such a weapon was to be one with war itself. To dance on the black rim of destruction, surrounded on all sides by a wine-dark sea. That was the dream of a Kel, the only dream worth seeing to fruition. An eternity of death and slaughter, spent among the funeral pyres of a thousand kingdoms. He laughed at the thought of it, and how close it was.

Khorne was no conqueror, no king. He was no lord, to be paid fealty to. Khorne was a tempest, a raw force, to be followed and filled with. Khorne was the war-wind, the blood-dimmed tide, sweeping over all things and subsuming them. Only in giving in to war could a warrior truly know victory. Only in fighting without purpose could one find the true beauty in battle. There was no purpose worth fighting for. Only the fight itself.

'And when war is all, what will you do, Ahazian Kel?'

Ahazian spun, skullhammer snapping out. It passed through the speaker's head, as if the skull in question were no more substantial than smoke. Volundr stared at him, red eyes gleaming within his monstrous helm, thick arms crossed over his chest. He'd wrought his sending from the steam rising from the cooling bodies of the dead. The warrior-smith glanced around. 'I had thought you smarter than this, hero of Ekran.'

Ahazian looked. The Vurm-tai were dead; thirty men, butchered like lambs. They had stood their ground and died to a warrior. He felt a flicker of remorse. Had he been wiser, he would have let one live, to pass his bravery down to further generations. It was the only way to ensure worthy opponents in the eternity to come.

'They attacked me,' he said, turning back to Volundr. 'Perhaps they were tired of life. It is a hard one, in these lands. Maybe a glorious death seemed preferable.'

'Or maybe you provoked them.'

Ahazian shrugged. 'And so? I emerge victorious.'

'Time is not our ally, boy.'

Ahazian frowned. 'Do not call me boy, warrior-smith. I left childhood behind long ago.'

'Then why don't you act like it?' Volundr pointed. 'The fragment sings – listen to it, and do not tarry! You are alone in a sea of enemies, and not even your vaunted strength will be enough to carry you through. Use your wits as well as your weapons, or you will fail.'

Ahazian bristled. 'I am a Kel of the Ekran. I do not fail.' He thrust his axe through his belt and reached up to grab the sliver of Gung on its rawhide thong. Volundr was right – it was singing, though he'd been deaf to it during the bloodletting.

Images passed through his mind, shadowy and undefined. Landmarks. A place – where? He blinked, trying to understand what he was seeing. He heard muffled sounds, smelled a verminous odour. Felt a wash of unnatural heat.

'You see it, don't you?'

Volundr's voice snapped him back to reality. 'You see where the spear is hidden,' the warrior-smith continued. His eyes blazed and his hands clenched. 'Find it – now. Or die in the attempt.'

'You have my oath,' Ahazian said.

'Aye, so I do. But oaths are fragile things. Better men than you have foresworn theirs. The former owner of that axe, for instance.' Volundr gestured to the axe in Ahazian's belt. 'Anhur made an oath to the Blood God, and to me, and reneged on it. He was prideful and foolish. Do not follow his example.'

Ahazian touched the axe instinctively. The axe was old and savage, imbued with a hunger that was almost equal to his own. Volundr had gifted it to him, as a sign of respect, he'd thought. Now, he wasn't so sure. He knew well the name of Anhur, the Scarlet Lord. Anhur of the Black Axe, who'd almost ripped open the belly of the realm, and who'd left a trail of destruction across the very face of Aqshy.

'And what happened to him?'

'Khorne took him.'

'To punish him, or reward him?'

Volundr was silent for long moments. His misty form thickened and thinned as the wind tugged at it. Finally he said, 'I do not know. But if I were you, I would be in no hurry to find out.'

'Consider me warned,' Ahazian said. Almost casually, he lashed out with his hammer and dissipated the sending. He laughed softly. The skullgrinder was an intimidating being. But a kel could not be intimidated. Not even by the gods.

Something croaked overhead. He looked up and saw several ravens circling the battlefield, their black eyes fixed on the dead. Or perhaps on him. He lifted his hammer in salute before turning to retrieve his now well-fed steed.

They had leagues to go yet, and as Volundr had reminded him, not much time to do it.

❧ ELEVEN ❧

GORCH

'Are you sure about this?' Volker asked. He stepped aside as a burly Kharadron, pulling a cart loaded with aethergear, bustled past him. The aerial docklands were busy. Trade winds were always blowing, and the Kharadron sought to follow them wherever they blew. Across the wide, flat platform, high above the streets of Shu'gohl, traders haggled with captains, seeking the best price for passage or delivery of their goods. Aether-vessels drifted to and fro above the great worm, crowding the heights.

Nyoka nodded. 'It will be better this way, I think. I have challenged Calva's authority once too often. Some time away will be good.' She wore her armour, but carried a travel satchel and a bedroll slung across her chest. In her hands was a heavy warhammer, its haft carved in the shape of a worm.

'For you, or for him?'

Nyoka smiled. 'Both.' She sighed. 'Once, the entire order might have accompanied you on this quest. Artefacts such as the one you – we – seek are too dangerous to be left unguarded.

Even Calva would agree with that.'

'Did you tell him about what we were after?'

While the freeguild warriors had escorted Volker and the others back to the aether-dock, Nyoka had conferred with the rest of her order, including Lector Calva. Her request to accompany Volker and the others had been agreed to with surprisingly little argument from anyone.

'No. And he did not enquire. I did not think it wise to volunteer the information, though I have no doubt he will find out soon enough.' She shook her head. 'He is not a bad man, but he has made his oaths, as we have made ours.'

'Let's hope we never have to see which is the stronger.' Volker turned as Lugash stumped towards them. 'Found him yet?'

'Just listen for the bellowing.' Lugash hiked a thumb over his shoulder. 'He's not happy, the cheating *wazzock*. Refuses to let us on board. Roggen sent me to get you.'

Volker sighed. He'd been afraid of this. Zana had insisted that Captain Brondt would be open to transporting them where they had to go. But given that they'd only just arrived, Volker had doubted that Brondt would be as amenable to the idea as Zana believed. Shouldering his rifle, he followed Lugash, Nyoka trailing after.

Adhema sat on a stack of crates, watching the confrontation. 'You're just in time,' she called out. 'I think they're going to shoot her.'

Volker shook his head. Zana stood at the foot of the *Zank*'s boarding ramp, staring up at its captain in obvious consternation. Brondt, for his part, seemed serene. 'I just got here. I haven't even got my cargo offloaded.' Brondt chomped on his cheroot as he spoke. Several of his crew stood below him, between Zana and the aethercraft. 'Haven't even taken on new supplies, for that matter.'

'Half a favour, Brondt,' Zana said.

'Flying off without my cargo is worth two, at least.' Brondt shook his head. 'I brought you here as an act of goodwill, Mathos. But that's as far as it goes. Find your own way off this ambulatory rock.'

Roggen strode towards Volker, Harrow plodding along behind him. 'He will not let us on the boat,' he said loudly. Brondt grimaced.

'It's not a boat, it's a ship,' he roared, jabbing his cheroot at the knight.

Zana snapped her fingers at him. 'Forget about the Ghyran-ite. Get back to telling me how you decided you weren't going to fulfil your oath.'

Brondt flushed. 'Woman, I am very close to using you as megalofin bait.'

'At least that way I'd get on the boat,' Zana shot back.

'It's not a boat!'

'I don't care what it is, I'm coming aboard,' Lugash rumbled. 'We need transportation, cloud-creeper, and you're the one who's going to take us where we want to go.' Lugash lifted his axe, and Brondt's crew tensed, glancing at one another nervously. They fingered their weapons, ready to draw them at their captain's command.

'And where might you be wanting to go, hot-blood?' Brondt sneered.

Lugash spat. 'Gorch,' he said.

Brondt stared at him. 'Gorch. The forest?'

'No. Gorch, the seaside village.' Lugash frowned. 'Of course the forest.'

Brondt's crew began to murmur amongst themselves. One of them gestured curiously, and Brondt snapped, 'Belay that, Tagak. I'll not have one of my crewmen indulging in that superstitious nonsense. And you, hot-blood, if you think I'm going to *Gorch* of all places...'

'Afraid, Brondt?' Zana shook her head. 'And here I thought I was bargaining with the man who once stabbed a harkraken in the brain from the inside of its gullet.'

'Gorch is a forest, woman. Nowhere to land. Nowhere safe, anyway.' Brondt blew a smoke ring towards her. 'I wouldn't risk it, even if you were paying me. Which you aren't.'

'But I can,' Nyoka said.

Everyone looked at her.

'You can what?' Brondt said, suspiciously.

'Fifty comets, per person,' Nyoka said. 'Seventy-five for the demigryph.'

Brondt goggled at her. 'What?' Even Volker was taken aback. That was a small fortune by Azyrite standards.

'Three hundred and seventy-five meteors. A fair price, I believe.' The priestess smiled benevolently. 'More than enough to cover passage to Gorch, captain.'

'Where would you get that kind of money?'

'My Order has deep coffers, captain, as you are likely aware. We are also always on the lookout for further investments. Like, say, a share in a prosperous cargo concern.' Nyoka's expression was serene. 'Do we have an accord?'

Brondt stared at her. He shook himself, took a breath and nodded. 'We'll leave as soon as we finish unloading. You – ah – you have the money on you?'

'Half,' Nyoka said. 'The other half will be provided upon our safe return.' She reached into her satchel and produced a small sack. It clinked as she dropped it into Brondt's hand. 'Is that acceptable?'

Brondt weighed the sack in his hand. 'Acceptable.' He glanced past her, at Adhema. 'Are you sure you want to bring that one?

Can't trust the dead, you know. Especially that kind.' He gestured to his mouth. 'They're biters.'

'As if I'd ever bite you,' Adhema said, from the foot of the ramp. She'd moved so swiftly that no one had noticed. Brondt twitched, his hand falling to his sword. His crew drew their weapons amid a bevy of curses. Adhema grinned. 'Can't squeeze blood from a stone, after all,' she continued.

'She's with us,' Volker said firmly. He ignored the looks from Zana and Lugash. Brondt shrugged.

'Fine. You know your business. I'll let you know when you can board.'

The next few hours passed slowly. Volker sat on the aether-docks and contented himself with stripping down and oiling his weapons. The others occupied themselves as they saw best. He left them to it. He wasn't in charge, and they weren't friends, really. Companions at best, allies of convenience at worst. But then, that wasn't anything new. Azyrites knew all about allies of convenience.

As he worked, Volker considered his situation, and calculated the angles. There were currents here that he could not perceive; he'd sensed that the moment he'd answered Grungni's summons. How long had the god been searching for the Eight Lamentations? And what would he do with them, once he'd found them?

To serve the god in this seemed the most natural thing in the world. The lessons of the Maker, as filtered through Oken, had been one of the central pillars of his life. But even so, he couldn't help but question why he'd been chosen. Why had any of them been chosen? Perhaps Oken would know.

'You're frowning an awful lot, Azyrite,' Zana said, startling

187

him. He nearly dropped the shot-cylinder he'd been cleaning.

'Not frowning. Concentrating.'

'Looks like frowning to me.' She sat down beside him on the cargo crates he'd made his seat. She watched the Kharadron work and whistled tunelessly. Volker glanced at her.

'Don't you have something you could be doing?'

'I am doing it.' She took one of his rags, spat on the side of her helmet and began to polish it. Up close, Volker could see the numerous dents and scratches. The helmet had seen heavy use. He supposed it wasn't surprising. Mercenaries weren't rare, by any means. Whole tribes of them could be had for a few coins, if you were of a mind. But lone sellswords were another matter. It took skill to survive alone.

As she worked, the coins attached to her gauntlet clinked. Volker indicated one. 'That's not a meteor, is it? Not ur-gold, either.'

'Torope-chaw,' Zana said, absently. At Volker's look of incomprehension, she sighed and held up her hand so he could see the coin more clearly. 'Torope gold. From the Black Marsh Barony, down south. They dig it out of the excrement of the giant turtles they live on.' She looked around. 'A lot like Shu'gohl, really. Fewer libraries, though. And the turtles aren't so big – about the size of a small castle.' She gestured. 'Tiny, comparatively.'

'Turtles?' Volker asked.

Zana nodded. 'They brew good beer there. And there's this fish-head stew...' She licked her lips. 'Delicious.'

'I thought you were from Chamon,' Volker said. 'What were you doing in a barony in Ghur?' For a moment he thought he'd asked one question too many. Zana stared at the coins on her vambrace, picking through them.

'A change of scenery,' she said, finally.

'Is that why you came to Excelsis? Was it at Grungni's behest, or…?'

She looked at him. 'No. I was heading there anyway. Business.' A grin flashed, almost too swiftly for him to see. 'And none of yours.'

'You're the one who sat down to talk.'

'Talk, not spill my guts. What about you, Azyrite? Why were you in Excelsis?'

Volker looked down at his uniform. Zana snorted. 'Not that reason. The real one.'

Volker sat back. 'Azyrheim – ever been there?'

'No.'

'You'd like it. Plenty of work for a sellsword.'

'That surprises me.' Zana held up her helmet, checking for any spots she'd missed. 'I'd heard it was one of the greatest cities in all the realms. The City of Alabaster Towers. Azyrheim the Eternal. Last and First.'

Volker snorted. 'I'm told the walls are alabaster, but I never saw them. The city's too big, you see. The walls stretch from sunup to sundown, moonrise to moonfall. You can go your entire life without seeing either edge. A lot of people do. They never leave their district.'

'Sounds boring.'

'Not that. Never that.' Volker sighed. 'It's a place of wonder and culture. Or at least, that's what we like to tell ourselves, in our little enclaves. Time stands still in places.' He saw her look and smiled. 'You laugh, but… it does. There are whole districts where people speak and dress strangely. Archaic, almost.' He hesitated. 'Familiar, yet not.'

Zana frowned. 'Did you ever visit those districts?'

'Once or twice. Their artisans were far beyond anything I'd ever seen then, or since.' He held up the cylinder of his repeater pistol. 'I learned what I could, though,' he added somewhat wistfully as he cleaned the chambers.

'Do you miss it?'

Volker paused. 'Sometimes. Some things. The sound of dragon wings splitting the morning air. The smell of the market district at midday.' He chuckled. 'The sound of a Makaisson-patented waste-extraction pump, hard at work beneath the better class of privy. I miss that one more and more every day.'

He began to reassemble his weapon. 'Other things, not so much.' He swallowed, remembering the midwinter processions of the Khainites. The dark nights, and the flickering aelfen shadows that crawled across the outer walls of his family's estate. He'd heard stories of what the celebrants got up to in the poorer districts. Of missing men and women, and screams in the night. He shook his head. 'Some things, not at all.' He looked at her. 'Do you miss Vindicarum?'

'No.'

'Not at all?'

Zana hesitated. Then, slowly, she began. 'I knew a lass there, a proper soothsayer. Folk came for leagues around, looking to make use of her gift. One by one, they'd tell her of their troubles and beg her to give them insight. Save us, soothsayer, they'd cry. And she'd weep, that girl. Because she was a girl.' She squinted up at the sky. 'She had no control over what she was seeing. But she'd tell them, and they'd go away happy, mostly. And the next day, there'd be more of them.' She looked away. 'More and more, every day, looking for some hope in a hopeless world.' She fell silent.

After a moment, Volker cleared his throat. 'What happened to her?'

'They killed her,' Zana said. 'Or someone did. She saw something not to their liking and paid the price. Some rich bugger, fresh from Azyrheim, who thought he could buy a better ending than the one he was destined for.'

'And what ending was that?'

Her grin was savage. 'My sword spilling his fat guts.' She hawked and spat. 'I challenged him to a duel. He accepted. A more merciful death than he deserved.' She looked at him, her dark eyes empty of anything save satisfaction. 'She saw her own, you know. Saw it and told me, and damn me if it didn't happen like clockwork.' She looked him dead in the eye. 'No, Azyrite. I don't miss Vindicarum.'

She fell quiet, and Volker didn't press the issue. They sat in silence for a time. Volker watched Brondt conduct an increasingly animated discussion with several other Kharadron captains. All bore the heraldry of the City of Shadows and all had a similar roguish look to them. One even had some form of darkly plumaged bird perched on his shoulder. Every so often, the bird would squawk out in crude mimicry of its master.

'I wonder what they're talking about,' he murmured.

'Nothing good, knowing Brondt,' Zana said. 'Speaking of which, I hope you know what you're doing, allowing her to come with us.' She jerked her chin at Adhema, who crouched nearby, atop a stack of crates.

'No one allows me to go anywhere, mercenary,' Adhema said, not looking at her. Given the noise of the aether-docks, the vampire's hearing was impressive. 'I go where I will, at my queen's command.'

'Then why not go by yourself?' Zana asked.

'Why should I, when the priestess has so kindly paid for my passage?' Adhema turned her head. She crouched in shadow, out of the sun. 'Besides, I was invited.'

'By him. Not by me.' Zana pushed herself to her feet. She

gestured with her helmet. 'And if you know what's good for you, you'll stay out of my way, leech.'

'And mine as well.'

Brondt stumped towards them. He glared at the vampire. 'You'll keep those dainty fangs of yours to yourself while you're aboard, or we'll see if you're the sort that can grow wings and fly.'

'I am well fed, I assure you.' Adhema sounded almost insulted.

'What was that about over there?' Zana asked. 'Gloating to the other captains about your good fortune?'

'Hardly. I was warning them about the Great King.' Brondt looked up, shading his eyes with one big hand. 'That beastie is still up there, somewhere. And we'll be far from the glowbeacons, where we're going.' He grinned. 'But if he shows his snout, we'll be ready for him.' He rubbed his hands gleefully. 'There's quite a bounty on him, you know. Every aetherport in Ghur has lost ships to that overgrown beast. And I aim to collect.'

'You offered them a cut of the bounty to shadow us, didn't you?' Zana asked. 'Clever, Brondt. Very clever.'

'I haven't got where I am by being stupid.' Brondt jabbed a finger into Volker's chest. 'Keep that long rifle of yours handy, Azyrite. If it comes to it, I want you to put a ball into one of those great black eyes of his.'

'I doubt it'd kill a leviathan like that,' Volker said.

'Don't need to kill him. Just sting him a bit,' Brondt said, as he stumped away.

Volker looked up at the sky. 'Do you think that thing is really still out there?'

'Oh yes,' Adhema said. 'Take it from me, poppet – once a predator has your scent, it will track you for as long as it takes.' She leapt down from her perch, causing Volker to stumble back. 'That was a lovely story, by the way. Perhaps you and I can share anecdotes sometime.' She flashed her fangs. 'I warn you though, I get bored very, very easily.'

Volker watched her as she walked away.

'Not too late to shoot her,' Zana said.

'I heard that,' Adhema called out, without turning.

'You were meant to,' Zana shouted.

Volker shook his head and looked towards the horizon, and beyond it, somewhere, the forest of Gorch. If Oken were there, he would find him.

One way or another.

The warrior slept.

And in his dreams, Gung spoke.

The spear... hungered. No, better to say that it... desired. It desired to be used. It longed for a whispered name, and the rush of air as it was cast towards its prey. It thirsted for blood, and the screams of its victim. All of these things, Gung desired.

It could not articulate these desires, for it was a weapon, and the soul of a weapon is no more complex than that of an insect. A thing of simple wants and brute incomprehension. It was enough that it desired, and in its desire, sang. Like its soul, its song was simple. A quavering paean to murder.

The oldest song, that. A song sung at the beginning of time, and at the end. A beautiful song, to the one whose head now echoed with its notes. It wrapped itself around him, like the coils of some enormous serpent. Enfolding him. Piercing him. Filling him. And beneath the song, crawling in its wake, came a voice. A harsh voice.

A weapon's voice.

...close...

...so close...

Ahazian Kel sat up, heart thudding. He clutched the fragment of the spear with one hand. A dull ache radiated through his fingers and palm. He opened stiff fingers and hissed in surprise. The black fragment nestled in the bloody meat of his palm like a maggot. As he watched, it squirmed, seeking to drive itself deeper into his hand.

Carefully, he pried it loose. 'Hungry little beast, aren't you?' he grunted. He squeezed the blood from his palm onto the fragment, rubbing it into the facets. It wasn't the first dream he'd had since claiming the fragment, but it had been the most vivid. He looked around. The campfire he'd built was burning low. His horse stood nearby, feeding on the body of one of the men he'd killed a few hours ago.

The Vurm-tai had followed his trail, harrying him. With vengeance on their mind, they had made for disappointingly easy prey. A dozen of their youngest and bravest had pitted their strength against his, chanting for his death.

They chanted no longer. Their cooling bodies lay scattered about in the thick grasses, and their steeds had scarpered, save the few he'd killed. He felt some regret at the rapidity of the confrontation. He had killed them too quickly, without savouring the deed. Once he might have toyed with them for hours, or days. But not now. Not with the song of the Spear of Shadows ringing in his head.

The spear was calling to him. Drawing him onwards, across the steppes. It wanted – needed – to be wielded and Ahazian was the one who would do so. The old wounds in his palms itched, not for the barbs of his weapons, but for something different. Something unique. His axe, buried in the skull of his last kill, hissed angrily. Its haft pulsed crimson, swollen with the blood of the slain savage. The barbs set into the haft flexed, their hooked tips gleaming thirstily. Like its master, the gore-axe was rarely satisfied.

'Settle down,' he murmured. 'I am not your first wielder, and you are not my first axe. One of us will outlive the other. This is how it is.'

His skullhammer grumbled agreement from where it lay near the fire. It was an old weapon and had belonged to many warriors in its time. And like all old things, it had its share of unshakeable certainties. He stroked its head, calming the ancient hammer. The axe resisted any attempts to placate it, however. It could hear Gung's murder-song, resonating through the dark places of his soul. And it didn't like it.

The axe too was old, in its way. Though it had been reshaped and forged anew by Volundr, it was still the same weapon it had been. Still the same black axe wielded by Anhur, the Scarlet Lord, in his conquest of Klaxus almost a century earlier. Ahazian had not been among the warriors of the Eight Tribes who had marched on the crater-kingdoms at Anhur's command, but he had met some who had, later. After Anhur had fallen, swept away by Sigmar's storm.

Those had been heady days, full of fear and glory. The armies of Khorne had grown fat and lazy on easy meat, and the servants of the Changer and the King of Poxes had retreated to their own demesnes, afraid to challenge the might of those who walked the Red Path. Ahazian had contented himself with seeking out and challenging the great champions of the Furnace Lands – warriors like Gadon the Ox, or the Lord-Razulhi of Salamandron. He had fought his way into the bloodstained pavilions of Havocwild, the Headsman of Thurn, and through the magmatic monastery of the Fireweed Sect.

He had collected the skulls of a hundred gore-handed heroes before he had heard the first whisper of the celestial storm or seen one of Sigmar's armoured slaves. And then, heroes had come seeking him. Warlords sought him out, with promises of wealth and glory, seeking to sway him to their banner. Having the services of a Kel of the Ekran was a symbol of high status among the fractious Bloodbound.

'And should it be otherwise?' he murmured. 'Are we not the deadliest killers in all creation?' He held up the fragment of the spear. 'Do we not sharpen our blades on worthy bone?' He rolled the fragment between his palms, enjoying the feel of it digging into his flesh. Once every eight years the surviving Kels met in the ruins of Ekran, to boast of their prowess, share tales of their victories, and match blades. A fair few of them were left, despite his best efforts. And theirs.

The time to return to Ekran was fast approaching. He interlaced his fingers, squeezing the fragment. It wriggled in his grip, like a leech, battening on the blood dripping from his palms. 'Drink your fill, little one. Drink, and show me the way.'

At first, he had thought to possess the spear for himself. Such a weapon would make him mighty indeed. Then, he had thought to take it for Volundr. The skullgrinder was odd, as masters went, but then he was one of the legendary forgemasters. Ahazian was prepared to overlook a certain amount of oddness.

But the longer the hunt went on, the more his mind turned down crooked paths. The more he began to think of his fellow Kels, in their solitude. The greatest warriors Aqshy had ever seen. It was said that even Khorgos Khul himself had admitted such, in a rare unguarded moment. The Eight Lamentations were the greatest weapons ever forged by mortal hands. Thus, was it not fitting that they be wielded by the greatest warriors?

And what might such warriors do, then?

He frowned. These were not proper thoughts for a kel. A true kel did not seek to conquer, or rule. Those were the tasks of lesser men. A kel cared only for battle. A kel sought only the pure heart of the flower of carnage, for in war was the truest peace. But… but. A nagging thought, like a wound that would not heal.

'What might we do then? And how best to do it?' He spoke softly, to himself, to the fragment, to his weapons. He did not know which of them seemed the most curious as to his answer. He opened his hands, and let the fragment swing from its cord. Its facets gleamed with blood – his blood. He flexed his hands, suddenly aching to kill something. Anything. He forced himself to his feet and retrieved his weapons.

His steed whickered softly and snuffled at his bloody hands. He shoved its head aside and climbed into the saddle. 'Come then, my friend. The night is cool and my blood is hot. Let us find something in need of killing.' The fragment shivered against his chest. He laughed, low and fierce.

'And then we will return to the hunt.'

∽⊂◯⊃ TWELVE ∽⊂◯⊃

GODS AND RATS

'How goes it, grandson?'

Jorik Grunndrak, cogsmith and Master of the Excelsis Arsenal, flinched. Not much. Not even visibly. More a twitch of the soul. Even the stoutest spirit could not help but do so, when addressed by a god. 'It goes well, Maker. The vermin are content to wait in their own filth, as is their nature. We are content to kill them, as is ours.'

The cogsmith stood at the highest point of the Iron Bulls Bastion, composing the calculus of battle. Arcs of fire competed with material estimations in his head as he considered the problem at hand. It was an old problem, but one that required a new solution every time. The skaven were devious. Cunning. But simple. They flowed away from strength, towards weakness. Like water in a tunnel, they had an unerring ability to find the thinnest point and attack it. The key was to turn that strength back on them.

'You don't seem to have killed many, grandson.'

'Well, they do eat their dead, Maker. Makes it difficult to assess casualties.'

Behind him, Grungni laughed softly. Even so, the sound of it pulsed through Jorik. He turned and looked up at the god. The Maker towered over him in a way no mortal being could. Grungni expanded outwards through all of Jorik's perceptions – he was not simply there, but everywhere, in every moment and every thought. Like smoke filling a flue.

'The lad?' Jorik asked, bending to tap out his pipe on his heel. Down below, General Synor had unleashed the *Old Lady*. The steam tank rumbled across the broken ground on four iron-bound wheels, belching a trail of smoke that stretched in its wake.

'Away, and about my business.'

Jorik nodded and began to scrape the bowl of his pipe. 'He is young yet, that one. In manling years, as well as ours.'

'We were all young, once.'

'True enough.' Jorik found the act of scraping the bowl comforting. It calmed him in moments like this. A simple ritual, easily done. A way to keep the hands busy. 'I have intimated that his absence is on my behalf. The others were most put out by his disappearance.'

'Were they now?'

'No,' Jorik said. 'I don't think they even noticed, the fools.' He looked down towards the tangled angles of the trench line, as the *Old Lady* gave a shout with its cannon and collapsed a rickety wooden structure, crushing the skaven within. Herzborg and the other gunmasters were down there somewhere, making their own calculations, closer to the battle. None of them had half the mind for it as young Volker. A good head for the algebra of chance, that one.

More cannons boomed below, a threnody of destruction.

Vast gouges were torn in the mutilated earth. Both god and duardin, aficionados of such brutal melodies, nodded in satisfaction. 'Good rate of fire on those helblasters,' Grungni said.

'Taught the gunners myself,' Jorik said, with some pride.

Grungni chuckled. 'You always did have an eye for destruction, grandson.'

'Why do you call me that?'

'What? Grandson?' Grungni frowned. 'Because you are, in a way. All of you, save those descended from my brothers or my sisters.' He leaned close, enveloping Jorik in the smells of the forge. Jorik's blade skittered, gouging the bowl of his pipe. 'You know this, cogsmith. What's wrong?'

Jorik grunted. 'There is talk.'

Grungni said nothing.

Jorik paused, gathering his thoughts. It was no easy thing, to question a god. Especially this god. 'Whispers, in the main. Heard at great distance, and unclearly. There are some in Azyrheim who mistake your absence for abandonment and your reticence for treachery. They say you have abandoned Sigmar's great purpose, and their mistrust spills over onto us.'

'And Sigmar?'

'Says nothing.'

Grungni nodded. 'Unsurprising. A god of few words, that one. Why explain, when he can exemplify? His fault has always been that he expects others to rise to meet him, rather than lowering himself to their level.'

'Is that what you do, then?' Jorik flicked a final bit of crusted ash from his pipe. 'Are we so much lower than you, Maker?'

Grungni smiled. 'Of course it's so, grandson. I lower myself, as an elder must, to the level of the child. How else will they understand, if we do not speak plainly and with no artifice? A lesson I learned from Grimnir, who was always one for plain speaking.' He sighed, and a stream of smoke escaped his lips, to join the cloud about his head. 'I wish...' He fell silent, and Jorik felt a sudden pang of sadness.

Gods were not supposed to die. And it was always hard when family passed. A double-seam of sorrow, then. He began to pack the bowl of his pipe with lichen and blackleaf. A god's sorrow was like a leak in the roof of the tunnel. It dripped on the just and unjust alike. But the Maker was not the only one who had lost someone. There was hardly a duardin living who had not known loss, and grief. Jorik had sung death-songs for siblings, cousins and friends.

And down below, even more were dying. Selling blood and bone to buy time. To buy back ground sold at a high price. Today, it was the ratkin. Tomorrow, it would be orruks, or some petty chieftain, with the Dark Gods whispering in his ear. They would keep coming, until the last wall fell and the last banner was cast down. It was their nature.

'Even as it is your nature to build,' Grungni murmured, his words piercing the shadows of Jorik's doubt. 'I know, for it is mine. To repair the cracks and set the foundations right, whatever the cost. As it is Sigmar's. That is why I swore my second oath to him, to prosecute his war as if it were my own.'

Jorik nodded. 'So it is written, so it must be. And if it must be, let it be done well. For that is the duardin way. Whatever else, whatever comes, let the thing be done, and well.' He looked up at the god. Alone, Grungni could end the battle below. With one swing of his hammer, he could smash the skaven and drive them from the field. But the gods of the duardin were not as the gods of men and they did not do for their children what their children could do for themselves. 'But is it worth it?'

Grungni did not look at him. Instead, he gazed at the

battlefield far below, the fires in his gaze quickening in time to those that raged across the ravaged ground. With every inhalation, Jorik smelled gunpowder and burning wood, as if the fires below were the same as the ones running through the god's veins.

'Worth can only be determined by time,' Grungni said, finally. 'In time, mayhap those who died here will be the heroes of generations unborn. Or they might be forgotten. Only time will tell.'

'And what of your work, Maker? Is it, too, at the mercy of time?'

'Mine most of all.' Grungni studied his scarred palms. His fingers curled into massive fists, each the size of a cannonball and twice as deadly. 'With these hands, I will fashion the tools by which we will uphold all that is, or I will craft a great folly and join my brother in the ignominy of oblivion.' He paused. Laughed. 'Those words were not meant for your ears.'

Jorik blinked. Grungni gestured. 'Not you, grandson. Them.' He pointed to a small group of ravens, perched nearby on the edge of the Bastion. He took a step towards them, and the birds croaked raucously, as if in warning. Grungni's smile was awful to behold. 'Where are the other ninety-five, then? Off and about some mischief, no doubt.' He made as if to reach for them. The ravens exploded skywards, startled.

Grungni followed them, without moving. His form expanded, like a cloud of smoke vented from a chimney. He reached up, growing ever larger, until he had caught the slowest of the birds in his hand. The creature shrieked, in an almost-human voice, as its feathers burst into flame and melted from its thrashing body. Grungni studied the pale, screaming thing he held with eyes as vast and as hot as distant suns, and chuckled. The sound was like thunder, momentarily obscuring the clamour of the battlefield.

'What a curious little thing you are. Like water, you flow from one shape to another, at a whim.' Grungni shrank, and the white thing shrank as well, still screaming. Jorik watched in silence. For all that Grungni was an ancestor, he was still a god, with a god's foibles and a god's temper. Come not between the Maker and his anvil was a common saying among the clans of the Dispossessed for a very good reason.

'And like water, the excess of you can be steamed away, until only what is required remains.' Grungni drew his hands, and what they held, close to his chest, as he resumed his former size. Jorik caught a glimpse of something small, like a baby bird, or a bit of bone, and quickly looked away. 'Cunning, in a crude way. Much artistry, the Architect, but precious little skill. So much so, I often wonder who named him.'

He placed the whimpering thing in the pocket of his forge-apron, and dusted his hands. 'The enemies of life march fast upon us, grandson. We share a quarry, and a desire. I hope the lad, Volker, is as capable as you claim.'

Jorik finished packing his pipe. 'If he were not, I would not have recommended him.' He cocked an eye at the god. 'And you would not have seen his face in the fire.'

Grungni laughed, and Jorik shivered. The sound was like a hammer, ringing down on hot metal. 'No. No, I wouldn't have, would I?' The god's gaze was as hot as dragon fire, as he turned back towards the battle. 'There's a daemon down there. Only a little one, but I can smell it from here. What does it want, I wonder?' He patted his apron pocket. 'I suppose we shall see.'

Jorik made to light his pipe. Grungni snapped his fingers, and a spark leapt into the bowl. Jorik puffed slowly, surprised. Grungni nodded.

'Yes. We shall see, soon enough.'

* * *

Kretch Warpfang, Grand High Clawmaster of Clan Rictus, looked out over the devastation and slumped back into the cushions of his palanquin with a sigh. Another dozen claw-bands cut to shreds. Another handful of clawleaders executed. The latest assault by his forces had been thrown back in dis-array and the trenches were still occupied by man-things.

A shambles, then. A man-thing word to describe an utter failure. A good word, Warpfang thought. Man-things made many good things. And skaven made them better. But not at this particular moment. They had got closer, this time. But not close enough. Never close enough.

Warpfang looked up at the Bastion, wrinkled his snout and spat. The air tasted of gunpowder and blood. The ancient war-lord gestured, and the palanquin shifted around, the slaves who carried it grunting and groaning from effort. Warpfang eyed his nervous subordinates stonily. 'Lucky-lucky, you are,' he growled. 'Lucky I have made contingency plans, yes-yes.'

His subordinates glanced at each other in confusion. Contin-gency plans? Warpfang licked his muzzle and chittered. They smelled nervous, as well they might. Skaven contingency plans often involved a purging of the ranks. He hunched forwards, clawed gauntlets resting heavily on the armrests of his seat. 'Your failure was foreseen,' he hissed. 'And planned-schemed for.' He swept a paw out in a dismissive gesture. 'We will pull-scurry back, yes-yes. Put a killing ground between us and the man-things. Fortify these ruins.'

His commanders nodded enthusiastically. This way of war-fare was more to their liking. Also, it would keep them busy, and away from each other's throats for the time being. Warp-fang had learned much, in his time. Most skaven armies were not defeated by the enemy, but rather the machinations of their own commanders. The constant in-fighting and back-biting led to a breakdown in discipline, which then spread like a rot to even the lowliest slave. Armies could unravel in a single night, if discipline was not maintained.

And if there was one thing Warpfang knew how to do, it was maintain discipline. A second gesture sent his officers scrambling to obey his orders. He twisted in his seat, taking a last glance at the Bastion. His lip curled over his teeth and his tail lashed.

It was said that the city was awash in prophecy. Such a thing could be useful to the Verminus clans, and Clan Rictus in particular. But for Warpfang it was more a matter of proving his own superiority. For almost a century, he had met every challenge, and, if not triumphed, at least survived. But here was the greatest challenge yet. And he was determined to meet it, teeth bared, and from a safe distance.

He snickered softly. Once, nothing could have kept him from leading the attack himself. But he was old now, and age brought wisdom. Let others lead the charge; he would reap the rewards they won. That was his right and privilege.

But for now, he needed to speak to Quell again. To see where his weapon was. He hissed a command and his slaves bore him away, back to the calm of his burrow. The slaves whimpered and moaned as they hurried the palanquin down the steep tunnel and into the hastily dug warrens that acted as Warpfang's field headquarters.

As the palanquin jolted along, Warpfang considered the situation. Quell had promised him a weapon of unimaginable power. Something fit to crack the walls of Excelsis and allow the skaven to plunder its portents and prophecies for themselves. Thus far, Warpfang had seen neither tail nor tip of the promised weapon. But he was confident Quell would hold to his end of the bargain. If he did not, Warpfang would throttle the life from him with his own paws.

This pleasant thought was interrupted by the smell of fear-musk and the nervous chittering of his guards. He blinked and focused on the entrance to his burrow. There were bodies there – several deathvermin, all in various states of mutilation. The rest of the elite warriors were huddled as far away from the entrance as they could get, weapons levelled at whatever lurked within. As they caught sight of the palanquin, one of them began to splutter an explanation, but Warpfang waved him to silence.

He sighed and barked a command. The slaves sank to their haunches, lowering the palanquin as gently as they could. Warpfang clambered down, grunting as his joints popped and creaked alarmingly. He was getting stiff in his dotage. Too much sitting, not enough killing. He rubbed the oily surface of the warpstone that covered his muzzle, and considered his options. Then, as ever, Warpfang seized fate by the dangling bits and bit down hard.

The aged skaven stumped into the burrow unaided and alone. The deathvermin chittered encouragingly, but made no move to follow. He hadn't expected them to. He moved slowly, not out of fear, but simply out of lack of urgency. 'They were expensive,' he said, without rancour. 'Many-many warptokens.'

'What is that to me?' the creature that waited for him growled. Skewerax, the Frenzy that Walked. The War-Shadow. The Verminlord Warbringer was a hulking nightmare, hairy, muscular limbs shrouded in serrated plates of scarred metal. Ruinous sigils were cut into the plates of the daemon's armour, and his sinuously curving horns, each larger than a clanrat, rose regally over his noble head. A shaggy mane, matted with the blood of thousands, spilled across his broad shoulders. Even one as jaded as Warpfang felt his heart quicken at the sight of so magnificent a murderer.

Skewerax glared at him from the deepest darkness of the burrow. The verminlord took up most of the space behind the throne, and over it. One pointed hoof was planted on the seat, a brawny arm braced across his knee. With the paw at the end of his other arm, he poked the cages full of rats, causing them to shriek and squeal in agitation. His talons were wet with blood, Warpfang noticed. The blood of his warriors. The daemon killed as easily as a mortal breathed.

Despite the blood, and the odour of homicidal mania seeping from the entity's pores, Warpfang remained calm. He had endured the creature's tantrums before, and always survived. The key was not to panic. Granted, this was easier said than done.

'Why have you chosen to bestow the honour of your presence upon me, most fierce and magnificent one?' he asked, eyes downcast. The daemon, like all his kind, went where he willed, and little could be done to gainsay him. Verminlords gnawed through reality as easily as a wolf-rat gnawed through bone, and they scurried through the realms-between-realms in their hundreds. That Skewerax was here now was likely more a sign that the creature was bored, than that he'd come for any real purpose.

'Coward,' Skewerax said flatly.

Warpfang grunted and peered at the creature. 'No. Cunning.' He tapped the side of his head. 'Cannot break through, must wait. So – wait.' He shrugged. 'Simple.'

'Are you calling me stupid, warlord?' Skewerax growled. Acidic slaver dripped from the rat-daemon's muzzle and scarred the surface of the throne. Warpfang watched the slaver fall and then looked up.

'No,' he said.

'Yes-yes, you are,' the daemon snarled. He leaned over the throne, planting his talons on the ground before it, and ducked his horned head. Red eyes blazed with fury. 'You think I am stupid-foolish, that I am blind-dumb. But I am seeing all things, warlord. I am scenting what you are hiding, yes-yes.' An accusatory talon jabbed forwards. Warpfang didn't move. To move would be to risk death, and Warpfang had lived too long to die now.

Occasionally, he wondered why he endured the daemon's attentions. There were ways of getting rid of such a beast, if warptokens were no object. Verminlords were beloved of the Horned Rat, true, but so was treachery. He had once contemplated binding the daemon into a blade or gemstone, so that he might put Skewerax's power to more efficient use. But he had never got around to it. Sometimes – now, for instance – he regretted that.

Skewerax crawled over the throne and hunched towards the old warlord. The daemon's long horns set the rat-cages to swinging. 'You think you are smarter than me, rot-jaw. Me – the greatest battle-fighter of the age!'

Warpfang looked away from those hell-bright eyes, unable to stand their gaze. 'No-no, great one. But this is a menial thing. Unimportant. Strategy, yes-yes?'

Skewerax made a disgruntled sound, low in his throat. 'Strategy?' The word sounded like a curse. Warpfang glanced up at the towering brute.

'Yes-yes, oh mighty one. Strategy. A necessary scuttling, most savage of all skaven.' Warpfang gestured. 'A sideways scuttling, yes?'

'Sideways,' Skewerax rumbled, uncertainly. Warpfang nodded encouragingly.

'Until the weapon arrives, yes-yes.' Quell's weapon. The weapon that would end this siege and see Warpfang master of the largest warren this side of the Blighted City.

'Yesss.' Skewerax's eyes narrowed. 'Quell must have the weapon. He said he would. He would not lie to me, no-no. Not Quell.'

It was Warpfang's turn to hesitate. There was something in the daemon's tone of voice he didn't like, as if they were talking about two different things. It wouldn't surprise him to find out that Skewerax was intent on treachery – such was its nature. And he knew Skewerax was in contact with Quell. The daemon was acting as the renegade's patron, in much the same way Warpfang himself was. Between them, they might even succeed in keeping Quell alive until winter. Warpfang had his doubts, though he kept them to himself. But would Quell betray one patron for the other? Maybe. It was not outside the realm of possibility. But would even Quell be that petulant? 'And then he will bring it here?' he asked, carefully. If the weapon was ready, he needed it sooner rather than later.

'Here? Yes-yes, he must bring it here, so that I might slay-swift the man-things!' Skewerax reared up, his horns gouging holes in the ceiling. The rats began to scream in their cages as an abominable heat pulsed from the verminlord's eyes. 'Where is Quell, stone-snout? Why is he not here-now?'

'Perhaps you should ask him, oh most dreadful of dooms,' Warpfang murmured. 'It might make him scurry-hurry faster, yes-yes.' The daemon had a short memory, and patience to match. The creature was useful on the battlefield, and a sign of the Horned Rat's favour, but a menace otherwise. Nonetheless, over the years of their acquaintance, Warpfang had learned the art of persuading the daemon to turn its less-than-keen insight elsewhere, leaving him to run the day-to-day operations of their various undertakings unhindered.

If Quell had some scheme of his own in mind, then throwing Skewerax at him might just derail it. The daemon was no subtle schemer. Skewerax was a berserker. Not stupid, no-no. But his thinking was a straight line, from desire to pounce. Perhaps Quell hoped that he would be easier to manipulate, without Warpfang's influence. Well, best to disabuse him of that notion, and swiftly.

'Why not speak to him, Great Ravager?' Warpfang indicated the rats in their cages. 'I'm sure Quell is eager to hear from you, yes-yes.'

Skewerax glared at the cages. 'Another device?' He tapped one, alarming its occupants. 'Why must he make so many?' There was an air of petulance about the daemon now. A simple creature, confronted with the impossibly complex.

'Would you like me to show you how to work it, oh most insightful of strategists?'

Skewerax growled. 'I am not stupid. I can work it.' He gestured. 'Leave me.'

Warpfang did, and not without some relief, though the daemon's disrespect gnawed at his vitals. It would take Skewerax some time to figure out how to work the far-squealer, which would, in turn, keep him occupied. And an occupied daemon was a daemon that wasn't interfering. Warpfang rubbed his paws together in satisfaction.

Soon, he would have his weapon. And then the city.

∞ THIRTEEN ∞

HUNTER OF THE SKIES

Adhema watched the crew of the aether-vessel scurry about their tasks, as the *Zank* glided far above the Amber Steppes. She leaned against the rail, watching the night pass by, and the shadow of the vessel trail across the grasslands far below. She peered down as a herd of wild horses galloped along, just ahead of whatever pursued them. Three days out from Shu'gohl and there was blood in the air, and death on the wind. Despite this, the heartbeats of the duardin around her were steady enough that she was almost lulled into hibernation. Only the smell kept her awake.

Due to the altitude, or perhaps because of the curious function of the aether-endrins, odour crystallised here. The sour rock stink of duardin hung frozen in the air, and she was unable to escape it. She resolved to ignore it as best she could. But it was hard.

It had been worse in the hold, with the others. The rank odour of the demigryph mingling with the stink of the duardin and the blood-song of the others, growing stronger day by day. Three days out, and she'd had enough. A confined space was too much like a tomb and she'd spent enough time inside one of those for one eternity. It wasn't much better out here, however. Duardin everywhere.

There were Kharadron traders in Shyish, though it was rare they descended past the highest mountain peaks, where their native kin dwelt. The duardin clans of Shyish rarely lived beneath the earth, instead preferring the heights. There were too many things creeping through the dark of the underworld for their liking, she suspected. Some risked it – the duardin of the deserts and wastelands of the south, for instance. But others made their nests in mountain peaks, away from the gaze of those who travelled below.

Wise, perhaps, given the incessant wars that still raged across the kingdoms of the living and the dead alike.

Now she speaks of wisdom. How droll, sister. And was it wise, then, in your considered opinion, to join your fate to those of these others?

'I was merely following your example, my lady,' Adhema whispered. The wind took her words, but she knew Neferata could hear them nonetheless. She was not startled by her queen's sudden interjection. She had been expecting it since leaving Shu'gohl. 'Strong allies make for high ramparts, as you have so often said.'

And are they strong, then?

'Strong enough. There are more hunters on the trail than we anticipated. Given that, I thought it best to eliminate competition and gain a few more swords at my back in one fell swoop.' She looked up, watching the clouds break like waves. 'I saw an opportunity and seized it. Am I to be chastised for that?'

Careful, Adhema. You dance perilously close to insubordination.

'I was often complimented for my dancing, in Szandor.'

So I recall.

Adhema sensed Neferata's amusement. 'They will serve well enough to ward my flanks, before the last charge. And when the day is won, and our enemy lies gasping out his life, I will claim that which I seek, as is only fair.'

And if they seek to stop you, as they must?

Adhema hesitated for a fraction of an instant. She felt no loyalty for the mortals. They certainly felt none for her. And yet, had not the Azyrite put himself between her and the warrior-priest? Perhaps that had only been repayment of a debt, but she did not think so. A strange folk, Azyrites. They held their honour sacred, in a way that was at once familiar and strange to her.

Honour had been all, to the aristocracy of Szandor. Even the highborn ladies would shuck robes and headdresses to match blades at dawn, in snowy fields. She smiled, thinking of the time she had lengthened her cousin's smile with a single, lucky slash. The girl had worn her gashed cheeks as a badge of honour – still did, as a matter of fact.

But the honour of the Azyrite was not as the honour of her kin – it was a plebeian thing, rough and simple. He trusted her because she had given him no reason not to do so. Trust was a precious jewel to her kind, rare and valuable. And not to be shared.

'I would leave their bodies beside that of our enemy,' Adhema said, at last.

Good. Do not lose sight of our goal, sister. You must acquire the spear – or see it destroyed. The Huntsman is too deadly to be allowed to fall into the hands of those who might use it against me – against us.

'I will do what must be done, my lady.' Adhema stretched,

enjoying the press of the wind against her body. She felt the dark tremor of the terrorgheist's sluggish spirit, some distance away. The great bat followed the aethercraft, though not closely. She would need the brute eventually, to make her exit – or to provide a distraction.

Perhaps it wouldn't be necessary.

Though it would be a pleasure to open the throat of the mercenary, and the doomseeker. They had insulted her, and only death would settle things there. She chuckled softly, imagining their bodies, pale and bloodless under a silvery moon.

Do not allow yourself to become distracted, sister.

Neferata's warning was like a spike driven into her brain, and she winced. The Queen of Mysteries had ways of ensuring the focus of her handmaidens, though she preferred gentler methods on the whole. 'I will not, my queen.' Adhema gripped the rail. 'I will succeed, and the spear will be yours.'

Good. Safe journey, sister. Neferata's velvet purr faded, leaving a familiar sense of emptiness. Adhema sighed and shook her head, trying to clear it of the echo of her mistress' voice.

'Something troubling you?'

Adhema blinked and turned. The Azyrite stood behind her, leaning on his rifle. She could taste his scent – gun oil and fresh water – on the air and feel the heat of his blood. She licked her lips and smiled.

Perhaps a small distraction wouldn't hurt.

Volker stiffened as the vampire turned. For a moment, her eyes had glowed red and he suddenly remembered the stories he'd heard as a boy. Of the thirsty dead, and the danger of meeting their gaze. He glanced away instinctively. She laughed.

'Scared, Azyrite?'

'No. But there's no shame in fear. Keeps a man alive.'

'Perhaps.' Adhema studied him. 'You serve the Crippled God,' she said, bluntly. 'Most unusual, for a human.'

'Is it?'

Adhema shrugged. 'I think so. And I have lived a very long time.'

Volker looked at her. 'How long?'

'Long enough. Why do you serve him?'

'Why do you serve your mistress?'

'I only have one mistress. You have two gods.' Adhema gestured to his medallion, which clinked against the rim of his breastplate. He hastily thrust it back beneath his armour.

'Grungni is an ally of Sigmar.'

'Is he? There is talk, you know. Whispers that imply otherwise. The dead murmur, and we hear.' She smiled thinly. 'They say the Crippled God has abandoned the old alliance, as others have done before him. That he too chafes beneath the rule of the God-King.'

Volker shook his head. 'That is none of my affair. I'm just a man, and I have enough to worry about. The gods can look after their own affairs.'

'If that were true, you would not be here, aboard this vessel, seeking one of the Eight Lamentations on behalf of your master.'

Volker was silent. In truth, he'd wondered that himself. Why had Grungni sent them, rather than hunting for the weapons himself? What could they do that a god could not? But as he wondered, the answer came to him. 'Action and reaction.'

Adhema frowned. 'What?'

'An action causes a reaction, yes?' He gestured. 'A blade enters flesh, a man dies. A loud noise starts an avalanche. Actions and reactions. If a god acts, other gods react. If Grungni seeks the weapons openly, so too will others. And the weight of their tread, the fury of their war, would crack the realms.'

'As if it has not already,' Adhema said.

Volker shrugged. 'True. Perhaps I'm wrong. But I suspect I'm not.'

'And so, you do his bidding.'

'It needs to be done.'

'How do you know he hasn't put the thought there, like a smith hammering a nail?' Adhema tapped her head. 'The gods speak, and mortals obey. You cannot help it. It is like a great wave bearing down on you, and all you can do is run ahead of it. Run where they want you to.'

'And is Nagash any different?'

'Nagash is… all,' Adhema said, finally. 'He contains multitudes. Even as Sigmar does. The gods are not men, and do not exist as men, confined to one life. I have seen Nagash unbound – a titan of death, striding across a field of corpses. Wherever his shadow fell, the dead rose and walked, hungry for the flesh of the living. And I have seen Nagash-Mor, calm and silent, weighing the hearts of dead souls against a feather. And there are other aspects, I'm told. The Forlorn Child, who leads those who die before their allotted time to gentle slumber, and the Black Priest, who gives succour to those whose deaths are too painful to be borne. All are one in Nagash and Nagash is all.'

'And which Nagash do you serve?' Volker asked.

'The one who can win the war for Shyish.' Adhema's fingers drummed against the pommel of her sword. 'The one who draws up the bodies of the enemy and hurls them back at their allies. The one who will not rest until the realm of death is scoured clean of false life. The Undying King, who leads the nine hundred and ninety-nine legions to war.' She grinned. 'He who walks in every man's shadow and wades in every man's blood.'

Volker felt a chill at her words. Nagash's name was a curse

among the armies of Azyr. Death itself was, if not a friend, then a familiar acquaintance. But the Master of Death was a terror beyond conception. A hungry shadow on a cave wall, stretching black fingers ever closer to those who huddled by the fire. Even the Ruinous Powers, horrifying as they were, were not so terrible as the entity known on the Amber Steppes as the Patient Hunter. And yet, what better ally against the nightmare forces that waited beyond the fire's light? Match terror against terror, and see which proved the stronger.

Volker acknowledged the pragmatism of the thing, even as his soul shrank from it. It was akin to loosing a volley into a melee – the risk to your own men was weighed against potential harm to the enemy. That risk was often the thin line between victory and defeat.

Adhema smiled. 'You understand.' It was not a question.

Volker nodded. 'Somewhat.' He paused. Then, 'Why did you help me?'

'Perhaps it pleased me to do so,' Adhema said. She leaned back against the rail. 'Perhaps I simply seized the moment for what it was – an opportunity.'

'That's oddly comforting.' Volker sighted down the length of his rifle. 'I'm not a fool, you know. I doubt there's a drop of mortal compassion in you. But you're honest, at least. That I can respect.'

Adhema chuckled. 'Blunt.'

'I've never been a very good liar.' He set his weapon down. 'Never seen a reason to learn. Lies are shoddy things, built on sand.'

'You sound like a duardin.'

Volker smiled. 'Don't let them hear you say that.' He looked at her. 'You have my thanks, regardless of your reasons. Our quest might have been over before it began if you hadn't intervened.'

'So I gathered.' Adhema knocked on the rail with her knuckles. 'You're not here for the weapons, though, I think. So why?'

'A friend.'

'Ah. Friends. I remember those. More trouble than they were worth, in my experience.' She shook her head. 'I have sisters instead.'

'Is that different?'

'Oh, vastly. Better and worse.' Adhema stared out into the dark. 'Sisters of blood, rather than flesh, but sisters all the same. We know each other better than we ought, my sisters and I.'

Volker joined her, watching the distant stars. 'Perhaps there's something to be said for that. My own family – well. We don't understand each other at all.'

'Small mercies.' Adhema straightened. 'Curious...'

'What?'

'The smell of your blood. There's a tang to it – a sharpness that puts one in mind of clean water and high peaks. Makes my teeth ache to contemplate it.'

Suddenly, Volker was very aware of her proximity. She smelled of something sickly-sweet, and this close, he could see the faint black veins running beneath her pale flesh. He was reminded that she was not human, and had not been so for many years, by her own admission. He took a slow breath, forcing himself to remain calm. 'Don't, then. I'd prefer my blood to stay where it is, frankly.'

'It's hard, though. If I lose control, I feed the beast within. Some days, I want nothing more than to shed my skin, and the last memory of what I was.' Her smile was ghastly. 'It would be easier that way. To be a beast, only concerned about the next meal. But I did not become what I am to forget. Nor to forgive.' She traced her fingers through the wispy trails of aether-gold that swirled just past the rail. 'Does that make me a monster?'

'Yes,' Volker said. 'But what sort of monster you are is up to you.' He lifted his rifle and braced the stock against his hip. 'With this rifle, I have taken more lives than I can count. Enemy lives, mostly. I reaped them, one at a time. I watched them first, though. Knew them, if only briefly. And then killed them.' He smiled, sadly. On bad nights, he saw some of their faces in his dreams – the freeguilder, caught by bloodreavers, begging for a merciful death before the savages began their feast; the old war-chief, leading his folk into a desperate charge against the metal monsters of the Ironweld, his only crime a refusal to bow to the highborn of Azyr; the proud queen, high on her palanquin, refusing to submit before the will of Sigmar's chosen, when they came demanding she cast down her people's idols.

He saw their faces, and screamed inside himself, until his mind shook itself calm. Or worse, he stayed awake, and wondered about the necessity of it all, and whether justice was a hard truth... or simply a fiction, invented by the gods to explain their whims. He looked at her. 'Is it better or worse to kill a foe who doesn't see it coming? A barbarian chieftain, carousing with his kin. A beastman, lapping at a pool. An orruk, dancing to the beat of tribal drums. They never heard the shot that killed them. They never saw the destruction that came after.'

'Where I come from, that'd be considered a mercy. My queen – and the one she serves – prefers it when the enemy fully understands the folly of their resistance. Death cannot be defeated, only postponed.' Adhema brushed a lock of hair out of her face. 'Even your thunder-god knows that.'

Volker touched his amulet. Before he could reply, he heard Nyoka say, 'Death is but one part of life, beneath the belly of heaven.'

He turned. The priestess inclined her head to him in greeting, and then studied Adhema. The vampire straightened. 'Come to check on us, priestess? Come to see that I have not beguiled him with my deathly charms?'

Nyoka chuckled. 'I do not think you are the sort to beguile a man, sister. You reek of predatory intent, and even the dullest wit cannot help but see it writ upon your face.'

Adhema frowned, but only for an instant. Then her smile returned. 'I'd be insulted, if I didn't know that you spoke the truth.'

'Lies serve no purpose in the world.' Nyoka had her hammer, though she held it only loosely. She swung it gently. A reminder, not a warning. 'There are some who say that vampires are lies made flesh. I do not think this, for I think that death loves lies no more than Sahg'mahr.'

'Death is the final truth,' Adhema said.

The two faced each other. Volker looked back and forth between them. He cleared his throat.

'Did you want something, Nyoka?'

Nyoka beamed at him. 'Zana asked me to tell you that Lugash has deciphered the rest of the bead book.' The fyreslayer had proven to have a remarkable memory, and they'd spent most of the trip attempting to align what he'd read, with what little was known of Gorch. Nyoka's contribution had been the most helpful, for she'd managed to liberate several maps, among other things, from her order. 'There is a fortress, at the forest's heart. A great tree, hollowed out to make a citadel.'

'That makes a certain sort of sense,' Volker said, dubiously.

Adhema gave a bark of laughter. 'Only a man like you would think so.'

Before he could reply, he heard a shrill whistle from the aft deck of the *Zank*. The crew began to shout to one another as some raced below. Volker made his way towards the rear of the vessel, wondering what the lookout had seen. A narrow plank extended from the aft deck, connected to the aether-endrins and the hull by steel guy-wires. At the end of the plank was a small cupola, in which a crewman could sit and watch the skies. At the moment, said crewman was hurriedly making his way back to the deck, using the guy-wires for support. He was pointing behind him and shouting as he came, but the wind whipped away his words.

Adhema hissed. Volker glanced at her, and then at the thick wake of clouds behind the *Zank*. An ocean of purples and blues, rolling in the black sky. And something else. Something was moving beneath the clouds at speed, and as he watched, something like the peak of a black mountain pierced the surface. It rose, accompanied by an omnipresent rumble, higher and higher, until it sliced through the clouds in its pursuit.

Volker stared at it for a moment, until he realised what it was. Not a mountain peak, but the top of an enormous dorsal fin. His heart sank.

Out in the dark, the Great King roared.

'I knew it!'

Brondt stalked across the deck, Zana and the others following him. The Kharadron lit a cheroot and grinned at the nearing shape. 'I knew it. I knew that bastard wasn't done with us.' He snatched up a speaking-tube hanging near the rail. 'All hands to stations. Man the belaying valves. The Great King has returned – and I intend to give him a welcome he'll never forget!'

The Great King roared, and the sky shook. Clouds parted and the stars shivered in the firmament. Or so it felt to Yuhdak, as he drew back on the reins of his sorcerous energy. Vast hooks of crackling magic dug tight into the immense megalofin's flesh, spilling gallons of ichor across the sky. The leviathan roared again, but turned at last, goaded by the pain. Even so, Yuhdak did not celebrate. A single moment of distraction would be enough to see him flung from the titanic creature's back.

He stood atop its skull, legs braced, held in place by his magic. His robes flapped in the wind, and the facets of his armour were frosted over. Only his sorcery kept the breath from freezing in his lungs at this altitude. He could see the soft glow of his quarry in the distance – the airship carrying the servants of the Crippled God. The Great King roared again, a vast exhalation of intent. The beast would have the scent of the aether-gold soon. And when it did, it would plunge forwards, eager to have its prey between its teeth. As Fate willed.

Ravens perched on his shoulders or high above on the rocky aether-barnacles that studded the beast's hide like small mountain ranges. They croaked out helpful suggestions as Yuhdak fought to keep the Great King aimed in the right direction. The endless hunger that swamped the beast's mind crashed against his mental defences, threatening to overwhelm him. 'Quiet please, friends,' Yuhdak hissed. 'This is difficult enough, without your well-intentioned contributions.'

The Kharadron airship crossed the horizon, heading south. Heading for the great spider-haunted forest of Gorch. He glanced at the leader of the flock. Unlike her followers, she was human, for the moment. She stood behind him, perfectly at ease despite the pull of the wind, and the instability of her perch. 'You are certain that is where they are heading?'

She stared at him, unblinking. He sighed. 'Yes, of course. Forgive me. I merely wished to be sure, before we disposed of them. It's getting harder to control our – ah! He's caught the scent.' The sorcerous chains flared to blinding radiance as the Great King suddenly surged forwards with a bone-rattling rumble. Yuhdak let the beast have its head. The chains and hooks dissipated and he stumbled back, shaking slightly.

She reached out to steady him, her black eyes studying him. 'You are ill.'

'Tired. Merely tired. It's like trying to control a storm.' He waved her back. 'Time to go, I think. The Great Fortress-Tree awaits.'

But even as he said it, the air burst wide with fire. The Great King bucked and roared as explosions peppered its hide. Yuhdak turned as much as he dared, a curse on his lips. He'd forgotten the first rule of dealing with the cloud-dwellers – never trust your first glance.

Bulbous shapes hummed out of the clouds, rising and falling like the jaws of a trap. Kharadron gunships, and at least a dozen. He'd seen them before, at a distance, during the blockade of Barak-Zon. The two-seater vessels were quick, and deadly in packs.

'They were ready for us.' The leader of the flock looked at him.

'Or for the Great King,' Yuhdak said. Angered, he loosed a pulse of sorcerous energy into the beast's brain. The megalofin shuddered as its blood burned with new strength. It lunged forwards, fins scraping the sky. 'They want a fight – fine. A fight they'll get.' He turned to the leader of the flock. 'Go. Remind the duardin what it means to confront the servants of Fate.'

She nodded and leapt into the air, her form twisting and shrinking. The Ninety-Nine Feathers took to the sky as one, and the whole flock swooped towards the approaching vessels. They would serve well enough as a distraction until he could destroy the Crippled God's emissaries. Then, perhaps, he would turn upon the gunships and let the Great King devour them as well.

Yuhdak crouched, drawing deeply from his reservoirs of strength. He would need every iota of power at his disposal to control the beast, and keep it from turning on the approaching vessels. Lashing cerulean and cerise chains, topped by cruel barbs, sprouted from the air about him and sank into the Great King's flesh. He had hoped to leave things up to fate. But sometimes a more direct approach was called for.

'Come then, my friend – let us hunt together.'

∞ FOURTEEN ∞

DUEL

'Ha-ha! Pepper that meat!' Brondt pounded on the rail as the night was lit by explosions. 'Worth every bloody coin, those lads. Look at them – the pride of the Grundcorps!' His crew seemed in similar good spirits. They cheered as the tiny shapes swooped about the megalofin and spat fire.

The massive beast rolled through the clouds, banking to escape the throng of vessels that had suddenly attacked it. Zana laughed. 'Gunhaulers. Look at them swarm that beast.' She grinned. 'You weren't just warning the other captains, you sold salvage rights to the bloody Grundstok Company, didn't you, Brondt?'

Brondt returned her grin. 'Let's see that oaf Brokrin think of that! The Great King is big enough that we'll all get a share – of bounty and glory both. The Grundcorps have been looking to put paid to his debts for some time – they just needed the proper bait.'

'Willing, you mean,' Volker said, grasping the captain's meaning. He felt a flush of anger, but quickly throttled it. There was

227

a certain brutal pragmatism to the Kharadron's plan, and he couldn't help but respect it.

Brondt peered at him. 'Aye. Two nuggets with one swing, as the saying goes.' He laughed and clapped Volker on the arm. 'Don't frown so, Azyrite. This is a glorious day – the day the skies were made safe for all honest – oh bugger.'

The explosion lit up the sky. One of the gunhaulers burst into weirdly coloured flames and plummeted from above with a shriek of abused metal. Brondt gripped the rail, all good cheer stripped from his face. 'Sorcery,' he growled. '*Kruk*!' He struck the rail with a fist. 'I knew it was too good to be true. I knew it.' He turned on Zana. 'What have you got me into, woman?'

'How is this my fault?' she protested.

'They're going to want hazard pay for this! Not to mention the bloody Thunderers taking up precious space in my lower holds.'

'Not if they all die,' Adhema said mildly. She peered into the dark. 'Which seems fairly likely, given that flock of ravens now attacking them.'

'Ravens?' Volker shoved past Brondt and flipped down his range-finder. He clicked through the lenses until he found the right one. The distant image leapt into stark focus. He saw several birds swarm a gunhauler, pecking and clawing at the pilot and gunner with an improbable ferocity. He cursed, and turned to the others. 'It's the same ones from the library. The shape-changers. I'm sure of it.'

'The what now?' Brondt looked from Volker to Zana. 'Forget to mention that, did you, woman? That's something I ought to know about, don't you think?'

'First rule of business, Brondt – always ask questions before signing the contract,' Zana said. She looked past him. 'Looks like they're running interference for the brute.' She frowned. 'But why?'

Volker lifted his rifle and braced it on the rail. Through his rangefinder, he could see the eerie glow of sorcery, bristling across the megalofin's massive skull. 'There's someone on his head.'

'What?' Brondt spluttered, turning to stare at the approaching leviathan. 'That's cheating!'

'That's life in the realms,' Zana said. 'He's getting closer, Brondt. Any other tricks up your sleeve? Maybe a flotilla or two?' She gripped her sword helplessly. Nyoka and the others looked equally nonplussed. Even Adhema seemed taken aback by the situation. But then, it likely wasn't every day that the vampire found herself on the wrong end of the food chain, Volker concluded.

Brondt glared at Zana, but vented his ire on the speaking-tube instead. 'I need more speed, Thalfi,' he roared. 'All ahead full, endrinmaster, and damn the stars.' A voice crackled in reply, and the soft glow of the aether-endrins began to brighten. 'All hands to the volley cannons and aethershot carbines. Brace for engagement.' The crew hurried to obey, shoving past Roggen and the others.

'I must see to Harrow – if she gets loose...' the knight said, as he hurried below decks.

'Leave that beast where it is. We might need you up here,' Zana shouted after him. 'Or at least wake up Lugash while you're down there!' When he didn't stop, she shook her head in disgust. 'I suppose we won't need him, at that. Not much any of us can do to that thing.' She glanced at Adhema. 'Not even you.'

'Keep talking, and you will see what I can do, mortal.'

'Quiet,' Nyoka said, her voice a whip-crack of authority. 'Discord is the sour in the meat. Thus spake Gu'ibn'sahl the Sage to the Conclave of the Third Segment.'

'Do you have any idea what she's talking about?' Zana asked Volker. He pointed at the Great King.

'She's saying we've got more important things to worry about than each other.'

The air shuddered as the Great King bulled through the clouds, drawing ever closer. Volker ignored the thrill of fear that congealed within him, and tried to focus on the tiny figure standing atop the creature. It was a man, he thought, but surrounded by a scintillating shroud of weirdly coloured flame. He shifted the rifle's position, ignoring the voices raised in argument behind him. He heard a soft murmuring and realised that Nyoka had begun to pray. The words gave him some comfort and he mouthed them along with her.

He'd faced sorcerers before, but always on the battlefield, and always at a distance. That was the best way to handle anyone who glowed strangely and shouted a lot. This one was controlling the Great King, if the ghostly chains and fiery lashes were anything to go by. Urging the megalofin towards them with pain and sorcery.

The Great King opened its jaws wide, obscuring the horizon. 'Vent the starboard belaying valves,' Brondt roared, clutching the speaking-tube as if to throttle it. The *Zank* lurched sideways, venting aether-gas from its starboard valves. Volker readjusted his aim to compensate, counting down. He had the range, barely. But he needed to be sure. A wounded sorcerer was a dangerous sorcerer.

The vast shape closed in, bringing with it the stink of death. Volker's vision was momentarily filled by teeth. Metal screeched, and the endrins' hum became erratic. The deck shuddered beneath his feet. He heard the rumble of the volley cannons, and the dark was lit up by bursts of fire. A gun-hauler swept past the *Zank*, guns blazing. Some of the smaller vessels were still in the fight, but they seemed helpless to stop the leviathan.

The craft shivered as the great teeth slammed down on the observation cupola, tearing it loose from the hull. Aethershot carbines barked, as Brondt bellowed orders to his crew. Explosions caressed the monster's hide. The megalofin swept past the *Zank*, shaking it down to its rivets. The Kharadron fired every weapon at their disposal, trying to discourage the beast, but whether due to sorcery or its own hunger, the Great King was determined to have them. It thrashed through the clouds, blotting out the stars, the moons, the ground below, each in turn as it circled its prey and sought to intercept it.

The aether-vessel rolled and banked, moving so swiftly that its straining endrins moaned like lost souls. The clouds were lit up by the fiery breath of the volley cannons. Belaying valves kept the *Zank* out of the Great King's jaws, but only just. The deck pitched and yawed, sending the crew, as well as Zana and the others, stumbling against the rails. Volker lashed himself to the rail by the edge of his coat, threading it around the metal and tying it in a knot. Through it all, he kept his rifle aimed, waiting for the shot.

'Fragmentation charges – seed the clouds,' Brondt roared, maintaining his footing on the rolling deck through sheer willpower. 'Do it!'

Volker heard the rumble-chunk of oscillating mechanisms. Housing plates on the hull sprang open, as crewmembers below decks rolled out the charges. Sputtering shapes vanished into the clouds, followed by the bone-deep boom of explosions. The megalofin roared in fury as the clouds erupted into a firestorm. Volker blinked tears from his eyes as a solid wave of heat rolled over him. The paintwork peeled from the rear of the *Zank*, and metal blackened. But the Great King emerged from the conflagration, jaws wide and hunger undiminished.

Brondt, cursing vituperatively, wrenched the speaking-tube around and drew his volley pistol. 'Stonehelm, get your Thunderers up here, on the double. I–' He was interrupted by a sudden lurch as the Great King passed close by, nearly throwing the vessel off course. The megalofin was drawing nearer with every circuit.

Volker tuned out Brondt's increasingly hoarse bellows and concentrated on his calculations. He followed the megalofin's progress, tracking it, accounting for windage and range. Waiting for the right moment. He blinked. There.

The Great King dived down, like the black thing from his dreams. It was too big for Volker to perceive it, save as a tidal wave of teeth and scarred flesh. But the figure on its head was easy to track. It was just a matter of seeing through the colours. A tremor ran through his legs. The *Zank* was turning in the air, and there was a sound like a dying animal. One of the endrins was venting aether-gas. Something had been damaged in the last pass, given the way Brondt was cursing. Guns thundered into the mouth of destruction. The Great King came on, remorseless. As inevitable as death.

'Azyrite, what are you doing – we've got to get below,' Zana said, grabbing his shoulder. 'If we're up here when that thing hits…'

'I'm concentrating,' Volker said, shaking her off.

'And we're crashing,' Zana shouted. He ignored her, took a steadying breath and pulled the trigger. The long rifle roared, but the sound was lost in the scream of the *Zank*'s dying. The aethercraft turned in the air, losing its hold on the sky, emitting aether-gas. Volker lost his balance and slid across the deck with bone-jarring force as his coat tore, crashing into Zana. She hit the rail and nearly went over. Volker wasn't so lucky.

Zana caught his hand, just before he left the deck. 'Hold

on, Azyrite!' She clung tight to the rail. Volker concentrated on gripping her hand, and his rifle. Everything was shaking, and he couldn't tell what was up or down any more. The ship seemed to be spinning end over end as it plummeted down towards a vast expanse of green below. His stomach lurched as his legs kicked out over the void.

The Great King had got below them somehow. The megalofin was burning, though whether due to sorcery or the Kharadron weapons, he couldn't tell. Whatever the cause, the fire crawling across its hide didn't seem to hinder the leviathan in any way. It plunged upwards to meet them, its maw growing larger and larger. Volker wanted to close his eyes, but couldn't look away from the yawning, tooth-studded chasm.

And then, it was gone. Surging past the dying vessel, towards the cold reaches of the firmament, perhaps in search of something to quench the flames. A last, spiteful lash of its wide tail caught the falling craft and sent it spinning further and faster downwards. He heard Zana yelling and Brondt bellowing commands, and then he heard only the howl of the wind and the frantic thrashing of his own heart, as the ground raced up to meet them.

Ahazian drew back on the reins. In the distance, the trees of Gorch rose high, like the wall of some incomprehensibly vast citadel. It was said that the smallest of those trees was equal to the greatest siege tower, both in height and sturdiness. That so little light could pierce the green canopy, that the roots of the trees and what dwelled within them did so in permanent gloom. His dreams had been green for some time. Green and murmuring, like the constant pacing of hairy bodies, moving back and forth just out of sight.

But the dreams had changed, as had the song. The Huntsman

no longer whispered of the cool, dark forest, but instead of – what? He didn't know. But his head echoed with the clamour of it, and his nose burned from the stink of spilled oil and reeking bodies.

Ahazian was no fool. Someone had got to the spear before him. There were other possibilities, but that was the most likely. Annoyed, he'd driven his steed hard across the Amber Steppes, barely pausing, save when the beast needed feeding. Luckily, there were orruks and nomads aplenty in these lands, and they all had more courage than sense.

But now someone was standing between him and his destination. A heavy chariot, of bone and black iron, was nearby, among the bloody grasses. A team of night-black steeds pawed at the ground, their flesh marked by bony encrustations and their manes matted and stiff, like quills. The horse-things snorted as he drew his own steed up short, and his mount bugled in challenge.

The tawny grasses hissed in the wind. Broken piles of rock pierced the surface, built in ages past by a now-scattered people. Great poles of wood, hung with bronze plates decorated with strange, vine-like sigils, jutted from them at odd angles. They were the remains of walls, perhaps, or barrows. Ahazian neither knew nor cared, save that they made an ideal spot for an ambush, as the broken arrows still jutting from his armour attested to. Ravens gambolled among the stones, croaking and squawking, even as they watched his approach with inordinate interest.

'The birds said you would be coming this way. They led me to this place.'

Ahazian turned, as the owner of the chariot stepped out from between the nearest stack of rocks, reeking of death. Strange charms and tokens hung from about his neck – death fetishes and shrunken heads. The breastplate of his black armour was etched with scenes of battle. His helmet was crafted in the shape of a skull, and the haft of his axe was a human femur. The axe rested over one broad shoulder as he set himself in Ahazian's path. The warrior gestured.

'Long ago, I learned the tongue of carrion birds. Today, it has served me well.'

'Or badly,' Ahazian said. His weapons stirred, scenting death. He slid from the saddle and gave his steed a slap, to send it trotting out of the way. He rolled his shoulders, loosening them, and cracked his neck.

'I know your scent, deathbringer,' the hulking warrior rumbled, watching him. 'I am Skern, the Gallowswalker. Gift me your name, so that I might etch it into my blade afterwards.' He lifted his axe for emphasis.

'Ahazian Kel, a Kel of the Ekran, and the doom of any who would stand between me and my destiny.' Ahazian studied the warrior. 'We have met before, in the Soulmaw.' The great weapons-smithy between worlds, where the tools of Khorne's wars were forged. Where Ahazian had learned of the Eight Lamentations, and been set on his current path.

Skern laughed, a sound like the clicking of bones against a tombstone. 'Yes. I would have taken your head then, had the forgemasters not separated us.'

'Perhaps,' Ahazian mused. This was an old rite, and one he knew well. Two deathbringers could not meet in peace. Such was the will of Khorne. No warrior could defy it. And no warrior worth his name would wish to do so. 'And which of them do you serve, Gallowswalker? From the stink of you, I'd say Zaar, the Hound of Shyish.'

'Aye, as you serve the Skull-Cracker,' Skern chortled. 'I have too long spilt the dusty marrow of the dead. I would have the taste of living blood in my mouth.' He lifted his axe and extended it. 'Yours, for preference.'

'We serve the same cause, brother. Khorne guides us.' Ahazian gripped his weapons tightly. He remembered the brute now – one of the deathbringers summoned by the forgemasters, even as he himself had been. There had been others, each chosen by one of Volundr's rivals to serve them in the quest for the Eight Lamentations. Only one champion would survive, as only one forgemaster could prosper.

'And Khorne cares not from whence the blood flows. But Zaar does, and he would see your master humbled in the eyes of the Blood God. He would see me take that trinket you wear, and claim the prize in his name.' He gestured to the fragment of the spear, dangling from its rawhide thong.

'And what would you see, Skern Gallowswalker?'

'Blood, Ahazian Kel. Freshly spilled and dripping from my axe.' Skern lunged, axe whirling over his head. Ahazian dived aside, avoiding the blow. He came to his feet in a crash of armour and swung his skullhammer, hoping to end the fight quickly. Every moment he delayed, the further away his quarry drew.

Perhaps that was the point. The birds watched in silence from the rocks, their gazes knowing and cruel. More than just the servants of Khorne were on the hunt for the Eight Lamentations. And some of them were known for subtlety.

Skern caught the head of the hammer on his palm, and held it. Ahazian blocked the brute's axe with his own and they stood for a moment, straining against one another. Skern leaned close. 'I nearly had you in the lowlands, before you fled Shyish,' he growled. 'I thought to claim the fragment then, but you had already reached the Jaws.'

'I did not flee, and you should have tried harder.' Ahazian

jerked his head forwards and cracked their skulls together. Surprised, Skern stumbled back. Their axes parted with a screech. Ahazian spun and drove his goreaxe into Skern's forearm. The warrior's hand spasmed and his axe fell to the ground. He roared and buffeted Ahazian with a tooth-rattling blow, knocking him sprawling. His weapons were torn from his grip by the force of the blow. Their frustrated screams rose wild in his mind, forcing out all other thought.

Skern snatched up his axe with his unwounded hand and whirled it around, chopping a chunk out of the rune decorating Ahazian's helm, as the deathbringer tried to rise. Ahazian fell back, dazed. Skern advanced on him, axe raised.

'I will hang your skull from my belt, in honour of your bravery,' Skern said.

'Don't count your skulls before they're collected,' Ahazian hissed. He swept his foot out, knocking Skern's legs from under him. Ahazian leapt onto the fallen deathbringer, clawing for his throat, even as he batted the axe from his hand. He tore the gorget away with a screech of popping rivets, exposing the leathery neck beneath, and sank his fingers into Skern's throat. Skern clawed at his head and neck, trying to heave him off or blind him, but Ahazian held him down. Throttling him, slowly but surely. It was not as satisfying as the axe, or the hammer, but it was just as effective.

Volundr had warned him of this, that the other forgemasters might resort to butchery when cunning failed. The skullgrinders could not strike at one another, for they had sworn an oath before the throne of Khorne to restrain their fury against each other, until such time as Khorne reigned supreme. But they could spill an ocean of servants' blood, if it suited them. The fragment of Gung was invaluable, and he'd known that he wasn't the only one seeking it. That Skern had been determined enough to pursue him this far was something of a surprise – but then, single-mindedness was a common trait among deathbringers.

Skern's fists pounded against his arms and shoulders as Ahazian squeezed his throat more tightly yet. The fire in the deathbringer's eyes blazed bright. Surrender was anathema to such as him – another common trait. But Ahazian had strangled stronger foes. He had throttled his sister's children in their cots, and his grandfather upon his throne. Skern was nothing, next to that.

And soon enough, that was proven true. The fire flickered, dimmed and was snuffed. Ahazian waited, counting the seconds. Waited until the fists uncurled, like dying spiders. Until the armour sagged with a clatter. Until the neck-bone crumbled. Breathing heavily, Ahazian stood. He snatched up Skern's axe and swung it down, separating the other champion's head from his shoulders. Just in case. Then he freed the horses from Skern's chariot and scattered them. The beasts would have freed themselves in any case, but he saw no reason not to aid them.

He embedded the axe in a rock pile and hung Skern's head from it, so that his ghost could watch as the carrion birds feasted on his body. He looked up at the black birds watching him from above. 'Well, then – did that work out as you hoped?' he asked, as he retrieved his weapons. 'Did you lead him here to kill me – or for me to kill him?'

The ravens croaked mockingly. Ahazian took a step towards the birds, and they sprang into the air, flapping away in a swirl of feathers. The deathbringer stared after them, but only for a moment.

He still had a quest to finish, and a weapon to claim.

∽∞ FIFTEEN ∞∾

SPIDER-HAUNT

Volker cracked an eyelid. The world had stopped spinning, but his stomach hadn't got the message yet. Blood dripped into his eyes, and his head felt like someone had tried to kick it off. He was lying against the railing, and everything was green. He smelled wet bark and something else – something acrid. It reminded him of Excelsis, and dark alleyways.

Spider webs. He coughed, trying to remember how to breathe. There were spider webs in the trees. The world had been reduced to a canopy of vines, entangled branches and thick, interwoven leaves. And there were thick mats of webbing spread liberally across all of it. So thick was the white substance that rainwater had collected in it, in places, and turned stagnant. Around these sour pools, patches of spongy fungus had grown and spread, like a cancerous infection, stretching from tree to tree.

Volker pushed himself up. Luckily, he hadn't lost his long rifle in the crash, but the weapon was tangled in the rail. He looked around, searching for the others. The *Zank* hung suspended in the monstrous canopy at a steep angle. Branches cascaded across the deck, clumped one atop the next, and vines hung down like curtains across the hull. Only the thickness of the greenery and the strength of the overgrown branches had kept the aethercraft from crashing to the ground far below. As Volker tried to stand, he almost lost his balance. The deck was tilted at a steep angle, the prow aimed downwards and the figurehead subsumed by the canopy. A thunderous creak echoed through the air as the deck shifted slightly, and pain shimmered through him.

He groaned and rolled over. His side ached where he'd struck the rail, but nothing seemed broken. He heard a sound he thought was rain, tapping against the metal. He looked up. Something with too many eyes and too many legs looked back.

The spider was the colour of rotten wood, and the size of a large dog. It clacked its mandibles and scuttled towards him. He rolled away from it, clawing for his artisan pistol. He whipped it out, but his vision blurred even as he pulled the trigger. The spider didn't slow as the ball whizzed past it, to ricochet off the hull. Volker cursed and stumbled back, triggering the built-in blade concealed beneath the pistol's barrel. The long blade extended with a click, even as the spider leapt. It struck Volker, knocking him flat against the sloped hull. The blade slid into its abdomen, and Volker twisted it as deep as it could go. Ichor spurted, covering his hand and splattering his face. There was a shrill sound – not quite a scream – and the creature spasmed. It flopped away from him, rolling down the tilted deck and vanishing into the thick canopy below. More tapping. More hissing.

'Don't move,' Brondt said, from somewhere close by. 'You move and they'll be on you before you can scream.' Volker froze. His skin crawled, as the sounds grew louder. The duardin was crouched in the branches that covered the deck, his white hair plastered to his scalp by blood. He aimed a pistol just past Volker. 'Don't move,' Brondt said again. He blinked blood out of his eyes. 'Sometimes they can spit poison.'

Volker's hand twitched towards his satchel. 'I said, don't move,' Brondt snarled.

'They're getting closer,' Volker muttered. 'And you can't see straight.' He took a firm grip on his satchel. He heard a hiss. Brondt fired, and Volker rolled aside, pulling his satchel around. Something heavy bounced off the bag and fell scrabbling to the deck. Volker lunged with his pistol-blade, nailing the spider to the wood.

He left it there and rolled back, just as a second arachnid scuttled towards him. A throwing axe bisected it. Volker glanced over his shoulder and saw Lugash clambering towards him through the greenery, the haft of his war-iron between his teeth and another throwing axe in his free hand. The fyreslayer grinned cheerfully around his weapon and let fly with the axe, smashing a third spider from the air. He retrieved his war-iron and laughed wildly. 'Some fun, eh, manling?' Kharadron crewmen, some wounded, but all armed, followed him. They took up positions with dogged efficiency, aiming volley guns and readying cutters.

'No,' Volker said, wrenching his pistol from the body of the spider he'd killed. He could hear shouts and the whine of aethercarbines. The webs that stretched across the canopy were alive with eight-legged forms, all converging on the downed craft. A screech from below alerted him to Harrow's survival. He hoped the demigryph's shifting around wouldn't unbalance the craft any further.

He stuffed his artisan pistol through his belt and drew one

of his repeater pistols. Taking careful aim, he emptied the weapon into a clump of spiders, tearing the hairy bodies to wet chunks. Swiftly, he reloaded and fired again. More spiders died. But there were still hundreds coming. Too many. He glanced back at Brondt. 'This craft of yours have any more tricks, captain?'

The duardin was huddled near the aether-endrin, along with several other battered looking crewmen, muttering. He glared at Volker. 'We used up all our tricks on the Great King, lad. Nothing left but fists and sharp sticks.' He stood and drew his cutlass. He rubbed blood out of his face, smearing it into his hair and beard. He grinned savagely, and for a moment, the divide between Kharadron and fyreslayer didn't seem so great. 'Sometimes, it's better that way.'

The first wave of spiders crawled over the rail, moving in eerie silence. Then, from below, came the loud clang of hull-hatches being slammed open, followed by the roar of massed aethershot rifles. The trees echoed with the bellowing of duardin guns, as Volker suddenly remembered the Grundstok Thunderers Brondt had brought on board. Brondt laughed and chopped through a spider.

'Worth every nugget, those lads,' he said. 'I was hoping they'd realise what was going on before we got swarmed.'

'I thought you said you were out of tricks?' Volker said, reloading his repeater pistol.

'That? That's not a trick. That's just old-fashioned duardin ingenuity.'

Lugash laughed and kicked a spider over the rail. The fyreslayer was covered in ichor, and was smiling widely. 'I remember hunting magma-spiders with my brothers, when I was naught but a child. Our runefather used to promise a lump of gold to the one who killed the most...' He laughed, and for a moment he seemed a very different duardin to the one Volker had become acquainted with over the past few days. The moment passed as quickly as it had come, however. Lugash made to chop through a spider, only to be beaten to it by Adhema, who darted out of nowhere, blade flickering.

The vampire moved quicker than the eye could follow, her sword making short work of the remaining arachnids. When she'd finished, she turned and snagged the edge of Volker's coat, using it to clean her blade. 'Feh. A waste of time. Barely even worth the effort.' Whether she was referring to the spiders, or the act of aiding them, Volker couldn't say. Before he could ask, he saw Zana chopping her way through the broken branches and vines that shrouded the deck, followed by Nyoka and Roggen. Harrow followed the knight, squalling loudly, fur fluffed up and feathers stiff with agitation.

'Keep that thing under control,' Brondt snapped, as the demigryph swiped at a Kharadron. Roggen caught the beast's beak and murmured softly to it. Nyoka pushed past Zana and began to move among the crew, seeing to the wounded.

Down below, the Thunderers moved out across the branches and thicker sections of canopy, establishing a rough perimeter. Gunfire echoed rarely. The spiders had retreated, or died, leaving the immediate area free of their skittering. Volker checked his gear for damage, while the others armed themselves, or made use of the *Zank*'s food stores. He looked up as Nyoka bent to check his wounds.

'I'm fine,' he said. 'Mostly bumps and bruises.' The cut on his head wasn't deep and had already dried up. Even the ache was fading, if slowly.

'Yes.' She lifted his medallion with a finger. 'Sahg'mahr provides.'

He took the medallion from her and tucked it back into his armour. 'Yes. Let's hope he continues to do so.'

She smiled at him. Her smile was a strange thing, at once innocent and wise. She was unlike any of the Devoted he'd met. There was a calm to her that reminded him of the eye of the storm. 'He will. He always does.' She turned, and frowned. 'The forest of Gorch,' she said, staring at the heaving sargasso of vines, branches and leaves. 'Legend says its first saplings were watered by the blood of Gorkamorka and so grew larger than any trees should. So large that they threatened to blot out the sky, until Gorkamorka hurled his spear through the sun, and hooked great Ignax, the god-beast of Aqshy. When he dragged Ignax into Ghur, through the tunnel of sunlight, the beast's fiery struggles scorched away the top of the forest, and stunted its growth forever.'

'Not by much,' Volker said.

'No.' She gripped his shoulder. 'But enough. The gods do what they can. No more, and no less.' She moved to check on Captain Brondt, who was inexpertly daubing at his wounded scalp with a rag.

As Nyoka bandaged his head, Brondt laid out the situation bluntly. 'We're done for,' he said. He drew a thumb across his throat. 'No sign of the gunhaulers, and no way of getting help, short of someone going and finding it.'

'Can you get us back in the air?' Zana asked. 'What about the endrin?'

'It's busted,' Brondt growled, tugging at the bandage Nyoka had just finished knotting. 'Not permanently, but for the moment we're stuck.' He turned and kicked the crumpled aether-endrin. 'Stuck upside down, in a canopy swarming with Grungni-be-damned spiders, and who knows what else.' He kicked the endrin again, showering it with curses.

'How long will it take to fix?' Volker asked.

'Hours. Perhaps days.' Brondt shook his head. 'If ever.' He spat over the side.

Volker straightened, and stared out over the canopy. He squinted. 'Then we may as well take the long way.'

'Where?' Zana asked. 'We don't even know where we are.'

'We're in Gorch.' Volker looked at Lugash. 'Now we just have to find a tree in the forest. Should be easy enough.'

Lugash nodded slowly. He peered out at the silent greenery. 'The *thunwurtgaz* - the Heartwood. Largest tree in the forest. Just follow the roots and branches, and we'll find it soon enough.' He squinted. 'Might take some time, though. Few days, at least.'

Zana laughed. 'You mean walk?' She glanced at Adhema. 'Can't you summon some bats to carry us?'

Adhema sneered. 'Myself? Surely. You? No.' She peered down into the darkness. 'We'll have to climb down.'

'I'm afraid she's right,' Volker said.

'So, we're just going to – what? – take a stroll in the forest? Have I mentioned that I hate the forest?'

'Several times,' Volker said. She had been complaining about it since they'd left Shu'gohl, though always in a somewhat jesting fashion. Now though, the humour had curdled into something less than mirthful.

'Just making sure,' Zana said. She hefted a coil of rope, one of several they'd taken from the ship's stores, onto her shoulder and peered out over the canopy. Roggen and Lugash had similar coils, though the knight had hung his from the horn of his saddle. 'Long way to go, if Lugash is right.'

'I am right,' Lugash snapped. He poked his brow. 'It's all up here, woman. Right where I put it.'

'That is very comforting,' Nyoka said. She smiled placidly at the scowling doomseeker. 'And if you forget, Sahg'mahr will surely provide.'

'Let's hope we don't have to bother him.' Volker picked up another coil of rope and glanced at Roggen. 'This must feel like home for you.'

'No,' the knight said, staring into the greenery. 'Not all forests are alike. This one is… hungry. But patient.' He pulled on his helmet. 'We will need to be careful. We are not welcome here.'

'Do forests anywhere welcome people?' Zana asked.

Roggen glanced at her. 'Some. Fewer, now.' He bent to check Harrow's saddle. 'A forest is like an animal. You must let it get used to you, before you can walk its paths. You must learn its moods, before you can do so safely.'

'Safe being a relative term,' Zana said.

Roggen nodded. 'Yes. If we move quietly, we should be fine,' he said, patting Harrow's flank. 'I have travelled through spider-haunts such as this before. Do not touch the webs, unless you must. Any excess vibrations will bring them, in their hundreds.' He hauled himself into the saddle. 'We will go first, and mark the path.'

Volker frowned. 'Are you sure that's wise? She's quite heavy.'

Roggen smiled. 'She is light on her paws. And we have done this many times.' He gave her a thump with his heels, and the demigryph leapt silently from the deck. The great beast moved with feline agility, springing from branch to branch, until it struck the slanted expanse of what appeared to be an immense bridge of wood below.

'This is a probably nothing more than an evening stroll to that murder-cat of his,' Zana muttered. Volker chuckled as he slung his rifle across his back and picked up the coil of rope. He looked at Brondt, who handed him a heavy, pistol-like device. Volker shoved it into his satchel with a nod of thanks.

'When you've found the place, fire this into the air. If we're able, we'll come looking.' He clasped Volker's forearm in a tight grip. 'Maker walk with you, Azyrite.'

'And you, captain.'

'Watch out for spiders, Brondt,' Zana called, as she clambered over the rail.

They made their way down slowly, and with much muffled cursing, using ropes, vines and outsized leaves for handholds. Adhema was the only one who suffered no difficulty, descending like a lizard, her armour making barely a clatter. When they reached the large pathway of wood below, Volker saw that it had, in some way, been shaped into what could only be an immense bridge, connecting one tree to another.

'They used heat and air to shape the branches into sky paths,' Lugash said, peering about him. 'Don't know why they bothered, when there's likely good stone under the dirt.' He frowned. 'They did to this forest what we normally do to mountain ranges – made tunnels from the roots and branches, and holds from the trees.' He shook his head. 'They were odd ones, no two ways there. But then, it isn't unusual for a lodge to go a bit funny, with isolation.'

'I've read that there are hot springs, somewhere below,' Nyoka said. 'Whole oceans churn beneath the ground, though most are deeper than any mortal can reach. Seas that carry the wealth of the deep dark within their waters. Perhaps that is why they came.'

Lugash shrugged. 'Maybe. Still odd.' He peered at a series of markings carved on the side. They made little sense to Volker, though they looked similar to the deep-cant used by the clans of the Dispossessed to mark their tunnels. Lugash extended his war-iron. 'We go east from here. Stay close.'

The branch-path swayed and creaked gently as they followed

Lugash. It reminded Volker of the stone bridges he'd seen beneath Excelsis – the secret roads of the Dispossessed, extending for leagues in all directions through the stultifying dark. The sides of the path were roughly carved, but burnt smooth and black. They rose higher than a man's head, and had been engraved with figures, maps and other, less identifiable shapes. One section was dominated by an intricate mural depicting the path's construction, and the builders' battles with spiders and worse things. Great bats had slumbered in the highest branches, as well as monsters with the heads of stags and the bodies of hawks.

The path travelled through the trees, rather than around them. Gate-houses and waystations, silent now save for the soft scuttling of unseen insects, enveloped the pathway at regular intervals. The wood of the trees had been bent away and pushed outwards, without cracking or breaking it, cultivated into a hollow space of curved walls and parapets. The interiors of these hollows were vast and empty, save for where they were dominated by thick curtains of webbing. More carvings decorated the walls, and statues as well, hewn from the interior of the tree and shaped with great care. But there was no sign of life or the activity that might once have echoed through them.

Often, Volker noted steps curving downwards or upwards in these places, leading somewhere out of sight. Heat rose from unseen depths, making the air muggy. Iron grates had been set into the floors of the waystations, and a damp warmth gusted up occasionally, as the group passed over them. 'They channelled the heat from an underground source,' Lugash had said, when Volker had questioned him about it. 'Easy enough to do, in a mountain. Harder in wood.' He'd glared at the statues then, as if questioning their propriety.

The sheer scale of it all was staggering. Only duardin would think to make a fortress, or a city, from a forest. To link each tree, and every branch, slowly, constantly, down the long road of years. They had carefully shaped their environment, bending it to their will with a determination greater than any he'd known. But then, that was their way. The duardin were like stones in the sea, unchanging and unmoveable. When they set their minds to it, the world had no choice but to bend to their will, or be broken.

But now, that will was gone. And in its place, something else had risen to claim the fruits of that ancient labour. The forest had not been tamed, at least not fully, and now it had gone savage. Monsters stalked the high places and the low.

Often, they heard the bellicose chortle of troggoths from within the belly of a ruined tree-structure, or the lumbering thud of enormous footsteps. Once, they were forced to stop as a troop of gargants plodded by beneath them, causing the branch-path to shudder and sway dangerously. The brutes were covered in spiral tattoos and ritual scarification, wearing shrouds of vine and web. Volker wasn't surprised. Where else would gargants live, but a gargantuan forest?

'They're on the hunt for something,' Lugash muttered, as the great beasts vanished into the gloom. 'Not us, but something.'

'As long as it's not us, I don't care,' Zana said. 'Let's keep going.'

They camped that first night in the hollow bulb of what had once been a waystation. A deep chamber had been cut into the trunk of a tree, the walls smoothed by heat and blade. Runes and pictographs covered the interior, though Lugash refused to share their meaning. Indeed, the doomseeker didn't even look at them as he lit a fire, using scraps of wood and vegetation, in the iron bowl set into a groove at the chamber's centre.

Rain began to fall as they settled in, striking the canopy with a rhythmic patter. Adhema sat well back from the fire, where only the barest edge of the light reached. Volker glanced at her every so often, and thought she looked as if she were listening to something no one else could hear. If the vampire noticed him watching her, she gave no sign.

'She is communing with spirits,' Nyoka murmured, from beside him. The priestess sat before the fire, her legs folded beneath her, back straight, her hammer flat on the ground before her. She had her eyes closed, and Volker wondered how she'd known who he was looking at.

'And you?'

'Only one spirit,' she said, without opening her eyes. Thunder rumbled distantly, and she smiled, as if she had received an answer to an unspoken question. Chilled, Volker turned away. The others spoke quietly among themselves. Roggen and Zana had the easy familiarity of old comrades. Even Lugash had thawed some. Or perhaps he was simply still in a good mood from killing spiders.

'What do you think happened to them? This lodge, I mean.' Zana took a bite of dried meat, and chewed thoughtfully. 'Are they still here?'

'No.' Lugash scraped a whetstone along the edge of his axe. 'If they were, those filthy spiders wouldn't be.' He paused, a wistful expression on his face. 'So many of the Far Lodges are no more. They vanished into the fires, forgotten, save in the records of their kin. We seek them still, though most think them no more than ash on the wind.'

'And what do you think?' Volker asked.

Lugash resumed sharpening his axe. 'I think it does not matter what I think. It is what it is, and no thought or wish can change that.'

Before anyone could respond, something rumbled, out in

the dark. Not thunder this time, but something else. Lugash was on his feet in moments, head cocked. 'Drums,' he grunted. Adhema chuckled.

'So, you finally heard them. They must be drawing close enough for mortal ears.' She stretched lazily. 'You are correct. They are drums. They've been banging away since the sun set.'

'If the duardin are gone, who's out there beating on drums?' Zana asked.

'Greenskins,' Roggen said, feeding Harrow a chunk of dried meat. 'We passed several of their curse markers earlier.' He looked around. 'Did I forget to mention that?'

Lugash laughed harshly. 'No need to mention it. I saw them.'

'I bloody well didn't!' Zana sat up. 'This is like that time you forgot to mention when we were being trailed by those one-eyed beasts in the Mistmere.'

'I did not want to worry you,' Roggen protested.

'They almost cracked open my skull!'

Volker spoke up before she could continue. 'Orruks?' he asked Roggen. He'd fought orruks before, and had little wish to repeat the experience. Lugash snorted.

'Grots,' he spat. 'Spiderfang.' He gestured to the webs that clung to the trees. 'Use your eyes, manling.'

'It'd help if you used your mouth, and let us know we were walking into enemy territory,' Volker said. 'What's got them stirred up? Us – or maybe Brondt and the others?' He felt a sickly sensation at the thought. The Kharadron were tough, and armed to the teeth, but that meant little to foes like the Spiderfang tribes. They would swarm and swarm again, so long as their shamans commanded it.

'No,' Adhema said. 'There's something else on the air.'

'She's right,' Lugash growled. 'They're on the war-road. We're not enough of a threat to get them that agitated.' He sounded disappointed.

'Then let's hope whatever it is keeps them occupied until we've found what we came for,' Volker said. They sat the rest of the night in silence, save for the thud-thud-thud of the drums.

Echoing like the heartbeat of something vast, unseen and hungry.

Neferata, Queen of Mysteries, Chatelaine of the Last High House, and Mortarch of Blood, watched the world through the eyes of her servant, and sighed. 'She persists still, our sister. I should not be surprised, I suppose. She possesses a certain raw vigour, that one.' She reclined on her divan and reached for a goblet filled with crushed ice and blood. Refreshing, in the proper proportions.

Proportion was everything. Too much or too little, and the balance was thrown off. Things went askew. Neferata believed in balance. With proper balance came possibility, and with possibility came opportunity. And Neferata hoarded opportunities like a miser hoarded wealth. She was rich in prospects, and doled them out where and when seemed most conducive to her benefit. But mostly, she collected them.

Such was the case now. The ancient weapons known as the Eight Lamentations were opportunity wrought in daemon-iron. The potential they represented was great indeed. With one, an individual might change the course of a battle. With two, a war. With all eight, one might – well. Best not even to consider that, until the day in question. Neferata sipped at her goblet, and pondered the possibilities.

A wide bowl sat before her divan, filled with blood. In the blood, she could see what her servants saw, if she wished. Slaves, shorn of all flesh and spirit, continuously refreshed the bowl from the great clay jugs balanced on their bony shoulders. Spirit-courtiers gathered about the bottom of the dais upon which her divan sat, their soft voices raised in a constant murmur. Mingled among them were representatives from the various mortal and death-rattle kingdoms seeking an alliance or some favour.

Skeletal warriors, clad in ragged mail and battle-scarred hauberks, stood guard to either side of her divan, their fleshless hands resting on the pommels of barrow blades. Her hand-maidens wafted through the crowd of living and dead souls, speaking quietly to some and ignoring others. They would collect those petitions they deemed most worthy of her attentions, to be mulled over at her leisure.

But for the moment, her interest was only in Adhema's quest. The blood knight was cunning, and savage, but prone to whimsy. That tendency would be the end of her, at some point, but not yet. Not today. The duardin aethercraft had crashed in the dense forest of Gorch, and Neferata found her ability to scry there less certain than she liked. Almost as if something were preventing her from seeing within the shadows of those great trees.

'There is a mind there. A force, hungry and aware, however dimly.' She spoke idly. The handmaiden sitting at the foot of her divan gestured.

'The spider in its web,' she murmured.

Neferata frowned, and nodded.

'Perhaps, Naaima. Gorkamorka was ever profligate with his power, bestowing it on every creature to draw his blood. But then, one cannot expect much in the way of sense from the personification of destruction.'

'It is not the only force peering into the gloom,' Naaima continued. She dipped a hand into the bowl and traced crimson birds on the stones of the dais. 'The crows gather.'

Neferata sighed. 'Yes. That is to be expected. When one of the four moves, the others do so as well, to counter or aid him, as the whim strikes them. Khorne roared his intentions to all the realms, and his brothers – and servants – react. Some more swiftly than others.' Naaima drew another shape in blood – three ovals, one set above the other two. 'And the gods are not alone in this. The Three-Eyed King seeks the weapons as well.'

'That was to be expected. His servants scour the realms for any item that might turn the tide in his favour, as do my own. The Eight are simply new notches added to a long list.' The detritus of millennia littered the realms – the graveyard wreckage of forgotten kingdoms, the tombs of ancient heroes, even the hidden prizes of daemonic gamesmen. Any of which might hold the key to victory in one of the thousands of wars being waged across the realms. Her servants had flooded into the mortal realms, seeking artefacts and grimoires, or information relating to such. Her armies fought battles all across Shyish to claim long-hidden treasure barrows or misplaced libraries. And her enemies fought just as hard to prevent her from doing so.

She rubbed her temple, considering. Adhema was no babe in the woods, and could take care of herself easily enough. She was not the only one of Neferata's handmaidens seeking the whereabouts of the Eight Lamentations. But she was the closest to her goal. Neferata leaned forwards, gesturing to her slaves to refresh the bowl.

With the Spear of Shadows in her possession, she could break the back of the armies that assailed Shyish, one after the next, by eliminating their commanders. Cut off the head and the serpent dies, as the saying went. Without their leaders, the servants of the Dark Gods were like so many sheep, waiting for the slaughter. Fierce sheep, true, but sheep nonetheless.

Her hands itched to hold that weapon, to speak a name and watch them die.

That was power fit for a queen.

Coldness leaked over her hand. She looked down at her goblet, and saw that she'd crushed it. With a moue of distaste, she handed it to one of the slaves. 'Fetch me another. Something older. I find myself in a contemplative mood.' Delicately, she extended her hand. A flurry of spectral courtiers rushed forwards at the invitation, their aethereal mouths suckling at her fingers, desperate for a taste of life, however far removed from the source.

Neferata watched them lap at the blood with fond indulgence. Then, with a curt gesture, she sent the spirits fluttering away. She glanced at the bowl and saw that the blood had gone murky again. Wherever Adhema was, Neferata could not advise her now. She sighed and sat back, annoyed.

'Fight well, sister. Or perish bravely. Either is preferable to failure.'

≫ SIXTEEN ≪

FOREST CITADEL

Time passed all but unnoticed in the eternal green twilight of Gorch. Days were shorter in Ghur, and nights longer. Or so it seemed to Volker. The forest had taken them into itself, and the outside world might as well have not existed at all. In the shadows of the great trees, the air congealed into formless clouds, dripping rain or sending fierce breezes gusting through the leaves. Animals hunted each other through the swaying, creaking ruins of a long-vanished kingdom.

Roggen and Harrow ranged ahead of the group, scouting the canopy above for any sign of danger and testing the strength of the branch-path ahead. Despite its sturdiness, the structure was not in good condition. Several times the group had to divert their course because of a gaping hole in the path, or a thick patch of thorny vines that resisted even Lugash's best efforts to hack through them.

Then there were the omnipresent webs. Everywhere Volker looked there was evidence of infestation. Whole pathways were entombed in white shrouds, and sheer walls of the substance stretched between the great trees like organic bastions. It was those that stretched across the canopy high above that were the worst. Volker could see the indistinct, scurrying shapes of spiders of all sizes moving to and fro. Sometimes, it even seemed as if the arachnids were following them. Obeying the orders of distant drummers, perhaps.

The drumming started up every night like clockwork. Sometimes it grew to a riotous cacophony, drowning out all other sound. Other times, it was but a dim pressure, just at the edge of hearing. It was as if they were searching for something. That worried him.

But there were other things, besides noise and skittering shadows. There was a familiar stink on the air, rancid and sharp. He knew it well, after all these weeks. Skaven-stink. The raw tang of their abhorrent machinery clung faintly to everything, and more than once he caught sight of char-marks and blood spatter, in out-of-the-way places. He made no mention of it to the others, though he suspected Lugash already knew. The duardin often had an intent look on his face, and he scanned the canopy above and the branches below often. Seeking enemies who might be lurking just out of sight.

Volker understood. At times, it was as if the forest itself were pressing down on him. Watching him, the way a predator might watch unwary prey. A feeling was building in him – a worry that they were too late. That something or someone had already beaten them to their goal. More than once, as the days passed, he caught himself looking for ravens perched in the trees.

On the fourth day, as the faint drip of sunlight dimmed, and the shadows crept out to glide across the canopy, fireflies swarmed up from secret knotholes. They danced in flickering waves across the muggy air, casting a pale glow over the ancient duardin paths. For a moment, the threat of skaven or shapeshifting sorcerers seemed distant.

'Beautiful,' Volker said. He walked along beside Roggen and Harrow, his long rifle resting in the crook of his arm. 'You forget, sometimes.'

'There is beauty in everything, my friend,' Roggen said. 'Even our dead companion.' He jerked his head back towards Adhema, who stalked along in silence. Behind her, Nyoka walked beside Lugash, the two of them in quiet conversation. Zana followed behind, whistling softly, one hand on the pommel of her sword.

'I'll take your word for it,' Volker said. Roggen chuckled.

'I have never fought beside a vampire before. There are few of them in the Jade Kingdoms. That we know of, at least.' He reached for the wineskin hanging from his saddle horn. He offered it to Volker after he'd taken a swig. Volker accepted gratefully. They'd brought what supplies they could carry, but there was no telling how long they would last. Harrow seemed content to eat spiders, but Volker couldn't say the same. When he mentioned it to Roggen, the big knight shrugged.

'Worst comes to worst, we can hack open a cocoon or three. There might be something worth eating in them.' He popped the cork back into his wineskin and hung it in its place. 'You learn to take what the forest provides, where I come from.'

'I've never been to Ghyran. Though I've heard we're not as welcome as we might once have been.' He glanced questioningly at Roggen.

'We did not always get along with you Azyrites, it is true,' Roggen said, cheerfully. 'When you first came, and began building your great cities, filling the air with smoke and noise. Not the best neighbours.' He pulled off his helmet and hung it from his saddle.

Volker shrugged uncomfortably. 'And now?'

'After Greenstone Vale, things are better.'

'Green...?'

Roggen gestured. 'The last stand of the old Ghyranic Orders. Their way had come to an end and they could not see it. The Jade Kingdoms were changing, and they had been abandoned by their lords. So they resolved to defy the will of gods and men alike.' He chuckled sadly. 'Five hundred warriors, from the ancient knightly orders, made a final stand at Greenstone Vale. Outnumbered sixty to one by freeguilder and Ironweld. So many arrows were loosed that they blocked the sun.' He fell silent for a moment. 'Later, men swore they had seen a daemon with a hundred faces and robes of every colour dancing among the dead, celebrating the success of the trick it had played.' He sighed. 'But that is a story guilty men tell themselves, I think.' He looked at Volker. 'Things are better now.'

'Were you – were you there?' Volker asked.

Roggen laughed. 'By the Lady, no. I was but a child. My grandfather, though... he saw the last ride of the Order of Seven Leaves, as they charged the gun lines with lowered lances. Mighty warriors, though not mighty enough in the end.' He stroked Harrow's neck. 'It is the nature of life, that the old ways must give way before the new. The realms cannot continue on as they are. Life itself is out of balance. So we must do what we can. All of us, from the greatest to the least.' A smile split his bearded features. 'The foundations of victory are ever built on the heroism of little men.'

Volker looked up at him. Roggen laughed. 'A saying of my order. Occasionally, even we need reminding of the importance of what we do.'

'A good saying.'

'I think so,' Roggen said. He pulled Harrow up short, as they cleared a bend in the path. 'By the Lady of Leaves,' he muttered.

Volker froze, as he spotted what had brought Roggen up short. The stakes had been shoved through deep gouges in the wood of the path ahead. The skulls that topped them were old, and of varying origin – human, some of them. Others belonged to orruks, or troggoths. But most… most belonged to duardin. Hundreds of them, lining the path ahead. Worse, some even still had their beards. Every skull had crooked green-skin symbols carved into them, or else had been painted with warning pictograms.

Lugash said nothing at the sight. He stumped past them, through the thicket of death, his gaze fixed straight ahead. The others followed more slowly, picking their way carefully through the stakes, careful not to disturb them. Adhema fingered a lank, rotting braid dangling from a small skull. 'Now we know what happened to them, I suppose.'

Lugash whirled, a fierce look on his face. His runes blazed up, so brightly that Adhema flinched back, lips writhing away from her fangs. For a moment, Volker thought he might attack the vampire. Adhema seemed to, as well, for she half drew her sword. But the doomseeker only said, 'Don't touch them. Don't any of you touch them.' His voice was quiet. Harsh. He spat onto the ground at the vampire's feet, turned and trudged on.

More skulls hung from nets of vine and woven scalps above the branch-path, clattering softly in the warm air between crumbled cocoons. Fetishes and curse-tokens were threaded among them, and these sent a thrill of unease through Volker. The grots had marked their territory well.

The webs grew so thick on the path that they were forced to hack through them, as if they were foliage. Spiders, disturbed by the intrusion, climbed higher, leaving the travellers to pass through a corridor of webs and clumped cocoons of all shapes and sizes unmolested.

Withered mummies, drained of all vital fluid by the spiders, screamed silently on each side of them. The brown shapes hung or slumped in their hundreds, within the glistening white strands. Volker kept his gaze resolutely to the fore, trying to ignore the empty stares of the dead. Finally, they came to a massive gateway rising up over the branch-path.

The gateway had been hewn from a tree trunk, and carved into a stylised representation of Grimnir, his fiery mane curling up and away from his fierce features. A grimace of fury contorted that wide face, and the entryway passed through the god's snarling mouth. There was no portcullis or door to bar their way. Only more webs.

Past the gateway was an immense plaza, ringed by great curving columns of split trunks. It appeared as if several trees had been bent together and then carefully hollowed out. The conglomerate trunk continued on undisturbed, high above the plaza, balancing on the massive columns. More gates, each shaped like the first, lined the ring of columns, the wide mouth of each marking the beginning or end of a path. Dozens of walkways crafted from tangled vines and slats of crudely chopped wood stretched net-like above the plaza.

There were more statues, carved into the bases of the columns and the inner walls of the gates. Ancient fyreslayers glowered woodenly at the thick masses of spider web that stretched curtain-like over every empty space. Even here, the infestation had taken hold. By the light of the dancing fireflies, Volker saw that these webs were occupied – hundreds of cocoons hung suspended above and around them as they entered the plaza through Grimnir's gaping mouth. Water from the previous day's rain cascaded in thin streams from the heights above, running along the strands of each web, to pool and stretch across the broken surface of the plaza.

Everywhere were signs of devastation. Whole sections of the web had been burnt away to nothing, and several of the gates had been charred black. Thick slabs of broken wood lay in smouldering piles, half obscured by new webs being woven about them. And among the rubble, scrawny, tattooed green shapes, as well as the broken bodies of spiders and other beasts. 'What happened here?' Zana murmured.

Lugash grunted. 'A fight.' He used the edge of his axe to lift a ragged strand of blackened web. 'And smell that? That's not normal fire-sign.'

The others sniffed. Volker frowned. 'Warpfire. The ratkin have been here.' For a moment, he imagined skaven scurrying along the network of immense branch-roads, flooding the canopy with hairy bodies.

Lugash nodded grimly. 'Yes, and not long ago.' He looked around and sniffed. 'All dead, more is the pity.'

'Yes,' Adhema said. Lugash glanced at her, frowning. Apparently satisfied that she wasn't mocking him, he turned back.

'They look in bad shape, most of them. Burnt, pulverised and punctured. The ratkin are efficient, when they want to be.' He said it grudgingly, and scraped the edges of his weapons together, making a ringing noise. 'I'd wager that's what the drums were about. The ratkin attacked, and the greenskins saw them off.'

'Or were exterminated, along with anything else that got in the skavens' way,' Adhema said. She pointed upwards. 'There's at least one gargant-sized cocoon up there, in the lower webs, and plenty of grots. Looks like the spiders are playing carrion bird.'

'It doesn't matter,' Lugash growled. Fireflies swarmed about the doomseeker, their glow giving him a deathly pallor. He lifted his war-iron. 'We are here.' He spoke quietly, almost reverentially. He scraped his weapons together and pointed.

A larger gateway, bigger than any of the others, dominated the plaza, behind swathes of fluttering web. Unlike the smaller gates, it was not carved to resemble a face, but instead a massive, stylised flame. To either side of this flame stood immense wooden statues – one was Grimnir, but the other was a great salamander – Vulcatrix, perhaps, the Ur-Salamander – rearing up over the god. The statues faced each other, as if preparing to do battle.

And beyond this gateway was what could only be their destination. They stopped and stared at the edifice that towered above and beyond. The Heartwood of Gorch. The hearth-tree of an extinct lodge. Lugash murmured softly to himself, his voice echoing strangely in the ruin. 'It's amazing,' Volker said.

'It's a tree,' Lugash said, flatly.

A tree, perhaps, but one almost as large as the Spear of Mallus, a mountain of bark and branches rising inexorably upwards towards the ochre sky, its highest branches stretching outwards for leagues. Its bark had been carved and added to – battlements and gateways studded its surface, connected to the other, smaller trees by branch-paths and swaying bridges of vine.

Great plazas, similar to the one they now stood in, were visible to the north and the south. The plazas served as courtyards for the citadel, warding the cardinal approaches. Far below the plazas, the roots of the great tree had been shaped, somehow, into massive roadways the likes of which Volker had never before seen. The root-roads stretched off through the forest in all directions, spreading outwards from the lower trunk of the hearth-tree. Following the roads, he sidled towards the edge of the plaza.

The heights were not so dizzying as he'd first thought. They were no higher than the Bastion, really. From where he stood, he could also see ancient trees, survivors of fire and flood, which had been snapped in two. Their descent had warped the canopy, tearing gaping holes in the green, and shattering several of the branch-paths in their descent.

He frowned as he studied the destruction below, in the dim radiance of the swarming fireflies. The ground had been visibly carved and gouged, as if by immense, trundling wheels. It had been burnt black, too, as though by some great heat. The trail led across several crushed root-roads, and right up to the base of the huge tree. Then it veered away, heading west, to judge by the fallen trees and gouged earth. He'd seen several skaven war-engines of the sort that might accomplish similar sorts of destruction, but none so large as this one must have been.

It made sense, however. The skaven, in his experience, rarely went anywhere without war-machines of some sort. If they'd brought one that size into the forest, especially one that caused such devastation, it was no wonder the Spiderfang tribes had been provoked, and were still agitated enough to be on the hunt.

'I noticed that trail before,' Roggen murmured, from behind him. 'It crossed our path at several points. A few days old, at least. As are the signs here.'

'Your eyes are impressive,' Volker said, glancing up at the knight. Harrow had a limp, green arm hanging from her beak. As he watched, the demigryph swallowed her meal with avian satisfaction.

'I am used to spotting trails among the green. Especially ones that look as if they were made by daemons of iron and flame. They entered the forest to the south, and vanished west.' Roggen frowned and turned in his saddle, studying the web-choked branches above.

Volker followed his gaze. Hundreds of small dark shapes wrapped in thick, gooey cocoons hung there, suspended above the plaza. Occasionally, one of the cocoons would twitch. He couldn't repress a shiver. If it had been the skaven, they hadn't won their battle without cost. 'What were they looking for, I wonder?'

'Perhaps the same thing we are,' Roggen said softly. 'They came with purpose, and recently. That cannot be a coincidence.'

'Of course it can,' Lugash growled, loudly. 'This is not a saga, beast-rider. We are not the heroes of some vainglorious song. I–'

He was interrupted by a thunderous snarl from below. The plaza shook slightly as something clawed at it from below. The duardin turned, eyes wide. A broken section of rubble shifted and burst upwards as a massive shape hauled itself to its feet. A giant face, like a stretched and swollen parody of a man's, pierced the thick webs that had covered it, and roared in anger.

Fingers like barge-poles slammed into the surface of the plaza, gouging deep canyons. Lugash dived back, out of reach of a groping paw. The gargant heaved himself up, until he loomed over them. Blood caked his gangly limbs and barrel chest. Burn marks dotted his torso, and the stink of infection wafted from him. The tiny eyes bulged with the madness of a wounded animal. Thick strands of webbing clung to the gargant's body, and spiders skittered along his shoulders and gut. Volker realised that the spiders had likely been in the process of cocooning the brute, until they'd woken him.

The creature wore a crude harness of leather and wood, much of which had been melted to his flesh by some intense heat. On his back was something that might once have been a primitive howdah, but was now nothing more than a blackened ruin. Burnt bodies, small and scrawny, flopped and tumbled in the ruin, or else were fused to the gargant's skin like blackened scabs. Jagged arachnid tattoos and scarified markings decorated the gargant's flesh, beneath his many wounds.

The gargant gave a simian roar and slammed his fists down, shaking the plaza. Volker lifted his rifle, wondering if he could put the beast down. The gargant started forwards, propelling himself by his knuckles, swiping webs and spiders from his flesh. Bellows shook the webs, and eyes glittered in the hollows of the high branches and beneath the leaves. 'That's torn it,' Volker muttered, swinging his rifle around. He fired, killing a spider even as it prepared to pounce on Nyoka. The priestess whirled, and then nodded her thanks.

'We need to get out of here,' Zana barked, as more spiders poured into view.

'Not with that brute in the way,' Adhema said, spitting a spider on her blade. The gargant was closer now, shaking the branch, his big feet flattening any spiders that got in his way. Roggen lifted his helmet and set it on his head.

'Now you will see why I brought her,' he growled. He leaned down, and murmured something to the demigryph. Harrow shrieked in challenge. Roggen straightened and drew his blade. 'Glory and death,' he roared, thudding his heels into Harrow's flanks. 'Phoenicium stands!'

The demigryph leapt down the trunk of the tree, bounding towards the gargant. The gigantic brute bellowed and spread his long arms. Harrow struck him like a mortar round, knocking the gargant backwards, into the crumbled remains of the nearest gatehouse.

'Not without me, you don't,' Lugash snarled, scrambling

towards the fray. The gargant screamed and thrashed, trying to pry the demigryph off. Harrow's talons had sunk deep, and it was all the brute could do to keep the demigryph's beak from reaching his throat. Lugash's war-iron sank into the gargant's knee, and the doomseeker hauled himself up, waving his axe.

Volker crushed a spider with the stock of his rifle, and turned, batting a second out of the air. They weren't much larger than stray cats, but then it might take the bigger ones time to make their way up the web. He didn't want to be around when they arrived. They needed to end this quickly. He started towards the brawl, reloading as he walked. It was tricky, especially with spiders swarming everywhere, but he had done it under more difficult circumstances. He sidestepped a scuttling arachnid and kicked it over the edge of the plaza.

Behind him, he could hear Zana and the others keeping the spiders away, with boots, blades and bludgeoning. The gargant's thrashing would make their efforts moot, however. The brute twisted, trying to dislodge Harrow, who now clung to his back, her beak embedded in his neck. Roggen stabbed at the gargant's head, as Lugash continued to chop the creature's leg. Even wounded as he was, the brute refused to fall. Instead, he knelt on hand and knees, free hand pawing at the demigryph, his blood raining down across the trees below.

Eventually, they would kill him. But by then, the plaza would be crawling with spiders. The gargant moaned loudly, garbling words in his own tongue. Threats, perhaps. Or maybe pleas. There was no way to tell, and no time to figure it out. No time for mercy, or hesitation. Only time to pull the trigger, and pray.

Volker got as close as he could, lifted his rifle, and pressed the barrel to the gargant's skull. In the moment before the hammer snapped down and the powder flashed, the creature rolled its agonised eyes towards him. He saw only animal suffering there. And then, nothing at all, as the echo of the shot faded and the gargant slumped with a disgruntled sigh. Harrow continued to tear at the body, screeching.

'You killed it,' Lugash roared. He waved his bloody axe in anger. 'Who asked you to interfere, manling?'

Volker snatched his artisan pistol from his belt and shot a spider off the doomseeker's shoulder. He put the weapon away and began to reload his long rifle. 'What did you say before? This isn't a saga, remember? We don't have time for this.' He turned. 'Let's go – move, now!'

Zana and the others raced along the branch, pursued by a horde of spiders. As they began to clamber up the gargant's carcass, Volker slung his rifle and reached into his satchel. He extracted a small clay pot capped with wax, and a scrap of fuse soaked in oil. Scratching the wax, he quickly inserted the fuse and turned to Lugash. 'Lugash – make a spark.'

The doomseeker scraped his weapons together, creating a spark. The fuse caught and began to burn. Volker turned, gauged the distance and lobbed the pot. It crashed down, just past the gargant's out-flung hand, and exploded into fire. Spiders retreated as the fiery liquid contained in the pot splattered across the plaza and began to spread.

Volker turned and chivvied Lugash up onto the gargant. 'Go, that won't hold them back forever. The wyldfire doesn't burn for long.'

'What was that stuff?' Zana demanded, as she caught Volker's hand and helped him up. 'I've never seen anything burn that fast.'

'You wouldn't, this side of Aqshy and the Cauldron.' Volker didn't look back as he clambered past the ruined howdah. 'There's a type of water there that bursts into flame when exposed to an igniting spark. We tried using it in greater quantity, but it's too unpredictable. Even for the Ironweld.'

'And you just carry it around with you?' She sounded horrified. Volker shrugged.

'It's not that dangerous.'

Zana glanced back. The flames had caught at the webs now, and were steadily creeping outwards, claiming anything the skaven warpfire hadn't.

'Bad luck, to burn healthy trees,' Roggen said, as Harrow loped ahead of them, her beak still wet with blood.

'It won't burn for long. It's too hot for that. Even with a ready source of fuel, it'll go out in a few moments. Another reason we don't use it.'

They moved quickly across the plaza towards the main gate, Lugash leading the way. Volker could hear the thump of drums, echoing through the trees. The fireflies swarmed in agitation, and the webs above them shook with the weight of scuttling bodies. 'They're beating those cursed drums again,' Zana said. 'I think we woke up more than that gargant. We'd best get out of the open, and swiftly.'

'Too late, I think,' Nyoka said. The priestess pointed her hammer at the sudden flurry of movement that was occurring within the main gateway. A moment later, a flood of spiders burst through the ragged curtains of webbing, the hunched forms of feather- and bone-bedecked grots clinging to their backs. The creatures urged their eight-legged mounts forwards with shrill screams. Volker's heart sank. There were too many of them.

'We need to find a place to fight it out, or we'll be overwhelmed,' Zana said. She looked at Volker. 'Unless you've got another firebomb in that bag of tricks?'

'Just one,' he said. In truth, he had one or two, but that wasn't going to stop them. There were too many, and they were too fast. He reached into his satchel for the pistol-like device Brondt had given him, and fired it into the air. It burst into a cascade of multicoloured lights, momentarily throwing back the shadows and dismaying the grots. Then, as the light faded, the grots urged their spiders up over slanted slabs of rubble and along the strands of webbing, closing in on the group from all directions at once.

'Was that it?' Zana asked, glaring at him.

He tossed aside the smoking device. 'Hopefully. If Brondt's managed to get his ship moving, we might just survive...'

'That doesn't get us inside, or had you forgotten that, manling?' Lugash snapped. 'I'll not be stopped here, and certainly not by any poxy grots.' He raised his weapons. 'I'm going in, even if I have to chop my way through every spider in this blasted forest.'

'And get yourself killed in the bargain,' Zana said. The doomseeker glared at her, but before he could reply, Roggen beat him to it.

'Leave it to me, my friends,' the knight said. 'Stupid beasts, to think we can be stopped so easily, hey girl?' He patted Harrow's neck. 'We have tilled tougher fields than this.' He leaned forwards in his saddle, his ironoak armour rustling softly. 'I will clear the path. Do not wait for us.' Harrow snarled and tensed, tail lashing. Roggen snatched up the heavy mace from his saddle with his free hand, and raised his sword in the other. He thumped Harrow's flanks. 'Hup-ya! Time to earn your keep, lazy beast.'

Harrow sprang forwards, moving far more swiftly than any animal that size ought. The demigryph shrieked, and her claws gouged the wood of the plaza, sending up a cloud of splinters and torn webbing. She sprang towards the closest spider, beak wide. The grot on its back stared up in wide-eyed horror as the demigryph crashed down, splattering both spider and rider. The other scuttling arachnids wasted no time, racing to attack.

Roggen bent and swayed in the saddle, lashing out at the grots and their monstrous steeds as they scurried towards him from all directions. His mace slammed down, pulping a green, feather-bedecked skull, even as his sword lashed out, slicing through hairy limbs. The grots uttered shrill, clicking cries as they urged their arachnids forwards.

Harrow did not wait for them. The demigryph pounced, cat-like, rending and tearing. Slowly but steadily the brawl spun away from the path, as Roggen's efforts drew the attentions of the grots from the others.

'Come on,' Lugash growled, darting towards the yawning gateway. He raced through the chaos, striking out at any spider or grot that sought to bar his way. Volker followed, repeater pistol growling. Spiders juddered and fell, torn apart by the volley of lead. He slung the weapon and reached for its twin without pausing.

Zana and Nyoka followed him, their own weapons dispatching any foe that avoided his shots or Lugash's bull-charge. A moment later, they passed through the gateway, leaving their companion to his lonely battle.

They floundered slightly, caught up in the strands of webbing that the spider-riders had so easily navigated. Volker thrust the stock of his rifle through the webs, tearing them aside. He and the others chopped or tore their way through, until at last they reached the entry hall. From behind them, Volker heard the crash of weapons and Harrow's snarling screeches.

'What about Roggen?' Nyoka said, looking back at the plaza.

'You heard him. He'll be fine.' Zana squinted. 'I can't see any-thing. Lugash?'

'Nothing to see,' Lugash rumbled.

'Wait a moment.' Volker turned, reaching into his satchel for a glow-bag. The small sack was filled with a paste made from the excretions of a particular worm, found only in the sea-caves below Excelsis. When pressure was applied to the paste, it glowed. He squeezed the glow-bag and tossed it to his left. A pale, yellow light rose up, washing away the gloom.

The entry hall was little more than a set of wide, slabbed steps, carved from the inner bark, and rising to a narrow landing. Large rusty braziers, each the size of several men, had been set into the edge of the landing, their clawed feet gripping the wood. The braziers were draped with dust and cobwebs, and had been cold for years. The walls behind them were covered in crude scrawling – the work of grots. The greenskins had defaced the entirety of the entry hall with their primitive efforts – brute pictograms and handprints covered the walls. The statues that had once stood sentry over the inner gate, at the opposite end of the landing, had been hacked from their pedestals and chopped to flinders.

Spider nests clustered in the corners and webs hung like drapery from the low roof and walls. Everything stank of grot and arachnid where it did not reek of skaven. For it was clear that the ratkin had passed this way, as well. Scorch marks undulated across the walls, and bodies hung silent and small in the webs. Blood had soaked into the steps and landing, staining them a deep, dark hue.

More stakes lined the steps, each one topped by a duardin skull, or decorated with chunks of effluent-encrusted gold. Many of these had fallen over during whatever skirmish had taken place, scattering bones and gold across the steps. A narrow archway, carved to resemble a crackling flame, occupied the landing. Beyond it – darkness.

Lugash led the way up the long stretch of steps, his frown

growing deeper with every step. The runes hammered into his flesh flashed and sparked, as if a volcanic heat was growing within him. Nyoka reached for his shoulder, but did not – quite – touch him. 'We will avenge your folk,' she said. 'Gryhm'neer's children are as dear to Sahg'mahr as his own.'

Lugash didn't look at her. 'Grimnir tests us with pain, and rewards us with fire,' he said. 'That is the way of it. The dead are embers, and this –' He held up his axe, '–this is the light of my flame.' He shook himself, and stumped on ahead. 'Besides, this lodge was not mine. These were not my kin. Let others avenge them. I have my own ghosts to appease.'

Nyoka blinked, and looked uncertainly at the others. Zana shook her head. 'Forget it, priestess. Easier to convince lead that it's gold, than comfort a doomseeker.' She looked around, eyes narrowing. 'Wait a moment… we're missing someone.'

'The leech,' Lugash said, without turning.

Volker looked around. They were right.

There was no sign of Adhema.

∞ SEVENTEEN ∞

THE HALLS
OF THE HEARTWOOD

In the halls of the Heartwood, Volker reached for another glow-bag, and sent it rolling across the landing of the entry, and through the archway. The soft glow illuminated a slender walkway carved whole from the inner bark of the tree. 'Hand me one of those,' he said, indicating the iron-framed lanterns hanging to either side of the archway. Zana brought one to him, and he emptied the contents of a glow-bag into it, smearing it across the inside of the frame. 'It'll last a bit longer, this way. Old miner's trick.'

'Not any miner I've heard of,' she said.

Volker shrugged. 'You don't know the right miners.' He hung the lantern from the barrel of his rifle and lifted it. Light swept out, illuminating the innumerable cracks and crevices that marred the inner bark of the Heartwood.

'Where do you think she went? Back outside?' Nyoka looked around, hammer gripped tightly. The priestess seemed at home in the cramped, shadowy space. Zana, on the other hand, looked like Volker felt. Despite his admiration for the deep-folk, he had little liking for tunnels or confined spaces. He turned, casting the lantern's glow over their surroundings, seeking any sign of the vampire.

Adhema wasn't anywhere to be found. She might have climbed higher than they could see, or slipped past them. No. She would be close. She might be ahead of them, or following, but she was nearby. He'd have wagered a year's pay on it. 'Hold this.' He handed his rifle to Zana and reloaded his repeater pistols quickly.

Distant shrieks echoed from the great, web-clogged holes that marked the walls and ceiling like old wounds. The webs pulsed, and Volker knew reinforcements were on the way. 'They've realised we're here.' He holstered his pistols and reclaimed his rifle. 'There's no time to waste worrying about Adhema. She'll have to fend for herself, just like Roggen.' He looked at Lugash. 'We need to keep moving.'

'Aye, and where?' Lugash said, peering about.

'You're the fyreslayer – where would you hide a bloody great spear?' Zana said.

'The vault,' Lugash said, after a moment, padding deeper into the gloom. 'Anything valuable is always in the vault. And that'll be at the heart of this place. Follow me.'

They followed the doomseeker through the archway, and onto the walkway. The freestanding path extended through a vast gallery, the upper reaches of which were lost to the darkness, or to enormous webs that occupied the open stretches. The space stank of greenskin and spider. By the lantern light, Volker saw immense support structures had been carved from the inner bark. All of them were hewn in the shape of duardin gods and monsters, curving around, following the circumference of the ancient tree. Smaller, more intricate carvings had been crafted beneath and between these vast effigies, though they were all but impossible to discern. These too had seen the attentions of the Spiderfang, and cascades of webbing covered them, connecting smaller figures to larger, or blanketing them entirely.

The walkway proved to be one of many – half a dozen others extended from all directions, out of the gloom, and all connected to a circular platform, through which was thrust a curving staircase that descended deeper into the tree. The upper tangles of the staircase reached towards the highest branches of the tree, and more walkways were visible above. Peering upwards, Volker could just make out the odd buttress or protrusion – high chambers and outer galleries, all of which showed some signs of infestation.

As he followed Lugash down the cramped stairwell, he wondered how long it would take to explore a place such as this properly. More time than a mortal man had, he concluded, somewhat sadly.

Lugash stopped suddenly. 'Here,' he said. 'The *Salamazgal-barak* – the Salamander's Road.' The aperture clung to the side of the stairwell. It was shaped like a salamander's snarling maw, and Volker had to stoop to avoid getting splinters from the protruding fangs. The path was wider than he'd expected, and appeared to have been cored through the deepest rings of the Heartwood.

It led to a large gallery, studded with balconies and intertwining pathways that rose and fell like roots. Stairways became ladders and ladders became tunnels, all winding back towards a central chamber, nestled at the tree's heart. 'It was the first place they carved – it's always the first place we carve,' Lugash said. 'The vault is the heart of a lodge, in more

ways than one. Our citadels grow outwards from it, generation upon generation.'

Everywhere were signs of battle. Pockmarked, scorched
walls and floors crumbling into ash. Dried smears of blood
and tattered webs. Volker had fought the skaven often enough
to recognise the signs of jezzail fire and warp-flame. They had
fought their way inside, likely supported by armoured beasts
and weapons teams. Ferocious as the Spiderfang were, they'd
been no match for the better-armed and equally numerous
ratkin.

'Hard to believe the vermin got this far,' Zana said, peering
at the damaged walls.

'They can be tenacious, when they want something,' Nyoka
said. 'And disciplined, besides.' Volker shivered slightly, remembering his time in the trenches and the chittering hordes
scuttling through the smoke.

'It's probably a good thing,' Zana said. 'Otherwise, we'd never
have got this far. The skaven must've knocked six golden bells
out of the greenskins.' A scream echoed up from somewhere,
and she whirled, sword drawn. The scream faded, its echo
bouncing from the walls and broken statues that littered the
corridor. They waited, weapons ready, but no grots showed
themselves. 'Occupied elsewhere,' Zana murmured.

'I'm sure Roggen is fine,' Volker said.

'Sahg'mahr watches over him,' Nyoka said. 'As he watches
over us.'

'It's not Roggen I'm worried about. It's that bloody leech. She's
up to no good.' Zana frowned and gestured at Volker with her
sword. 'You made a mistake, letting her come with us, Azyrite.'

'How was it my decision?' he protested. 'I'm not in charge.'

'Well, someone is in charge, and it's not me,' Zana snapped.
They both looked at Nyoka, who seemed bemused.

'I am but a humble priestess. Not a leader of men.'

'Quiet, the lot of you,' Lugash snarled. He'd stopped at the entrance to a balcony, overlooking the tree's heart. The thick rail had been torn apart, possibly by a skaven weapon. Lugash sank to his haunches. 'There was a fight here,' he said, rubbing a bit of grit between his fingers. 'A dozen duardin, by the boot-prints. We've crossed their trail several times now. Must've cut their way in, and fought their way up. Tough.'

'Oken,' Volker said. His heart leapt. If Oken had made it this far, perhaps he'd already found the spear. Volker touched one of the powder burns on the wall and tasted the residue on his finger. 'It was definitely him.'

'How can you tell?' Zana asked.

'I recognise the mixture.' He hawked and spat, clearing the taste from his mouth. 'We're on the right trail.'

'They must've used the skaven attack as a distraction. The grots would've been too preoccupied fighting the ratmen to see off a small group like that.' Zana spoke clinically. Calculatingly. 'Good plan.'

'It didn't work,' Nyoka said. She traced the wall with her hand. Her head was cocked, as if she were listening for something. 'The skaven fought their way down from above and up from below, trapping them.'

'They pressed on, from here,' Lugash growled. 'Look – they blew down a walkway, used it to cut across. Risky, that.'

'Not for Oken,' Volker said. The balcony had ended at the entrance to one of the twisting walkways. Someone had used explosives, planted at the opposite end and likely lit by use of a powder trail, to send the walkway crashing down a level and creating a makeshift ramp. It would have been a difficult descent, but preferable to fighting their way through the entangled tunnels and corridors. 'Look, rock-claws.' He nudged a metal grapple, sunk deep into the ruptured wood. 'And they've left the ropes.'

'They expected to come back,' Zana said.

'They didn't,' Lugash said.

'That's why we're here,' Volker said, extending the lantern out over the fallen walkway. He hefted one of the ropes and gave it an experimental tug. 'And that's why we're going down.' He hooked the lantern to his belt, slung his rifle and took hold of one of the ropes. 'Stay up here if you like, but I'm taking the light with me.'

Zana chuckled. 'And that's why you're in charge.'

Yuhdak of the Ninefold Path, last prince of the City of Tiers, pulled his blade from the body of a grot, and sighed. Small green bodies littered the wooden corridor behind him, stretching back to the entrance he'd made, in various states of destruction. Curtains of tattered webbing fluttered about him as he stepped over the newest body and pressed on.

His landing had not been an easy one. The mortal's rifle ball had struck him in the head. The crystal of his helmet was cracked and broken in places and his ears still rang. Only the magics wrought into his armour and woven into his robes had saved him when he'd slipped from his perch atop the Great King's head.

He had crashed into the canopy of Gorch and been set upon by hungry spiders. Hundreds of them. He had burned them from the trees, and their webs with them. The survivors had recognised the fire for what it was, and fled. He had followed, trusting in the Changer of Ways to guide his path, even as the rulers of the forest had dogged his trail.

Yuhdak had fought his way down through the forest, by spell and blade, until he reached the highest branches of the place he sought. The duardin had colonised the forest, one tree at a time. They had travelled through branches, hollowed out to make sky-bridges, or along roots smoothed and flattened to make roads, stretching between immense towers of bark. An industrious folk, though blind to the greater cosmic truth.

Every branch and root stretched back to this place – the oldest and greatest tree in a forest of such trees. Higher than the tallest spires of the City of Tiers, with roots sunk more deeply than any skaven burrow, it was a place unlike any other. But as with the rest of the realm, it had suffered. The duardin who had hollowed it out and made it over into a citadel were long gone, and a new folk had claimed it.

Yuhdak spun, his sword licking out to remove a creeping grot's head. Two more lunged at him from bore-holes in the walls and ceiling, clutching stone blades. Another burst from the webs, tattooed fingers gripping the haft of a crudely made spear.

The scrawny shapes fell one by one, joining the rest, as the sigils on his blade glowed more brightly with each death. The weapon stretched in his grip, pleased. The daemon bound within the iron was a thing of simple hungers. Or it had been, once. With every life it took, it grew stronger, testing the sigils that held it trapped. Soon it might even resist him, or worse, seek to turn in his hand. The only trustworthy thing about daemons was that you couldn't trust them, even with your heel on their throat.

The thing in the blade whined in sudden agitation. The hilt squirmed in his grip. He murmured softly to it, wishing his murder-flock were here. He had not seen a single raven since his fall from the Great King. He did not think they had abandoned him. Then, like the daemon in his sword, they were not truly trustworthy. The blade whined again. Improbably, something had frightened it.

And that something was watching him. Yuhdak could feel the weight of its attentions now. It was no daemon or sending. Nor was it simply a beast. But something else. He turned, lifting his hand. Witchfire crawled about his fingers, casting its strange light to the far corners of the ruin. In the flickering glow, he could make out the barbarous markings daubed on the walls. The grots were possessed of a manic creativity, when they weren't busy eating each other. Curious despite himself, Yuhdak examined the markings.

The symbols were easy to decipher. His glowing fingers traced markings relating to the weather, and great battles – mostly ambushes. But there was something else, one symbol repeated over and over again. That of the spider. Not unexpected, perhaps, given the nature of the grots' particular breed of savagery. But there was something...

He touched one of the eight-legged symbols, and froze. Whatever was watching him was no longer doing so passively. Instead, it was studying him with the cool gaze of a hunter that had sighted its prey. The sword quivered in his hand, the daemon screaming a warning in his head. He whirled, slashing at shadows. Shadows with too many legs, too many eyes.

In the dark, something spoke.

Yuhdak shuddered as that awful voice scraped against the walls of his soul. It was not the voice of a thinking being, but instead that of a force of nature. It battered at him, and he stumbled back, shaking his head, desperate to clear it. The voice continued to scythe into him, peeling his thoughts back. He tried to resist, but it was too powerful. This place belonged to it, as all places like this belonged to it.

He dropped to one knee and hastily carved sigils in the

rough bark of the floor. As he turned, still carving, the voice grew dim. When the last protective mark had been carved, it fell away, like the sound of a distant storm. But it did not disperse. Breathing heavily, he tried to gather his scattered thoughts.

There were spiders watching him. Hundreds of them. Small ones mostly, no bigger than his finger, but with a few larger, fist-sized ones mixed in. All of them clung to the webs, their glittering eyes fixed on him. And whatever he'd felt was watching him through those eyes. He felt a chill as he realised what it was he faced. The Spider God. Not a true god, but as good as, in the places where it chose to spin its webs. Places like this.

True god or no, it was as much a predator as the Great King. And just as dangerous.

Yuhdak forced himself to remain calm. There was no profit in panic. To run or flee would only see him brought low. He needed to think. To–

The weight of the god's attentions suddenly shifted. Yuhdak stared into the dark as he heard a familiar croak and the flutter of wings. A stream of avian bodies filled the corridor, racing forwards to swoop down on the spiders. The ravens spun about him, a typhoon of feathers and talons. He felt the awful weight of the Spider God retract, with the instinctual wariness of a beast confronted by something new.

Then, it was gone, scuttling away, back into the dark places, to seek easier prey. He looked up as the leader of the flock extended her hand. 'Are you injured?' she asked, hauling him to his feet.

'Only my pride. Your flock?'

She shrugged. 'We persist. The Kharadron do not. All is as the Great Raven wills.' She peered at the webs. For the first time, he heard a flicker of emotion in her voice. 'We have incurred the wrath of something old. It has retreated, but is still close by.'

'The Spider God,' Yuhdak said. 'A facet of Gorkamorka.' He hesitated. 'I think.' He felt the old lure of forbidden knowledge. Part of him yearned to study this place and the presence he felt here. To unpick the strands of its web and see what crouched at the centre. But there were some cocoons best left unravelled.

He passed a hand through the air, and murmured a few words. The air throbbed, and his senses with it. He could taste the magic of the spear, inundating the ancient wood like damp rot. The weapons were things of divine favour, forged in the heat of a god's wrath and cooled in blood. They could not be hidden by mortal means. Not for long, anyway.

He pointed. 'That way.'

'Is it here?' she asked, one hand on the hilt of her sword. Her warriors stood around him now, though he had not noticed them changing shape. Their black eyes bored into his own, expectantly.

'It must be,' Yuhdak said, warily. 'Where is the Kel? Close?'

'Not close enough,' she said. 'We led him astray, even now, and into the path of another. The survivor will be easy meat.' She drew her sword. 'We should keep moving.' She looked pointedly at the thick folds of web that clung to the walls. More spiders were gathering anew, in the high strands.

Yuhdak nodded. 'So we shall.' He held out a hand, palm flat, over the body of a grot. He spoke three bleak words. Something like steam rose from the scrawny corpse – the last memories and thoughts of the dead creature, trapped in its cooling flesh. Swiftly, he shaped them into a crude approximation of a spider, and set it free. The glowing white arachnid scuttled away.

'Come. It will take us by safe roads to that which we seek.'

⤞ EIGHTEEN ⤝

PIT OF THE SPIDER GOD

The climb down was arduous and took longer than Volker had thought. The air grew thick and warm the lower they went, and the smell of greenskins grew stronger. Oken and his party had been forced to defend themselves several times during their descent, by the looks of it. Dead spiders hung mangled in their webs, their green-skinned riders dangling beside them. But they were not alone – at the end of one rope on the bottom of the slope, a dead clansman slumped, arrows jutting from his flesh. He had been small for a duardin, and his beard had been dyed a vibrant green, for reasons he had taken with him into death.

'A few days,' Nyoka murmured, examining the body. 'Not long ago.' She looked at the others. 'He was among those who visited the Libraria Vurmis with Oken.'

As Volker knelt to examine the body, Zana grabbed his arm. 'Don't. If these greenskins are anything like the grots in the Quicksilver Basin, they steep their weapons in poison. No reason to risk it.'

Reluctantly he stood, and looked around. He didn't know what he'd been expecting. Something more than just what appeared to be the mouth of an enormous cistern, occupying the centre of a large, semi-spherical chamber. 'This is a vault?' he asked. His voice echoed oddly in the strange proportions of the chamber.

It was shaped like a hexagon, with each facet carved to represent what Volker thought must be some pivotal event in the lodge's history, from its founding to the birth of the first runeson. Each facet faced towards the cistern at the centre. Great chains hung from the concave, multifaceted ceiling, dangling down into the cistern from a complex pulley system. The mechanisms that controlled the system hulked nearby, surrounded by a thicket of stakes, topped by skulls clad in the tarnished helms of fyreslayer warriors.

More stakes occupied the entirety of the chamber's floor space, and heaving shrouds of web suffocated the upper reaches. Lugash seemed to hunch in on himself as he led them through the grisly field of death. 'Greenskins have funny ideas about ghosts, and the dead,' Zana said softly, studying one of the skulls. 'They probably thought they were honouring them, rather than desecrating them.'

'Why are they all facing the pit?' Nyoka murmured. 'Look – not one of them is staring outwards. As if…' She frowned. 'As if in reverence for something.'

'They died defending the vault,' Lugash said heavily. 'Some would have survived, escaping through hidden paths, carrying what they could. But the rest would have made a stand here.' His face was set and stiff, as if it too had been carved from wood. 'How many times must we die thus, father?' he demanded suddenly, his voice loud. He looked up, weapons in hand. 'How many times must your sons and daughters die, defending the ruins you left behind as your bequest?'

Volker followed his gaze. Above, just visible through the webs, was a carving of what could only be Grimnir. The god was scowling down protectively at the vault – or what was left of it. Lugash shook his head and cursed softly. 'They didn't even take it.'

'What?' Volker moved to the edge of the cistern, and looked down. Something gleamed in the depths. He set the lantern down, so that its light reached the other side of the cistern, illuminating more stakes. More skulls. All staring into the pit.

'It is an old way, little practised these days. The lodge's gold is held suspended on a scale. If it is too light, the lodge knows it is time to walk the war-road. If it is too heavy, it is time for the lodge to send out its sons and daughters to form new lodges. A steady flame burns longest.' Lugash looked up. 'The chains were cut – see? The gold dumped into the guts of the tree, where no one could get it easily. The last act of this place's runefather, I'd wager.'

'It should have been easy enough, for the spider-riders,' Zana said, peering over the edge. 'But then, what would little savages like that know about gold?'

'Or maybe something else got to it first.' Volker peered at the chains, and then down at the rim of the pit, where a second set of chains was visible, extruding from knotholes in the lip of the cistern. These stretched down into the glittering dark below. 'More chains, leading down. Another pulley system?'

'The vent,' Lugash said, studying them. He gestured to another, smaller mechanism nearby – a collection of cogwheels, pulleys and levers. 'That'll be the control. It opens a shaft below. Probably drops the gold deep into some underground river or other.' He frowned. 'They must've not had time to open that one. It could be our way down.' His frown deepened. 'What–?'

Volker looked. A warm breeze swept over him, and he could see something glittering in the dark below. Ragged shafts of light pierced the gloom, showing huge gouges in the belly of the cistern, as if something had torn great wounds in its shell.

'They smashed into the vault from the bottom, and gutted it. All that gold...' Lugash peered down into the glittering depths, his eyes blank. 'So much of it,' he continued, absently. 'They just... left it.'

Volker felt a chill as he realised what Lugash was saying. The skaven had fought their way up from below, and burrowed into the vault. 'Maybe they weren't after gold.' If the spear had been with the gold, it would possibly have been dumped into the depths as well.

'You think Gung is down there,' Nyoka said. It wasn't a question.

He checked the chains and found that they seemed sturdy enough. 'Only one way to find out,' he said. And perhaps find out what happened to Oken, as well, though that hope was becoming dimmer with every passing moment. He wondered what he would do if the old duardin were dead. He pushed the thought aside. He would think about it later... if there was a later.

'You can't go down there alone,' Zana protested.

'I'll go with the manling,' Lugash said. He tugged on one of the chains, tested it. 'I'm the only one who knows what might be waiting down there, if there's anything left of the vault.' He glanced at them. 'Some lodges set little surprises for would-be thieves.'

'We should all go,' Zana said, stubbornly.

'Hsst.' Nyoka turned, gripping her hammer tightly. 'Hear that?'

'What?' Volker asked. Then, he did. The persistent thud-thud-thud of drums, sounding in the hollow places of the tree.

'Drums,' Lugash muttered. 'Drums in the dark. They must've finished off the manling and his beast. Every tribe of spider-riders in this place will be on our trail now, and they're probably spoiling for a fight, after what the skaven did to them. Their chieftains will be looking for a victory to save their own skins.'

'We're hardly a victory,' Volker said. 'There's only six of us. Well – four.'

'Good odds, from a grot's perspective.' Lugash smiled humourlessly. 'It'll take them some time to mobilise properly. If we're going, we need to go now.'

'No – you will not.'

A flash of blinding light stunned them. There was a shriek of tearing air, and the smell of hot metal. A coruscating typhoon of azure fire swept out, surrounding them and driving them back from the edge of the cistern. The witchfire coiled about them, making strange, nauseating shapes before fading away into winking motes. Volker's vision cleared. A shimmering figure strode towards them, surrounded by a croaking cloud of ravens.

'Fate is a jester,' the newcomer said, almost gently. 'That I should find you here can be nothing else, save an expression of cosmic humour – a jape, a merriment, an infinite jest, composed by the mind of a god.' He cocked his head. 'Don't you think?'

He was tall, almost abnormally so, and clad in crystalline armour, over robes of blue. A sword hung loosely in one hand, and one eye was visible through a great crack in his helm. Ravens perched on his shoulders, or hopped at his feet.

Volker swung his long rifle around and fired. The sorcerer waved a hand and, impossibly, the ball stopped in mid-flight, halfway between barrel and target. The Arcanite gestured, examining the lead ball from every angle. 'A thousand ripples from a single stone. You cast it so freely, seeing only the intended path. As if by belief alone you might make it so. But, it can be diverted, like… so.' Fingers twitched and the ball sped away to the side. It struck a skull on its stake, shattering it into jagged shards. 'Fate is not a tool to be wielded by the hands of the ignorant. The gods suffer only a craftsman to make something of it.'

Volker ignored the sorcerer's ranting and began to reload. The others spread out, weapons ready. The sorcerer and his ravens watched, seemingly in no hurry to dispatch them. He laughed softly. 'Can you feel it, I wonder? We are being watched – all of us. An awful wisdom sits in places such as this, and finds us wanting.' The Arcanite paced towards them, sword hanging loosely from his grip. 'The god of all spiders has set his shadow on this place, hiding it from the gaze of god and man alike. Fitting, then, that it took vermin such as the skaven to find it.'

Volker hesitated, remembering what Grungni had said, about being unable to see Oken. Did the Arcanite speak the truth? Was something else here, watching them? The echo of drums grew louder and the shrill shrieks of grots grew closer. The air in the chamber became still and heavy, and the shadows seemed to thicken in anticipation.

The Arcanite peered at him. 'You. You're the one who shot me. Before, I mean.' He touched the crack in his helmet. 'An impertinence I could forgive, under other circumstances. But today I am running low on mercy.' The Arcanite raised a gilded claw and started to speak. The air throbbed with the power in his words, and a sickly glow suffused his hand as he began to gesture.

The world slowed to a crawl as Volker levelled his rifle,

hoping his next shot would play out better than his first. He knew, even as his finger closed on the trigger, that he would not be able to pull it in time.

Something dropped down on the Arcanite from above. Not a spider, as he thought at first, but something equally dangerous. Adhema rode the sorcerer to the floor, one arm pressed against the back of his neck. He yelped in shock and pain. His spell lashed the air and the vampire sprang away.

She slid back towards Volker, laughing harshly. Arrows studded her armour, and there were cuts on her marble cheeks. 'You're welcome, by the way,' she tossed over her shoulder.

'For what?' Volker asked, incredulous.

'Finding reinforcements, of course,' she crowed. A moment later, the walls and ceiling were alive with swiftly moving forms. Spiderfang grots poured into the chamber, their ululating calls filling the air. The sorcerer staggered to his feet and sent a wave of sorcerous fire washing over the first knot of scuttling shapes. He barked a command, and his ravens twisted and swelled into black armoured warriors, who raced to cut down the approaching grots. Several peeled off from the flock and sped towards Volker and the others. At their head was the woman who had led the raid on the Libraria Vurmis.

Adhema met her, sword to sword, moments before she reached Volker. 'Hello, poppet. Come to finish our dance?'

The raven-woman said nothing, but the ferocity with which she met Adhema spoke volumes. The two traded brutal blows, before splitting apart.

Adhema glanced at Volker. 'You look surprised to see me, Azyrite.'

'I thought you'd abandoned us,' he said.

'Only briefly. Someone needed to keep the greenskins inside the citadel occupied, and I'm quite fast, even on foot.' She parried the raven-woman's blade and shoved her back. Volker made to fire, but the Arcanite was already gone, in a twist of shadow and feathers. He tried to track the raven, but it was impossible.

The chamber had become the scene of a three-sided battle. The black-clad warriors and their soft-spoken master were mostly preoccupied with the grots, but several traded hits with Zana and Nyoka. The priestess ducked beneath an attack and sent the raven-warrior stumbling back with a crushing blow. She spun, whirling her hammer up and about, cracking the Arcanite in the knee, and then catching him full in the face as he bent forwards. Lugash rampaged among the grots, laughing wildly, his runes sparking. Volker tried to draw a bead on the sorcerer, but the Arcanite was moving too much – he flickered in and out of sight, like a mirage.

Cursing, he gave up. 'Can you hold the line here?' he demanded, looking at Adhema. She nodded, even as she beheaded a grot with a casual sweep of her sword.

'Until I get bored,' she said, booting a spider into the air. 'Best hurry, though.'

'She's right,' Zana called out. She jerked her head towards the chains. 'The priestess and I will keep the path clear. You and the doomseeker go.' She snagged a knife from her belt and whipped it into a grot, plucking the greenskin from its spider.

Volker nodded and hurried towards the edge of the pit, calling for Lugash. The doomseeker was covered in blood and ichor, none of it his. 'Thought you'd forgotten, manling,' Lugash said, grinning. 'Thought I was going to have to go claim the spear myself.'

'You thought wrong.' Volker slung his rifle and took hold of the chain. 'Now let's go.' Lugash chortled and slid down the chain, into the dark. Volker waited until he'd vanished into the gloom before following. The links were large enough that he could get several fingers between them.

'Coming, manling?' Lugash called up.

Volker took a breath, and then started down.

Grungni held the white thing in the palms of his hands, and watched it twist and change itself, as if by warping its form, it might escape him. He smiled, almost gently, and clucked his tongue. 'No, no, my little soul. There is no escaping me. I am behind you and before you, all at once and suddenly. However far you fly, however long you live, I will still be here. I will persist unto the guttering of the last star. For that is my nature, as this contortion of flesh is now yours.'

The thing screamed. A tiny sound, a wail of discontent stretched over octaves. Grungni closed his fingers, silencing it. He considered what to do with it. He had put the question to it, after a fashion, and learned what it knew – precious little, in fact. Though, in his experience, it was the little things that wound up mattering most.

'What will you do with it, grandfather?'

He glanced down, his smile fading. 'I do not know yet, Vali. Perhaps I will try my hand at reforging it, as my brother has done.'

'Is such a thing worth so much effort?' Vali said, sourly. The old duardin frowned thunderously, his pinched features settling into a familiar expression of discontent.

Grungni sighed and placed the white thing into his apron. It squalled piteously, begging an uncaring god for salvation. Somewhere, that god was possibly laughing. It was in his nature to do so, being a great one for japes and tricks.

'Better to ask whether any task is worth any amount of effort. The answer is inevitably… possibly. We won't know until we're done.'

Grungni looked down at his bondsman, and felt a flicker of – not quite guilt, but something like it. Vali was old. Older than he should be, and it weighed on him. Every decade he grew a little more gnarled and knotted, body tightening against itself as the spark within him sought more fuel to keep itself alight. He'd been kind once, had Vali. A great teacher and student, in one. Now...

'This is not worth doing,' he said. It was not quite a sneer. One did not sneer at a god. Vali clung to propriety the way a drowning man clung to a broken spar. 'It is a waste. We could make new weapons in the time we spend searching for these... these lamentable devices.' He grimaced. 'Foolishness.'

Grungni snorted. Vali had ways of calling him a fool without stating it outright. 'And if it is, it is my foolishness. Besides, I prefer to think of it as a gamble.' He sighed, and looked around his smithy. The first smithy, and the last. Forges flickered with fires first set millennia ago, which had never been doused. And never would be, if he had any say in it. It was in these fires he had forged the first weapons of sigmarite, from the core of a dying world. He smiled, revelling in old satisfactions.

'Have I ever told you how I met Sigmar, Vali?'

'Many times,' Vali said, bluntly.

Grungni blinked. 'Ah. Well, he's a good lad, for all that. Bit headstrong, bit rough around the edges, but there's a good seam there, running through him.' He frowned. 'Not like the other one, hiding there at the centre of all that is, like some great spider.' He sighed. 'Though even in him, something gleams. It's the way of mortals, I think. They're weighed down with possibility, even when they don't see it.'

Vali spat. 'The Three-Eyed King lost any claim on mortality a long time ago. Before the realms even existed.' He shook his head and clenched his hands. 'Would that I had his head here, bent over an anvil, and a hammer in my hands.'

'And would you kill him, Vali?'

'In a heartbeat.'

Grungni stared at him in silence, pondering his servant's words. Vali's kin, he recalled, had been slain by Archaon, in those last, fateful days before the end of the beginning. 'And what if he, too, could be forged anew? Would you kill him then, or make of him something better?'

Vali shook his head. 'He is rusted through. Him and all his kind.'

'It is said that there is worth, even amid the rust.'

Vali snorted. 'Who says?'

'Well, me. I said it.' Grungni sighed. 'Leave me, Vali. There must be something you need to take care of. Some poor soul in this vast smithy surely requires chastising.' He turned away, to select a hammer from among the plethora on a nearby rack. He heard Vali shuffle off in a cloud of discontented muttering.

'You're cruel to him, old one.'

'Who are you calling old, white-beard?' Grungni said, striking an anvil. Sparks danced through the air, twisting into new and interesting shapes. They fluttered about the hooded head of the cloaked duardin who sat nearby, perched on an old, splintery stool, smoking a long pipe. A massive overflow of white beard spilled out of the hood and down across a barrel chest. Broad arms, thick with ancient muscle, were crossed over the chest. A heavy foot was propped up on an overturned bucket.

'True. I always forget which of us is older. Are you my grandfather, or am I yours?'

Grungni winced. 'I wish you wouldn't pose riddles like that.'

'A riddle is a whetstone for the mind, Maker. You know

that.' Smoke spilled upwards out of the bowl of the pipe. For a moment, Grungni saw tiny figures there, working, fighting, dancing, and felt something that might have been sadness. The old duardin waved a hand, dismissing the images. 'And nostalgia only serves to dull the wit.'

'Like strong drink. Yet we indulge regardless.'

The pipe-smoker chuckled. 'So we do.' The chuckles faded, and the ancient figure leaned forwards. 'This world moves faster than I am used to, Maker. Faster than we expect, at times. Years fall like rain, and the manlings rise like grain.'

'Poetry, my friend?'

'Nothing wrong with that.' The white-beard sniffed. 'I've a fair singing voice, as well. Beat me a tune with that hammer of yours, if you doubt me.'

'I beg thy pardon, old friend,' Grungni said, with elaborate courtesy. 'Now, did you come here to brag about your voice, or to tell me something?'

'Both.' The heavy boots thudded to the floor. The sound they made was heavier than it ought to have been. The ancient had a gravity to him. He was somehow more real than the world around him. Where he walked, it bent itself into pleasing shapes, and time flowed in rivulets, rather than as a mighty torrent. He was an impossibility. Or perhaps – an impurity. Something old, which had staggered onto a new shore, wet with the blood of a dead world.

When Grungni looked at the old one – really looked, as opposed to a glance – he did not see a mayfly spark, soon extinguished by the passing of years, but a snarling light, which would resist even the ultimate darkness. A fire as old as time and as hot as a realm's core. The light was so bright that even a god could not long stare into it without blinking. He did so now, slowly and with great thought.

The old one spoke, bluntly and with no hesitation. 'Drums beat in the Varanspire. The call to war might last a day, or a century. None can say. The hand of Death stretches out from the amethyst realm, gathering souls the way a miser gathers coins. Rats gnaw at the roots of all the realms, scuttling between the walls of all that is, seeking crumbs from the table of the gods. All these things are happening, and have always happened. But now, the eyes of some are turning to you, Maker, and your scheme.'

'Is that an accusation, white-beard?'

The ancient duardin shrugged. 'A warning. The threads of fate grow more tangled, the harder you pull on them. And this is a mighty tug indeed.'

'The Eight Lamentations cannot be allowed to fall into the hands of the enemy.'

'They were in their hands before.'

Grungni paused. He ran his palm over the surface of the anvil, feeling the residual heat from his earlier blow. 'Now is not then. As you well know.'

'No. It isn't. And your enemy isn't who he was, then.'

Grungni turned, a frown creasing his features. 'Careful, old one. I will allow a certain amount of familiarity, but I am still he who forged the sun, and hammered the spine of the world into shape.'

'Are you? Or are you merely the shadow of him, cast on the far wall of a smithy?' The ancient duardin tapped his chest. 'We all might be shadows, in the end. Not for me to say, of course.' He rocked to his feet and stood, with a slight groan. 'Though I wager a shadow wouldn't ache so.' He pointed the stem of his pipe at Grungni. 'I will keep my eyes and ears open, Maker. If I see or hear anything related to your quest, I shall send word.'

Grungni nodded. 'My thanks, grandfather.'

The ancient duardin laughed. 'Not that old, I think.'

He was gone a moment later. Grungni made no attempt to watch him leave. There were limits, even to a god's power, and if the old one did not wish to be seen, he would not be seen. Instead, he turned his attention to the anvil, and the hammer in his hand.

One rang down on the other, and Grungni listened to what the sparks had to say.

∞⇽ NINETEEN ⇾∞

WEB OF THE ARACHNAROK

The web stank.

Volker had wrapped a rag about his face, but it did little to help with the smell. It was also difficult to traverse, being exceedingly sticky. He was glad he was wearing gloves and boots. The web would have torn his flesh if he hadn't been. The chain was slick in his grip, and several times he almost fell.

Lugash seemed to have no difficulty. His runes steamed, and the web seemed to shrink away from his blades. He was using his axe as an improvised piton, when necessary, descending on the strength of his arms and shoulders alone. Volker got the feeling this wasn't the first time the doomseeker had done this sort of thing.

When he said as much, Lugash glared up at him. 'You talk too much, manling.'

'My apologies – just trying to pass the time.' And to keep

from thinking about what was going on above, though he wasn't having much luck.

'Keep it up and we'll be knee-deep in spiders.'

'Spiders don't have ears,' Volker said, tearing his hand free of the web. He shook it, trying to dislodge the sticky strands. Above, a flash of witchfire briefly illuminated the mouth of the cistern, and he murmured a silent prayer.

'What?'

Volker gestured absently. 'No ears.'

'Then how do they hear?' Lugash demanded.

'They sense vibrations. Through their hair.'

Lugash stared up at him. 'That's ridiculous.'

'They also have a keen sense of smell. Through their pedipalps.'

Lugash blinked.

'On their legs,' Volker continued. He tried to concentrate on the chain, one hand after the next. His arms and legs were beginning to cramp.

'They smell... through their legs,' Lugash said heavily.

Volker nodded, stopping to rest. 'Quite fascinating, your average spider. Like a very intricate mechanism, of sorts.' He looked around. 'That's why I'm not worried about alerting them, by the way. They already know we're here.' He flicked a strand, causing it to quiver. 'They felt us the moment we started our descent.'

Lugash growled something low in his throat. Volker didn't ask him to repeat it. Instead, he said, simply, 'Thank you.'

Lugash didn't look at him. 'For what?'

'Helping me. Helping Oken.'

Lugash laughed harshly. 'Is that why you think I'm doing this?' He looked up, an incredulous sneer on his rough-hewn features. 'Or any of us?'

Volker frowned. 'No – I know you're doing this on Grungni's orders, but–'

Lugash threw back his head and guffawed. 'I do not serve the Maker, manling.' He grinned savagely. 'The woman, yes, and the beast-rider, aye, but I am Lugash. I serve only the memory of my people.'

'Then why–'

'Are you deaf?' Lugash growled. 'You came to help your friend, I came to help my people,' he continued. He unhooked his axe and dropped down to the next strand.

'What do you mean by that?' Volker asked. While he didn't care for the fyreslayer's tone, he was intrigued. Lugash had barely spoken more than three words in a row to him since they'd met. And most of those had been insults.

'I made an oath. My people are scattered. They have no purpose, nothing to lead them into the coming age. They build walls out of tradition, and suffocate behind them. The fire in our belly has grown dim, and our actions are but rote memory.' Lugash stopped, head bowed. 'We fight, but we do not know why. Only that we have always fought.' As he spoke, the runes hammered into his flesh began to glow softly. 'I would see my folk made whole. So I work with the Maker, and together, we might repair the soul of my people.'

Volker stared down at the doomseeker. Lugash shook himself and looked up. 'I do not expect you to understand, manling. Your god still lives, after all.' He looked down. 'There – look!' From down below, the glint of gold reached up to caress their eyes.

It lay scattered singly and in clumps across a thick web, woven amid the remains of an enormous, shattered platform. Piles of coin and ingot shifted gently among the sticky strands of spider-leaving, sliding into the dips and valleys of successive layers of web. From below, the muffled susurrus of water was just audible. Great holes had been bored through the cistern above and below the web, their edges blackened. Cracks ran upwards and outwards from these holes in striated fashion, the much abused wood smeared with a tarry, glistening substance that Volker recognised all too well.

'The skaven did this,' he said, as he tossed a glow-bag onto the gold below. 'There's lubricant from their engines splattered all over the walls. They bored in with warpgrinders, chewing tunnels through the wood, until they reached the cistern.' He refrained from stating the obvious. They were too late.

The Spear of Shadows, if it had ever been here, was gone.

Lugash snarled a curse and dropped down, landing amid a cascade of coinage. The sound echoed loudly in the circular space, and the web shifted. Cocoons were revealed amid the gold. Withered snouts and tails poked through these in places, but others were more sturdy. As Volker joined him on the gently bobbing web, Lugash sliced one open. A shrunken, mummified face stared up blankly. There was not a drop of fluid left in the unfortunate duardin within. Even his beard had turned brittle.

'Filthy spiders,' Lugash spat.

Volker began tearing at another cocoon, his heart a lump of ice in his chest. 'Help me get these others open. One of them might still be alive.'

'Doubtful,' Lugash grunted, but he stooped to help anyway. One by one, they tore open the cocoons, exposing the withered remnants of duardin and skaven. Several of the skaven proved to be still alive, or were, until Lugash silenced their squeals with brutal speed. Volker grew more frantic. There was every likelihood that Oken hadn't even made it this far – that he was dead in a spider's web, in the forest somewhere. But Volker couldn't, wouldn't, accept that. Not yet.

'Not yet,' he hissed, ripping open a cocoon. Something glinted in the light of the glow-bag. A pair of iron-rimmed spectacles. Volker's heart leapt. 'Oken...' he whispered. Then, more loudly, 'Oken!'

The duardin was old, his beard and hair the colour of ice and almost indistinguishable from the webs that ensnared him. Vivid scars ran across his broken features, souvenirs from an exploding cannon. Behind the spectacles, eyes blinked. Oken groaned. 'Lad...' he murmured.

'It's me, old man,' Volker said. 'Rest easy – we'll get you out of here. Lugash, come help me.' The doomseeker started towards him, shaking his head.

'Luck of the Maker, this one.'

'Maybe the gods are watching out for us,' Volker said. But even as he said it, in the dark, something uncoiled itself from the depths of the web. A deep, unsettling clacking echoed through the pit, and the strands began to shudder and jerk. Volker turned from the half-opened cocoon and drew one of his repeater pistols. He thumbed back the hammer and scanned the dark. A smell rose out of the depths, like corpses bloating in the sun. Clack-clack-clack. A warning sound.

The webs bulged, and then tore with a soft sound. Something rose, eyes blinking against the light of the glow-bag. 'Arachn-arok,' Lugash breathed. 'Get him up, manling. I'll hold it off.'

'You're stronger than I am. You're the only one who can get him up the chain.' Volker took aim at the massive shape, wondering if he could get to the remaining pot of wyldfire in his satchel before the gigantic spider was on them. 'Besides – it's just a spider.'

'A big spider,' Lugash said.

'Just get him up the chain, Lugash.'

The doomseeker looked at him, for just a moment. Then he

nodded. 'There's gold in your veins, manling. And iron in your spine.' He began to hack away at the strands holding Oken's cocoon in place.

'I'd settle for powder and shot in my guns,' Volker muttered, keeping his eyes on the arachnarok as it crept closer. He doubted the repeater would penetrate its hide. But if he could hit it in one of its many eyes...

The monster struck, moving more quickly than he'd thought. Like the gargant they'd faced outside, the creature was wounded. Something had burned it, and badly. But it was still fast, and lethal. He held his ground and fired. The repeater pistol bucked, splitting the dark. The arachnarok twitched back with a sound like a shriek. Volker clawed a second shot cylinder from his satchel, counting the moments under his breath. One... two... three... He slammed the cylinder home and locked it into place. Cogwheels clicked into position, and he snapped the barrel up, even as the spider lunged forwards again.

'Bastard – back,' he snarled. Another burst of fire, another not-quite shriek. The light of the shot hurt it more than the shot itself, he thought. He reloaded, eyeing the beast as it crept around them, moving slowly. When he'd finished, he reached into his satchel for another glow-bag. Crushing the paste against his cuirass, he smeared it across the metal. The glow brightened and the great spider retreated, eyes glittering evilly.

'Manling – get over here,' Lugash called, one hand on the chain. He had Oken's cocoon over one shoulder and his axe in his free hand.

'I thought I told you to get up the chain,' Volker called out.

'And when did I start listening to you?' Lugash snarled. 'I've got an idea.'

'Oh, well, if you've got an idea,' Volker said.

The arachnarok had stopped its circling. It was readying

itself for another lunge. He reached into his satchel, feeling for a clay pot. When he found it, he muttered his thanks to whatever gods were listening. Grungni, perhaps. Sigmar, hopefully. He took aim at the arachnarok, watching it quiver in anticipation. He would only have one chance.

He tossed the wyldfire, levelled his pistol, and fired. The explosion deafened him momentarily, but he'd been on enough battlefields not to let it cost him time. He was up and moving, head ringing, blinking sparks from his eyes, before the first splatter of fire caught. The arachnarok was thrashing in agitation, startled and possibly blinded by the sudden flash. It wouldn't be distracted for long.

As he stumbled through shifting piles of gold towards the chains, he felt the web tremble beneath him, disturbed by the giant arachnid's distress. Heat kissed his back as the fire roared up, licking greedily at the cocoons and wood. He lunged for the chain at Lugash's urging. He caught hold of it as Lugash chopped through the chain, and the fires spread rapidly across the webs. The ancient mechanisms began to clatter as the chain shot upwards, jerking Volker and the doomseeker off their feet and up with it, at great speed. Volker concentrated on holding on, as below him the arachnarok retreated from the flames, shrieking.

'Get ready to jump,' Lugash hollered as they approached the rim of the cistern. Volker's heartbeat thudded like thunder in his ears. The chain clattered thunderously as it zipped upwards, and then Lugash was leaping, and Volker followed. His gloved hands slapped down, seeking purchase on the wood. He found it at the last moment, digging his fingers into the rough bark. He glanced aside and saw that Lugash had hooked himself to the rim with his axe. The doomseeker laughed wildly. 'Some fun, eh?'

'No,' Volker said, through gritted teeth. He looked down. The fire was raging through the webs below, speedily devouring every strand. He couldn't spot the arachnarok, and hoped that meant it had perished or retreated deeper into the cistern. Muscles straining, he hauled himself out of the cistern. Lugash scrambled up, still carrying the cocoon.

The battle for the vault was raging on. Volker spotted Zana and Adhema trying to cut their way towards the sorcerer as he flung an eldritch bolt into a rearing spider twice his size. Nyoka fought nearby, on the edge of the pit, her voice cutting through the noise of combat like a knife. Her prayers rose and fell like a song and her hammer pulped green skulls with abandon. A black-clad shape darted towards her.

Volker swung his long rifle up and fired. The raven-warrior twitched aside, distracted. Nyoka spun and smashed him from his feet, knocking him over the edge of the cistern. She nodded her thanks. 'A timely return,' she said, extending her hand. Volker caught it and she hauled him to his feet.

'We have to get out of here,' Volker said. Arrows pattered against the ground at his feet, and they ducked behind the mechanisms controlling the vault-chains. Spiders skittered towards them, their greenskin riders practically gibbering in eagerness to come to grips with an enemy they easily outnumbered.

But just before the spiders reached them, they suddenly scattered, retreating swiftly. Horns blew and the grots shrilled warnings. The chamber shook as a gust of heat billowed up from the cistern. Volker turned, a curse dying on his lips.

The arachnarok surged up out of the pit, its hairy body aflame and its great legs stabbing down with ballista-like force, to crack the wooden floor. It emitted a scream of frustration and pain, casting about blindly. Driblets of fire splashed across the floor, turning the wood black. 'Looks like there's still some fight in her,' Lugash said, eyeing the creature. 'Not for long, though.' He sprinted towards the beast before Volker could stop him. Volker hooked Oken's cocoon and dragged it into cover.

'He's going to get himself killed,' he said.

'We can but follow the paths the gods have laid out before us,' Nyoka said. She peered up at the arachnarok as it stepped over them. 'Still, that is a very big spider.'

The creature wailed as one of its legs slammed down, narrowly missing the sorcerer. He rolled to his feet and hacked at the monstrous spider, ignoring the flames that licked at his robes. The monster turned, following him. Volker grunted in satisfaction, hoping they'd kill each other – or at least give him time to reload.

Smoke flooded the chamber, rising from the now burning webs and crackling wood. Everywhere the arachnarok trod, it spread the flames. 'Mixture was off,' he muttered to himself. The fire wasn't going out, as it should have. Instead, the whole chamber was rapidly becoming an inferno. Burning strands of web drifted down from above and the atmosphere grew stifling. He saw Zana staggering towards him, beating at flames on her clothing. He reached out and hauled her into cover.

Between coughs, she said, 'This is your doing, isn't it?'

'The mixture was off,' he said. 'Where's Adhema?'

'Staying out of the way,' the vampire said, from her perch atop the mechanism. 'The birdies are flying the coop, poppet.' She pointed.

Volker saw a storm of ravens spiralling away towards the safety of the tunnels. Some of them didn't make it, and were caught by the flames, or the arachnarok's snapping mandibles. 'Where's the sorcerer?'

'I lost track of him once that creature started blundering

around. If he's smart, he's already run...' She twisted, bounding from her perch as a blade thudded down, chopping into the wood.

'No one has ever accused me of intelligence,' the Arcanite said, stepping through the smoke. He motioned, and a line of flame drove Volker and the others back, separating them from Adhema. Within the flames, hateful faces leered and gibbered, hissing curses and whispering secrets. The sorcerer tore his blade free of the mechanism as Adhema lunged for him. He parried her blow and gestured, spitting syllables, and she screamed as an amethyst light suffused her form. Her marble flesh was suddenly riven by black cracks and her armour squealed and began to flake away into rust. She staggered back, clutching at her head. Her hair was going white, even as her face shrank in on itself.

'But then, perhaps I am not alone in my foolishness,' he continued. He raised his sword, intending to bury it in Adhema's heart. 'First you, and then the rest.'

The smoke behind him billowed and burst wide, disgorging a massive feline shape. The sorcerer turned, visible eye widening. Then he was falling backwards, buried beneath the bulk of a snarling demigryph. Roggen leaned forwards in his saddle and brought his mace down, smashing the sword from the sorcerer's grip and sending it clattering away. 'My apologies for my tardiness, my friends. It took me forever to find my way through this maze.'

The knight looked much the worse for wear, his armour battered and scored by blows, and his helmet missing. Blood matted his hair and arms, but his strength seemed undiminished. Harrow too was covered in blood and wounds. The broken shafts of arrows stuck out of her hide, and her beak was chipped. The demigryph snapped at the sorcerer's head. As she did so, his form wavered like moonlight and bled away into a radiant fog, which soon became lost in the smoke and flame.

'Coward,' Roggen said. 'Always, they run.' He slid from the saddle, stumbled, straightened. He was breathing heavily. 'Still, for the best, I think. We could do with a rest.' He glanced at Adhema. Her hair had darkened once more, though black veins still marked her cheeks. 'Do you yet persist, my lady?'

'I persist,' she rasped, ignoring his proffered hand. 'Only my pride was injured.'

'I'm sure it will heal quickly,' Zana said. Adhema hissed.

The vampire looked at Roggen. 'You saved me some pain, mortal. I'll not forget that.' She cocked her head. 'Unless I do.'

Roggen bowed his shaggy head in acknowledgement. Before he could speak, the arachnarok screamed again, reminding them that it was somehow, improbably, still active. The great spider staggered back towards the pit, flames dripping from its massive shape. It was dead, but didn't know it yet. A brawny shape clung to its abdomen, hacking away. Lugash, Volker realised with a start.

The fyreslayer seemed utterly unperturbed by the flames licking about him, as he chopped at the arachnarok's flesh. The monster staggered, slamming into a support column. Wood cracked and smouldered. Lugash was thrown from his perch. He rolled across the ground, narrowly avoiding the arachnarok's legs as it flailed about, trying to regain its balance. It screeched again, a subsonic wail of confusion and agony.

By some instinct, it managed to home in on the stunned doomseeker. It rose up over him as he clambered dazedly to his feet. Volker lifted his rifle, knowing it was useless. Before he could pull the trigger, the chamber began to shake. The ceiling cracked, not from the heat of the rising flames but from something above.

A moment later, an explosion tore open the chamber, splitting the ceiling and sending immense shards of burning wood hurtling down. One of the largest pierced the arachnarok through, like a well-thrown spear, pinning the giant spider to the floor of the chamber. The sudden updraught drew the fire aloft, simultaneously snuffing much of it out. Dust and splinters rained down, mingling with the smoke.

Heavy ladders, made from chains and metal slats, clattered down from above. Weighted on the bottoms, they struck the floor and anchored themselves. Armoured figures clambered down quickly, weapons on their backs. As they dropped to the ground, they assumed a defensive formation. Any grots that hadn't already fled were shot down with ruthless efficiency by the Grundstok Thunderers. The armoured Kharadron spread out, moving to secure the chamber.

A moment later, Captain Brondt climbed down to join them. 'Still alive then? Good.' He stumped towards them, grinning widely around his cheroot, his head still bandaged. 'That's a favour you owe me, Mathos. For an even three, I'll even give you transport out of this forest.'

'Three? You dirty chiseller!' Zana was on her feet. 'Two, and I won't say anything about that night in Haar-Kesh.'

Brondt blanched. 'You swore you'd take that secret to your grave,' he said. He pointed his cheroot at her. 'Two and a half, and I'll forget you broke that vow.'

'Two, or I'll break more than that.' Zana sheathed her sword with a flourish.

Brondt grimaced. 'Fine. Two.'

Ignoring them, Volker dropped to his knees beside the cocoon. Nyoka was already working on it, carefully stripping the rough strands away from Oken's semi-conscious form. The old duardin stirred with a groan. 'O-Owain?'

'It's me, old one.'

'Thought… dreaming…' Oken slurred. 'Spider…'

'It's dead. And you're alive.'

'Gung,' Oken said. He gripped Volker's arm tightly and tried to haul himself up, despite Nyoka's protestations. 'They took it, boy,' he croaked, eyes wide and wild. 'The skaven have the Spear of Shadows. And gods help whatever fool gets in their way.'

∞ TWENTY ∞

WARP-WHEEL

The massive conglomeration of rusted iron, bronze and steel sped along the Amber Steppes, leaving the grasses aflame in its wake. It resembled nothing so much as an immense wheel, spinning about a central sphere. The wheel was as wide as a castle wall and lined with gouging teeth of iron, which caught the earth and tore it apart wherever the machine passed. It roared like a wounded animal as it ploughed ever forwards, emitting green-tinged smoke from various vents and orifices, which poisoned the air just above the burnt grasslands.

A herd of wild horses stampeded ahead of the monstrous engine, their screams of terror lost within the mechanical cacophony. Some of the animals, slower than the others, were caught and dragged beneath the wheel, their thrashing bodies ground to a bloody mulch. Others were incinerated by the occasional bursts of warpfire that blasted from the dripping cannon muzzles studding the central sphere. Raging wildfires spread outwards from the wheel, sweeping across the steppes.

'Well?' Warlock Engineer Quell, formerly of the Clan Skryre, now a clan of one, hissed, staring at his assistant. The device currently juddering its way across the steppes was both his crowning achievement and the current object of his frustration. He sat in his throne within the command chamber. Whistling pipes, sparking conduits and trembling control devices filled the compartment, each one an invaluable part of a magnificent whole. His crew-rats scurried back and forth, seeing to the needs of the great machine, keeping it on course and intact.

Just like Vex was supposed to be doing. Quell's assistant rubbed his blistered snout with a gloved paw. 'Spiders everywhere,' he grunted. The acolyte wore heavy goggles over his eyes to protect them from the light of the engines. He was ugly, even for a skaven. His ears had been burnt to raw nubs and most of his hair had been scorched away, leaving him a scarred, hunched thing. A bandolier of tools, mostly filched from other acolytes, hung across his scrawny chest, and he played with them constantly, much to Quell's annoyance. 'Need to burn them out, yes-yes.'

'No-no,' Quell chittered, in frustration. 'Fool! Idiot! No fire. Too many gases, too much pressure – you might kill us all.' He threw up his paws in despair. 'Surrounded by idiot-fools, yes-yes! Punishment from the Great Horned Rat! Doomed. Doomed!'

'They're just spiders,' Vex muttered.

'This engine is impregnable,' Quell snarled. Saliva spattered the lenses of Vex's goggles. 'It was sabotage. Do not lie!' He pointed an accusing talon at his assistant. 'I will know-sense if you are lying.'

'Not lying, no-no, most impressive of tutors,' Vex assured him, unctuously. Vex did everything unctuously. It was his single redeeming quality as far as Quell was concerned. Quell believed him, for Vex was too stupid to sabotage a work of genius like the warp-wheel, the spawn of Quell's magnificent intellect. The greatest weapon the realms had ever seen, or would see. He slumped back on the mouldering cushions of the command throne, idly chewing on a cracked talon. Despite a few mishaps, the first test of the war-engine had been completed successfully.

The tree-citadel had been easy enough to crack, though not without some difficulty. The gyroscopic actuator needed fine-tuning, for one. Climbing the Bastion of Excelsis would be a far more perilous prospect than rolling up the side of an overlarge, spider-infested tree. And the warpfire throwers had not performed to expectations.

But all in all, he was pleased. As Warpfang would, no doubt, be pleased. He yanked on his whiskers, annoyed by the thought. Warpfang – that decrepit, dismissive old beast – did not deserve such a glorious weapon as this. Cruel fate had bestowed unearned gifts upon the Grand High Clawmaster, and Quell longed to snatch at least one of them back.

A small movement caught his eye. His paw slammed down, squashing the spider. His good mood evaporated. There were spiders everywhere, lurking in the ducts, spinning webs in his precious mechanisms, laying eggs, eating his rats, poisoning his slaves. The warp-wheel was inundated with eight-legged vermin. Not to mention grots. Somehow, in some way, a pack of the scrawny greenskins had got on board. Now the majority of Quell's crew were busy trying to hunt them down, rather than exterminating the spiders.

Quell ground the twitching remains of the spider to paste. 'Handle it, Vex. Or I will.'

Vex bowed, snivelling respectfully. He hurried from the bridge, snarling at the slaves chained to the bulkhead on his way. Quell sank back into his cushions, snout wrinkled in frustration. They were off schedule, thanks to the infestation.

The only solution was to return to his lair at Lion Crag and commence a full extermination procedure, one level at a time. The warp-wheel would need to be cleansed of the infestation before he could allow it back into the field. Warpfang wouldn't like that. Quell snickered. All the more reason to do it, then.

He flinched, suddenly. A strange tone quavered through the hull, startling his slaves and inciting the sudden release of fear-musk. Pawing at his snout, he thrust himself out of his throne with a hiss of annoyance.

It had been singing since they'd found it sitting down there in the dark. Right where Skewerax had said it would be. Quell's lip curled, at the thought of the daemon. His other patron. Skewerax was influential, if stupid, and all too willing to share what he knew with others. A fool, but a mighty one. And murderous – extremely murderous.

He padded towards a ladder descending into the heart of the war-machine and slid down it with a chitter of annoyance. Slaves and crew-rats scurried out of his path as he loped along the narrow gantry leading to the engine chamber.

Two armoured, fume-masked stormvermin guarded the chamber. The black-furred warriors stepped aside at Quell's gesture, though not without some hesitation. He hissed at them in annoyance, but chastised them no further. They were still Warpfang's warriors, and far more afraid of him than of Quell. Soon that might change, but for the time being the warlock engineer was content, if not happy.

After all, without Warpfang's generous supply of expendable bodies, he would never have managed to acquire the last element his glorious machine needed. He slunk into the chamber, and the oscillation overgrinder pulsed in its housing, as if in welcome. The dimensional orrery was composed of seven hundred and eighty-four separate parts, all handcrafted by the most dexterous of slaves, to his specifications.

The great orrery whirred perpetually, one ring within the next, even as the dais turned, thanks to the efforts of the slaves chained to its base. The motion of the gyroscopic orrery was what propelled the warp-wheel along on its course, keeping it balanced. But it was the artefact within the orrery that would make the warp-wheel the most dangerous war-machine in the mortal realms.

The spear hung suspended within the oscillating rings of the orrery. It was a long, black serpent of a thing, made from dark wood and darker iron. It seemed to drink in the light, and where its shadow fell, skaven slumped, listless. The blade was broad and leaf-shaped, like a hunting spear – meant for stabbing, as much as throwing. Strange sigils, which smouldered with a blue heat, were etched along the edge of the blade, and there were gouges on either side that resembled eyes.

Sometimes, he thought it might be looking at him.

The spear's song changed as he entered the chamber, and became almost mocking. Quell ground his teeth, annoyed. Inanimate objects shouldn't be able to look, or sing, or laugh, but somehow, the Huntsman did all three. The song was caused by a slight internal vibration, he thought, though he could only speculate as to the cause. He snatched up an iron discipline rod from nearby, and jabbed the weapon with it. 'Hush-quiet, you!'

The spear spun in its chains, and the song rose up like the growl of an irritated animal. Quell jabbed it again. The spear couldn't be hurt – it was just an artefact, after all – but it made him feel better to give it a whack now and then.

He tossed the rod aside with a satisfied growl. The spear was still singing, but much more quietly now. It was quite temperamental, for a weapon. Another thing Skewerax had forgotten to mention. Like the duardin who'd tried to steal their prize in Gorch, or the spiders even now infesting his machine.

In fact, the daemon had left a lot out. Quell peered at the weapon, studying it with an engineer's eye. The dull metal of the wide, leaf-shaped blade reflected no light and absorbed no heat. Indeed, it was cold. Colder than the waters of Gjoll, colder even than the void between stars. A cold fire, ever hungry, never dimming.

There was a terrible strength in the spear. A ferocity that even Skewerax acknowledged and respected. Quell knew little of the weapon's origins – only what his patron had deigned to share with him – yet he knew enough to recognise that the hand of a god had aided in its crafting. But its origins were of little interest to him.

No, what was interesting was that the spear was a transdimensional object, occupying all realms simultaneously. That much Skewerax had told him, though in words of fewer syllables. Cast the spear, and it would strike its target, wherever they were. It would pierce the veil between realms and travel endless leagues to find its prey. But it didn't return to the hand of its wielder – a serious design flaw, Quell felt.

Therefore he had improved it. It had taken him months to make the calculations, even as his agents – and Skewerax's – hunted for the spear's location, but he had completed them as the warp-wheel thundered through Gorch. With the spear connected to his oscillation overgrinder, it would carve a path through the realms and drag the warp-wheel in its wake. There would be no citadel he could not crush, no kingdom he could not grind to rubble. And Excelsis would be the first.

Warpfang had employed him to design a weapon capable of breaching the Bastion. And Skewerax had tasked him with finding and acquiring the Spear of Shadows. Quell, like any halfway intelligent warlock engineer, had combined both tasks, thus saving himself valuable time and energy. Only a skaven of his unmitigated brilliance could have conceived of it – a self-propelled weapon, capable of crossing the realms in the blink of an eye and crushing anything that got in its way. And soon enough, he would have the opportunity to commence the first true trial run.

'Yesss,' he hissed, gazing at the spear. 'We shall not waste you on a man-thing or a duardin-thing, no-no. We shall cast you at a city-burrow, yes-yes, and you shall take us there. The warp-wheel shall crush the walls of Excelsis, and then – the walls of every other man-thing city in the mortal realms!' He threw back his head and cackled wildly, shaking his paws in excitement. His laughter turned to curses as a spider fell onto his face from above, and his dreams of destruction were forgotten as he struggled to crush the skittering arachnid.

And in its nest of chains, the spear hummed to itself, and thought sharp thoughts.

'Greetings, Ahazian Kel.'

Ahazian jerked his steed's reins, forcing the animal to rear up as a shape wavered into being before him. A brightly coloured shape, delicate-seeming and crystalline, save where it was scorched black, and badly tattered. 'Sorcerer,' he snarled. He could smell the magics bleeding off the Arcanite.

'Barbarian,' the Arcanite replied. He stood in Ahazian's path, hands folded over the pommel of the curved blade planted before him. 'Any further insults to share, or might we speak as civilised men?'

'I see only one man here,' Ahazian said, calming the restive stallion. 'But speak your piece, sorcerer, and be quick. Some of us have things to do.'

'Yes. You seek the Spear of Shadows. As do I.'

'And who are you?'

'Yuhdak of the Ninefold Path.'

'Never heard of you.'

Yuhdak chuckled softly. 'No, I expect not. But I have heard of you, Ahazian Kel. Last hero of the lost Ekran. Kinslayer and regicide.'

Ahazian shrugged. 'What of it?' The sorcerer's image wavered in the steppe wind, like smoke from a fire. A sending, then. It was to be expected. Such creatures were cowards by nature, preferring to let others do their fighting for them. 'I know who I am, and I don't care who you are. State your business, or step aside.'

'I wish to make a bargain with you.'

Ahazian frowned. He briefly considered riding through the phantasm and continuing on his way, but decided to hear the creature out. 'What sort of bargain?'

'One that will enrich us both.'

'Speak plainly, or not at all.'

'I shall keep to simple words, then. We seek the same thing. With my help you will find it and claim it, in Khorne's name.'

Ahazian grunted. 'And what is in it for you?'

'The Three-Eyed King wishes to add the Eight Lamentations to his arsenal. After you have claimed them, you will wield your pick of them at Archaon's command.'

Ahazian laughed. 'And why would I do that? I do not serve him.'

'And who do you serve?'

Ahazian shook his head. 'That is my business.'

Yuhdak nodded obligingly. 'No matter. The two are unrelated. The master you serve today is not necessarily the one you serve tomorrow.' The Arcanite gestured, as if in invitation.

'Think on it, Ahazian Kel. You are a warrior without a war-lord. Archaon could be that warlord, and the wars you would wage in his name would be glorious indeed. Especially if you wielded one of the Eight.'

'And who are you to make such offers? Do you sit at his right hand, trickster?'

'I am no trickster, Kel. I am a pilgrim of chance, and a student of fate. I do not seek to bend or alter what is. And I do not make offers – I merely put forth possibilities. A wise man must keep all possibilities in mind, lest he be taken unawares.'

'And a brave man has no need of wisdom, for courage is a keener blade than any other.' Ahazian straightened in his saddle. 'What prompts this offer?'

'You are distrustful.'

'Of you?' Ahazian laughed. 'Certainly.'

Yuhdak chuckled. 'Wise.' He gestured to his blackened armour and tattered robes. 'My trail has been… difficult. I cannot overcome such obstacles alone. Thus I require aid to complete the quest the Three-Eyed King has given me.'

'If Archaon wishes for these blades, let him bargain with the Blood God.' Ahazian smiled. 'Or with me.' He glanced about, noting the dark shapes gliding through the air, high above. Ravens, watching. Circling. And he thought, ah, the nature of the game had changed again. So be it.

'Well, the sooner they are acquired, the sooner such negotiations can begin,' Yuhdak said. He reached up and touched the cracked surface of his helmet. 'The quicker the better, ideally. I am offering my aid, child of Khorne. Will you accept it?'

Ahazian pondered the being before him, and the vagaries of fate. 'It seems to me,' he said, 'that it is not I who needs aid, but yourself. Else you would not have come to me.' He leaned over the horn of his saddle. 'It is something I am not unfamiliar with, for many have sought my aid down the long road of years. And I say to you what I said to them – my arm is yours, for the right price.'

Yuhdak was silent for long moments. 'Archaon–' he began.

'Is not here, Arcanite. You wish my help? Then what do you offer? Will you help me achieve my goal?'

'Our goal is the same.'

Ahazian shook his head. 'I did not say which goal.' He laughed and straightened. 'I find myself considering the future, sorcerer. Too much time riding, not enough killing. Softens a man's certainties, and makes the path ahead seem fluid. Makes one consider – what did you call them – possibilities?'

'Ah,' Yuhdak breathed. 'I had heard that the Kels of Ekran were a single-minded lot.'

'Rumour and innuendo,' Ahazian said, bluntly.

'As you say,' Yuhdak murmured, bowing low. 'Let us bind our fates, blood-brother, even as the gods themselves once did. Who can say whether or not this is even as they intended? Not me. And I would not be so foolish as to try.'

'And the spear?'

'Khorne is a reasonable god, when all is said and done. And you are a reasonable man. We shall cross that bridge when we come to it.' Yuhdak lifted his blade. 'Do we have an accord, Ahazian Kel?'

'We do, Yuhdak of the Ninefold Path.'

Even as he said it, the sending wavered and vanished. He felt the flat of a blade tap against his leg, and looked down. His own reflection, stretched and distorted across the cracked facets of Yuhdak's helmet, looked up at him. Somehow, while he'd been distracted by the sending, the Arcanite had crept up behind him, and so silently that not even his horse had noticed. Ahazian growled, already annoyed with his decision.

'Good,' the sorcerer said, and Ahazian could almost hear his smile. 'I think this alliance shall prove fruitful for both of us, my friend.'

Volker leaned forwards and filled Oken's mug. 'Drink slowly, old one. There's plenty more where this came from.'

They sat once more in the hold of the newly repaired, much battered *Zank*, which was creeping its way through the skies above the Amber Steppes. The endrins did not hum like before, but instead rattled and groaned. The aethercraft did not slide across the sky, but instead wobbled and limped.

How Brondt and his crew had managed to get their vessel back into the air, let alone flying somewhat steadily, Volker hadn't dared to ask. It had been difficult enough convincing the Kharadron captain to follow the black trail the skaven had left, rather than returning to Shu'gohl as he'd intended. Only a promise of payment had seen him agree, however grudgingly, to press on.

Oken looked better than he had a few hours ago. Much of the colour had returned to his face, though he still looked abnormally thin. But then he'd never been heavy. He was broad, like all duardin, but age had sapped some of his mass. Shaggy hair, the colour of iron filings scattered across the snow, was held back from his sharp features by a simple rawhide thong, and his beard was plaited and bound by a copper cap. His spectacles balanced precariously on a nose that had lost all shape after one blow too many, and his hands trembled slightly as they clutched the mug.

Brondt had broken out something from the crew's stores – a strong mead, made in the northern hill-country of Chamon. There were flakes of gold floating in it, and it smelled strongly of honey. Oken sniffed it. 'Not my usual,' he grunted. 'But needs must.' He took a deep swallow. He looked at Volker. 'Grungni sent you, I suppose.'

'You're welcome,' Zana said. She sat nearby, with the others, save Roggen, who was on the other side of the hold tending to Harrow. The demigryph had sustained numerous minor wounds, but seemed little the worse for wear despite this. Her rumbling purr provided a quiet accompaniment to the conversation.

'I'll not waste thanks on someone who's getting gold for their trouble,' he said, casting a weary glare at her. She smirked and saluted him. The gesture was vaguely offensive, and Oken chuckled.

'Get on with it, grey-beard,' Lugash growled. 'You've wet your lips, now use them. Where's the blasted spear?'

Volker shot a glare at the doomseeker, but Oken seemed unaffected by the other duardin's tone. 'I told you. The skaven have it. Though Maker alone knows how they learned of it. But they did, and they came in force – hundreds of them, swarming through the branches and roots, burning anything that got in their way.' Oken closed his eyes and took a gulp of mead. 'We kept our distance, tried to stay ahead of them, but the forest was swarming with grots by then. We were forced to climb higher, to avoid getting caught in the crossfire.' He frowned. 'It didn't work. We lost Thunor and Kjarlsson on the second day. Skaven were everywhere by then, scampering after that blasted machine of theirs.'

'We saw the tracks – what was it?' Volker asked.

'Some sort of wheel, but armoured and big – bigger than it ought to have been. It rolled over gargants like nothing and left a trail of mashed spiders for leagues. Even the giant ones were no match for it. It just ground on, setting fire to the trees and tearing apart webs. If Gorch were drier, the whole forest would have gone up.'

Oken emptied his cup and extended it for a refill. Only after Volker had complied did he continue. 'We made it to the Heartwood Citadel in time to see the attack begin. Decided to take advantage of it, and slip in. The skaven beat us to it.' He sagged, tired. 'We fought them in the vault, but they had it before we even realised. And then...' He trailed off. 'None of the others survived, I suppose.'

Volker shook his head.

'Ah, well. Good lads, those. Their spirits will need singing into the Deep Halls.' Oken looked up. 'The ratkin have the Huntsman. Maker alone knows what their plans are, but we need to find them, and stop them before they do it.' He drained his cup and set it aside. 'Or worse, someone else gets to it first.' He frowned. 'It was... singing, down there, in the dark. Not so you could hear it, but you could feel it, deep in your bones. A sort of sick feeling.'

'The grots were frightened of it,' Nyoka said softly. She looked around. 'The stakes, remember?' Oken nodded and patted her hand, fondly.

'Aye, my lady. That they were. They could hear it themselves. That's why they sought to bind the ghosts of their enemies to stand guard over it, and left that big bastard spider down there in the pit.'

'What were they worried about?' Volker asked. 'The spear?'

Oken shook his head. 'Not the spear, but whoever it was calling for.' He frowned. 'The weapons seek out strong wielders. Like parasites, they're always on the lookout for a stronger pair of hands, a keener mind, a tougher body. They'll turn in a weak warrior's hand, if his opponent catches their fancy.'

'You make it sound as if they're alive,' Volker said.

'They are, in a way. Not smart, but... cunning. An animal cunning. That's why those old Khazalids, in their wisdom, decided to lock up the ones they had rather than try to put them to use. Can't trust a weapon with a mind of its own.' Oken pulled off his spectacles and held them up. The glass was scratched and cracked, and he sighed. He folded them carefully and slid them into his coat. 'And the Thunwurtgaz Lodge felt the same way. But it's out now, and in the hands of the enemy. The ratkin won't hold onto it for long, no more than the grots could. It's probably still singing – calling out for someone, anyone to wield it...'

Volker frowned. 'I think I know who's coming for it.' Quickly, he filled Oken in on their encounter with the shape changers in the Libraria Vurmis, and the Great King's sorcerous rider. The old duardin shook his head, his expression sour.

'We need to get to it first. If some Chaos filth gets it, and worse, knows what it is, they could very well decide to hurl it at Sigmar, or Grungni.'

'Or Alarielle,' Roggen said softly. 'The Lady of Leaves has been hurt much, these past centuries. I would not see her hurt again.'

'How chivalrous of you,' Adhema murmured. She smiled crookedly. 'You're missing the obvious target, of course.'

Volker looked at her. 'Who? Nagash, I suppose.'

Adhema laughed. 'No, fool. The Three-Eyed King.' She leaned forwards, her face half in shadow. 'This is not a war with two sides, or even three, or four. The enemy is not united, and there are those in their ranks who would see Archaon toppled from his throne just as surely as we would. It could be that our foes are his foes.'

'And so?' Lugash rumbled. 'What of it? They are still our foes.'

'As you say,' Adhema said, leaning back. 'It might be wise to consider all possibilities, though. Just in case.'

'And who does your mistress seek to slay?' Oken asked.

'I should have thought that would be obvious,' Adhema said. 'Anyone who gets in her way. A spear that can strike any target, even one in a different realm? My lady could change the course of entire wars with one death. Efficient, no?'

'That depends entirely on the death in question,' Roggen said.

Adhema smiled lazily at him and shrugged. 'Perhaps we see these things differently than you.' Her smile faded. 'Each of the Eight has a purpose. Gung kills, Sharduk breaks, so on and so forth. Who better than the Queen of Mysteries to see that they serve those purposes properly?'

'I can think of several people,' Volker said.

Adhema sat back. 'I bet you can, poppet. Starting with yourself.' She looked around. 'Let's not pretend any more, children. We are not friends. We are allies of convenience, at best. The gods fling us about and we dance at their command. This is but the newest game. And I intend to win it.'

'You're wrong.'

Volker blinked, realising suddenly that he was the one who'd spoken. He cleared his throat. 'You're wrong,' he said again. 'It's not a game. Not to me. Not to us – any of us. To them, maybe. To the enemy. But not even Nagash thinks this is a game. This is a war, for the fate of all things, and all who have ever lived or died are combatants. And the gods cannot win without us, even as we cannot survive without them.' He looked around. 'Some of us are here for pay – for honour – for promises made and desires unfulfilled. But all those things can be settled after the fact. Right now, we have common cause and an enemy standing in front of us. And that's enough.' He hesitated. 'Or it should be.'

Adhema laughed softly. 'Pretty words.' She lay down, hands clasped behind her head. 'Wake me when we find the enemy, Azyrite. Perhaps I'll have decided whose side I'm on by then.'

∞ TWENTY-ONE ∞
LION CRAG

Quell peered up at the monstrosity looming over him. It was not really there, being merely a trick of the warp light, but he thought it best to bow anyway. Prudence was the armour of the cunning. Especially against a being like Skewerax, the Frenzy that Walked.

The image of the Verminlord Warbringer was not so impressive as seeing such a creature in the flesh, but it was still quite imposing. The image rose from the crackling web of warp lightning being emitted by Quell's mechanisms. Quell's slaves and guards cowered, banging their snouts against the floor of the engine chamber or gnawing their tails to keep from screaming as the green light washed over them. One of the unlucky slaves working the oscillation overgrinder's dais was now utterly mad, and writhed mindlessly, foam dappling his jaws, as the others heedlessly trod him into paste. Quell poured a line of powdered warpstone across the knuckles of his gauntlet. He snorted it and thought calming thoughts.

It was hard. Just the sight of Skewerax was enough to drive lesser skaven into a killing frenzy. He crouched on powerful legs, his mighty claws braced on his knees, and glared at Quell, eyes blazing with divine madness. There were entire realms separating them, but Quell still felt the weight of that glare.

'Well?'

The word emerged from the daemon's mouth like a ballista bolt. Quell pawed at his nose for a moment, sniffling, trying to regain his composure. 'We have found it, oh Great Stabber-Slicer. Just where you said it would be.' It hadn't been, exactly, but Quell saw no reason to point that out. Skewerax had little patience for excuses, and less still for recriminations. One argued with the brood of the Great Horned Rat at one's peril.

'Yes-yes, of course it was. Am I not the most cunning of war-fighters, the most brilliant of planner-thinkers?' Skewerax pounded his chest with each assertion. 'None rival me. None can compare to my cunning-wisdom.'

'As you say, most murderous one,' Quell said, bobbing his head subserviently. Privately, he considered the verminlord's grasp of any strategy more complex than 'scurry-hurry' to be tenuous at best. But one couldn't be picky when it came to patrons. Especially patrons as generous – and as stupid – as Skewerax.

He glanced at the gift in question, checking to make sure it was where it was supposed to be. The spear still hung in its chains, its black tip hungrily soaking up the light.

The image of Skewerax leaned forwards. 'Give it to me.'

Quell's snout twitched. 'As you command, most assiduous of assaulters.' He paused. 'Did you mean now?'

The daemon's eyes narrowed. 'Yesss.'

Quell hesitated. 'It will take some time.'

'No. Throw it.' Skewerax bristled. His bifurcated tail lashed. 'Throw it, fool-fool.'

'At you, oh most puissant potentate of pain?'

Quell pre-emptively flinched, knowing what was coming next. Skewerax shrieked, baring his fangs in a grimace of frustration. He reached out, as if to throttle Quell. The daemon lacked Warpfang's patience. The old warlord was the soul of serenity compared to the Frenzy that Walked. Quell didn't particularly like either one of them, but he knew which he preferred.

But still – one couldn't afford to sneer at a daemonic patron. It was only by the good graces of Skewerax that Quell had managed to survive this long. The world was a dangerous place for a renegade skaven; even more so when one took his various crimes into account. He inhaled another lump of powdered warpstone.

He hissed in pleasure, eyelids fluttering. It wasn't his fault that the explosives he'd used to eliminate his rivals had collapsed an entire district of Blight City. And set the remains on fire. And then left it adrift in the void. There had been any number of unforeseen elements at play. Shoddy masonry. Substandard materials. Sabotage. It was obvious to anyone with half a brain that he was a victim of circumstance.

'Quell!'

Quell blinked and looked up. The verminlord had finished screeching. Skewerax held a struggling skaven dressed in gaudy armour in one paw. Quell didn't bother to wonder where the newcomer had come from. Skewerax had a tendency to wander into burrows and take command. The wriggling captive was likely one of old Warpfang's unlucky warlords. 'Yes, oh savage one?'

'You will hurl-throw the spear at this one – what is your

name, fool-fool?' Skewerax snarled, shaking his captive with bone-rattling force. The skaven whimpered something, twitched, and expired. Skewerax blinked and glared at the carcass dangling from his grip. 'Wait a moment – I will find another one,' the daemon grumbled, after what might have been an embarrassed silence.

'Or I could bring it to you in person,' Quell interjected. The powdered warpstone was singing in his veins now, crackling through him, lending him courage and cunning in equal measure. 'It will take some time, but you will be pleased, yes-yes.'

Skewerax peered at him. The daemon had only a dim grasp of the concept of time. 'Why?' he growled. Ropes of slaver dangled from his narrow jaws.

Quell gestured to the spear. 'See, oh mighty lord of war – by my genius have we made this infernal weapon into a source of power!' He threw back his head and cackled. 'Its realm-bending abilities have been bent to my – our, *our* – will.' He raised his fists and hopped from one paw to the other, excited.

'What?'

Quell paused, one paw lifted. 'We can throw it – and follow it,' he said, gesturing. 'The spear tears a – a hole of sorts in the membrane between realms, yes-yes? Which we can then roll through, mulching anything in our path!' Another cackle, wilder than the first. 'No fortress can stand before us, no mystical barrier or warded gateway! I – we, we – shall be supreme!'

'We can already gnaw holes, Quell,' Skewerax said heavily. 'Why do we need a new way to gnaw the holes?'

Quell twitched. 'Bigger holes,' he said hesitantly. Then, with a more certain tone, 'Bigger and more startling holes, yes-yes. In uncomfortable places, for the enemy.'

Skewerax stared at him. Then, 'I will find a new warlord. You will throw the spear at him. Then I will have the spear, yes-yes?'

'Or we could just bring it, and then you could see for yourself. I shall use it to crack the very walls of Excelsis.' Quell shook his fists at the sky, snout thrown back, whiskers a-tingle with righteous indignation and warpstone. 'The warp-wheel shall ride-crush the man-thing city, mighty Skewerax, and you shall be there to seize victory from their unworthy, hairless paws, yes-yes!'

'What is a warp-wheel?'

Quell twitched. 'A... weapon?'

'Another weapon? You have *two* weapons?' Skewerax's features swelled, and the rats shuddered in their cages. 'Give me the weapons!'

'I will bring them to you post-haste, oh mighty colossus of war,' Quell said, flailing in what he hoped was a placatory manner. 'Just as soon as we finish the de-infestation procedures. Any time now, yes-yes, quick-soon.' He hesitated. 'Relatively.'

'Relatively?' Skewerax snarled.

'Just as soon as we finish killing all of the spiders.'

Skewerax's reply was lost to the aether, as one by one the rats making up the farsquealer burst in their cages. Quell wiped blood from his robes and sighed in relief. Hopefully they'd be on the move by the time a new connection was established.

Outside the comforting confines of the warp-wheel, Lion Crag was a-buzz with activity. Repairs were being made to the outer hull, even as the last of the stowaway grot corpses were mulched and fed to the rat-ogres who operated the great bellows that kept the forge-fires burning. Smoke billowed from hidden vents as the warp-wheel was repaired, restocked and rearmed for the campaign to come. Soon enough, they'd be ready to leave.

Quell rubbed his paws together in excitement as he gazed up at the spear. 'Soon-soon, yes-yes, you will take us to the

killing ground. And then my genius shall be obvious to all.'
He bared his teeth.

'Even to stupid-stupid daemons and impatient warlords.'

'Tell me then, sorcerer, how badly did you lose your last fight?'
Ahazian Kel stared across the steppes towards Lion Crag. The
shock of stone rose high above the surrounding grasslands,
vomiting smoke from its various hollows and crannies. 'Must've
been very badly indeed, given the state of your armour and
robes. Was it the skaven, then?'

'No.'

Ahazian nodded. 'Good. I'd hate to think you were as weak
as that.'

'Weakness is in the eye of the beholder.'

'Yes. And I say you look weak.'

One of the ravens croaked warningly. Ahazian glanced at
them. The flock studied him watchfully; Ahazian returned the
favour. 'Are there really ninety-nine of them?'

'You know, I've never actually counted,' Yuhdak said. He
turned, head cocked. 'I suppose I should, at some point, just
to make sure I'm not being cheated.'

'But there might be more of them,' Ahazian said. 'Best not
to, unless you fancy being held to account for all those extra
blades.'

Yuhdak stared at him. 'Yes, thank you. Might I trouble you
for your opinion on our enemy?'

'There are a lot of them.'

'You can count. Well done.'

Ahazian chuckled. 'Careful, sorcerer. I might take offence
one day, and then where would you be?'

'Right back where I started, I expect.'

Still chuckling, Ahazian sank to his haunches and peered

again at the distant crag. It was a jagged fang of rock, shaped like an animal's tooth. It had been called Wolf Crag once, though how and why the name had changed, Ahazian couldn't say, and didn't care.

The crag rose over smaller hillocks of rough stone, an island amid the sea of grass that stretched out around it. The skaven had not attempted to hide their presence – the stony slopes had become riddled with tunnel mouths and bore holes. Smoke gouted from unseen vents, curling through webs consisting of rickety walkways and bridges strung between the natural turrets of the crag.

A heavy palisade of sloppily assembled wood and stone occupied one slope, but there was an open, black path right into the heart of the fortress. Something big had gone that way, likely the great war-machine he could see crouched among the highest cliffs. The ratkin had an appalling fascination for such devices, as if right weaponry would make up for their numerous shortcomings. 'It's a nest,' he said, finally. 'Probably a staging post, from the look of that machine. The skaven are fond of such things. Useless vermin with their useless schemes.'

'You mean like supply lines?'

'Exactly. What good's killing an enemy if you don't then eat his food and children?' Ahazian gestured dismissively. 'No sense of tradition, the ratkin.'

Yuhdak nodded. 'So I gather. What are your thoughts?'

Ahazian peered up at the sun, sniffed, and spat. 'Frontal assault would be easiest.'

Yuhdak waited, saying nothing. The deathbringer chuckled. 'No, didn't think you'd like that one.' He tapped the ground with the edge of his axe. 'But it's the most efficient means of accomplishing our goal. I can draw their attention, and you can swoop in and make the kill.'

'Where is the spear?'

Ahazian reached up to clasp the fragment. The song had grown louder and now echoed through every bone in his body. A murder-song, enthralling and divine. The spear was shouting to him, demanding that he find it, and wield it properly. He shook his head. 'Close. It's down there somewhere. I suppose you'll just have to follow me to find it, eh?'

Yuhdak nodded slowly. 'I suppose so.'

Ahazian stood and approached his steed. The coal-black stallion whickered in anticipation. It snapped at him, in friendly fashion. 'One last ride, my friend,' Ahazian said, stroking its neck. 'And then, perhaps, I shall set you free, to gallop these steppes and feast to your heart's content.' Or perhaps not. When a man found a horse worthy of him, it was foolish to let it go.

He swung himself into the saddle. 'Be quick, sorcerer. Or I shall kill them all before you get a chance to wet that growling blade on your hip.'

Yuhdak spread his hands. 'It will be as it will be, barbarian. I shall come on wings of shadow, with an army at my back.' He began to gesture, murmuring softly, and Ahazian felt the air grow stale and thick. Vague shapes became visible, capering silently all about them. Neverborn, drawn by the scent of fates aligning and opportunities seized.

Ahazian frowned and spat, then kicked his steed into a trot. Let the sorcerer play with daemons, if he liked. Ahazian preferred his own tools. He rode down the incline and turned his horse towards Lion Crag. The song of the spear rose riotously, drowning out all thought. He drew his skull-hammer and kicked his horse into a gallop. The black horse flung itself forwards, racing flat out, moving faster than any normal animal ought. The horses of the dead ran swiftly. Ahazian laughed.

He was still laughing when he passed through the first picket of skaven sentries, camped out in the blackened, crushed grasses. The ratkin gaped at him as he rode them down. Great gongs sounded, somewhere on the outer slopes of the crag, as someone noticed his approach. He bent low in the saddle and leaned left, sweeping his hammer out to catch a skaven warrior in the chest. The vermin tumbled through the air and fell with a crunch as Ahazian galloped past. He removed the head of another with a casual swipe of his axe.

Ratkin swarmed into view, scampering across the slopes and ledges of the crag as he reached the rocks. Gongs sounded and horns blew. Ahazian clashed his weapons together and bellowed a wordless challenge, drawing every eye.

As he passed through the shadow of the crag, he saw the first of the ravens dart down, swooping towards the ledges and caves. He smashed aside a barbed spear as it was thrust at him. His steed reared, shrieking in fury. Skaven raced towards him, chittering vilely. A dozen, two, a hundred. A tide of hairy bodies, boiling out of their warrens.

There was nothing to see then, but blood and slaughter.

'We're making good time,' Volker said, leaning over the rail. The trail below was as evident as it had been since they'd left Gorch. The skaven were not subtle creatures, for all their cunning. Their war-machine had burned a black swathe across the steppes, setting fires in its wake that choked the horizon with smoke. Wild fires roared below, engulfing the grasslands. It would take them days to burn out.

'We'd be a damn sight faster if the endrin wasn't on its last legs.' Brondt sounded gloomy. 'Took me a decade to hoard enough to pay for this heap. All gone now.'

'Grungni will make good on his debts, Brondt. He always

does.' Zana ran a stone across the edge of her sword. She sat on the rail, balanced against a strut. 'Trust me.'

'I'd rather trust the leech,' Brondt said.

Zana laughed, then coughed, as the aether-vessel passed through a column of smoke.

Volker eyed them, wondering, not for the first time, how they'd met. He said nothing, though. Oken joined him at the rail, still wrapped in his furs. He looked old and frail. 'A fine crew, lad. I bet you're starting to regret not staying in Azyr, eh?'

Volker smiled. 'Not yet.'

Oken chuckled. 'It'll happen.' He sighed. 'I regret it myself, sometimes.' He leaned against the rail, eyes half-closed. 'I'm worn out, lad. Rubbed thin and raw by this life.'

'But you're alive,' Volker said softly. 'Grungni sent me after you.'

'Grungni sent you after the spear,' Oken said flatly. He looked at Volker, his gaze hard. 'Never mistake pragmatism for compassion. The gods have an excess of one and precious little of the other, I've found.'

Volker touched the amulet around his neck. 'If they did not have compassion, they would not be fighting for us now. And they would not inspire us to fight for them.'

Oken shook his head. 'Stubborn. Like your mother.'

'You're as much at fault as she is.'

Oken laughed. 'True enough.' He shook his head. 'Perhaps I shouldn't have taught you so many of our ways.' He patted Volker on the arm. 'Ruined you, probably. Fragile minds and bodies, you humans.'

Volker smiled. 'You kept me from becoming someone neither of us would have liked, I suspect. Another spoiled Azyrite brat, looking to carve his name on the heart of the world.' He laughed. 'And now, I am in service to a god.'

338

'As are we all,' Nyoka said, from behind them. She smiled down at Oken. 'I am pleased that you survived, Oken. This harsh realm would be poorer for the loss of a scholar such as yourself.'

'And a fine compliment that is, from yourself.' Oken grunted suddenly, and staggered. His face was white and worn. Volker moved to catch him, but the duardin waved him back. 'I'm fine, boy. No need to fuss.'

'You are still weak, from the arachnarok's venom. You should rest.' Nyoka spoke firmly. Oken frowned at her.

'Not you as well. I am no beardling. I need no nursemaids.' He pushed past them. 'I'm going below. Not because you said, mind. Just because I'm tired of the view.' He pulled the furs tight about himself and stumped off.

'He is strong. He will recover, in time.'

'If there's time.' He looked at her. 'Do you hear Sigmar's voice?'

'Sometimes.'

'Now?'

'No.' She looked away. 'I hear him in my dreams, I think. A great voice, tolling down like the peal of a bell, made from starlight and thunder. He showed me things, in my dreams. Showed me what must be, and what will be.'

'Aren't those the same thing?'

'Not always,' she said. She rubbed at her eye, as if it pained her. 'That is why I came, I think. He spoke to me, before your arrival, and told me that I must go. That if I did not, what must be would be rewritten. That I must be prepared for what was to come, and ready to do what must be done.'

'I don't think I understand.'

'Nor do I. But I have faith.' She gave him another placid smile. 'You are worried.'

'Aren't you?'

'No.' She lifted her hammer and held it up to the light. Volker saw a worm coiled there, with the face of a god; Sigmar's face, on the body of a great worm. He shivered – it was no wonder Calva was as upset as he was. Nyoka continued, seemingly unaware of his unease. 'Worry is for those who lack faith, Owain. My faith guides me in all things. That Sahg'mahr does not speak, does not mean that he does not show me the way. Even when the realms were sealed away from one another and caught in the chains of Chaos, he was with us.' She brought the hammer to her lips and kissed the face emblazoned on it. 'We have but to listen, and hold fast to our faith.'

'Easier said than done,' Volker said.

'If it were easy it would not be a matter of faith.' Nyoka tapped the head of her hammer against his chest. 'Always remember that.' She smiled again, widely. 'Faith is the road on which the righteous march to victory.'

'That one I've heard before,' he said. She laughed, as alarm bells sounded. Someone had spotted something. Volker saw a looming rock formation, sharp and jagged, rising from the grasslands ahead. He looked for Brondt. 'Captain…?'

'Ha! I thought so.' Brondt stood nearby, leaning over the rail. 'They've repopulated Lion Crag, the vermin. I knew the Azyrites hadn't dug deep enough. The one thing about the ratkin you can count on, there're always more of them than you expect.'

'Lion Crag,' Volker muttered. He hadn't been there, but he'd heard the stories of the fang-like splinters of rock rising from the steppes. The free-standing tower-like mesa resembled nothing so much as the jaw of a beast, with crooked turrets of stone, in place of teeth. It was hollowed through by curving tunnels, worn smooth by the passage of feet. It had been occupied, in one form or another, since the Age of Myth, its name changing to suit its owners.

It had been called Wolf Crag during the Realmgate Wars, before three warrior chambers of the Lions of Sigmar Stormhost had decimated themselves purging it of its bestial masters. The Hundred Herdstones that had been raised in the crag's shadow had been toppled, and the Wolf-Kings with them, but with the beastherds gone the skaven had moved in. The ratmen had burrowed up from below, as the forces of Azyr built their defences. When the ratkin had at last erupted into the half-finished citadel, a new war had been waged on the ashes of the old.

It had not been the sort of victory that bards sang of. More, a grudging stalemate. Lion Crag had been left a scalded ruin, the last Volker had heard. Apparently, that was good enough for the skaven. Brondt glanced at him. 'Your folk are good at the destruction, but not the follow-through. It takes more than collapsing some tunnels and burning a few vermin to exterminate the ratkin.'

Struck by a sudden thought, Volker began to calculate distance. He cursed. Nyoka nudged him. 'What is it? What do you see?'

'The old trade roads.' Volker pointed. 'It's a straight line from Lion Crag to Excelsis. That's why we had to drive the beastherds out in the first place – it was the only way to re-establish those early trade routes with the worm-cities. It was why the skaven wanted it, as well. At least that's what everyone thought. But they never made any raids that anyone knew of.' He looked at Zana. 'What if they had different plans in mind?'

She groaned. 'Of course. They wanted some place to construct that device of theirs. And close enough to Gorch to use it to claim the spear.' She rubbed her face. 'They've been planning this for a while.' She shook her head. 'Grungni isn't going to be happy. If the ratkin have known about the weapons this long, there's every likelihood that they're looking for the others as well.' She frowned. 'They might even have already claimed some of them.'

'So? Just sounds like it makes them easier to find, to me.' Lugash strode across the deck, scratching his cheek with his war-iron. The doomseeker had been prowling about since they'd left Gorch, unable to relax. Volker knew how he felt. 'Skaven are sneaky, but not that sneaky.' He peered over the rail. 'How many are down there, do you think?'

The explosion lit up the sky, sending a ragged scar of reds and yellows across the black. Zana whistled. 'Fewer now, I expect.' Another explosion followed the first. Something was happening. Volker looked at the others.

'Looks like we're not the only ones who followed them.'

TWENTY-TWO

BATTLE OF THE CRAG

Volker looked at Brondt, as another explosion lit up the sky. Whoever – whatever – was attacking Lion Crag, they weren't being quiet about it. 'We need to get down there.'

'Are you mad?' Brondt demanded. 'I just got this thing sky-worthy – I'm not taking it down there to be destroyed!'

'You won't have to. Not for long, at least.' Zana had a speculative look on her face.

'You've got a plan, I expect.' Brondt shook his head. 'What am I saying? Of course you do. Well, we're out of most everything that burns or explodes.'

'You've got a contingent of Grundstok Thunderers on board,' Zana said. 'And your crew.' She scratched her chin. 'Besides, once the skaven get a look at this heap heaving to out of the clouds, they'll scatter. If they're not busy fighting whoever is already down there. All we have to do is find the spear – we're not trying to win a battle.'

Brondt puffed on his cheroot in silence for a moment. Then,

'You can put it to them yourself. Stonehelm isn't a member of my crew, and I can't order him to do anything he doesn't want to do.'

'I thought what the captain said goes,' Zana said.

'And if he wants to remain captain, he'll make sure he says the right thing.'

The Thunderers gunnery sergeant was a bluff, burly, shaven-headed duardin named Stonehelm. He had a sharply cropped ginger beard shaped like a spade, which he tugged on as Zana made their case. Stonehelm had a hard look in his eye, one Volker normally associated with freeguild officers – a sort of flat acceptance of the world, and all its obvious faults. Especially those standing in front of the officer in question.

Stonehelm frowned as Zana finished her pitch. The Thunderer held his helmet under one arm and tugged on his beard again. 'It's suicide. Worse, we're not being paid for it.' He glared at Brondt, who glanced at Zana, and gestured.

'The Grundstok company can bill the Azyrites for services rendered,' Zana said. She knocked her knuckles against Volker's chest. 'He's a gunmaster. He'll be a witness.' She grinned. 'Better, he's your employer.' She shushed Volker as he made to protest. 'Besides – think of it as a social obligation. You see a fire, you put it out. You see a skaven – kssht.' She ran her thumb across her throat. 'It's just neighbourly.'

Stonehelm laughed. It wasn't a pleasant sound. He looked at Brondt. 'She has a point, your human.'

'Not mine.' Brondt was nodding, though. 'There's still a bounty on skaven tails in the worm-cities,' he added, speculatively.

Stonehelm laughed again. He spat in his palm and held it out. Zana did the same. 'We have a contract,' Stonehelm said. 'We'll kill rats for you, but the rest...'

'We'll handle it, never fear,' Lugash growled, running a thumb along the edge of his axe. A bead of blood welled up on his thumb and he stuffed it into his mouth. He looked at his thumb. 'Still not clear on how exactly, though.'

'Horns of the bull,' Volker said. 'A two-pronged assault – one group on the ground, the other by air.' Before Brondt could protest, he continued. 'I've seen Kharadron land troops atop walls before. Landing on that war-machine shouldn't be much more difficult.'

Oken laughed and slapped his knee. He'd come back up on deck with the others, unwilling to sit out preparations. 'That's the Azyrite way. Why attack one place, when you can attack two?' He bent over, coughing, and Volker went to him. The old duardin caught his wrist. 'I'm fine. Bit of venom left in me. Stop worrying.'

'I'm not worried,' Volker said.

Oken snorted. 'You've always been a worrier. It's why you make a good gunmaster.'

Volker hesitated. Then, 'We haven't had much chance to–'

Oken waved him to silence. 'I taught you better than that. There's a time and a place, and down in a mine isn't it.'

'We're in the air.'

'Same difference,' Oken said, dismissively. He looked at Volker and tapped the side of his head. 'Concentrate, boy. Eyes on the target. Nothing else is important.'

'Eyes on the target,' Volker said. He turned. 'I'll lead the attack on the machine. Captain…?'

'Aye, lad. We'll see to it.' Brondt expelled smoke through his nostrils. 'Bit of cut and thrust never bothered us.'

'I'll go as well,' Zana said, before Adhema could speak.

Lugash clashed his weapons together. 'And I as well, man-ling.' The doomseeker was almost vibrating with excitement.

Roggen crossed his arms. 'I will go with Stonehelm. Harrow will be of more use in the open than in some cramped machine.'

Nyoka rested her hammer in the crook of her arm. 'I will accompany Roggen.'

'As will I,' Adhema said, finally. She grinned at Zana. 'Three and three, eh? Gives us all an equal chance of finding what we came looking for.'

'And if you find it first, you're welcome to try to escape with it,' Volker said, cutting any argument short. He thumped the deck with the stock of his long rifle. 'I suggest running very swiftly.' He looked around. 'And I suggest we make ready. And pray.'

'Save your prayers, lad,' Brondt said, bluntly. 'I've found that the gods are usually on the side of those with the most guns.'

Volker nodded. 'And failing that, the best shots.'

Once the decision had been made, things moved quickly. The *Zank* swung east, manoeuvring to approach Lion Crag from the cover of the clouds. Adhema winced slightly as the sun crept across the deck. The day was brighter here, the light fiercer, than in Shyish. Age lent strength to the body of the soulblighted. She could walk in the light, though not for long. Armour helped. Shadows helped more.

Despite the annoyance, she was excited. The promise of battle always had that effect. Even more so when victory was within her grasp. She licked her fangs, thinking of the celebration to come. Perhaps Neferata would allow her to cast the spear, as a reward for her diligence. She could think of a hundred possible targets, and was imagining one such when the big knight interrupted her. Roggen leaned forwards, hands gripping the rail. His eyes were on the fire below. 'The Lady of Leaves has

346

little tolerance for your kind. Something that is not dead, but should be – it is offensive to her.'

'And what do you think?' The question came unbidden to her lips. Curiosity, perhaps. The knight had saved her. Unthinking bravery, or simply a coincidental destructive urge? 'Am I offensive?'

Roggen grinned. He was missing teeth. Not through neglect, she thought. A history of violence was writ on his features. A more interesting story than that of the Azyrite, at first glance. 'Not to me. But then, I am a simple man. I fight. I do not judge.' Another explosion from below drew his attention and he leaned forwards intently. His pulse jumped, and she felt something close to kinship, even as she imagined the taste of his blood on her tongue.

'Simplicity is best,' she said. 'Leave judgement for the gods.'

'Yes,' he said, tearing his eyes away. 'Come. We go below. It is almost time.'

She gestured elegantly. 'Lead the way.'

Down below, in what the Kharadron called a deployment hold, they found Nyoka awaiting them, alongside Stonehelm and his Thunderers. The duardin glared at her, but none of them protested. She noted with some amusement that they gave both her and the demigryph an equally wide berth. 'Predators of a feather,' she murmured. The demigryph grumbled at her, its tail lashing. Animals rarely tolerated the scent of the undead.

As the *Zank* lurched into position, the sides of its hull scraping against the jagged cliffs of the crag, the Thunderers braced themselves. The ready-orb, mounted high above the cargo hatches, blinked, and Stonehelm began barking orders to his warriors. There were more than a dozen of them, divided into two fire-teams. 'I want a fast drop. Ironwall formation, centred on Nhar. Eyes up and out. If you see anything bigger than a jezzail, give a shout. We all know the ratkin like their toys. Hamfist…?'

'I'll keep the big yuns off'n, gunnery sergeant,' a heavy duardin, hunkered behind the blast shield of an aethershot cannon, answered. 'Me an' Helga.' He patted the cannon fondly. Adhema snorted and traded looks with Roggen.

The big knight sat in the saddle, the reins gathered in his hands. He patted the demigryph's neck, calming the restive beast. 'We shall take the lead, I think.'

'Aye, if you like,' Stonehelm said. 'Just don't get in our way. I want a clean deployment zone. No foul-ups.' He turned, fastening one of his warriors with a glare. 'That goes double for you, Big Mad Drengi. Don't think I don't see you fondling that cutter of yours. We stay out of the chop, lads. That's for greenskins and manlings.'

Drengi, a smallish duardin, muttered something, but nodded as Stonehelm's glare remained steady. 'Aye, gunnery sergeant. No chop.'

'I trust you don't have any aversion to us doing so, however,' Adhema said. Her keen hearing had picked up the whining ping of small-arms fire ricocheting off the lower hull. The skaven had realised by now that a new player had entered the game. Stonehelm fixed her with a stare. Then he smiled.

'Oh no, by all means – chop away. Just stay out of our line of fire.' He shrugged. 'Or don't. Your choice.' The ready-orb pulsed again, washing the hold in crimson light. 'That's it. Get ready. Blowing hatches in three… two… and…'

The trio of hatches set into the slope of the hull swung open with loud clanks and the grinding of unseen cogs. The sound of battle was no longer muffled, and Adhema could hear the crackle of warpfire and the screams of the dying. The landscape below was a blur of sandy brown, split by green streaks and azure slashes. Roggen thumped Harrow into motion before the first Thunderer had moved, and the demigryph sprang through an open hatch with a snarl. Adhema followed, laughing.

She struck the ground lightly, and was moving before the dust of Harrow's landing had settled. She relished her speed, and the way the ratkin twitched and fell to pieces in her wake. In Shyish, the skaven were considered abominations – Nagash had declared them unworthy of life, or what came after, and they were to be destroyed utterly. Exterminated like the vermin they were.

From behind her, she heard the clatter of the descent-ladders unfurling. She glanced up and saw the Thunderers descending, their gauntlets sparking as they slid to the ground. Nyoka was among them, mouth moving in what Adhema assumed were prayers. She shuddered slightly. Prayers had no place on the battlefield. Death ground belonged to Nagash, whatever the inclinations of the combatants.

She stepped aside as Roggen galloped past, roaring out a war-cry. The demigryph bowled over a trio of skaven before lunging to meet a bellowing rat-ogre. Skaven scuttled in every direction, throwing up clouds of dust, fighting black-clad warriors or daemonic shapes. The stink of Chaos hung heavy over the slopes, and warp-flames raged in the depths of the crag, causing stockpiled ammunition to cook off and ricochet about the battlefield.

A high-pitched cackle caused her to turn, and she saw gambolling pink-fleshed daemons swing and leap among the walkways and gantries above. The creatures were fleshy night-mares, with leering features marking their wide torsos, and massive, grasping hands flapping at the ends of too-long arms. They stuttered forwards on bowed legs, chortling and shriek-ing. One mass of shifting, gangly limbs bounded towards her with an excited squeal.

She ducked beneath its lunge and chopped through its torso, splitting it in half. Pink flushed purple, before fading to blue, and the chuckling monstrosity collapsed into two smaller, squabbling shapes. She kicked these aside and turned, as the shadow of the *Zank* passed overhead, sliding towards the rounded shape of the skaven war-machine.

Yuhdak gestured, and a skaven screamed as his spell twisted it into a new and more monstrous shape. Its flesh burst and boiled, erupting in scabrous tendrils, even as its torso split, revealing a newly made maw of dagger-like teeth. The skaven-thing fell on its comrades, ripping and tearing with unnatural hunger. Yuhdak left the spawn to its feeding and pressed on, trailing warpfire from his hands.

He felt a strange sense of peace at times like this, when there was no greater objective in the moment than to ride the wave of chaos over the enemy. He felt the strands of binding that connected him to the daemons he'd summoned twitch and hum, as the creatures set about indulging themselves. The writhing lesser daemons were fashioned from raw warp stuff, and eager to entertain themselves with the more solid inhabitants of the mortal realms. They served to occupy the skaven well enough, while the Ninety-Nine Feathers saw to more pragmatic concerns.

He'd considered summoning such creatures earlier, but the effort was tiring, and he had no intention of making any more pacts with the Neverborn than was absolutely necessary. While some adepts could drag daemons from the Realm of Chaos through sheer brute strength, he was not one of them. Instead, he bargained – or failing that, wagered – with them. This for that, tit for tat. A favour here, a favour there. Luckily, lesser daemons were rarely capable of thinking beyond their own immediate gratification.

Yuhdak turned, unleashing a gout of coruscating flame with a twitch of his fingers. A rickety-looking wooden watchtower convulsed and bent, becoming something horrible and hungry. It gnashed the skaven who'd occupied it to red, wet rags with splintery teeth, before lurching awkwardly after new prey. Yuhdak laughed gaily. It pleased him no end to bring new life into the world.

A different sound intruded on his good cheer. The hard bark of duardin guns. He spun, searching the battlefield, and cursed as he saw a familiar shape sliding through the sky above. He lifted his hands, intending to bathe the vessel's hull in witch-fire and send it crashing to earth. But before he could loose the spell, something struck him in the belly, driving the air from his lungs and the words from his mind.

He staggered, wrenching his sword from its sheath, driving his attacker back. Words lashed at him – holy words, spoken in a panting rush. The woman came for him again, two-handed hammer raised. A blinding aura suffused her, making him wince. The power of Azyr flowed through her, and it made his soul ache to be near it. He recognised her, if dimly – a priestess, then. 'Vampires, lunatic duardin, and now a fanatic – the Crippled God chooses strange tools,' he said, backing away.

'It is not for us to question the gods,' she said. She paced after him. 'I know your stench. You sent your feathered assassins to desecrate our holy fane, witch. For that, you must deliver an accounting.'

'And who are you to judge me?'

'You have already been judged,' she said, with a serenity that irked him. 'And I am the sentence.' Her hammer snapped out, almost faster than he could follow. He ducked back, startled. She whipped towards him, allowing him no respite, giving him no chance to gather himself. She spun, catching him in the side. He skidded, barely managing to remain on his feet, and whistled once, sharply.

A pink horror leapt for her, out of the smoke. She struck it in the face, pulping it. Its unnatural flesh smoked where her weapon struck it and it sagged back, deflating with a maudlin sigh. Two more daemons flung themselves at her, chortling. As she fought, the light within her grew brighter, almost blinding, and he felt a shiver in his soul.

This was no simple fanatic. This was something else. As she moved, something moved with her – a great shape, guiding her, lending her strength. A shape made of starlight, and the sound of rattling swords. 'Changer give me strength,' he murmured. Was this a test, then? Had he been sent here for some reason other than the obvious? The sword in his hand wailed as it sensed the god-light.

A daemon burst into flame and crumpled. She stepped over its burning remains. 'Judgement cannot be denied, only postponed.' Her voice struck him like a barb, and he tensed. 'Perhaps Sigmar has guided me here to be the instrument of his wrath. I make no assumptions. I merely follow his will.' She sprang forwards in a swirl of robes and a rattle of armour, hammer raised.

The air split as several black, feathered shapes shot past him, intercepting the priestess. The ravens swooped and pecked, causing her to falter. Several twisted into bipedal shapes, attacking with blades rather than beaks and talons. The priestess spun one way and then the next, holding them back through sheer momentum. But only for a moment.

A raven darted in, swooping towards her face. An instant later she screamed. The hammer fell from her grip and she stumbled, clutching at her face. A sword blow scraped sparks from her war-plate and knocked her to the ground. Black boots pinned her arms. Yuhdak laughed softly.

'Then it is his will that you die, I suppose.' Ravens settled on his shoulders as he strode towards her, lifting his blade.

Ahazian Kel cursed, and split the stormvermin's skull with a single blow. Without bothering to wrench the axe free, he hauled the twitching body up and swung it at the other skaven, knocking several sprawling. He was on them a moment later, skullhammer snapping down. The survivor tried to crawl away, squealing in terror. Ahazian took two steps and caught up with it. He stamped on its back, pinning the black-furred ratkin to the ground. 'That was the best horse I ever stole,' he growled, before removing its head.

He turned, watching as the black stallion-thing kicked its last. The skaven's jezzails had been lethally accurate, and even the horses of the dead weren't immune to warpstone bullets, fired at high velocity. The animal lay amid the remains of its killers, having crashed into them in its death throes. Ahazian felt a flicker of regret. Soon enough, it was snuffed out by the relentless song hammering through his soul. The hunter's song, the murder-song. It tugged at him, drawing him towards the towering wheel-like war-machine that loomed amid a network of rope bridges and temporary gantries, stretching from the surrounding rocks.

Skaven seethed in its shadow. Armoured stormvermin had formed up into disciplined phalanxes, their shields planted, awaiting him with spears lowered. He laughed softly. He'd broken shieldwalls before. Jezzail-fire plucked at the ground near his feet, kicking up dust. He glanced up, eyes narrowing. Skaven slunk across the high ledges, moving to better positions. As they did so, black-clad shapes dropped down among them, blades singing. The Ninety-Nine Feathers were moving again, even before the bodies fell. The ravens swooped overhead, croaking, seeking further prey.

Ahazian grunted and shook his head. He took a step towards the stormvermin, but was beaten to the punch by a raucous pack of horrors. The pink-fleshed daemons capered past, filling the air with oily flames of a hue drawn from the mind of a lunatic. The flames splashed against the raised shields of the skaven, causing them to run like water and drenching the rat-kin with splatters of molten metal.

With an annoyed growl, Ahazian loped through the carnage, leaving the daemons to their play. Let Yuhdak's pets enjoy the fruits of the killing field. He had greater rewards to reap, at any rate. The fragment rattled against his chest-plate and tugged at its rawhide thong. He followed its pull, killing anything, skaven or daemon, that got in his way.

Daemons crawled over the machine's hull, and were unceremoniously shot off by skaven snipers, or burnt to greasy motes by the machine's weaponry. But more pink horrors swung chuckling about the guy-wires that held the immense wheel firmly anchored to the rocks, or scaled the crag, seeking skaven to burn or throttle. Yuhdak had summoned a small army, though some of them were already wavering back into the void from which they'd sprung. Daemons couldn't long maintain their hold on the realms, even in places like this, befouled as it was.

When he reached the machine, he took the crude wooden steps up to the closest open hatch, two at a time. Jezzails fired from the upper walkways, and a bullet struck his shoulder-plate, nearly knocking him from his feet. He snarled and hurled himself through the hatch, just in time to meet the skaven rushing to close it.

'Too late,' he growled. The skaven immediately scrambled in the opposite direction, biting and clawing each other in an attempt to be the first through the closest bulkhead. Ahazian followed. That was the direction in which the fragment was pulling him in. The slowest of the vermin died first, then the next slowest. Whip-wielding overseers goaded panicked clan-rats through cramped corridors into his path. He met them with savage elation, and his weapons hummed in his grip, well-pleased with the slaughter. The axe in particular seemed to be enjoying itself.

Ahazian tightened his grip on the weapons, and felt the thorns dig into his flesh, somewhat affectionately. 'Do not worry, my friends, I shall not forsake you when I have the spear. You shall taste blood – seas of it – when the Huntsman is mine. We will carve a hole in the realms, you and I.'

He pressed on, hacking through squealing skaven and trampling the rats that fled across his path. Warning klaxons screamed, warring with the spear's song for his attentions. And then, sooner than he'd expected, he was there.

The spear hung suspended in a nest of chains, screaming his name above a dais being turned by a number of hunched slaves, beneath a whirring orrery around which warp light-ning crackled. As the rings of the orrery passed through one another, Ahazian saw strange sights stretch, solidify and fade into crackling excrescence. At one point, he thought he saw the familiar sight of the Felstone Plains in Aqshy, but dismissed it as more skaven trickery. Several stormvermin raced forwards to intercept him. The big, black-furred skaven leapt upon him, hacking and screeching.

Ahazian met them, the spear's song on his lips.

There were enemies everywhere. Just… everywhere.

Quell felt as if he were going to vibrate to pieces, so intense was his anxiety. Warning klaxons squealed and his assistants ran back and forth, attempting to look busy. He hunched forwards, gnawing on his tail, trying to focus. The warp-wheel shuddered, and sparks cascaded down from the rat-cages above, carrying with them the stink of burning hair and flesh. The battle outside was taking its toll on his lair. He could hear it, even through the thick hull of the warp-wheel. He shouldn't have been able to. That meant some of the hull plates hadn't been reattached.

They also weren't moving. That was more important than the hull plates. As long as the warp-wheel was moving, nothing could stop them. No foe could catch them, and any who got aboard could be run down and killed by his warriors. But when they weren't moving… well. That didn't bear thinking about.

Quell spat out his tail and reached for a squealing-tube. 'Vex! Where are you, fool-fool? Have you cornered them yet?'

'No, most worshipful warlock,' came the static-y reply. Vex sounded nervous. Quell's anxiety redoubled. He'd sent his assistant out to take command of the defence personally. That Vex had time to reply was a sure sign he was hiding somewhere, rather than seeing to his duties. Understandable, but annoying.

'Why not?'

'They've – ah – they've cornered us.' A crash reverberated through the squealing-tube, causing Quell to wince. 'But we are regrouping, your magnanimousness! We will have them soon enough, yes-yes.' Another crash followed this boast. And screams. Many-many screams. And daemonic giggling.

Quell flung the tube away with a panicked snarl. He bared his teeth at the crew, trying to reassert his superiority. He was beginning to suspect that some among them might be responsible for the current predicament. That was the time-honoured way of advancement among the Clans Skryre, after all.

He snorted a knuckle's worth of warpstone, trying to induce brilliance. The dust blazed through him, as thoughts coalesced.

The warp-wheel was trapped where it was, for the time being. Unless… yes. Yes! That would work. 'Geniussss,' he hissed.

The spear was the answer. Where it went, the warp-wheel would travel as well. If he could just get the machine moving, then they could escape, possibly even relatively intact. Whatever else, the warp-wheel must be preserved. And its creator with it.

'Alert-command the engineers,' he screeched. 'Whip-lash the slaves! Activate the oscillation overgrinder! Set the warp-wheel into motion, now-now!'

'It's starting to move, lad,' Brondt yelled. 'We'll have to be quick. If they catch us before we're down…' He trailed off. Volker didn't need him to finish. The *Zank* hung just above the war-machine. Through the open hatch below him, he could see the immense, wheel-like machine shuddering into motion, preparing to propel itself away from Lion Crag. Temporary walkways twisted and shattered, hurling unlucky skaven and giggling daemons alike to the ground far below. The great, grinding wheels began to churn against the ground as exhaust ports vomited a noxious smoke.

He swallowed and took hold of the ladder. The weighted ends thudded against the hull below, unable to find purchase. With a quick prayer, he began to descend. Halfway down, he let go and dropped to the hull. The vibrations shook up through his legs and wrenched his spine, knocking him onto all fours. He began to crawl towards the hatch. He heard the others descending behind him, but he kept his attentions focused on the hatch. Just as he reached for it, the hinges squealed and it flipped open. A snarling, verminous snout poked out. Volker lunged.

He slammed into the skaven and followed it down through the hatch. The creature gave a strangled screech and flailed at him. As they struck the gantry below, it clawed for the blade thrust through its belt. Volker wrapped his arm around its neck, braced himself, and twisted. Bone popped and the skaven went still.

He heard a whistle and looked up. Zana crouched at the top of the hatch. 'Well done, Azyrite. I thought you gunmasters didn't like getting your hands dirty.'

He shoved the carcass away. 'We work with what we have.' He hauled himself to his feet as the others climbed down.

Lugash dropped to the gantry and gave the corpse a cursory kick. 'Neatly done, manling.' He stepped over the body, weighing a throwing axe in his hand. Alarms were blaring somewhere. 'Sounds like we're late to the feast.'

'Or right on time,' Zana said. She stepped to the edge of the gantry, sword drawn.

Volker looked up at the hatchway. 'Brondt...?'

Zana shook her head. 'We barely made it down ourselves. This thing is already rolling away from the crag. Feel it? We're on our own. We'll be lucky if the *Zank* is waiting for us when it's time to go.' She looked around. 'Now, if you were a magic bloody spear, where would you be?' She started down the corridor, after Lugash. Volker hefted his long rifle and followed.

'Somewhere under heavy guard,' he said.

'Good,' Lugash grunted.

They found the first bodies a moment later, and Volker realised the skaven he'd killed had likely been trying to escape the slaughter. The stink of death hung heavy over everything, and blood painted the hull and deck. Mangled skaven lay everywhere, in various states of mutilation. Someone – or something – had torn a path straight through them.

They followed the trail of dead down through the swaying, rattling corridors of the war-machine. Sparks rained down occasionally, cascading across them, and more than once Volker was forced to brace himself against the wall as the machine lurched one way or another. The internal lighting system flickered, and entire passageways were plunged into darkness, lit only by the warpstone tumours flickering on the flesh of the rats in the cages that hung above certain junctions.

To Volker, who knew the sound of a healthy mechanism, the whole construct seemed one step from flying apart. The dank corridors, leaking pressure pipes and nonsensical gauges stuck at seemingly random junctures offended him in a deep and somewhat spiritual way. 'How is this thing even in one piece?' he muttered, as they picked their way through a thicket of badly patched hoses made from reinforced intestine. Some sort of faintly glowing lubricant spurted through the hoses, going gods alone knew where.

'Luck of daemons, the ratkin,' Lugash said, shoving a loose pipe aside. It cracked, venting a foul-smelling steam that instantly corroded a nearby section of wall. 'Like orruks, only worse. I've seen them cobble together fire-throwers from three rats, some bellows and a bit of warpstone.'

'Well they can't tighten a rivet to save their lives,' Volker said, as his foot went through a section of gantry. Zana caught him before he fell. 'Look at this – shoddy construction. I'm surprised it doesn't shake itself apart.'

'It might well do. Feel the way it's juddering? And listen to those klaxons – I think something's very wrong.' Zana looked around. 'Do you hear that?'

Volker did. It was like a leaky boiler, building to full steam. But there was another sound beneath it – a low, feral sort of hum that resonated in his bones and at the base of his skull, and he felt a chill as he remembered what Oken had said about the spear. About how it had almost seemed to be singing. The air had turned greasy, and motes of off-putting colour danced before his eyes. He was beginning to feel nauseous.

Lugash licked his lips and spat. 'Sorcery.'

'Worse,' Volker said. 'We should hurry.'

'We don't even know where we're going,' Zana reminded him.

'Follow the singing,' he said, only half in jest.

Several times they ran across panicked skaven, hurrying one way or another. The ratkin rarely made a fight of it, and Volker found himself thinking of an old saying of Oken's – rats deserting a flooding mine. The skaven were heading for hatches, fighting one another to be the first one through the narrow apertures. Though just where they thought they were going, given that the machine was moving, he couldn't say.

The trail of death ended at the entrance to what could only be the engine room. Heaped corpses lay scattered about the bulkhead, and the air was thick with a yellowish steam from several ruptured pipes. The sound had grown so loud that Volker feared his teeth might rattle loose from his jaw. Tendrils of crackling energy raced through the steam cloud, as they warily entered the chamber beyond.

Volker's eye was immediately drawn to the teetering shape of the massive orrery that dominated the heart of the chamber. Its spinning rings dripped incandescent smoke, within which blisters of flickering light took shape. The air heaved with shifting, phantom images – places and things that Volker couldn't identify. He felt a hot breeze blowing down from Aqshy, and a chill wind howling up from the depths of Shyish.

At the heart of the orrery, a black shape twisted, like a shadow caught in a cage of light. As it writhed, the orrery sparked and the images faded, only to be replaced – jungles rose from dissipating lava flows, castles crumbled and were replaced by black pyramids, swirling, star-born palaces turned, dissolving into brute barrow-lands. One image after the next, faster and faster. 'The spear,' he muttered, as he realised what he was looking at. 'They're using it as a-a power source?'

'Skaven, manling, you have to ask?' Lugash said. 'And not for long – look.'

They were not the only intruders – a towering, crimson-armoured figure fought through a crowd of desperate skaven, wading towards the dais and the orrery. 'That's not who I was expecting,' Zana said, ducking aside as a chunk of skaven struck the wall behind her. 'Who in the silver hell is that?'

'Does it matter?' Volker said. He spun, thrusting the stock of his rifle into the snout of a skaven as it lunged towards him. More of the ratkin had noticed them now, and seemed to prefer fighting them to dying at the hands of the hulking warrior.

'Not particularly,' Zana said, parrying a serrated blade and driving her elbow into a hairy windpipe. She plunged her sword through the skaven's heart as it staggered back, clutching at its throat. 'Lugash – make us some room.'

'Gladly.' The doomseeker bounded forwards, runes gleaming. Skaven scattered, losing their sudden eagerness for battle. Volker moved quickly towards a section of the deck that had been ripped up, likely by the crimson warrior's axe. He'd seen Bloodbound before, but usually not so close. The servants of the Blood God were best kept at a distance. He was close enough to smell the miasma of old slaughter that clung to this one – a deathbringer, as some of the steppe tribes called them.

As he took up his position, the deathbringer clambered up onto the dais and thrust his weapons into the orrery. The axe and hammer caught the whirling rings, and in a shower of sparks, he pried them apart. The mechanisms that controlled the motion of the device whined in protest, and ground uselessly against one another, belching broken cogwheels and warpfire as the deathbringer forced them wide. Metal bent as he wedged the hafts of his axe and hammer in such a way as to pin the orrery rings in place. Then, with a guttural laugh, he reached for the spear.

'He wants a spear now,' Lugash growled.

'*The* spear,' Zana said, as she tore her sword free of a dying skaven.

'I see that,' Volker said. He balanced his rifle on the section of broken plating, and cocked it. 'Now let me concentrate.'

Lugash cursed and scrambled forwards, chopping skaven from his path. 'Sit there if you want, manling, but I'm getting that spear.' Zana cursed and reached for him, but he was too quick. He hurtled towards the monstrous warrior, bellowing a challenge.

Volker didn't waste breath trying to stop him. He just had to hope that the doomseeker wouldn't get in his way. He took aim – and fired.

∾⊂⊃ TWENTY-THREE ⊂⊃∾

THE HUNTSMAN

Adhema crept across a ledge high on the southern face of Lion Crag, her mouth thick with the taste of arcane blood. She'd fed on one of the raven-warriors to sate her growing hunger, and the blood had been spiced with sorcery. It was a curious taste, lacking in the sourness one usually found in such corrupted individuals; perhaps it was down to the form the corruption took. Something to investigate another time, she suspected, as she paced along above the battle.

The skaven had, for the most part, fled the moment their great war-engine had begun to lurch away. Between the daemons and the Thunderers, they'd quickly lost whatever stomach they had for battle. Now the three-sided struggle had narrowed to two, as Stonehelm's warriors pitted their accuracy against the capering changespawn.

Despite her disdain for the cloud-grubbing duardin, Adhema was forced to admit that they were formidable, in their way. Stonehelm's warriors had formed a compact firing line on the ground, and were keeping the daemons at bay with an efficiency born, no doubt, of experience. Even so, the end was clear enough to one with the wit to see it. The duardin, for all their prowess, would be overwhelmed eventually or forced to retreat.

She looked up, searching for the *Zank*. The aether-ship was in pursuit of the slowly rolling war-machine. She wondered, briefly, whether the others had made it aboard, and whether they'd found the spear. It hadn't been in any of the caves she'd searched during the fighting. She hissed in growing frustration and turned her attention back to the battle below. A tawny shape caught her eye, and she leapt from the ledge, down the slope, following it.

The demigryph bounded from rock to rock, moving with animal grace. Her fur was matted with blood and ichor, but her strength was undimmed. Roggen hunched low in the saddle, a weapon in either hand. The knight had fought with brutal joy, and Adhema had come away with a wary appreciation for his skill. Part of her wished to see the carnage a full lance of such warriors could inflict.

The knight seemed to have found new prey. She followed from above, curious. The demigryph pounced, bearing a daemon to the ground and crushing it. Roggen lashed out with mace and sword, driving back others, until he'd cleared a path to – ah.

Adhema sank to her haunches and smiled. The priestess. Nyoka was down, surrounded by raven-warriors, her face a crimson mask. Roggen had spotted them. Harrow crashed among them, scattering the feathered warriors. A blast of sorcerous fire alerted her to the presence of the crystal-helmed sorcerer – Yuhdak, he'd called himself.

She crouched, watching as Harrow was knocked sprawling

by the blast, hide smoking. Roggen staggered free of the saddle as the raven-warriors converged on him through the smoke wafting across the field. She sprang quickly down the rocks, intercepting one. Her blade punched through the warrior's back and out his chest before he registered her presence. She could not say why she was bothering to intervene. The fewer of Grungni's servitors who lived, the fewer she might have to kill later.

But the thought displeased her. It grated against the shards of honour that remained to her. And in any event, she owed the knight a debt. He'd saved her. So she would save him. Fair was fair.

She crossed blades with a second warrior as Roggen dispatched a third. He hadn't noticed her yet, his eyes locked on Yuhdak. He crushed his opponent's skull and sprang at the sorcerer, roaring. Yuhdak gestured, and purple fire enveloped Roggen's hand and forearm as the mace descended. The weapon burst like an overripe fruit, and the haft coiled about the knight's arm. It burrowed into his flesh, sprouting pale thorns.

Adhema winced as Roggen screamed and fell back, his arm burning with the raw heat of change. The flesh of his hand ran like water, merging with the weapon, sprouting delicate gossamer fins and clumps of blinking eyes.

'No,' Roggen snarled, and raised his sword. He brought it down, chopping through his own forearm with one blow. She blinked in surprise, impressed despite herself. Few mortals had the stomach for such measures. His malformed limb flopped like a dying fish as it sprouted jointed legs and the bleeding stump ruptured into a leech-like maw of glinting teeth. Cradling his wounded arm to his chest, he hacked at the pulsing lump of meat.

'Fascinating,' Yuhdak said as he watched. He extended his hand. Changefire quickened about his fingers, and motes of purple and azure swirled through the air. 'What will you do, I wonder, when I transform your other arm? Will you gnaw it off, like a beast?'

'If I must,' Roggen panted, face pale with pain. The smell of his blood, like sweet nectar and wet bark, wafted towards her. She beat aside her opponent's blade and caught him by the throat. A flick of her wrist was enough to snap his neck. She let the body fall, intent on getting to Yuhdak.

Before she could, however, Harrow, her fur blackened and her feathers seared away, gave a screech and leapt. Her iron-hard beak clamped down on Yuhdak's shoulder and he gave a startled cry as the demigryph jerked him from his feet and flung him aside. Before he could rise, the beast was on him, her talons tearing through armour and robes alike. Yuhdak screamed and lashed out with his blade. Harrow squalled and lurched back, before slumping wounded to the ground.

Yuhdak clambered to his feet. 'Filthy animal,' he hissed, gesturing with his bloody blade. 'I'll make something more useful out of you, beast.'

'You will do nothing,' Roggen roared, as he lunged forwards. Their blades crashed together. Even wounded, the blood draining from him, Roggen was fast. And strong. Every blow rocked the slimmer, lighter sorcerer back. But for every one blow Roggen landed, Yuhdak landed two. It was taking its toll, Adhema saw. A few moments later, after a wild blow, the knight staggered and sank to one knee, chest heaving. Yuhdak raised his blade.

Adhema darted forwards, through the smoke. Her blade slid up, between the plates of Yuhdak's armour. He grunted in shock and made to backhand her. Adhema ducked nimbly beneath the blow and stabbed him again. Another thrust, and the sorcerer staggered. She grinned as the circling daemons began to thin and fade.

She paced after him as he stumbled away. 'You're not the one I am after, but given the insult you delivered me in the forest, I'll settle. Perhaps I'll draw up what's left of your soul afterwards, and make it my hound.'

'No,' Yuhdak hissed. He flung out his hand, staining the air with his blood. The substance of reality bubbled and split, revealing giggling, grinning pink faces. Long arms, topped by overlarge paws, stretched out, clawing for the vampire, gripping at her arms and legs, drawing her inexorably towards the gap in the air. A voice rose up a moment later, and the faces wavered and vanished as the spell was broken. Adhema staggered, off-balance, and turned, seeking the cause of her salvation.

Nyoka was on her knees, leaning against the haft of her hammer, one eye a swollen ruin, but the other gleaming with fervour. Voice hoarse and cracked with pain, she croaked the words of a prayer. The few remaining daemons wavered and burst, like soap bubbles. Adhema met her gaze and nodded in thanks.

When she turned back, Yuhdak was gone. She snarled a curse, and whirled, seeking any sign of him. But the sorcerer had vanished. She turned back to the others. Nyoka had dragged herself towards Roggen, who lay limp on the ground. Adhema went to them, the smell of the knight's blood thick on the air. Nyoka had torn off a section of her robe, and was using it to bind up the knight's wounded limb.

'Will he live?'

Nyoka looked up. 'If Sahg'mahr wills it.' She gave a weak smile. 'He is strong, though. Like a tree. He can afford to lose a branch or two.'

Adhema sneered and bared her teeth. 'Good enough, I suppose.' She heard a clatter and saw bulky shapes moving towards them through the smoke. Stonehelm and his Thunderers – those who'd survived their fight with the daemons. A sudden explosion caused her to turn.

The skaven war-machine hadn't got far. It wobbled on its axis, venting fire and smoke, seemingly about to topple over. She glanced at Nyoka as another explosion ripped through the great machine. 'Best keep praying, priestess. I have a feeling Volker and the others might need it.'

Volker fired. He cursed a moment later as Lugash slammed into the deathbringer, knocking him back, and out of the ball's path. The ball struck the rim of the orrery and ricocheted into the device, bursting the chains that held the spear in place.

The great black blade swung down, slicing the air with a lingering hiss of what might have been satisfaction. Lugash roared and reached for it, leaving his war-iron embedded in the deathbringer's shoulder. The deathbringer caught his wrist and wrenched the doomseeker away, slamming him face-first into the dais. The Khornate warrior drove a bone-rattling kick into the dazed duardin's side, sending him rolling down to the deck. He turned and reached for the spear. Gung twisted in its chains, stretching towards the warrior.

'Zana,' Volker shouted as he tossed aside his rifle and drew his repeater pistols. Skaven scampered past him, seeking to escape. The former freeguilder was already darting up onto the dais, sword out. Her blade slashed down, drawing blood from the warrior's thickly muscled arm. He roared and reached for her throat, catching her next slash with his bare hand. Her sword snapped in his fist as she ducked beneath his clawing grip. Still holding the jagged stump of the hilt, she went for him again, seeking to drive what was left of her blade into his exposed throat.

The deathbringer slammed the broken tip of her blade down, through her forearm. Coins clattered free of the vambrace as Zana screamed. She snatched a knife from her belt and sank it into her opponent's exposed thigh. 'Shoot him, Volker,' she gasped.

The deathbringer roared and slapped her from the dais, to join Lugash in a heap on the floor.

Volker shot him. Both repeater pistols exploded in fire, filling the air with lead shot. The deathbringer jerked back with a bellow of pain and surprise. He flailed backwards, hand groping. Even as Volker tossed aside his emptied weapons and clawed for the artisan pistol in his belt, the Spear of Shadows slid unerringly into its new wielder's hand. The warrior's fingers snapped shut about the black haft and he tore it free of the remaining chains with a triumphant snarl. 'Mine,' he howled. 'Mine – at last.'

He turned to Volker, his eyes burning with a fierce mirth. He fingered one of the impact craters that now marked his war-plate. 'That didn't work out like you hoped, did it?'

Volker said nothing. He cocked the artisan pistol.

The deathbringer paused. 'You think you can beat me, little man, with your silly little guns?' he said, contemptuously. 'I am Ahazian Kel. I have weathered the fire of the Tollan Cannonade, and the Thunder-wagons of Kursk. What can one gun, or two, do to me, that a thousand could not?'

'Depends whose finger is on the trigger,' Volker said, as calmly as he could.

Ahazian chuckled. 'Maybe so. But I don't have to get close to you, to kill you.' He raised the spear and looked down at Zana. 'What did she call you – Volker? Yes.' He whispered to the quivering black blade. Volker felt a wrenching sensation deep within him, as if something had torn loose. The eldritch runes carved into Gung's wide blade glowed with cold fire. Time seemed to slow. Volker levelled the pistol, his finger tightening on the trigger. Ahazian Kel swung the spear about. It left his grip with an eager hiss. The air parted before it, peeling away from that hateful blade.

Everything stopped. Volker stared at the spear, so close and yet so far away. His death, frozen in time. Gung had not fed in a thousand years, and it wished to enjoy its meal. Time and space were nothing to it, and they folded about it like ragged shrouds. It crept towards him, stealing through the moments between them like a ghyrlion slinking through the tall grasses. His limbs felt leaden, heavy with years yet unlived. It was all he could do to finish pulling the trigger. Thunder boomed. Fire burst from the barrel of his pistol, momentarily blotting out the shadows clinging to the spear.

Gung undulated closer, slithering towards him like some great black snake. Time was narrowing. Volker watched his pistol ball spin slowly past the spear, firm on its trajectory. He took a step back. Then another. It was like swimming through mud. And with every step the spear got closer. Closer. Until, at last, he could feel the heat of the blade. Time, stretched to the breaking point, snapped back. Only one chance.

Volker darted towards the oscillating rings of the orrery, towards the hazy images of other places, other realms. The spear hissed over his shoulder with a snarl of frustration. He took the steps of the dais two at a time. Gung hurtled after him with a hungry scream. He caught at the thorny haft of Ahazian's axe, still holding the quavering rings pinned, and threw himself forwards, ripping the axe free as he fell.

He felt a lurch, as if he were being pulled in several directions at once. Colours filled his vision and he was enveloped in heat and ice all at once. Frost dappled his coat and a fiery heat burned his skin. He saw stars, red clouds and amethyst wastes, all bleeding into one another, and vanishing in the blink of an eye. Something black and hateful shot towards him through the shifting madness. It was not a spear, not really. It was something else, masquerading as a spear. A mote of cosmic filth, stretching out towards him across every realm, hungry for his death.

Desperate, he flung a hand out and caught hold of one of the now spinning rings. The metal burned through his glove and blistered his hand, but he held on regardless as he was wrenched upwards, towards the throbbing orifice in the fabric of space. His arm and shoulder protested and he felt muscle tear, deep inside. He let go at the apex of its circuit, and fell through the hole. Somewhere below him – or perhaps above him – he heard a frustrated cry, as Gung plunged deeper into the ever-shifting realms.

Volker hit the deck hard and rolled limply, his uniform steaming, his heart hammering. He'd lost his pistol in the jump, and the axe as well. He tried to push himself up. As he did so, he heard a scream. Blearily, he scanned the chamber, and saw Ahazian Kel stagger back, clutching at his eye. Volker's last shot had struck home. The deathbringer sank to one knee, still howling. Blood poured between his fingers and puddled on the floor.

'Still alive, Azyrite?'

Volker looked up, into Zana's bruised features. She wiped blood from her chin and offered him her good hand. He took it, groaning as the burns on his palms flared agonisingly. 'We need to get out of here,' he coughed, leaning against her. The arm he'd used to hang on sagged limply by his side. Even as he spoke, the oscillating portal creaked on its dais. Energy lashed out, tearing through the walls and floor, reducing metal to slag. Volker shoved Zana aside and fell over her, as a lash of energy swept through the air where their heads had been. She screamed as he jostled the blade that still pierced her forearm. 'That thing is going to blow,' he said, by way of apology.

'I guess you'd know,' she said, trying to haul them both to their feet. Everything was coming apart around them. Conduits burst and pipes ruptured, spewing a noxious steam into the air. The orrery was spinning off-kilter now, wobbling madly on its dais, casting warp lightning in every direction. A strong wind tore at them, howling, as if the orrery were trying to draw them into the shimmering vortex growing within its spinning rings. 'Come on, Azyrite – get up!'

Volker bit back a scream of his own as he jostled his injured arm. He wasn't able to stop himself a moment later, however, as a red-armoured hand burst through the steam and smoke to latch onto his arm. Ahazian Kel's grisly features appeared a moment later. 'The spear,' he snarled. 'Where is it, maggot?'

He wrenched Volker from his feet and hurled him to the floor, hard. Something snapped inside Volker and he felt like a punctured water skin. As he rolled over, he saw Zana bring a knife down against Ahazian's vambrace. The blade snapped, and the deathbringer caught her by the throat, slamming her back against the wall. 'Where is my spear?' the warrior roared.

'No spears here, filth. Just axes.'

Ahazian turned and staggered as one of Lugash's throwing axes sprouted from his chest. The doomseeker barrelled through the smoke, bloody mouth twisted in a wild grin, his beard whipping wildly in the wind. 'Did you think we were finished, daemonspawn? We're only getting started!' Axe in hand, Lugash drove the deathbringer back, one wild sweep after the next. Debris flew through the air about them as they struggled, drawn into the void within the orrery.

Zana crawled towards Volker. 'What does it take to put him down?' she hissed, as she tried to drag him upright with her good arm. Volker cursed and clutched at his side. The wind caught at them, nearly pulling him off his feet. He saw the corpse of a skaven tumble past and fly into the void, on a journey to gods alone knew where.

'More than we've got. Hopefully Lugash can keep him busy.'

The doomseeker's body bounced past them, to vanish into the smoke. Volker couldn't tell whether he was still alive or not. He and Zana stared as Ahazian staggered towards them, fighting the pull of the vortex, bleeding, missing an eye, chopped to the bone, but still standing. The deathbringer flexed his hands.

'I won't kill you, mortal. Gung will come for you, sooner or later. It's a matter of when, not if. But by the end, you'll be praying for its arrival, this I swear.'

Volker glanced at Zana. 'Can you find Lugash, and get to the hatch? Any hatch?'

'I – yes, maybe. What are you planning?'

'To give him what he wants. I need this.' He caught hold of the shard piercing her forearm and jerked it loose. She yelped in pain as he shoved her towards the bulkhead, and turned, letting the current of the vortex catch him. Palming the chunk of steel, he tumbled towards the deathbringer. Ahazian staggered back, startled, as Volker crashed into him.

'Are you mad?' he growled.

'No, just desperate,' Volker gasped. He flicked the chunk of metal up and rammed it into the deathbringer's ruined eye socket, twisting it as deeply as he could manage. Ahazian screamed in agony and clubbed Volker to the deck. Pain exploded through his arm and head, but as he fell, Volker swept the deathbringer's feet out from under him. Ahazian fell, and then was hurtling backwards, unable to stop himself. He caught the edges of the orrery and for an instant Volker thought the deathbringer might manage to drag himself free of the howling void. Then the orrery rings bent and burst, and Ahazian Kel was gone.

A moment later, Volker was on his way to joining him. Even with the orrery crumpling in on itself, the vortex was still there, still growing. And he couldn't muster the strength to fight its pull. He closed his eyes as he began the slide to oblivion.

His eyes sprang open as he jerked to a sudden, painful halt. He twisted, looking back, and saw Zana holding onto the back of his coat with her good hand. Lugash held her wounded one, and had his axe embedded in the frame of the bulkhead. 'That's two favours you bloody well owe me, Azyrite,' she shouted. 'Now shift yourself, you great lump.'

Despite the black spots crowding the edge of his vision, Volker did. Slowly, they hauled themselves out into the corridor, the void-born wind clawing at them with increasing ferocity. Inside the chamber, warp lightning erupted from the remains of the device, running across the walls and floor. Metal crumpled in on itself as it was ripped from the frame and drawn into the whirling vortex at the heart of the orrery.

They staggered to the closest hatch as the war-machine shook itself to pieces around them. Volker couldn't tell whether it was part of the ceiling or the wall, as everything around them seemed to be changing position rapidly. Lugash smashed it open, leaving bloody prints on the metal. The doomseeker was a mass of shallow wounds, his helmet lost, a bloody gash matting the hair on his head.

He gave a bark of laughter and flung out a hand, as if signalling for something beyond the hatch. A moment later, he caught hold of Volker and dragged him up. 'Reach, manling – your life depends on it.'

Blearily, Volker saw a dangling ladder, and the familiar face of Brondt, hand extended. The *Zank* was keeping pace with the war-machine, but only just. Aether-smoke gouted from the vessel's endrins, staining the air. 'Hand, lad, give me your hand,' Brondt shouted over the roar of the wind. Volker reached and nearly fell. The ground raced by below, smashed into broken chunks by the war-machine as it sped along, even in its death throes. 'We can't keep pace for long,' Brondt roared. Lugash cursed, caught hold of Volker and flung him out of the hatch. Volker hit the ladder and tried to grab hold, but his arm refused to cooperate. Brondt caught him and dragged him up. 'Where's Zana?' the Kharadron demanded.

'I've got her,' Lugash snarled. He leapt from the shuddering hatch, Zana clinging to his neck. He scrambled up the ladder after Brondt and Volker.

Zana grinned up at Volker from Lugash's back.

'Some fun, eh, Azyrite? Never a dull moment, working for Grungni.'

'Is it always like this?' he said. The *Zank* pulled slowly away from the war-machine. The great engine was folding in on itself, as if it were deflating. He winced as the metal screamed and buckled.

'Sometimes it's worse,' Zana said. She flinched as the war-machine gave a shriek of bending metal and popping rivets. Volker blinked stars from his eyes and sagged against the ladder, feeling more tired than he could ever remember. He looked down at Zana as another explosion sent chunks of the dying skaven war-engine hurtling in all directions. 'Two favours, huh?'

'Two,' she said. 'And I will collect, Azyrite, you mark my words.'

'Glad to see you're happy,' Brondt called down. He grinned at Zana, and her own smile faltered. 'And speaking of favours, you owe me three now, Mathos.'

Aboard the dying warp-wheel, Quell realised something had gone catastrophically wrong when he felt his throne beginning to pull loose from the deck. Metal groaned and burst. His crew squealed in panic. Deck plates were ripped free of the frame and drawn away from the command chamber, deeper into the warp-wheel. Everything was shaking, coming apart at the seams.

Rivets burst from the hull, whipping backwards. Several of his warriors fell, heads and chests pierced by the flying rivets. Their bodies rolled across the floor, sliding back into whatever was growing within his war-machine. Quell clutched his throne tightly, as if he might be able to keep it in place through sheer will.

A section of the hull frame slammed down close by. The massive beam bent backwards with a screech, nearly taking his head off. He could hear the familiar roar of the oscillation overgrinder now. Something had caused a power surge. Instead of propelling the warp-wheel through the dimensional membrane, it was drawing it in – and not as a whole, but piece by piece. He slammed a paw down on his throne.

'Sabotage,' he shrieked. His throne rocked back, caught in the pull of the overgrinder. It was the Blighted City all over again. Someone was trying to deny him his rightful glory. 'Was it you?' he demanded, glaring down at the crew-rat clinging to his throne. The skaven chittered a protest. Quell crouched on his throne and kicked the hapless creature off. The skaven squealed piteously as he was dragged away to his well-deserved doom. A moment later, he was joined by several other members of the crew, most of whom were still clinging to their seats, or part of the hull.

The hum was growing louder. The overgrinder, chewing away at the fabric of the realm. Quell ran the calculations. Definitely sabotage – but who stood to gain? Warpfang? No. Skewerax? Possibly. Daemons were sneaky, even the stupid ones. Perhaps especially the stupid ones. The warp-wheel was doomed, regardless.

The thought made him want to gnaw his tail to a bloody stump. He had wasted precious months building the device, only to have it snatched away now, on the eve of his greatest triumph. Someone would pay. But first – escape. Quickly, he dropped into his seat and reached for the straps. His was the only seat with them, for a very good reason. It was the only seat designed to be anything more than what it appeared to be.

The first rule of being a warlock engineer – always have a way out. He tightened the straps and tore away the padding on the frame, revealing a heavy switch. He hesitated. He'd only ever tried this on slaves, and it hadn't ended well for them. Then again, what choice did he have? He looked up as the top of the hull peeled away, revealing open sky. Baring his teeth in fright, he thrust the switch down. Fat sparks stung his paw as the hidden launching mechanism growled to life. Warpstone springs contracted with a screech. Quell closed his eyes as his throne exploded upwards, towards the sky.

As he hurtled to safety, his invention at last surrendered to the inevitable and exploded with an ear-splitting shriek. Fading tracers of lightning shot across the steppes following the chunks of wreckage, scorching striated paths through the grasses.

He tumbled skywards, caught in the updraught of the explosion, paws fumbling at the controls of the ejector seat. He had to deploy the parachute before gravity caught him in its treacherous grip. As the sky and ground juxtaposed themselves with dizzying speed, Quell caught sight of an aether-craft pulling away from the funeral pyre of his genius.

A faint thread of satisfaction pierced the all-consuming fear. He had been right after all. It had been sabotage. Well, they would pay. They'd all pay. He shook a fist at the departing craft, even as he caught hold of the lever to deploy the chute.

Another gut-churning lurch and he was spinning gently towards the ground. Below, only a smoking crater dotted with wreckage remained of his grand design. The war-machine, and all that it had contained, was gone.

But Quell still lived. And while he lived, he could–

Something croaked above him. He twisted in his harness. A raven perched atop his throne, watching him with a beady black eye. It croaked again, and he wondered why it sounded so much like laughter. More croaks echoed from all around him.

Quell turned, glands clenching.

The rest of the ravens were waiting for him.

TWENTY-FOUR

SEVEN WEAPONS

Several days later, Owain Volker placed his hand palm-up on an anvil.

He'd been drifting in and out of consciousness for days since their return to Excelsis. Even now, he was sleeping more than he was used to. But he still felt tired. The pain was to blame for some of that, he thought. The ache of healing bones and bruised flesh. But the rest of it was due to the dreams. Nightmares, really. Of something seeking him, across the dark seas of infinity. Sometimes it was the Great King. Other times, Ahazian Kel.

But mostly, it was Gung. The Spear of Shadows had his scent and was on the hunt.

'Will this work?' he asked.

'If it didn't, we wouldn't be wasting our time,' Vali said. The ancient duardin caught his wrist in a vice-like grip and placed a rune, crafted from gold, right in the centre of his hand. 'Now hold still,' he said. He looked up at Grungni. The god stood nearby, waiting, his hammer over his shoulder.

'You may proceed, grandfather.'

Volker closed his eyes, and forced himself not to flinch away as the god raised his hammer. There was a sound like the bark of a cannon, and pain plunged through him, up his arm and into his brain. He staggered, but Vali refused to let him fall. The hammer struck again, and again, and Volker couldn't help but scream as the rune was driven deep into his flesh. After the third strike, he was allowed to slump. He cradled his hand. Despite the pain, nothing was broken.

Vali sneered down at him. 'No stamina.'

Volker caught hold of the anvil and pushed himself to his feet. He didn't bother to reply. Instead, he stared at the rune embedded in the meat of his hand. It flickered strangely, taking on a new and different hue with every flex of his fingers. The old duardin stepped back, and turned to Grungni. 'If you're done, I have duties to attend to.'

'Go, Vali.' Grungni watched his servant stump away and then looked down at Volker. 'Gung will hunt you, until it has you. That is its purpose. But its captivity weakened it, and your quick thinking saw it lost to the seas between realms. It will seek you, but this rune will change your scent, in a manner of speaking. Whatever realm you stand in, the spear will think you are in another. Thus it will pursue, but never catch.'

Volker looked at the god. 'Runes like this don't last forever, do they?'

Grungni frowned. 'No. But for the time being, it will do.'

Volker nodded, trying not to think about it. 'The others?'

Grungni set the head of his hammer atop the anvil. 'More or less in one piece. Roggen has returned home, so that he might heal in familiar surroundings. I offered him a hand of silver, to replace the one he'd lost, but he declined. He claimed he would plant the seed of a new hand himself, and return when it had sprouted.' He shook his head. 'A funny folk.'

Volker shook out his hand, trying to ease the ache. 'Zana and Nyoka?'

Grungni leaned forwards on the haft of his hammer. 'Somewhere. Both seem disinclined to leave my service at the moment, despite everything.' He paused. 'The priestess is healing, though I'm told a missing eye takes some getting used to.'

'Did you offer her a new one as well?'

Grungni smiled. 'I did. She seemed less than enthused by the idea. Mayhap Sigmar will tell her it's all right to accept gifts from other gods, when he gets around to it.'

'And Oken?'

'Here, boy.' Oken stepped out of the shadows of the smithy, leaning heavily on a cane of iron and bronze. 'Still in one piece, unlike some others I could name.' He looked up at Volker. 'I thought I told you to be careful.'

'I'm not dead.'

'That's not the same thing.' The old duardin shook his head. 'You didn't ask about the vampire, I noticed.'

Volker frowned. Adhema had vanished before they'd returned for Roggen and the others. She'd simply... slipped away. 'No. I didn't.' Then, 'Any sign of her?'

Oken snorted. 'No. Though I have no doubt she'll show up again, like a bit of grit in the gears.' He looked at Grungni. 'How long?'

The god sighed. 'I do not know. If he keeps moving, perhaps forever.'

'You don't know?' Oken said. He frowned and rubbed his face. 'My apologies, Maker. I did not mean...'

Grungni smiled. 'You did, but it is understandable.' The smile faded. 'There is much about these weapons of which even I am ignorant. They are mysteries, and I do not like mysteries. They must be studied before they are reforged.' He looked at Volker, and there was cool speculation in his gaze. 'So long as he lives, Gung will seek him. And as long as Gung seeks him, no one else may claim it.'

'I'm bait,' Volker said, mouth suddenly dry. 'Bait, and a failsafe in one.' He looked at the rune in his palm, and wondered at how such a small thing would keep him hidden from the black hunger that hunted him.

'Aye,' Grungni said, ignoring Oken's glare. 'You are. Is it a burden you are fit to bear, gunmaster?'

Volker hesitated. Then, he nodded. 'It is, Maker. However much time is left to me, is yours.' He flexed his hand, and then pulled on his glove. 'There are seven other weapons out there. Seven shots, to turn the tide, for one side or the other.' He smiled thinly.

'A gunmaster only needs one.'

And why did you choose to slip away, rather than stay?

Neferata's voice pierced the din of Excelsis at night. Adhema rose to her feet, smiling. She stood high above the Veins, perched on wet slates, revelling in the scents that unfolded beneath her. It had been too long since she had visited a city – a proper, living city.

'A spur-of-the-moment decision, my lady. One I suspect you will agree with, if you but hear me out.' When Neferata did not reply, Adhema continued. 'The spear is gone. Once thrown, it will not allow itself to be bent from its purpose until it makes its kill. You yourself told me that.'

So, you will stalk this Azyrite until his almost certain demise?

She sensed her mistress' amusement, and allowed herself a

polite chuckle. 'No. Grungni will find some way of preserving his life, of that I have no doubt. But it is what they will do next that I wish to see...'

Silence. Then a soft laugh. Adhema shivered. There was malice in that laugh, and some slight admiration. *The other weapons,* Neferata murmured. *And will you help them claim the Lamentations, sister? Will you play the guardian angel for them?*

'If I must,' Adhema said, frowning. 'Grungni will seek to gather them. He will stop at nothing, and neither will they. They are determined, for mortals.'

You admire them.

It wasn't an accusation. Not quite. But almost. Adhema hissed. 'They are a means to an end, my lady – nothing more. They will gather the weapons for us, in a safe place, and then we will take them, as our rightful due.'

And you know where this place is?

Adhema smiled and looked down. In the crooked, cramped alleyway below, an ogor stood, half-slumbering, on guard. She'd considered attempting to get inside herself, but saw no benefit to announcing herself so brazenly just yet. She knew where the entrance was, and that was enough, for now. 'I might have some idea,' she said. She sniffed. 'I will keep a watch on it, and them. And when the time is right... well.' She shrugged.

A good plan, sister. But do you have the patience for it? Would it not be better for me to send someone else... someone more subtle, to do this thing?

'No,' Adhema snarled. She clutched the hilt of her sword. 'This is my quest. I will bring the weapons to you, my queen, whatever obstacles arise. That is my oath, upon the ashes of Szandor.' She looked up at the moon. 'Let me do this?' she asked softly.

The only reply she got was a mocking laugh, which soon

faded away into the night, leaving her uncertain and irritated. The Queen of Mysteries did so enjoy her little jokes. Adhema shook her head, and went back to studying the alley below.

After a few moments, she sighed.

Neferata had been right. She didn't have the patience.

Something clattered on a nearby rooftop. She turned, seeking the source of the noise. She smiled a moment later. 'Ha,' she murmured. Two swift steps brought her to the edge of the roof. Across the way, a roof-runner gang slowly but easily pried away slates, so that they might slip in through the eaves of the building below. They were young, and thin. Children, really, but feral. Like alley cats with opposable thumbs.

She crashed down behind them, startling them. One slipped and slid with a squall, nearly falling. She caught the boy by his ankle and pulled him up as she stood. Dangling him over the edge, she looked into their pinched, starveling faces, and smiled.

'Hello, children. I am Adhema. And there is something I need you to do for me.'

Kretch Warpfang, Grand High Clawmaster of Clan Rictus, sighed and shifted on his throne. He rubbed his snout tiredly. It had been a trying few days, since he'd ordered the retreat from Excelsis. The expected in-fighting had taken its toll, and he was running low on subordinates as well as patience.

It was all Quell's fault, of course. When his wondrous war-machine had failed to materialise, Warpfang had come to the unhappy conclusion that Excelsis would remain unplundered for the time being. He'd struck camp and retreated inland, towards Lion Crag, and the supply warren he'd built there, only to find it on fire and full of corpses. Not entirely full – there had been some survivors, one of whom was crouched before him now.

'Where is Quell?' he growled, glaring down at the cowering skaven.

'Almost certainly dead-eliminated, Grand High Clawmaster,' the snivelling creature before him said. The warlock engineer stank of scorched hair and fear, and his eyes were hidden behind cracked goggles. He and a few followers had stumbled into camp that morning, looking as if they had been through a war. 'You need have no worries-fears on that score, no-no. He has paid for this most disappointing of failures with his life.'

Warpfang tapped one talon against his warpstone tooth, deep in thought. 'Your name is Vex, isn't it?' he growled, finally.

'Er...' Vex peered up at him, his beady eyes owlish behind the goggles. 'Yes?'

Warpfang leaned forwards. Vex bobbed, wanting to retreat, but prevented from doing so by the hulking shapes of the deathvermin standing behind him. Warpfang crooked a talon, beckoning him forwards. Vex hesitated. One of the deathvermin prodded him with the blade of his weapon. The warlock engineer scurried forwards, leaking fear-musk. Warpfang took an almost gentle grip on Vex's whiskers.

'What about the weapon?' he hissed softly.

Vex blinked. Swallowed. 'Weapon, your worship?'

Warpfang nodded heavily. 'Weapon, Vex. Quell promised me a weapon. A weapon I paid him well for, yes-yes. Where is this weapon, Vex?' As he spoke, he began to twist Vex's whiskers. Tears came to Vex's eyes, smearing across the inside of his goggles.

'Destroyed,' he shrieked.

Warpfang snarled and tore loose a handful of whiskers. Vex collapsed with a squeal, clutching his bloody snout. Warpfang let the whiskers fall, to join their former owner. He sagged back into his throne with a sigh. 'Destroyed,' he murmured.

He'd feared as much. When he'd lost contact with Quell, he'd assumed something had gone wrong. But if Vex was to be believed, there were layers to the failure. And Warpfang was intent on peeling back said layers, until he discovered what Quell had been hiding from him. So far, he'd learned that there had been, in fact, two weapons. One funded by him, and one – an ancient artefact of some sort – sought by Skewerax. Quell, with the relentless optimism of a warlock engineer, had decided to combine the two into one, while hiding that fact from both of his patrons. Warpfang looked down at Vex. 'What about the other one?'

'Other one, oh potentate of pain?' Vex looked up. A cunning look, that. Badly disguised. Warpfang reached for his remaining whiskers. Vex clapped a paw to his snout and shrank back. 'Other one – yes-yes, the other one, it is gone-vanished. Lost-lost in the void-black between worlds!'

'A shame,' Warpfang murmured. 'If you had known where it was, I might have spared you.' Vex's eyes widened, and the cunning was replaced by sudden desperation.

'There are others,' he squeaked, throwing his paws up pleadingly.

Warpfang paused. 'Others?'

'Other weapons, your most magnanimousness. Many weapons. Skewerax said so, yes-yes, Skewerax – he's the one, he said–'

Warpfang reached out with a startling swiftness and caught Vex by the throat. 'Speak-quick, yes-yes,' he growled, his claws digging into the cowering skaven's throat.

'He cannot speak, if you strangle him,' a deep voice rumbled. Warpfang sighed and released Vex. The warlock engineer squeaked plaintively and crawled away, casting darting glances at the new arrival. The deathvermin were nervous as well, and the faint odour of their fear tickled Warpfang's nose. He looked up.

'Skewerax,' he said, in greeting.

'Where is my weapon?' the verminlord hissed, slaver dripping from his fangs. He loomed over the back of the throne, his claws dug into the top of it. 'Why is Quell not here?'

'Quell is dead, according to this one.' Warpfang gestured to Vex, who'd curled into a tiny ball on the floor.

'That is no excuse,' Skewerax said. 'My weapon?'

'Gone, beyond the reach of any skaven.' Warpfang laughed. 'Mine as well.'

Skewerax leaned forwards, acidic drool spattering Warpfang's armour. 'Where?'

'Does it matter?' Warpfang looked at the daemon. 'There are others, after all. Or was he lying about that?'

The verminlord slid back, eyes narrowed. 'If he wasn't?'

'Then perhaps you had best tell me, oh mighty one, so that together we might claim them for the glory of the Rictus, and all the Clans Verminus.'

The daemon stared down at him, as if considering. Then, slowly, a smile crept across the verminlord's scarred muzzle.

'Very well. Have you ever heard tell of the Eight Lamentations?'

Ahazian Kel erupted from the smouldering wreckage. Shards of metal jutted from his bloody form, and his armour was blackened and steaming. He wrenched off his bent and twisted war-helm with a groan, exposing badly battered features, and a bloody socket where the Azyrite's shot had burst his eye. A lucky shot, that. He tossed the helmet aside and looked around, squinting with his good eye.

There was no way of telling how far he'd fallen, or how long he'd been buried. The warp energies had torn the war-machine apart, scattering it across the mortal realms. Caught by the explosion of the warp-portal, he had been sent somewhere else – somewhere unfamiliar. The air tasted of burnt metal and the landscape was jagged and gleaming. Strange birds with iridescent, silvery feathers swooped overhead, their raspy cries echoing down. The remains of a number of trees, broken by the sudden arrival of a section of the skaven war-machine, poked up through the wreckage, their coppery branches shimmering eerily in the firelight, as the leaves blackened and drifted away on the wind.

Chamon, perhaps, or somewhere in Aqshy. In the distance, he saw signs of industry – great clouds of smoke staining the pale sky. He could hear the dull murmur of machinery, and every so often a rumble shook the air. A mine, perhaps. Whatever it was, there would be people there, and food. Not to mention weapons.

Ahazian swayed on his feet, hands clutching instinctively for the weapons that were not there. He had no weapons. No spear. He growled angrily, and pawed at his aching socket. The Azyrite would pay for that. They would all pay. 'I swear it,' he snarled, glaring about him with his good eye. He was a Kel of the Ekran, and his oath was as iron.

Then a treacherous voice within him whispered that he had also made an oath to acquire Gung, and look how that had turned out. Rage flared anew, burning the ache from his wounds and the weariness from his limbs. He had failed, and the loss of his eye, of his weapons, was but the price of that failure. 'Volundr,' he said. Then, more loudly, 'Volundr! Where are you, warrior-smith?'

Volundr must have seen. Must be listening. But there was no reply. No sound, save the crackling of flames and the screaming of birds. Ahazian grunted, weary again. Abandoned then. So be it.

He started towards the smoke on the horizon, shoving wreckage from his path. He would find the spear again. He still had the shard, could still feel the echo of the Huntsman's song in the depths of his mind. Once he had regained his strength he would begin the hunt anew. And then he would seek out the others, one by one. But he would not deliver them up to distant masters or faithless allies.

Instead, he would put them to use. He had fought other men's wars for long enough. He had sought peace in the shadow of lesser warriors, and paid the price. Only the Kels of Ekran knew how to properly wage war, and Ahazian would see to it that all the realms remembered why his people had once been feared. Aye, even the courtiers of Chaos, in the high halls of the Varanspire, would know and tremble. The last Kels of Ekran would march against the Three-Eyed King himself, and cast down all delusions of sanity and purpose. The realms would again be drowned in war – war, eternal and unending.

Ahazian stopped and raised his bloody features to the sky. Somewhere far above, amongst stars that glowed like hot metal cooling in dark waters, Khorne sat on a throne of skulls. Or so the sages of blood claimed.

'Khorne, I have never prayed to you. A god who needs prayers is no god at all. But if you listen, I ask a boon of you, here, today. Grant me revenge – grant me an eternity of slaughter beneath the laughing stars. Grant me this, and I will drown the realms in blood. And if you do not, then you had best strike me down now, for I will not forget.' He spread his arms, waiting.

Behind him, a raven croaked. Ahazian lowered his arms and turned. Black birds perched on the wreckage, watching him. His fingers curled into fists. 'Come to finish the job, then, carrion crows?'

Metal creaked. Ahazian froze, listening. He heard hissing voices, and the rattle of weapons. The wind shifted, and he smelled a rank scent. The smell of vermin. His torn lips split in a red grin as he nodded his thanks to the birds. 'My apologies. It seems our alliance still holds.' One of the birds dipped its beak, as if in acknowledgement.

The first of the skaven burst from the tangle of wreckage, moving quickly. It wore tattered yellow vestments beneath its rusty mail, and carried a round, crudely forged shield of bronze and gold. It slid to a stop at the sight of him, one paw twitching above the blade thrust through its wide leather belt. From the scabrous insignia daubed on its shield, he deduced that it belonged to a different clan than those he'd fought earlier. Scavengers, then, looking to strip the wreckage of any valuables.

More skaven joined the first, swarming out of the wreckage – a dozen, two, thirty, forty – on all sides. The sound of their squealing was deafening, and their reek drowned out even the harsh acridity of the fires. Red eyes glared at him, and warriors chittered, each one urging its fellows to lead the way.

Ahazian spat, wiped the blood from his mouth and stretched. He rolled his neck and loosened his shoulders. He cracked his knuckles and gave the skaven a ghastly smile. 'Come on then. What are you waiting for?' He made a beckoning gesture. 'Let us be about it, vermin. Some of us have places to be.'

The skaven scurried towards him, as one.

And Ahazian Kel leapt to meet them.

Yuhdak sat back against the rough rock with a sigh. The image he'd conjured faded, as did all thought of aiding his ally. There were realms between them, and Yuhdak was exhausted, besides. He stretched, trying to get comfortable. He'd got as far from danger as possible, but even so he could still see the column of smoke that denoted the final fate of the skaven war-machine.

'A shame. But then, the best alliances are inevitably the shortest.' He pulled off his helmet with a muffled grunt, exposing his features to the wind. He still resembled the prince he had been in his youth, though only vaguely. His face had no real shape, and those who looked upon it inevitably could not describe it. As if it were more the idea of a face than the definite thing. Yuhdak rarely thought about it. It was a face, his face, and that was all.

He set his helmet down and leaned back. His body ached and his wounds throbbed. That was good, for it meant he was alive. Pain was the seed of hope – hope that it might end, hope that there would be a reward on the other side.

Hope was the truest gift of the Changer of Ways. All plans, all schemes and tricks were born of hope. 'While we yet hope, life is worth living,' he murmured. A hoary saying, but a truth nonetheless, and one he'd clung to throughout the long, silent years of his childhood. He dabbed at the blood staining the facets of his armour and shook his head. 'Oh my brothers, if you could see me now. What would you make of silent, gentle Yuhdak?'

They would have laughed, he thought. His brothers had been harsh shadows, cunning and cruel. He had loved them, as they had loved nothing save themselves. 'But they were me, and I them, so perhaps it would be better to say that I loved myself.' He laughed softly, and then winced. The vampire had nearly killed him. A more savage part of himself desired to find her and return the favour.

But he was not a savage. Revenge was nothing, unless it served a greater purpose. The Three-Eyed King had taught him that, among other things. Archaon was a philosopher-king, wise and wicked. He grasped the immensity of existence with ease, and thought in terms of epochs, where others stumbled on centuries.

Ravens croaked nearby. He looked up, and the leader of the flock met his gaze. She crouched above him, holding something in her hand. 'Hello.'

'Hello, my lady. I am glad to see that you survived.'

'Hold out your hand,' she replied.

He did so, and she daintily dropped a bloody eye into his palm. Yuhdak clasped it gently, feeling the strands of life that still connected it to its owner. 'The priestess,' he breathed. 'You took her eye. I had forgotten.'

The raven-woman smiled. 'A gift, from servant to kindly master. One of several.'

Yuhdak nodded absently. 'A fine gift, my lady. And one I will put to use, most gratefully.' He rolled a palm over the eye, whispering softly. A bit of bone or flesh was as good as a hook in the heart. And the eyes were called the windows to the soul for good reason. He held it up, considering. Then, decision made, he reached up and plucked out his own eye. There was some pain, of course. But pain was the inevitable price of victory.

Squinting his remaining eye, he rolled the two loose orbs together, muttering. The rolling became swifter, and rougher, until both were squelching into one another. Sparks danced across his hands as he clasped them tight, squeezing his palms together. His servants watched in silence, their expressions unreadable.

He spread his hands. Where there had been two eyes, there was now only one. With trembling fingers, he pressed it back into its socket, wincing as the torn nerves reattached themselves. Blinding pain radiated through his skull, but only for a moment. Then he was blinking, sight restored.

The world had changed, subtly. His surroundings were overlaid with the ghost of somewhere else, and he heard the murmur of familiar voices. He sat back. 'Ah. There you are.' What the former owner of the eye saw with her remaining one, he too would see. A spy in the enemy camp, unaware and undetectable. He rubbed the raw rim of the socket, massaging it. It would take some getting used to, of course. But it was worth it. 'You mentioned multiple gifts?'

One of her warriors stalked forwards, dragging the limp body of a skaven. The creature was unconscious, possibly half-dead by the smell. From the raiment and the battered armour, he judged the creature to be a warlock engineer. The raven-warrior dropped the creature in front of him. Yuhdak leaned forwards, wondering what the Changer of Ways was trying to tell him, by delivering up such an unassuming prize. 'What a curious thing.'

He looked up at the raven-woman and smiled.

'Good fortune comes in the strangest forms, doesn't it?'

There was no sign of Ahazian Kel.

No matter how often he stirred the embers or peered into the flames of his forge, Volundr could not find his champion. If the kel was not dead, then he was well hidden. Or lost somewhere, in the realms. The skullgrinder gave a rumble of discontent.

It had all gone wrong, and so swiftly. Too many moving parts, that was the problem. He'd never been good with complex mechanisms. But then, neither had his fellow forgemasters. Zaar, too, was out a champion, for the moment. The thought brought some satisfaction, though not much.

Angry now, he swung up his war-anvil and brought it down upon the flames with a great roar, scattering embers through the smithy. Volundr kicked rolling coals aside and turned, searching for his slaves. He would need to make the appropriate sacrifices, to strengthen the reach of his gaze. He would find Ahazian Kel, or what was left of him, and hold the deathbringer to account for his failure.

'So angry, and at such a little thing.'

Volundr stiffened. A familiar voice, that, and unexpected. There was sadness in it, as well as anger. He had expected one, but not the other. He turned from the fire pit, tightening his grip on the anvil-chain. 'What are you doing here?'

'This place was once mine,' Grungni said heavily. 'I set its foundations, and carved the deepest flues. A hundred lifetimes, it took me. It was to be the greatest smithy in all the realms, its forges heated by the lifeblood of Aqshy itself.'

'I remember,' Volundr said.

'Aye. You watched me set the foundation stones. A wee lad, you were then. A scrawny thing, the marks of the lash fresh on your hide. But there was strength in you.'

Volundr spread his muscular arms. 'And I am still strong, Crippled One. Have you come to test me?' He lifted his war-anvil and gave it a tentative swing. 'I am ready. I will meet you, hammer to hammer, god of worms.'

Grungni said nothing. But his form seemed to swell, to fill the smithy, and his eyes drew in all the heat from the fire pits. They flickered and were snuffed out, one by one. Volundr stepped back, instinctively. 'Hammer to hammer, is it?' Grungni's voice was like the rumble of a fire-mountain, on the cusp of eruption. 'Ready, are you?' A great hand set itself on the large anvil before Volundr. The thick fingers, each as large as Volundr's arm, glowed with heat. The ancient metal began to hiss and bubble. The god's fingers sank through the anvil, until the whole thing collapsed.

Volundr felt the first flicker of fear. Appropriate, perhaps, given that the last time he'd felt fear had also been in the presence of the Crippled God. But he resisted the urge to give in to it. He was a Forgemaster of Khorne, and fear was only fuel for the fire inside. 'If I must fight you, Maker, I will.'

'Do not call me that, boy. You lost that right the day you cast your soul into the all-consuming fire. The day you chose a collar of brass, over loyalty and honour.' Grungni's gaze blazed brightly, almost blindingly so. Volundr stared into the light, though it stung his eyes, and burned his flesh.

'A chain by any other name binds just as tightly,' he said, flatly.

'I broke your chains.'

'And bound me in new ones, though you called them otherwise.'

Grungni fell silent. The god's presence scorched the walls black and caused the stones of the floor to run like water. His gaze beat down on Volundr like the heat of the sun. Then finally he said, 'You cannot win. I will not let you.'

'Our victory was certain the day Sigmar took the field,' Volundr said. 'All things end, and even the hottest fire is eventually snuffed out. You taught me that.' He shaded his eyes against the glare and laughed bitterly. 'You taught me much, and for that I thank you, old god. But some lessons are worth more than others.'

'Gung is out of your reach.'

Volundr shrugged. 'And so? There are seven more weapons to find, and eventually the Spear of Shadows will find its target, whatever obstacles you put in its path. And on that day I, or another, will claim it.' Deep, black thunder rumbled, somewhere far above. Volundr looked up. 'Your presence has been noted, Crippled One. Khorne has smelled your stink and come stalking down from the blood-red stars to find its source.'

More thunder. The roof of the smithy cracked, and dust

and rock spattered down. The fire pits flared to wicked life, hissing like enraged serpents. The flames were the colour of fresh blood. Grungni looked up, and frowned. The big hands clenched, curling into hammer-like fists. Volundr tensed, as the moment stretched. Part of him, the part long ago driven mad by the life he'd chosen, wanted to see what would happen. What could be more glorious than two gods going to war?

But a more rational part whispered that such a conflict would consume him and all he'd worked for. The gods would crush him in their struggle, with no more thought given to his fate than a man might give to that of an ant.

Grungni laughed, slowly, harshly. 'Not here. Not now. But soon, glutton.'

Volundr heard the sky split and roar, in rage at the insult. Everything was shaking now, trembling in anticipation of Khorne's approach down through the blood-dimmed skies. Grungni's smile was horrible to behold. 'Soon enough, I will take from you, in equal measure to what you have taken from me. Aye, you and your brothers.'

There was steel in those words. Duardin steel. An oath, in all but name. The words reverberated through Volundr and he felt a chill, cooling the heat of his blood. Grungni's gaze fell over him, freezing him in place. Not hot now, those eyes, but as cold as an abandoned forge. As cold as the highest peaks, and the silences between stars.

This, then, was the gaze of the god who had saved him. The god he had betrayed, whose kindnesses he had trampled, whose secrets he had stolen. Volundr met that gaze without flinching, and distant Khorne bellowed his approval.

A moment later, the Crippled God was gone. Somewhere, far above, Khorne roared in sudden frustration as his challenge was denied. Indeed, thrown back in his face. Sigmar would have fought. Nagash would have fought. But Grungni was not a war-god, nor a death-god, and had no interest in a contest of strength. He was a crafty god and as old as the realms themselves. Cunning and wise, was Grungni.

'Cunning you may be, but this game has just begun, old god,' Volundr growled. He reached for his tools, to stoke the flames. 'I will match my skill against yours, and we shall see who is the true master-smith here.'

And as he spoke, the fire pits raged up, casting sparks into the air, and making weird shadows dance on the crude stone walls. Shadows of past and future. Shadows of possibility. All dancing to the sound of hammers ringing down on anvils.

Dancing, as if in celebration of the slaughter to come.

ABOUT THE AUTHOR

Josh Reynolds is the author of the Horus Heresy
Primarchs novel *Fulgrim: The Palatine Phoenix*,
the Warhammer 40,000 novels *Lukas the Trickster*,
Fabius Bile: Primogenitor, *Fabius Bile: Clonelord*
and *Deathstorm*, and the novellas *Hunter's Snare*
and *Dante's Canyon*, along with the audio drama
Master of the Hunt. For Warhammer Age of Sigmar
he has written the novels *Eight Lamentations: Spear
of Shadows*, *Hallowed Knights: Plague Garden*,
Nagash: The Undying King, *Fury of Gork*, *Black Rift*
and *Skaven Pestilens*. He has also written many
stories set in the Warhammer Old World, including
the End Times novels *The Return of Nagash* and
The Lord of the End Times, the Gotrek & Felix tales
Charnel Congress, *Road of Skulls* and *The Serpent
Queen*. He lives and works in Sheffield.

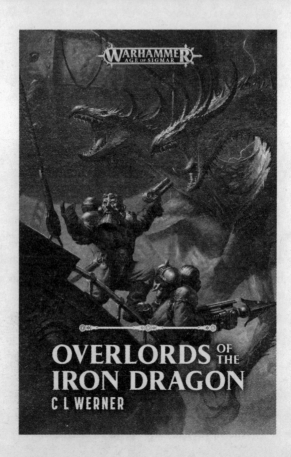

OVERLORDS OF THE IRON DRAGON
Written by C L Werner

Brokrin Ullissonn, a down-on-his-luck duardin captain, has a change in fortunes when he finds an untapped source of aether-gold – but is the danger that awaits him and his crew worth the prize, or are they doomed to further failure?

Find this title, and many others, on blacklibrary.com